Berkley Prime Crime titles by A. M. Stuart

The Harriet Gordon Mysteries

SINGAPORE SAPPHIRE
REVENGE IN RUBIES
EVIL IN EMERALD

EVIL IN EMERALD

◆ *A Harriet Gordon Mystery* ◆

A. M. STUART

BERKLEY PRIME CRIME
New York

BERKLEY PRIME CRIME
Published by Berkley
An imprint of Penguin Random House LLC
penguinrandomhouse.com

Library of Congress Cataloging-in-Publication Data

Names: Stuart, A. M., 1959– author.
Title: Evil in emerald / A.M. Stuart.
Description: First edition. | New York : Berkley Prime Crime, 2022. |
Series: A Harriet Gordon mystery
Identifiers: LCCN 2021051765 (print) | LCCN 2021051766 (ebook) |
ISBN 9780593335482 (trade paperback) | ISBN 9780593335499 (ebook)
Subjects: LCGFT: Novels.
Classification: LCC PR9639.4.S78 E95 2022 (print) |
LCC PR9639.4.S78 (ebook) | DDC 823/.92—dc23/eng/20211029
LC record available at https://lccn.loc.gov/2021051765
LC ebook record available at https://lccn.loc.gov/2021051766

First Edition: March 2022

Printed in the United States of America
1st Printing

In loving memory of my mother-in-law, Patricia (1933–2021). Pat was a voracious reader who could knit like the Furies, with a book balanced on her knee, and for many years was my number one reader and copyeditor.

Author's Note

In choosing to write a story set in colonial Singapore, I am conscious that I am portraying a time and characters with views and attitudes that are repugnant to our modern sensibilities. In every level of society there are the good and the bad, and characters like Lionel Ellis are grounded in historical reality. I hope there is sufficient reflection to be found in other characters within the story to provide balance.

EVIL IN EMERALD

✇ ONE

As the last strains of a waltz died away, Harriet Gordon looked up into Simon Hume's handsome face. Her heart skipped a beat as he bent his head toward her and whispered, "It's too early to go home and it's a lovely night, let's go for a walk."

"Yes, let's," she whispered back.

After a wonderful dinner and a few turns around the dance floor at Raffles, a walk in the warm tropical evening seemed the perfect end to a perfect night.

With the lights of the hotel and the bright music of the band behind them, they strolled arm in arm across Beach Road to the beach itself. Away from the hotel, the soft night enfolded them. Harriet threw her head back to look at the stars bright in the inky velvet blackness of the sky. She had had, maybe, one glass of wine too many, but she didn't care.

The peaceful sea sighed as it lapped gently onto the white sand and Simon pulled her away from the solidity of the palm groves toward the water.

"Simon. I'm not dressed for beach walking," she protested.

"Then take off your stockings and shoes," he said, and undid his own boots, hanging them from the laces around his neck. He rolled up his trousers and held out his hand.

"Coming?"

Harriet looked down at her expensive gray leather evening shoes and her one pair of silk stockings.

"Oh, hang it all," she said, and while Simon discreetly stood with his hands in his pockets looking out to sea, she pulled off her shoes and stockings. She rolled her stockings into the toes of her shoes, and holding the shoes in her left hand, she indecorously hitched her skirts almost to her knees, gathering the fabric into the wide velvet belt, before stepping gingerly out onto the sand.

Simon caught her spare hand and tugged at her, pulling her down toward the water.

"Simon!" Harriet protested as he swept her into his arms and waded out into the sea. "My dress!"

"It's only ankle-deep, and it's wonderfully warm."

He set her down but didn't release her, his arm circling her waist. The water embraced her bare calves, her toes sinking into the sand as he pulled her closer. She slid her free hand beneath his jacket and closed her eyes, but even as she leaned into the warmth of his hard body beneath his shirt, the memory of another man intruded, a man who had rescued her from kidnappers and carried her to safety. She had pressed her cheek to the hard, damp khaki cloth of his uniform, grateful for his strength and the staunch heart that had driven him to risk his life for her and a small boy . . .

"A moonlit night, a beautiful girl, and a tropical breeze. It doesn't get any better," Simon whispered into her hair before bending his head and kissing her, lightly at first.

The heady effect of wine and the romance of time and place swept over Harriet, and she sent all other traitorous memories spinning across the water like a stone. She wound her arms around his neck and abandoned herself to the moment, allowing herself to respond to his kiss. She tasted the saltiness of his lips and breathed in the scent of soap and man.

This should have been a magical moment, their first proper kiss after months of stepping out together. She held her breath, waiting for the sense that this was it, this was him.

But she felt . . . nothing.

She pushed away from him, but he caught her hand, his brow creased as he studied her face.

"Harriet, that was presumptuous, I . . ."

Presumptuous? They had been keeping company since August. Presumption was not the issue.

She smiled. "It's fine, Simon. Really. I'm just a little . . . out of practice."

He brushed her cheek with his forefinger. "I know how hard it must be, but your husband has been gone a few years, Harriet. It's not fair that you should be alone."

She stood quite still, unsure how to respond. Her hesitation came not from a loyalty to the memory of James Gordon. It was not James, but that other man who slid like a shadow between them.

"I just need time, Simon. I like you, I really do—"

"Enough to—?"

She stared at him. "To . . . what?"

He looked at her, and in the moonlight a thousand conflicting emotions crossed his face before he shook his head. "It doesn't matter. The last thing I want to do is put pressure on you."

Despite the warm night, she shivered. "I think I should get home, Simon. It's getting late and I have a rehearsal tomorrow."

Simon laughed. "Oh, not that damned show. It's bad enough I have to put up with Maddocks rehearsing 'I am a Pirate King' in the bathroom every night. I'll be glad when it's over."

"I shall ensure you have front row seats. I would hate for you to fall asleep," Harriet chided.

"*With cat-like tread . . .*" Simon sang as they strolled hand in hand back along the beach, barefooted in the warm water, the soft sand sliding away beneath their feet. When the lights of Raffles came into view and distant music once more spilled across the road, they ran up the beach to the tree line and sat on a fallen palm tree to pull on their shoes. Harriet grimaced as the lingering sand rubbed against the hard shoes, but it would never do to saunter back into Raffles barefooted.

As they walked back to the car, Simon slid his arm around her shoulder, leaving her with no alternative but to slide her own arm around his waist.

He swung her around to face him, lightly clasping her chin between his thumb and forefinger and raising her face to his.

"Harriet. I've never known a woman like you—"

"I should hope not," she said with a laugh, gently disengaging his hand and climbing into the green Maxwell tourer, the greatest love of Simon Hume's life.

He shut the door, and they drove in silence through the quiet streets, back to St. Thomas House, where a kerosene lamp had been left on the verandah to light her return.

Simon opened the passenger door, and as she stepped out, Harriet looked up at him and smiled, her hand on his chest.

He'd done nothing wrong. Nothing at all. Apart from the kiss, he had, as always, been the perfect gentleman. He was handsome, single, kind and considerate and from wealthy landed gentry in Australia. The perfect suitor in every way.

"Thank you for a lovely evening, Simon."

He bent his head and lightly kissed her again. She did not protest, closing her eyes and allowing herself to enjoy the moment.

"I'll be back from Kuala Lumpur in a couple of weeks. I can hardly wait to see you again," he whispered, curling a lock of her hair in his finger.

"It seems like a long time to be away," she said.

"I know, but the story's a big one. I will need the time."

"You haven't told me what the story is about—"

He silenced her with a kiss. "Another time, Harriet."

He vaulted back into the motor vehicle and, with a wave of his hand, turned the vehicle onto St. Thomas Walk.

Harriet stood at the top of the steps and waited until she could no longer hear the noise of the engine, discordant among the familiar sounds of insects and animals in the tangle of jungle behind the school.

She sighed and turned to pick up the lamp, smiling as she pushed open the door of the slumbering house.

Something in their relationship had changed on the beach tonight, and despite her initial reaction, a small tingle of excitement ran down her spine. Her friendship with Simon Hume had crossed an unspoken line and Simon was right; James Gordon was dead, and he would be the last person to grudge her a new relationship. If she was ready to allow another man into her life, then why not Simon? If she felt no choirs of heavenly voices when he kissed her, that didn't matter. They were neither of them green youngsters and love would come as friendship deepened.

As for the other . . . ? The khaki-clad shadow . . . ? That was an illusion that had no more substance than the shifting sands beneath her feet.

☙ Two

H e kissed you?"
"Shush!" Harriet laid a hand on Louisa's arm as she glanced around, hoping no one else on the verandah of the old McKinnon plantation, now known as the headquarters of the Singapore Amateur Dramatic and Music Society, was within earshot of Louisa's exclamation.

Rehearsals for the Christmas production of *The Pirates of Penzance* had been ongoing for several weeks and, mercifully, the pirates were all in the rehearsal room belting out "With cat-like tread" while the policemen's chorus waited to join in. The girls were at the far end of the verandah, reclining on battered chairs, fanning themselves as the torpid heat of the Singapore afternoon leeched whatever energy they needed.

"He kissed you?" Louisa repeated sotto voce. "I hope you kissed him back."

"Louisa!" The heat rose to Harriet's cheeks.

"Of course you did, and it's about time. How long have you been stepping out together?"

"Only since the end of August."

Louisa rolled her eyes. "And now it's October. Harriet, really!

You are still young and James has been dead for over three years now. He wouldn't expect you to be carrying a torch for him. It's time to start over."

James Gordon, like his friend Euan Mackenzie, Louisa's husband, had lived for his work as a doctor. He valued Harriet's share in his vocation and she had worked with him in the Bombay slums, but most of the time he wouldn't have noticed if he had missed a meal or his shirts were unlaundered. She had spent many evenings alone waiting for him to return from a difficult birth or an urgent surgery. Many nights she had gone to an empty bed.

No, Louisa was right, the Australian journalist Simon Hume was not James and it was unfair to compare them. She had loved James and he her, but now, maybe, just maybe, she had a second chance at love.

"I . . ." She struggled to find the words. "I like him very much, Louisa, but there is no . . ."

"No what? Bells and angelic choirs singing? Harriet, you know very well that sort of romantic nonsense only belongs in books or silly operettas." Louisa narrowed her eyes. "Or is there someone else? I always thought you and Griff—"

"Griff?" Harriet all but shot out of her chair. "Definitely no bells and angelic choirs with Griff!"

"Did someone mention my name?" Griff Maddocks, getting well into character as the Pirate King, sauntered out onto the verandah, wiping his brow with a handkerchief while his other hand rested on the hilt of a wooden sword.

"I was just telling Louisa that it is entirely your fault that I allowed myself to be talked into this production," Harriet lied.

Griff snorted. "I didn't twist your arm."

"No. You just said you couldn't play tennis on Saturdays for a few months, leaving me without my doubles partner," Harriet complained.

Griff grinned. "Oh, come on, old girl, you make a simply

splendid Kate and deep down you have to admit you're enjoying mingling with a different crowd."

Harriet's gaze swept the verandah where the company of the Singapore Amateur Dramatic and Music Society, or SADAMS as they referred to it among themselves, were spilling out of the rehearsal room for a well-earned break.

They were certainly a different crowd, drawn from the expatriate community and coming from all walks of life: from lawyers, such as the company's president and director, Charles Lovett of Lovett, Strong & Dickens, to the Straits Settlements Police Constable Ernest Greaves, typecast in the policemen's chorus. SADAMS existed on the understanding that a love of Gilbert and Sullivan united the British Empire, even though the cast had been drawn entirely from the British expatriate residents of Singapore.

Harriet had to admit that she was enjoying the experience. She had tried to enlist Julian, but he declared he detested Gilbert and Sullivan. To find himself dragooned into the chorus of *Pirates of Penzance* as a policeman, when he would rather be spending his Saturday afternoons playing cricket or comfortably ensconced on the verandah of St. Tom's House reading Virgil, was a trial beyond bearing and he had refused point-blank.

"Oh, there you are, Mrs. Gordon."

Elspeth Lovett, wife of Charles Lovett and the company's secretary and costumier, came out onto the verandah, clutching a large bundle of white cloth. She thrust the top garment at Harriet. "That's your nightdress for Act Two. The lace ruffles on the neck and wrists have come loose and need a stitch or two. I'm sure you can manage the repair."

Harriet shook out the voluminous garment. "I'm sure I can, Mrs. Lovett."

"Same for you, Mrs. Mackenzie." Elspeth dropped the nightdress on Louisa's lap. "And we have decided that the sisters will each have a color assigned to them. Kate—you, Mrs. Gordon—will have green, and Mrs. Mackenzie, you will have yellow. Mabel will have blue. Where is Alicia?" Elspeth Lovett cast a glance down the verandah where the principal soprano playing Mabel, Alicia Sewell, had just come out of the rehearsal room in conversation with Elspeth's husband, Charles Lovett. "I am getting in some lengths of ribbon to trim the nightdresses," Elspeth continued, and before either Harriet or Louisa could say anything, she had already moved on to a group of women farther down the verandah.

"I bet Alicia Sewell doesn't have to mend her own costume," Louisa remarked with some acerbity, her gaze moving to the leading lady, who had adjourned to a rickety planters' chair and reclined there, languidly fanning herself with her libretto.

Griff laughed.

"Would you like a cup of tea?" Eunice Lovett came out onto the verandah, balancing a tray with two cups of heavily stewed tea and a plate of digestive biscuits.

Harriet had not appreciated how heavily involved the Lovett family were in the society. Apart from Charles and Elspeth, their only daughter, seventeen-year-old Eunice, was a familiar sight at rehearsal. Eunice tagged along to every rehearsal in the role of general dogsbody, doing everything from serving teas to organizing props. Unlike her handsome parents, Charles Lovett and pretty, blond Elspeth, Eunice was dark haired, pale, painfully thin and easily overlooked.

Harriet thanked the girl and took the offered cup. Louisa held her hand out for the second cup but Eunice moved it out of reach.

"This is for Mr. Dowling," she said, her gaze scanning the verandah for the company's leading man, Tony Dowling, who leaned against the verandah rail holding court with a group of young ladies. Eunice trotted across to him and he took the cup without even looking at the girl.

Louisa tutted. "Bit too fond of his own importance," she said, referring to the handsome leading man.

"But he is very good," Harriet said.

She'd gone to see the July production of *Iolanthe* at the invitation of Constable Ernest Greaves, who had joined the company not long after he had arrived in Singapore. Happy to be in the back row of the chorus, being part of the SADAMS company had fired some life into the shy young constable and Harriet had been happy to support him.

It had been a pleasant evening. Charles Lovett had proved to be a fine comic actor with a good singing voice and brilliant timing in the patter song, but it had been Alicia Sewell and Tony Dowling who had stolen the show as Phyllis and Strephon. They were both born to be leading players.

Louisa had told her that before her marriage, Alicia had been a celebrated actress on the London stage but it had surprised Harriet to learn on joining the company that the famed Alicia Sewell was quite a few years older than her. There was, in the words of one of the characters in *Pirates*, "*the remains of a fine woman*" about Alicia. Even if Alicia might have been past the first blush of youth, once she was on the stage, she quite literally shone, and when she played the role of Phyllis or Mabel, the audience would be fully invested in her character.

Tony Dowling, the company's leading man, must have been at least ten years younger than Alicia and he made a dashing male lead with his chiseled good looks, dark blond hair and a fine tenor voice. The perfect Frederic, in fact.

Charles Lovett, red-faced and sweating, appeared at the door and rang a large handbell. Tall, gray haired and aging well, he had the sort of mobile face that lent itself to the older comedic leads, this time playing the Major-General.

"Ladies and gentlemen, chorus only," he shouted.

The chorus members set their cups down for Eunice to collect and filed into the rehearsal room. In its day, it had probably once been the main living quarters for the plantation house, with long, elegant French doors opening up onto the verandah that wrapped around two sides of the house. Set high on Emerald Hill, it afforded a lovely view across the island.

The battered piano struck up and the still-uncertain chorus began with the policemen singing "When a felon's not engaged in his employment." Being principals and having no desire, or need, to return to the stuffy rehearsal room, Louisa, Griff and Harriet remained on the verandah.

Griff pulled up a chair, rested his feet on the rails and opened his libretto, mouthing his lines.

"Do you want me to test you?" Harriet asked.

Griff handed her the libretto, and Harriet began with the first scene. As she fed Griff his cues, out of the corner of her eye, she caught sight of Tony Dowling and Elspeth Lovett at the far end of the verandah, in what looked to be an indistinct but heated conversation. Tony's brows were drawn together, and his hands bunched at his sides. Elspeth, by contrast, looked to be pleading with him. An argument over Frederic's piratical costume, Harriet wondered.

"Harriet, what's my next line?" Griff demanded, jerking Harriet back to her task.

"*I object to pirates as sons-in-law,*" read Harriet.

"*We object to major-generals as fathers-in-law . . .*" continued Griff.

But Harriet wasn't listening. Whatever Tony and Elspeth were discussing, it was not costume. Elspeth grasped Tony by the forearm, her face white and her shoulders stiff.

Tony threw off her hand. "No!" he said.

The word ran down the verandah, causing even Griff to look around. Elspeth turned and flounced through the nearest door into the rehearsal room. Tony watched her go before picking up his discarded libretto. He flicked through a couple of pages and looked up, his gaze lighting on Harriet and her friends. He waved, with a smile and a deprecatory shrug of his shoulders, dismissing the altercation as just a minor disagreement of no consequence.

"Mrs. Gordon is just going through my lines." With an encouraging smile Griff waved the man toward him. "I wonder what that was all about?" he added under his breath.

"Excellent. Do you mind if I join you?" Offstage, Tony spoke with the flattened vowels of a New Zealander, making the word *excellent* sound more like *ukcellent*.

"Words with the grandam?" Griff, always the journalist, asked.

Tony laughed. "She wants me to wear the most ridiculous costume. It involves skirts or some such. Apparently, it was proper piratical wear. Damned if I'm going to wear a skirt." He glanced at Griff. "And I'm pretty sure she has the same planned for you."

"Good God! I'll have her keelhauled if she tries to get me into something like that."

Tony drew another chair up on the other side of Harriet. "If you don't mind, can we start at the beginning of Act One?"

Harriet turned the pages back to the end of the opening song and began with "*Hurrah*."

She didn't for a moment believe the argument between Elspeth and Tony had anything to do with differences over a costume.

Lovett stuck his head out of the nearest door and summoned Griff and Tony Dowling to the rehearsal room, and Harriet and Louisa, who were playing Mabel's sisters Kate and Edith, returned to her own lines.

Harriet looked up at the sound of quick, light footsteps and a whiff of expensive perfume. Alicia Sewell smiled and came forward to lean her hands on the rail of the verandah. She greeted them both and stood gazing out over the overgrown garden to the view of Singapore beyond, perfectly poised had a passing photographer wished to capture an image of wistful imagining.

"How long have you been out, Mrs. Gordon?" she asked.

Out being shorthand for "out in the Far East," Harriet replied, "I arrived in January."

Alicia turned to look at her. "I've been hearing rather strange stories about you. Is it true that you were involved in that terrible case of the sapphire and rubies in March?"

Harriet nodded. "Quite true."

Up close, Alicia Sewell could not quite hide her age. There were lines at the corners of her eyes and her neck that put her in her early to midforties, but with the rosebud pout of her lips and the large blue eyes, she was still, and probably always would be, a beauty.

She sat on the chair vacated by Griff Maddocks and pulled a heavy tortoiseshell comb, inlaid with an intricate pattern in silver, from her head, allowing the heavy knot of gleaming light-brown hair to fall. She tossed her head, running her fingers through the thick tresses before twisting them into a knot and securing it again with the comb with a practiced art that made Harriet quite envious.

"That's better," Alicia said, wincing. "I get headaches. I wish I could just cut my hair short like a man and be done with it." She sighed. "I've been here for eight years but I still long for seasons, don't you?"

Harriet thought of the gray, miserable London winters and shook her head. "No. I lived in India for ten years. I am used to this climate."

Alicia tilted her head. "This is your first show with the society?"

"It is. I would rather be playing tennis but my doubles partner is Griff Maddocks. He and Louisa talked me into joining the cast."

Alicia laughed, a pleasant tinkling sound that echoed around the verandah.

"Alicia?" The three women turned to see Elspeth Lovett standing in the doorway. "You girls are on next."

Alicia rose gracefully from her chair and smoothed down the skirts of her cream muslin dress.

"Time to shine," she said, and sashayed into the rehearsal room as the pianist struck up "Climbing over rocky mountain."

❧ THREE

Inspector Robert Curran of the Straits Settlements Police, Detective Branch, strode out of the Singapore Police Court, his anger barely contained beneath what he hoped was a veneer of icy professionalism. He had just seen Lionel Ellis, the perpetrator of what should have been a straightforward case of aggravated assault that warranted a sizable prison sentence, given a slap on the wrist and a mild telling-off. If it had been any other judge . . . but the magistrate, Claude Bowman, was a known sympathizer when it came to cases brought against the Anglo population. White men could do no wrong in Bowman's world.

"A three-hundred-dollar fine," Curran seethed at his sergeant as they stood on the steps of the courthouse watching the plantation manager, Ellis, in high good humor, leaving, surrounded by a bevy of sycophantic friends. Seeing Curran, Ellis pushed through the crowd and remounted the steps. He leered at Curran and with a large stubby finger poked the policeman in the chest.

"That will teach you to go after hardworking planters, Curran."

Curran didn't flinch. He wouldn't give the man the satisfaction.

"You almost beat a man to death," he said between gritted teeth. "An innocent, hardworking man with a family to support. He will probably never work again."

Ellis bared his teeth. "The lazy bastard was late for work and had the cheek to talk back to me. I had to show him a lesson. Show all the coolies a lesson."

"He was late because his wife was ill."

Ellis snorted. "And she saved me a problem by conveniently dying."

Curran could barely contain the white-hot rage boiling in his chest. "And what of his children?"

Ellis shrugged. "Not my concern. I've paid my fine, but you, Curran. I won't forget how you dragged my name through the dirt. Watch your back on a dark night. Your pretty uniform won't protect you."

Curran narrowed his eyes. "Are you threatening me, Ellis?"

Ellis turned to his supporters. "Did any of you hear me threatening him?"

His friends met the question with jeers and denials.

Sergeant Gursharan Singh said in a low, quiet voice, "I heard you."

Ellis looked the Sikh sergeant up and down. "And who's going to take the word of a native?"

"I heard you too." Griff Maddocks, standing on the steps of the court, behind Ellis, pointedly took out his notebook and pencil. "Would you care to elaborate, Mr. Ellis?"

Ellis shot the reporter a quick glance. "Meant nothing by it. Just a joke," he mumbled. "And if you say otherwise, tell your editor I will sue the paper for defamation."

Maddocks, inured to the ways of bullies, merely smiled. "And I suppose you will request Mr. Bowman try the case? How deep are your pockets, Mr. Ellis?" he said.

The color rose in Ellis's face. "Are you implying—"

Charles Lovett, Ellis's lawyer, pushed his way to his client. "That's enough, Ellis. You've had your day in court. Let it go."

"Go home, Ellis," Curran said. "And God help you, if you so much as lay a finger on another one of your workers."

Ellis's chin rose. "And what, Curran? I'm untouchable. Not a court in this land will convict a white planter on the word of a filthy native."

One of Ellis's supporters clapped him on the shoulder. "Come on, Ellis, old chap. Let's get a drink."

Curran watched as Ellis and his cronies swaggered away in the direction of the Singapore River and, no doubt, one of the less reputable drinking establishments on the waterfront.

Curran let out a deep, frustrated breath and shook his head. "It makes a mockery of the law. One law for the whites and one for the natives. If it had been his worker who had taken to him, the man would already be dead."

Maddocks pocketed his notebook. "It's the way of the world," he said. "Doesn't make it right though."

"No, it bloody well doesn't," Curran agreed. "Come, Singh, we have real work to do."

They crossed the busy South Bridge Road to the Police Head-quarters and the Detective Branch, which occupied the first floor of a wooden annex at the rear of the substantial building that faced South Bridge Road.

The only person present, the departmental clerk, Nabeel, informed him Cuscaden wished to speak with him. Curran sighed. Any interview with the inspector general of the Straits Settlements Police never boded well.

He found Cuscaden standing on the balcony outside his office, watching the bustle of humanity passing below him on South Bridge Road. The man had a clear view of the police court and Curran wondered if he had witnessed the distant altercation on the steps of the courthouse.

"I heard the decision in the Ellis case," Cuscaden said without turning around.

"Bowman," Curran said. "I'm sorry, sir—"

Cuscaden turned to look at him. "Sorry for what? I'm damned proud of you for pursuing the case, Curran . . . and I expect you to keep on doing exactly what you're doing."

"It doesn't win me friends," Curran said.

Cuscaden shrugged. "We're not in the business of making friends. You know that. Carry on and don't let Ellis's threats bother you."

Curran stared at his boss. "You heard?"

Cuscaden smiled. "I'm a policeman, Curran. I make it my business to hear."

A rapid knocking on the office door made both men turn. Sergeant Singh stood in the doorway.

"My apologies, Inspector," he said, "but I have a message from Superintendent Pett of the fire brigade. He requests your attendance at a premises on Emerald Hill. There has been a fire and there is a body."

Cuscaden nodded. "Off you go, Curran. Nothing like a corpse to take your mind off your own problems."

Curran cast his superior a quizzical glance before turning and shutting the door behind him.

❧ Four

Curran had heard the property on Emerald Hill described as "the old McKinnon plantation" but the sagging gates through which they had just driven bore a hand-painted sign that read simply SADAMS followed by a rough impression of a theatrical mask. At the end of the steep drive, the original plantation house, with its rusting iron roof and unpainted mossy boards, still presided over several acres of overgrown plantation. Being no botanist, Curran didn't recognize the species of tree. Cut into the side of Emerald Hill, the old house rose from the overgrown carriageway, with a long flight of wooden steps, without a handrail, leading up to the wide, wooden verandah, but closed off from access at the top by a gate.

The Singapore Fire Brigade's pride and joy, a gleaming new motorized Merryweather fire truck, stood parked in front of the house, and the blue-uniformed firemen with their polished brass helmets were busy reeling in hoses from what looked to be the service area to the right of the house.

Curran found Superintendent Montague Pett, the chief fire officer, contemplating the burned ruins of an outbuilding that had once fronted a bricked courtyard. Since he had come to Singapore five years previously, Monty Pett had revolutionized the fire brigade, turning it from a haphazard collection of poorly trained, and led, men, most of whom were in prison, or had just come out of prison, to a professional unit. The firemen now wore a proper uniform, brass helmets imported from England, and operated from an impressive new fire station on Hill Street.

Curran's and Pett's professional paths had first crossed over a spate of suspicious fires in Chinatown the previous year and a comfortable camaraderie had grown between them. The two men were much of an age, with more in common than either would admit. Like Curran, Pett had served in the military in South Africa and professionally they wore the same rank. Pett also played cricket with an abiding passion, but for the Singapore Cricket Club's mortal enemy, the Balmoral Club.

"Monty," Curran greeted the fireman as he came to stand beside him.

"Curran. That was a fine half century on Saturday," Pett said, without looking around.

"Thank you." Curran surveyed the still-smoking ruins. "What am I looking at?"

The building had probably once been a warehouse for the plantation. Only two half-collapsed brick walls and warped roofing iron lying among the broken beams indicated that a solid structure had once stood on the site. The fire had been fierce and comprehensive.

"It was fortunate that a storm during the night doused the worst of the flames or we probably would not have this much to look at this morning."

"Where's the body?"

"In the middle of the inferno," Pett said. "Want to see?"

Not particularly, Curran thought.

"This way, Curran, and watch your step."

Pett had already moved into the ruin, carefully pushing the remains of still-glowing wooden beams aside with his axe. The rain had turned the ash into a sticky paste that adhered to Curran's boots and trouser legs. His dhobi would not thank him for tomorrow's laundry.

One of Pett's men stood in what had probably once been the center of the room. As his boss approached, he gingerly lifted a sheet of metal roofing material. Curran had to stop himself from physically recoiling. There was something about burned corpses, more than any other, that turned his stomach. Maybe it was the smell, the sickly stench of decomposition mingled with an unsettling odor of burned meat.

The man—or woman—lay facedown in the embers. All humanity reduced to a grotesque, blackened thing.

"The watchman on our tower spotted the blaze about midnight," Pett was saying, and Curran had to force his attention back to the fireman. "The place was well alight, so we did what we could to make sure it didn't spread to the adjoining buildings, and the rain saved us. I left one of my men on watch and came back for a recce in the daylight. That's when we found our friend here." He paused. "If you want my professional opinion, the fire was deliberately lit."

"What makes you think that?" Curran asked.

Pett gave him a withering glance. "Can't you smell it?"

Curran could smell only burned timber and burned flesh.

"Kerosene," Pett prompted.

Now he knew what he was supposed to be smelling, Curran caught the faint sweet scent of the familiar household fuel.

"So, is this an arsonist caught in his own blaze?" he suggested.

Pett shrugged. "You're the policeman, not me, but if he is an arsonist, I'd be surprised. Look at his lower limbs." He nodded to his man, who pushed the metal away from what would have been the lower limbs of the corpse.

Surprisingly, and probably because the roofing iron had fallen on the body before the fire had taken good hold, the lower limbs were relatively undamaged. The feet were shod in what looked to be boots and the remains of linen trousers. Curran crouched down and studied the handmade European boots. Definitely male, he concluded.

Beneath the legs were the remnants of what looked to be a cloth or a carpet. Curran touched the fibers . . . wool. A blanket?

"What do you want me to do?" Pett asked.

Curran turned and gestured to his men, who stood in the courtyard waiting for his orders.

"Constable Greaves, to me. Get some photographs and then we'll get him out of here."

"We'll get out of your way." Pett signaled to his man, and they both retired to the courtyard to leave the policemen to their work.

"Nasty," Constable Ernest Greaves editorialized as he stood looking down at the body, leaving Curran unsure whether the young man referred to the corpse or the gloopy mess of sodden ash and burned rubble in which he had to work.

While Greaves organized his camera, Curran poked around what was left of the building.

Hard against one of the freestanding walls were the remains of unburned canvas nailed to frames that would once have been enormous. The top one appeared to have the trunk of a tree painted on it. He flicked through the others . . . rocks, walls . . . more trees.

"What is this place?" He addressed Pett, who stood watching them from the courtyard, but it was Greaves who answered without taking his eye from the viewfinder of his new Kodak Autographic.

"It's the headquarters of the Singapore Amateur Dramatic and Music Society," Greaves said.

"How do you know?"

Greaves looked up, a frown creasing his brow. "If you recall, Inspector, I am a member of the company. I was in *Iolanthe* earlier this year. I invited you to attend opening night."

Stung by the reproach in the young man's voice, Curran cleared his throat. "Oh yes. Couldn't get away."

Curran loathed operetta and had found an excuse to avoid sitting through an evening of dainty little fairies stomping around the stage of the Victoria Hall.

"Are you still involved?"

"Yes, sir. I'm in the policemen's chorus for *Pirates of Penzance.*"

"Typecast?" Monty Pett said.

Greaves looked across at the firemen. "I would rather have been a pirate than a policeman," he said.

"*A policeman's lot is not a happy one*?" Pett quoted, and smiled at his own joke.

Greaves groaned and returned to his camera as Sergeant Singh joined Pett in the courtyard.

"Should I fetch Dr. Mackenzie?" Singh asked.

Curran shook his head. "I don't see any point in him coming out here. Send for the mortuary cart though. Pett, do you know who is responsible for the property?"

Before Pett could respond, Greaves answered for him. "There's a committee. The president is Charles Lovett . . . the lawyer."

Curran sighed. He'd had his fill of Charles Lovett over the Ellis case. Most of his dealings with the law firm of Lovett, Strong & Dickens were with Clive Strong, and as far as he knew, Lovett concentrated on the commercial and property side of the law and had fewer dealings with the police. For some reason Lovett had taken on Lionel Ellis and, Curran conceded, done an excellent job.

"I've already sent for Lovett," Pett said. "He should be here soon."

"Got your photographs?" Curran inquired of Greaves, who nodded. "Let's get him off this bonfire and turn him over," Curran said.

No one moved.

"You," Pett ordered one of his men. "Fetch the stretcher from the truck."

Pett's men unceremoniously rolled the corpse onto the canvas and carried it across the wreckage to the courtyard.

Curran hunkered down and pulled the canvas away from the man's face. Because he had been lying on his stomach, the fickleness of the flames had left his face relatively untouched.

A young European man stared back at Curran from burned-out eye sockets.

Greaves took a step back, the color draining from his face. "Good God, I think it's Tony Dowling."

Curran looked up at his constable. "And he is?"

"The leading man . . . playing Frederic . . . excuse me . . ."

The normally phlegmatic Greaves bolted for the nearest bush. He returned, ashen and sweaty, a handkerchief pressed to his mouth and his round, wire-framed glasses steamed up.

"Sorry, sir," he said. "It's just I never . . . not someone I know. What's he doing out here? We don't rehearse until next Saturday."

"That," said Curran, "is a very good question. When did you last see him?"

"At the rehearsal on Saturday," Greaves replied.

Curran forced himself to look down at the corpse. As he had surmised, where the man's body had been in contact with the floor, shreds of a tartan woolen blanket and unburned cloth still adhered to relatively undamaged skin, but if there was any trace of an injury, it was not readily visible. Hopefully Mac, in his cool, dispassionate manner, could glean something of the young man's story. He flicked the canvas back across the body and stood up.

"What did he do when he wasn't treading the boards, Greaves?"

Greaves shook his head. "It was something in the commercial area . . . banking or insurance . . ." He shrugged. "I am but a lowly chorus member, sir, not the sort of chap Dowling would choose for a conversation."

"There's a hierarchy in the society?"

Greaves rolled his eyes. "Oh yes."

Charles Lovett arrived shortly after the mortuary attendants. He drove a dark-blue motor vehicle that glistened with loving care. Lovett removed his driving goggles and dismounted from the vehicle. He still wore the well-tailored light-beige linen suit he'd worn to court that morning.

He came hurrying up the carriageway and greeted Curran, who introduced Pett.

"What's happened?" Lovett asked, his gaze swinging from one man to the other. "Your message said there had been a fire."

Pett used his axe to point at the destroyed building.

Lovett groaned. "Damn it. That's the scenery store. This is a disaster."

Curran indicated the shrouded corpse being lifted onto the back of the mortuary cart. "I think this is a slightly more serious matter than the loss of your scenery, Lovett."

Lovett shrugged. "Some derelict using the building for shelter. It's happened before."

"I need an identification, Lovett."

"If it's an intruder, I won't—"

"I believe he was a member of your company."

Lovett's gaze shifted to Greaves, who nodded.

Lovett had a mobile, expressive face that probably served him well on the stage and his grimace was pure theater. "Very well then."

"I warn you, it's not pretty," Curran said.

Lovett pressed a handkerchief to his nose. "I can work that out for myself. Let's get this over with."

Pett flicked the canvas back from the man's face.

Lovett recoiled. "Oh, good God," he blasphemed. "It . . . it's Anthony Dowling, our leading man."

Pett restored the canvas, and Curran nodded to the mortuary assistants. "You can take him now," he said.

Lovett had gone a frightful shade of gray with beads of sweat breaking out across his forehead and nose. He pulled a large pristinely white handkerchief from his pocket and mopped his face. Curran walked the man away from the scene of the fire to a bench in the shade of a large rain tree that stood in what had once been the front garden of the house. Lovett pulled a silver hip flask from his pocket and unscrewed the lid. He sat looking at the object for a long moment before holding it out to Curran.

Curran declined, and Lovett took a long gulp of whatever was in the flask, brandy by the smell. The color returned to his face.

"Please forgive me. I'm not used to dead bodies . . . or at least not one like that," the lawyer said. "How do you do it, Curran?"

Curran nodded. "It's a particular shock when it is someone you know. Was the building insured, Mr. Lovett?"

Lovett shot the departing mortuary cart a quick glance. "Yes. Dowling recently arranged us new cover with his agency. Caldwell & Hubbard Insurance. They're a New Zealand company. Got an office in Finlayson Green." He frowned. "When did this happen?"

"About midnight. Do you know why your leading man would have been up here at that hour?"

Lovett shook his head. "No idea at all. It seems a strange sort of accident."

"We think it was deliberate," Curran said.

Lovett frowned. "Why would Dowling want to burn down our scenery store?" He mopped his face again. "Sorry, this is all a shock. I can't think of any reason why Tony Dowling would be in the scenery store on a Sunday night."

"Except to burn it down?"

Lovett cleared his throat. "That was a foolish response. The value of the insurance is negligible. The price of a man's life, however . . ." He pressed the handkerchief to his mouth. "This is very distressing, Inspector."

"Need me for anything else, Curran?" Pett joined them.

Curran shook his head and waited until Pett had gathered his men and returned to the fire truck. He watched the impressive fire engine drive away and turned back to Lovett.

"Are you aware of anyone with a grudge against Dowling?"

Lovett shook his head. "Tony was adored. No one would wish him harm. Are you implying this is murder, Inspector?"

Curran ignored the question and continued. "Was the outbuilding habitually locked?"

"Of course. We had some valuable stuff in there, paints and the like, so we kept a stout padlock on the door."

"What about the house itself?"

Lovett shrugged. "It's always locked when we're not using it, but enough people have keys, Tony included. Tony used to come up here to practice." His face brightened. "Maybe that's it. He just wanted to practice and thought he'd get some peace and quiet up here and disturbed an intruder?"

Curran could not answer that question. Instead, he asked for a list of all the key holders.

The lawyer nodded. "Of course. My wife has the records. She's secretary of the society." He looked down at his hands, twisting the handkerchief as he shook his head. "This is terrible, Curran."

Curran was on the point of murmuring another suitable aphorism when Lovett continued, "Where am I going to find another Frederic?"

Curran looked at him. "Frederic?"

"Yes, Dowling was playing Frederic in *Pirates of Penzance*. He always plays the lead. Hard to find a good tenor. Don't know who we'll get to replace him."

Curran steadied himself before responding. "A man is dead, Lovett. That is all that matters to me."

"Of course, yes, terrible thing, but the Victoria Hall is booked. We're already selling tickets."

The differing priorities were not something Curran felt deserved a comment. He asked to see the house itself.

Lovett jumped to his feet and fished in his pocket and held up a large, old-fashioned key. "Key to the back door," he said. "All the other doors, except the front door, are fastened by internal bolts."

Curran followed the lawyer to the side of the house. The key turned easily in the well-oiled lock and Lovett strode through the open door.

"This is a sort of service room," he said. "There's a bathroom through there . . ." He pointed to a door leading off the service room and led the way through a second door into a small corridor. As he passed, Curran scanned the cluttered shelves in the service room. Swords and lamps jostled with other items that could only be props. On the bottom shelf were two cans of kerosene with a sizable gap between them. Curran hunkered down and looked at the gap. The dust and the width of the gap showed that a third can had stood between the remaining cans until very recently.

He looked up at Lovett. "Any idea where the third can is?"

Lovett shook his head. "Nothing to do with me. We keep the kerosene just in case we have a late rehearsal and need the lamps and I think we use kerosene for the stove in the kitchen to boil water for teas. Again, my wife—"

"Will have the details?"

Lovett flushed. "Busy girl, my Elspeth. This way, Inspector."

Their boots echoed in the empty spaces. There was a particular stillness to the fusty rooms that smelled of mildew and the peppery scent of gecko droppings.

"Our rehearsal room," Lovett said, throwing open a door.

A haphazard semicircle of unmatched chairs had been placed around the old upright piano in one corner of the largest room. Other chairs, including a worn red velvet daybed, were lined up against the walls, and chalk marks, some fresh and some faded, on the old floorboards marked out placements for the staging of the shows. Five glass-paneled French doors appeared to open out onto the verandah and Curran reflected that, in its day, it would have been a pleasant room with the open doors catching the sea breezes.

Curran inspected the internal bolts fastening the doors and found them still secured. As Lovett had said, only the door that faced on the original entrance had a keyed lock.

The second large room, which had probably been a bedroom, smelled of mothballs and stale sweat. Racks of costumes with shelves of hats and assorted costume pieces occupied every wall. The paraphernalia of sewing industry—scissors, pattern pieces, pins, spools of thread, ribbons and lace—littered a large table in the middle of the room and a heavy-duty treadle sewing machine occupied the area in front of a window.

To Curran's eye every space seemed to be a jumble of dust, clutter and confusion, so he asked Lovett if he noticed anything unusual or out of place.

The lawyer shook his head. "Not that I can say, but my wife would know. This is her domain. She's in charge of costumes."

Busy woman indeed, Curran thought, and asked to see the verandah area.

Lovett unbolted one of the French windows in the rehearsal room and the two men stepped onto the wide verandah. Curran crossed to the railing and stood looking out over the old plantation to the rapidly expanding city beyond.

"This is some view," he said.

"Yes, we're lucky to have it," Lovett said. "It's an old peppercorn plantation. Dates back to Raffles or close enough. One of my Chinese clients owns it. He's intending to develop the site into high-quality terrace houses, but until he judges the time is right, he lets us have it for a peppercorn rental . . . no pun intended."

As Curran had surmised, a roughly built gate, secured with

a flimsy bolt, barred access to the flight of steps leading down to the carriageway, where Singh was directing a search of the grounds.

"You don't use these stairs?"

Lovett shook his head. "The committee was concerned that they may be unsafe," he said, with a small self-deprecatory smile. "Liability and all that."

That's what came of having a lawyer as president, Curran thought.

He walked the length of the verandah, avoiding the carelessly placed clusters of chairs and ashtrays filled to overflowing with cigarette stubs and pipe ash. As he returned to Lovett, Singh hailed him from below.

The police sergeant held up a wickerwork picnic basket. "Found this thrown in the bushes, sir."

Curran leaned on the verandah rail. It creaked beneath his weight. "Good work. Keep looking." He turned back to Lovett. "Let's get back to Mr. Dowling. Did you say his name was Anthony?"

"Yes, but we all called him Tony." Lovett shrugged. "What do you want to know?"

"Is he married?"

Lovett gave a snort of ironic laughter, his face straightening when Curran cast him a curious glance. "No. Rather one for the ladies is our Tony . . . was . . ." He cleared his throat and schooled his face to appropriate seriousness. "He shares a bungalow with a couple of other young chaps off Orchard Road somewhere nearby. Elspeth will know the address."

"Friends?"

"Everyone liked him."

"Anyone in particular?"

Lovett shook his head. "No. Like I said, everyone liked him. He and Alicia had a very good rapport, which is important when you are playing the lead romantic roles, but it was nothing more than a professional friendship."

"Alicia?"

"Alicia . . . Mrs. Sewell. Our leading lady. She lives in Eltham, a bungalow off Cairnhill Road, just below here."

Curran nodded. "And you, Mr. Lovett?"

"Cairnhill House. It's up the hill behind this property." He pulled a watch from the pocket of his waistcoat and snapped it open. "If there's nothing else, Inspector. I need to get back to the office."

Curran held out his hand. "Do you mind leaving me the key while we finish up here?"

Lovett handed it over, and the two men returned to the courtyard.

Curran locked the door behind him and stood for a long moment, weighing the key in his hand. "So what was he doing out here by himself?"

Lovett shook his head. "I really don't know, Inspector."

Curran saw the man to his motor vehicle and watched him drive away before joining Singh at the scene of the crime. Singh had two men combing through the ashes with long sticks.

"Find anything else of any interest?"

"We found this in the ruins," Singh said, pointing to a metal can that had been placed on the ground near the motor vehicle. Any labels had been burned off, but it was clearly identifiable as a commercial can of kerosene, similar to those remaining on the shelf inside the house. Next to it, still attached to a piece of wood, which might have once been the door, was a bolt secured by a padlock. Curran hunkered down and picked up the iron bolt. The padlock was in the locked position.

His blood ran cold. If Dowling had still been alive when the fire had been set, the killer had secured the door, leaving Dowling to burn with no hope of escape.

He returned to the scene of the crime and stood in what would have been the doorway, but was now no more than a half-burned doorjamb and a portion of wall. He kicked around the ashes near the doorway with the toe of his boots and was rewarded with a flash of red. He stooped down and picked the object up, blowing the ash from it.

He shook his head and handed it to Singh.

"Matches," Singh said.

There was enough left to identify what had once been a packet of Takasima safety matches with its distinctive red-and-gold dragons. A common enough brand, but it did not require too much of a stretch to imagine the killer had stood in the doorway and tossed the matchbox into the inferno he had created. Despite the heat, Curran shivered.

He returned to the picnic basket Singh had found, lifting it onto the bonnet of the vehicle and being careful to use a handkerchief to handle it, although he doubted Greaves would find any useful fingerprints. The wickerwork was damp as if it had lain out in the rainstorm. It contained an empty bottle of champagne and two glasses, an opened jar of caviar containing only a few scrapings of the expensive treat, a silver caviar spoon and a sodden white linen cloth. Curran shook his head and allowed himself a smile. A young man would surely have only one thing on his mind as he packed these delicacies.

"A romantic tryst?" he said aloud.

Singh snorted. "I would hardly call this place romantic."

"But you have to admit it is private," Curran replied, looking up at the still, silent building. "Picnic basket . . . picnic blanket? Is that what he was lying on?"

"It would make sense," Singh agreed.

Curran sat on the lower step of the old house, smoking a cigarette, as his men did one last abortive search of the grounds.

The potholes on the rutted carriageway were still full of water and he reflected that it had been a spectacular tropical storm in the middle of the night. Certainly a sufficient downpour to quench a fire.

Curran had been awake when it broke, thinking about the morning's court case and watching through the window as the sky was rent apart by lightning. He had drawn Li An into him, kissing her hair, and despite the suffocating humidity she had snuggled against him, always afraid of the thunder.

He smiled at the memory as he stubbed out his cigarette, grinding it into the mud with the heel of his boot as he brought his thoughts back to the present.

Had Dowling come up here in the mistaken belief he was making a romantic tryst and been ambushed by his killer? But that did not explain the empty champagne bottle and caviar. No, Dowling had met a woman up here . . . if so, who?

He hauled himself to his feet, straightening his jacket beneath the Sam Browne. Time to get to work.

❧ FIVE

Harriet's contract to provide secretarial services to the Detective Branch meant her hours were irregular. As with any client, she was paid when she worked, and it could sometimes be a delicate balancing act between her unpaid administrative obligations to her brother's school, St. Thomas Church of England Preparatory School for English Boys, and her paid employment with the Straits Settlements Police Force.

On Monday morning she had been detained at the school typing up letters for overdue fees. She arrived at the South Bridge Road Police Headquarters in the early afternoon to find the large airy office, which comprised the Detective Branch, deserted except for Nabeel, the departmental clerk, who told her Curran and his men had been called out to investigate a fire at a property in Emerald Hill.

Emerald Hill being a populous corner of Singapore, Harriet had thought little about it as she settled to her work, a long report from Curran, written in his illegible scrawl, on a recently solved spate of thefts.

The department's staff erupted back into the office just before five, bringing with them a smell of smoke and sweat. Harriet looked up. From their flushed, dirt-streaked faces and damp uniforms, it had been a long afternoon at Emerald Hill.

Curran tossed his helmet onto his desk and leaned against the door to his office with his arms crossed, watching as Greaves and Musa laid out the evidence they had gathered on the large table in the center of the room, which Curran used for this purpose.

Unable to contain her curiosity anymore, Harriet stopped typing and wandered across to the table. A picnic basket, a padlock and bolt, a burned jerry can and in a small cellophane packet, the remnants of a box of safety matches.

Curran pushed himself away from the door and joined her at the table, bringing with him the odor of smoke and something else, sweet and sickly.

"What's the case?" she asked.

"Victim of a possible arson," he said. "The thing about fire is it destroys any useful evidence. This is all we could find."

"Nabeel said the fire was on Emerald Hill?"

"An old property rented by the Singapore Amateur Dramatic and Music Society."

Harriet's surprise must have registered on her face. He frowned.

"You know it?"

Constable Greaves looked up from his work on the evidence table. "Mrs. Gordon is one of the current cast. She's playing Kate."

Curran's eyebrows rose. "You? I didn't know musical theater was one of your interests."

"It's not normally, but Griff Maddocks is also in the company so our regular Saturday afternoon tennis is out for the time being. Where exactly was the fire?"

Again, Greaves answered. "The scenery store. Destroyed. Poor chap was in it."

Curran turned to glare at his constable. "Get on with your work, Greaves."

Greaves mumbled something that might have been "Yes, sir."

"Do you know who . . . ?" Harriet ventured, hoping against hope it was a stranger who had wandered onto the property.

"We believe it's a member of the company. One Anthony Dowling," Curran said. "Did you know him?"

She stared at him. "Tony Dowling? Of course I know him. He is—was—the leading man." She frowned. "Did you say it was deliberately lit?"

In a rare, unguarded moment she saw the horror of Tony's death in Curran's eyes.

Harriet's world tilted. Tony Dowling? The charming young man she had helped with his lines on Saturday? There had to be some mistake.

"I'm sorry," Curran added. "Was he a friend of yours?"

Harriet shook her head. "No. Just someone I met at the society. Was he . . . was he . . . did he suffer?"

"I hope not," Curran said. "As for arson, that's Superintendent Pett's professional opinion. Kerosene was used to start the fire." He indicated the can. "I suspect this was taken from inside the old house. There appears to be a can missing. Was he liked?"

"Very well liked. Why would anyone want to kill him?" She paused. "And what was he doing at the property on Sunday?"

Curran shrugged. "We don't know. There doesn't seem to be anything of value worth stealing up there and it begs the question you just asked, what indeed was he doing there on a Sunday night?"

Harriet looked at the picnic basket. "Did you find that on the property?"

"Yes. Have you seen it before?"

Harriet shook her head. "No. It's not one of the props. It's too new."

She threw it open and they peered at the remains of the repast.

"The contents would indicate a romantic tryst for two," Curran said. "Was there anyone in particular he was involved with?"

Harriet and Greaves exchanged glances. "Not obviously," Harriet said at last. "Have you spoken with Charles Lovett? He's the society's president."

Curran frowned. "I have, but I would be interested in your opinion. Who knew him best?"

Harriet thought for a long moment. "Alicia Sewell is the most obvious. She's starred opposite him in at least three or four productions. They seemed to have developed a friendship off the stage."

Curran raised an eyebrow. "Just a friendship?"

Harriet shrugged. "I couldn't possibly say. You'd have to ask her."

"Anyone else?"

She shook her head. "He was a very popular young man but I haven't been involved in the society long enough to say with any certainty." She glanced across the room at Ernest Greaves, who had subsided onto a chair, mopping his face with a handkerchief while he sipped from a freshly shucked coconut, no doubt bought from one of the sellers on the street outside. "This is Ernest's second production, he may have some useful observations."

Hearing his name, the constable looked up. "I've already told the inspector everything I know."

"And for a young man in your position, you are distinctly unobservant," Curran said.

"My talents lie in other areas. When it comes to people . . ." Ernest Greaves shrugged.

Curran turned back to Harriet. "I'm asking you, Harriet, because I know you have a keen eye and a nose for gossip."

Harriet bridled at the implication. "I do not gossip!"

"That's not what I meant . . . I mean you are observant, unlike Greaves." He shot the young constable a sharp, reproving glance. Greaves pretended an interest in a piece of paper on his desk.

"When I said he was popular, maybe I should have added—with the ladies. He was an extremely attractive young man and I would not be surprised if most of the girls were a little enamored of him, but beyond some harmless flirting, I never saw anything untoward," Harriet said.

Curran raised a questioning eyebrow and Harriet, now knowing him so well, smiled despite herself. "Are you asking me to do your job for you?"

"I would never be that presumptuous," Curran said.

She returned to her desk and picked up the report she had been transcribing. "While you're standing there. What on earth is that word?"

Curran peered at his report. "I think it's *egregious*," he said. "It's late, Mrs. Gordon. These reports can wait. Get home and we will talk some more tomorrow morning. It's been a trying day and I have to track down the lad's employer and residence before I see my dinner."

"A grim end to their day . . . and yours," Harriet said with sympathy.

Breaking bad news was the worst part of Curran's job, she decided as she picked up her hat and bag and bade him a good night.

Harriet returned home to find Louisa Mackenzie installed on the verandah, drinking tea with Harriet's brother, Julian.

"Oh, there you are," Louisa exclaimed, rising to her feet. "I was just about to give up hope and go home."

"What brings you here?" Harriet asked, feigning innocence. She knew exactly what Louisa was after.

Louisa rolled her eyes. "Harriet, it's all over the island. A body found at the old McKinnon plantation. Is it true? Is it Tony Dowling?"

"Yes," Harriet said, folding herself into her favorite chair. The cat, Shashti, promptly jumped on her lap.

"Oh, poor Tony . . . such a terrible thing . . ." Louisa subsided back on the chair and fumbled in her sleeve for her handkerchief.

"I think you both need something stronger than tea," Julian said with some obvious relief, and disappeared inside, returning with glasses of his precious whisky for them all. His brother-in-law had sent over a crate of the best Scotch at Christmas and they were down to their last bottle.

"What have you heard?" Harriet asked her friend.

"I was taking tea this afternoon with some friends and Edie Pett, Superintendent Pett's wife—do you know her?"

Harriet nodded. She had met Edie Pett through St. Andrew's Cathedral.

"So," continued Louisa, "she mentioned a fire at Emerald Hill and a body being found."

"So why did you think it was Tony Dowling?" Harriet asked.

Louisa blinked. "I—just a guess."

Harriet, knowing her friend well, frowned. "Louisa," Harriet said, "do you have any idea what Tony would have been doing up at the property on a Sunday night?"

Louisa didn't look up. "Perhaps he went up there to practice?" she suggested. "He had his own key and there was no piano at his lodgings." She looked up, "Yes, that would be it. He went up there to rehearse and encountered an intruder—"

Harriet interrupted this train of hastily cobbled thought. "Was he in the habit of meeting anybody else for these practice sessions?"

The momentary silence spoke volumes.

"Louisa?" Harriet prompted.

Louisa looked away, propping her chin on her hand. It seemed a long moment before she brought her gaze back to Harriet.

"Oh, very well, it was well known in the cast that Tony would meet . . . friends . . . up at the old house on Sunday evenings," she said.

"Lady friends?"

Louisa didn't meet Harriet's eyes. "Mostly but sometimes there would be larger gatherings."

"Louisa . . . have you . . . ?"

Louisa's head shot up. "No! That's not to say I wasn't curious. Tony was a very attractive young man and . . ." She glanced at Julian, who failed to hide his shock. "I would never dishonor my marriage vows."

"Then whom did he meet up there?" he said.

"I really don't know," Louisa said, and when Harriet said nothing, she added, "His taste was for older, married ladies."

"They are easy prey in this climate," Julian observed. "Absent husbands. All care and no responsibility."

"Quite," Louisa said. She set the empty glass down and rose to her feet. "I must get home. I can't bear to think of him, burned . . . too horrible."

"I presume that will be the end of the production?" Julian said.

Harriet shrugged. "With no leading man . . ."

Louisa shook her head. "I think hell would freeze over before the production is canceled. For Charles Lovett, the society is everything. He'll find someone."

"Good evening, Aunt Louisa." Harriet and Julian's ward, Will, arrived at the front steps, covered in mud from head to foot.

"Good heavens, William, what have you been doing?" Louisa asked.

"Rugby," Will replied, his teeth a startling white in his muddy face as he grinned. "I scored two tries."

"Good show. Did we win?" Julian asked.

"We did, sir."

It was Julian's turn to grin. "Always a pleasure beating Prince Edward's," he said.

"I think you should go around to the back door and change your clothes and have a wash before you go inside," Harriet said.

Will nodded. "I say, Aunt Louisa, are you going to let Roddy join the Boy Scouts?"

Louisa rolled her eyes. "He's talked about nothing else since that wretched man came to talk to you all. What was his name, Julian?"

"Frank Cooper Sands."

Sands, a leader in the fledgling Boy Scouts movement, had arrived in Singapore recently and had persuaded Julian to allow him to give a talk at the school aimed at recruiting keen boys to join the first troop of Boy Scouts in Singapore. It had been all Will could talk about.

"I really, really want to join." Will looked pleadingly from one guardian to the other. "Simpson's parents have agreed and if Mrs. Mackenzie lets Roddy join."

Will had found the winning argument and one Harriet and Julian had no answer to . . . if Will's best friends could become Boy Scouts, then it would be churlish of them not to agree. No one had said how much this little exercise would cost, but they would find the money.

"I think it sounds like an admirable thing," Louisa said. "I know Roddy is keen to join too."

Will hopped from one foot to the other. "We get to go camping and learn to read maps and tie knots and all sorts of larks and fun. There's going to be a camp on an island in the harbor. I can go, can't I?"

Julian held up a hand. "One thing at a time, Will. Now, get cleaned up. Supper will be ready soon."

After Louisa had taken her leave and they were alone, Julian sat back in his chair, steepling his fingers. "Do you really want to keep going with this music society?"

Harriet smiled. "I have been rather enjoying it," she said. "They're certainly a different crowd."

"I have a bad feeling about this chap getting himself killed up there. Not sure I like that, Harri."

Harriet shrugged. "I doubt it had anything to do with the society. As you might have gathered, Mr. Dowling was not above using the property for his own private reasons."

Julian rolled his eyes. "Ah yes . . . that was what Louisa implied, romantic trysts and more? Do you have any thoughts about whom he could have been meeting?"

Harriet mentally ran through the cast and shook her head. "No idea."

Huo Jin appeared at the door. "It is very late and Lokman says dinner is spoiled if you don't eat now."

Harriet glanced at the watch she wore pinned to her blouse. "Goodness, it is late. My apologies to Lokman. Let's eat."

❧ Six

It was well after six in the evening before Curran made it to Finlayson Green on the off chance he might catch Anthony Dowling's employer still at his desk. The address he had been given was in the commercial district of Singapore, just off Raffles Place, and the building comprised small offices for shipping agents, insurance companies, rubber brokers and similar, each glass-paned door proclaiming the incumbent in gold lettering.

At the end of a corridor on the second floor, he surprised a gentleman in the act of locking the door that proclaimed CALDWELL & HUBBARD INSURANCE. In smaller letters below it read FIRE, MARINE AND LIFE INSURANCE. J. HENRY MANAGER.

"Mr. Henry?"

The man looked up at Curran and pushed his glasses up his nose.

"Yes? What can I do for you, Sergeant?"

"Inspector," Curran corrected. "Inspector Curran of the Detective Branch. Could I have a word?"

The man blinked several times as if deciding whether he should give the policeman the time of day when no doubt all he wanted to do was to get home to his dinner.

"Is it important?"

"It is. I won't keep you long," Curran said.

Henry unlocked the door and ushered Curran into a cramped office space, almost filled with three desks and a tall cupboard secured with a hefty lock. A typewriter stood on one desk and the other two were pushed together in what Curran would describe as a partners' arrangement. The employees sat on hard chairs upholstered in leather, leaving no room for a visitor's chair.

Of the partners' desks, one was a study in orderliness, the blotter and pen stand arranged in perfect symmetry. The blotter on the other desk was torn and much stained with ink blots, and a haphazard pile of papers and files in the box marked IN TRAY betrayed a somewhat less orderly mind.

Henry turned to face Curran. "What's this about?"

"Do you have a Mr. Anthony Dowling working for you?"

Henry frowned, causing his glasses to slip down again before resuming the veneer of professionalism. "I do." He glanced at the disorderly desk. "Unfortunately, he has not been in today." He clicked his tongue in disapproval. "Not a word to say he was ill or inconvenienced."

The lack of surprise in the man's voice led Curran to conclude that Dowling's unexplained absence was not all that unusual.

"When did you last see him?"

"Saturday," Henry said. "If you wish to speak to him, I trust he will be in tomorrow—" He broke off, scanning Curran's face. "Has something happened to him?"

"He was found dead this morning."

"Oh." Henry subsided onto one of the desk chairs and pulled a neatly folded handkerchief from his pocket, pressing it to his mouth. "Dead? How?"

"He appears to have been caught up in a structure fire on Emerald Hill last night."

Henry blinked. "Good Lord, a fire? I live off Orchard Road

and I thought I smelled smoke last night. It wasn't his lodgings, was it? That's up toward Emerald Hill."

"No. It was on the land used by the musical society."

Henry stared at him. "The old McKinnon place? Oh dear, I believe we handle the insurance on that property. Was there much damage?"

"One of the outer buildings, but Mr. Dowling was found inside the burned-out building."

Henry shook his head. "Dear, oh dear . . . how awful. Was it an accident?"

"Too early to say," Curran replied. "However, as his employer, I am hoping you will be able to provide me with the details of his next of kin and his residential address."

Henry pressed his handkerchief to his forehead. "I suppose his father will need to be informed. Do you . . ." He swallowed. "Do you need me to identify him?"

Curran shook his head. "No. He has already been identified, but in the absence of any local family, we need someone to take responsibility for his body, after we have done the autopsy. A burial or return of his remains to his family will need to be arranged."

Henry's relief at not having the gruesome task of identifying a burned corpse was palpable. "Of course, of course. I can certainly do that. I doubt his family will be able to afford to bring him home. Best done locally."

"I believe he was originally from New Zealand?"

"Yes. He has a sister and father in Hamilton. Should I . . . ?"

Curran shook his head. "No, I'll see that they are advised."

A telegram had to be sent to New Zealand. The New Zealand police would be the best ones to advise the family of Tony Dowling's death. They wouldn't thank him. No policeman liked the "death calls."

The manager produced a leather-bound address book and a

pencil and paper from the drawer of the orderly desk. He wrote out the information Curran needed and handed it to him.

Curran slipped the paper into his notebook and took a moment to look around the stuffy office. "What sort of work do you do, Mr. Henry?"

"General insurance. Fire, theft, flood, commercial . . . that sort of thing."

"And which aspect did Mr. Dowling cover?"

"Dowling did most of the maritime and transport insurance. I do fire and life." He pointed at the desk with the typewriter. "We have a local clerk to do our typing and filing. Fire, eh?" He gave a snort of humorless laughter. "What did you say about the damage to the Emerald Hill property?"

"Just an outbuilding. The scenery store, I believe."

Henry tutted and shook his head. "The scenery can be worth a fair bit to replace. I will contact Mr. Lovett in the morning."

Curran slid his notebook back into his pocket. "Thank you for your time. I'm sorry to have been the bearer of bad news. Dr. Mackenzie will be in touch with you tomorrow to make arrangements regarding the body."

"Yes, of course. I will contact the undertakers in the morning. Was there anything else I can help you with?"

"Not for the moment."

Curran thanked the man and returned to the street, grateful for the comparatively fresh air after the stuffy office. He glanced at his watch and grimaced, thankful that Li An never questioned his erratic hours. He still had one more visit to make before he could return home.

Darkness descended punctually at seven o'clock and the streets were bustling with hawkers and locals come in search of an evening meal. Tantalizing smells of curries and spices wafted toward him as the ricksha he had hired passed along Orchard Road, reminding him that he had hardly eaten all day.

The bungalow he sought was on the road that wound around Mt. Elizabeth, although the sobriquet of *Mt.* seemed a rather overblown description of a relatively small hill.

Curran paid off the ricksha wallah, adding in extra cents and a suggestion that the man find some food, then he strode down the short path that led to the address for Dowling that Henry had given him.

Two young men lounged on the verandah of the bungalow. They were dressed in sarongs and open-necked shirts, beers in hand and a table between them with a kerosene lamp illuminating the newspaper one was reading and the book the other had in his hand. A servant in a white tunic and anachronous red fez came hurrying out to greet him, and the two young men rose to their feet, curiosity written on their faces.

The taller of the two, a slender dark-haired man in his midtwenties with a half-grown moustache and no chin, introduced himself as John Butcher. His shorter and rounder housemate went by the name of Percy Fraser. Curran asked about their occupations. Fraser worked for one of the banks and Butcher for another of the insurance agencies.

"Is this the lodgings of Anthony Dowling?" Curran asked.

The shorter man nodded. "Yes, but he's not at home. Haven't seen him all day, come to think of it. What's he been up to?"

"I regret to be the bearer of bad news, but he was found dead this morning."

They both stared at him with wide, horrified eyes.

"Tony?" Fraser shook his head.

"No, there must be some mistake . . ." Butcher said. "Was it an accident?"

"We don't believe so. His body was found in a burned-out building on an old estate on Emerald Hill."

"Sit down, Inspector." Butcher gestured at a chair. "Can I get you a beer?"

Curran would have killed for a beer, but he declined the offer. He'd be home soon. For now, he was still on duty.

"Was it the music society's property?" Fraser asked.

Curran nodded. "Do you know what he would have been doing at the property on a Sunday evening?"

Butcher and Fraser looked at each other.

"He used to go up there to practice. We don't have a piano and it's walking distance," Fraser said.

"And he found it a useful spot for assignations," Butcher said.

"I say, Butcher, that's telling tales out of school." Fraser glared at his friend.

Butcher glared at his friend. "He's dead, Perce."

Fraser sniffed and looked down at the beer he was holding.

"Did he have such an assignation arranged last night?"

Fraser nodded. "I believe so."

Curran stiffened. "Do you know whom he was meeting?"

Both men shook their heads.

"We only share a house, Inspector. It's no business of ours what he gets up to in the evenings," Fraser said.

Butcher grinned. "Lucky devil, had a number of lady admirers but he was always discreet. A proper gentleman."

"I suspect some of them may have been married ladies, Inspector," Fraser added.

"Anyone special? Someone in particular he may have talked about?"

Butcher and Fraser looked at each other and shook their heads.

"Anyone you might have met?"

"No. Like Butcher said, he was discreet," Fraser said. "The only woman he mentioned regularly was his leading lady in the society productions, Alicia Sewell."

"But that was only when he was talking about rehearsals or performances." Butcher rolled his eyes. "He could be a crashing bore on the subject of Gilbert and Sullivan. He loved the society."

"When did you last see him?" Curran asked.

"Before he went out last night. It was probably about nine thirty because he had supper with us." He turned to the servant who stood in the doorway. "That would be about right, wouldn't it?"

The man inclined his head. "That is correct. I had cleared the dishes when he came into the kitchen looking for a tablecloth."

"Did he have anything with him when he went out?"

Butcher nodded. "Yes, he borrowed my picnic basket. My aunt gave it to me when I left England. Thought life in the Far East was going to be genteel Sunday picnics. I haven't used the damn thing in all the time I've been here."

"What did he have in the basket?"

Butcher shook his head. "No idea, but if he was off to meet a lady, I imagine he'd laid in some bubbly." He snorted. "I don't know why you'd bother. It'd be warm and flat by the time you got to drink it. Horrible stuff." He held up his bottle of Tiger. "Give me a good honest beer any day."

"So, he left about nine thirty carrying a picnic basket?" Curran fixed the time in his mind. "Transport?"

Fraser shook his head. "On foot. If he was going up to Emerald Hill, it's only a ten-minute walk."

Curran moved on. "What were his interests outside of women and the society?"

Butcher laughed. "That's about it. Like I said, he lived for the music society," Fraser said. "That took all his spare time, and let's face it, what better way to meet desperate women than a jolly old musical. Dowling told me once that the way to a lonely woman's heart was through a sickly love song. I think he fancied himself as a modern-day troubadour."

Unbidden, one of Gilbert and Sullivan's ditties about a wandering minstrel came to Curran's mind. Which one of the appalling operettas had it belonged to? He dismissed the memory and asked to see Dowling's room.

Fraser showed him into an airy bedroom at the front of the house and stood watching as Curran searched the room with practiced efficiency. He found nothing of any great interest in the man's wardrobe, desk or bedside cabinet, but when he lifted the mattress, he almost laughed aloud. Several dozen letters, still in their envelopes, were concealed under the mattress. He gathered them up, shaking his head at the pale-violet ink, the girlish hands and the sickly traces of different perfumes that still clung to the missives.

"Did you know about these?" he asked Fraser.

Fraser shrugged. "They arrived. Occasionally he'd read one out and he'd laugh. I thought they were a bit sad, really."

Curran placed the envelopes in his pocket and went through Dowling's writing box and collected all the correspondence he could find from the young man's family and friends in New Zealand along with a collection of business correspondence.

He thanked Butcher and Fraser and left them to their own thoughts on their housemate's death.

Curran returned to South Bridge Road to deposit the evidence he had collected from Dowling's lodgings and retrieve his chestnut gelding, Leopold, from the stables at the rear of the property. Saddle horses were not that common a sight these days, but it didn't bother Curran to be thought of as "that eccentric policeman on the horse." He found Leo a convenient form of transport and he had no great love for machines, whether they were the newly popular motorcycles or the increasing number of motor vehicles that were adding to the traffic problems in the older part of town.

It was a brief ride from the Police Headquarters in South

Bridge Road to his bungalow off Cantonment Road. He left Leopold with his syce, Mahmud, who tended Leopold's stable at the turnoff into the narrow lane that ran up to the bungalow he shared with Li An. As he walked up the dark lane, flanked on either side by thick jungle, he all but ran into someone coming in the opposite direction. He jumped back, his hand instinctively going to the butt of his Webley.

"My apologies, Inspector. I did not mean to startle you."

In the gloom Curran could make out a slight man, the moonlight reflecting off round tortoiseshell glasses. The man removed his hat, a western bowler, from his head and bowed slightly.

"I will bid you good night." His voice carried the soft intonations of the Straits Chinese.

Before Curran could respond, the man replaced his hat and continued on his way, passing him without a backward glance. Curran turned and watched him pick his way around the potholes in the unkempt lane.

The only house on the lane was his bungalow, and he and Li An never, or at least hardly ever, had visitors and certainly not at this hour of the night. He ran the rest of the way, letting out a sigh of relief when the bungalow came into view and he could see Li An, not in her usual place, curled up on a chair on the verandah with a book, but standing, leaning against one of the verandah posts, looking down the lane.

She straightened as she saw him.

"Curran. You are late tonight."

"I have a new case," he said, tossing his hat onto the table. "A young man murdered at a property on Emerald Hill."

"*Ang mo?*" She used the disparaging word for a European.

He smiled and nodded. "Yes, *ang mo*. Who was that man I passed in the lane?" he asked, trying to keep his tone casual as he unbuckled his Sam Browne.

Li An took the belt from him, running the well-polished leather through her fingers. "My cousin Ah Loong."

Cousin?

Curran ran through her complex family tree. He had a vague recollection of meeting the man during his time in Penang. Had it been at a party at her brother's substantial property?

"Teo Gum Loong," Li An said.

He remembered now. Teo Gum Loong belonged to Li An's mother's side of the family and was a prosperous commodities trader in Penang. Rubber, tin or silk, Ah Loong, as the family called him, had an interest in it.

But what had brought him to Singapore . . . to Li An? In the two years since Curran and Li An had fled Penang, no member of her family had, to his knowledge, visited their prodigal daughter. To do so would incur the wrath of her brother, and few were willing to do that.

Premonition prickled at the back of his neck. Something had changed.

"Why was he visiting?"

Li An set the Sam Browne down beside the hat and curled up on her own chair, winding a lock of her long dark hair around her finger. Altogether affecting an attitude that was too casual and only served to heighten Curran's unease.

"He was in Singapore," she said with a shrug. Curran let the silence lengthen between them until Li An let her hand fall. "He brought me news of my mother."

"Ah," Curran responded. "What was the news?"

Li An's mother, Teo Fuan Peng, still loomed large in her daughter's life, despite having publicly disavowed Li An when she had taken up with an *ang mo* and disobeyed her family to the point of betrayal and disloyalty. Despite the public disavowal, Fuan Peng had remained in contact with her daughter. Letters and parcels would arrive for Li An from Penang, and along with them the news that Fuan Peng's health had been declining.

Li An quivered like bamboo in a wind as she wrapped her

arms around herself and lowered her head. Her hair fell like a silken curtain around her face.

"She is dying, Curran," she said, her voice muffled.

"I . . . I'm sorry," he said, wondering if that was the correct sentiment.

She sniffed and looked up, pushing back her hair.

"Death is inevitable," she said, rising to her feet. "She will go to eternal life and we will meet again."

Curran had never got to the root of Li An's spiritual beliefs. Sometimes she embraced Buddhist philosophy, but he suspected at heart, she favored the Taoist beliefs of her ancestors. It seemed to Curran's poor understanding of a non-Christian world, that the belief in life after death was echoed across many belief systems.

Fuan Peng was not dead yet and that ripple of unease he had sensed on his encounter with Ah Loong recurred.

"What do you want to do?" he asked.

She looked up at him, and her fingers brushed his face. "Do? There is nothing I can do, Curran."

"Even if your brother were to allow you to see her?" he ventured, knowing even as the words came out that he could not have said anything more fatuous.

Li An would never be safe anywhere near Zi Qiang.

As if she read his thoughts, Li An said, "Zi Qiang could not prevent me from being with her if that is my mother's wish, but she has told me to stay away . . . stay safe. That is what she told Ah Loong, and that is what he came to tell me."

Curran took her hands and drew her close, wrapping his arms around her. Holding her, providing what poor comfort he had to share.

After a little while, Li An pushed away from him, her nose wrinkling as she said, "You smell of smoke and death."

He pushed her hair back behind her ear and bent and kissed her. "And you smell of frangipani."

"Come, you are late and you have not eaten."

He changed and poured himself a large whisky while she put their supper together. Ah Loong's visit was not mentioned again, but the man's slight shadow fell across them both, and that night as they lay together he reached for her, but she turned away from him.

Beyond the window, a breeze blew up from the south, rustling the trees around him and causing the resident troop of macaques to chatter in the swaying branches of the trees around the bungalow. Li An's past had returned, bringing with it something intangible and vaguely threatening. He lay, stricken, watching lightning illuminate the dark sky beyond the window. Tropical rain once again lashed at the iron roof of the bungalow, and an icy fear knotted in Curran's chest as he recognized that something in his world had changed irrevocably.

❧ SEVEN

Tuesday, 1 November

Curran disliked starting his day with an autopsy, but Dr. Euan Mackenzie preferred to get the unpleasant task done in the relative cool of the morning, so Curran abstained from breakfast and made the Singapore General Hospital, where Mac served as the chief medical officer and part-time police surgeon, his first commitment of the day.

Even as Curran approached, the stench of burned, rotting flesh in the mortuary seeped out from under the closed door. His stomach lurched, and he wondered how Mac always remained so phlegmatic. The Scot had told him on more than one occasion that he rose to the challenge of solving the puzzle of death, particularly unexpected death, and in that at least, Curran agreed.

He pushed the unlocked door open and found the mortuary deserted except for a shrouded body on the slab and the mortuary attendant, who told him Curran would find the doctor in his office.

He made his way through the bustling hospital to the chief medical officer's office, where he found Euan Mackenzie, glasses perched on the end of his nose, writing hard and fast. He looked up at Curran's knock.

"Just writing up my notes, Curran. I've already done the autopsy on young Dowling. It was not something that could wait and it was not very pleasant, I can tell you. Have you found a next of kin to deal with the body?"

"His employer." Curran handed him a note with Joshua Henry's details. Mac scanned the note and called for his clerk, delegating him the task of liaising with Mr. Henry and the undertaker.

Curran sat down and pulled out his cigarette case, proffering it to the doctor. Mac accepted the cigarette and sat back in his chair, watching the smoke rise to the ceiling.

"Who are his people?" Mac asked.

"He was a New Zealander," Curran said. "He's left behind a father and sister."

Mac pushed a singed leather wallet across the table. "It always amazes me the things that fire will miss. I found this in his pocket."

Curran glanced through the wallet. It contained a few banknotes and a letter in an envelope with a New Zealand stamp from someone called Dolly. In the missive she talked about life on a farm and news of Dowling's father. A sister's gossipy letter rather than that of a lover. One brief paragraph caused Curran to pause. *Thank you for your recent contribution. I was able to get down to the doctor in Wellington and he has given me some new medicine. I don't know how we would manage without your help.*

He replaced the money and the letter and returned the wallet to Mac. "Looks like he was sending money home," he commented. "I must ask Henry what he earned."

Mac shrugged. "Your job, not mine. Now, are you going to ask me what else I've found?"

Curran smiled. "What have you found?"

Mac flicked ash into a marble ashtray and took another draw on the cigarette. "Someone wanted him dead. He had been stabbed in the neck." Mac indicated the vulnerable point beneath his jaw. "Got the carotid artery. He would have been dead when he was doused with an accelerant and set alight."

Curran grimaced. "I suppose that was a mercy. Any idea of time of death?"

Mac gave him a withering glance. "What time was the fire reported?"

"About midnight?"

"And what time was he last seen alive?"

"Nine thirty."

Mac's moustache twitched. "Sometime between nine thirty and midnight, Curran."

Curran allowed himself a smile. "Thank you. Very helpful."

Mac stubbed out his cigarette. "Unfortunately, I was not issued with a crystal ball when I became a doctor, and in this climate it's almost impossible to be accurate, particularly if the body is in the condition young Dowling was found," he said. "Do you want to see him?"

"I suppose I better have a look," Curran said with little enthusiasm.

Mac stood up. "After you, Curran."

Once they reached the morgue, Curran steeled himself as Mac flicked the stained sheet off the body on the slab. Curran grimaced, resisting the urge to cover his mouth and nose.

Mac proceeded with a detailed explanation. "He was found facedown, and you can see that where his body was in contact with the ground is relatively unburned. One interesting thing . . ."

Curran grunted and wondered if he was going to disgrace himself by throwing up. He felt decidedly wobbly.

"The body was lying on what looks to have been a tartan blanket. I've got a good piece of it preserved here." He indicated a table on which sat the man's boots, what little remained of his clothing and a ragged piece of blue-and-red tartan rug.

"It looks like a picnic rug," Mac continued.

That confirmed Curran's thoughts and he made a note to ask Butcher if his picnic set had included a rug.

"How can you possibly tell he was stabbed?" he asked, steeling himself to look at the man's head.

As he had noted the previous day, the man's face itself had survived relatively intact, but the back of the head and the neck had been badly damaged.

"The blade nicked the spine," Mac said.

"What sort of blade?"

"That I can't tell you beyond the fact it was long, probably about a good inch wide and went in from below." Mac put a hand on Curran's shoulder and mimed a blade striking upward into Curran's throat.

"So, whoever killed him would have had to be close enough to him to get the knife in," Curran said. "Maybe not a stranger?"

"You're speculating, Curran, but that's why you're the detective and I'm just a humble doctor."

"Thanks," Curran said in a tone heavy with sarcasm.

Mac gave him a quick smile. "If I have any further thoughts, I'll let you know. Meanwhile, I'll have the report finished by this afternoon. My assistant took some photographs and I'll have those sent across to you when they are developed. Anything else you want to see?"

Curran gave the sad remains one last look before he emerged into daylight, feeling decidedly queasy.

He rode slowly into Chinatown, stopping for a restorative coffee and a steamed bun at a shop. He smoked another cigarette, trying to eliminate the stench of decomposing flesh from his nostrils, and thought about Tony Dowling in life, by all accounts talented, handsome, charming and a man with an eye for married women.

He lingered on the last thought. A jealous husband? A jealous lover? Jealousy and lust were often at the root of a murder, but this had been particularly nasty. Dowling had been stabbed and subsequently set alight. Someone had really hated young Dowling.

He stubbed out the cigarette and pushed his empty coffee glass to the middle of the table, leaving a few coppers for the shop owner. Taking a deep breath of the noisome air of Chinatown, he mounted Leopold and turned toward New Bridge Road and the new fire station on Hill Street.

The magnificent redbrick-and-cream fire station, commissioned by Pett, had been opened only the previous year and still smelled slightly of fresh paint as Curran led Leo into the engine bays. Apart from the Merryweather truck, the brigade still had several horse-drawn wagons and Curran left Leo with the stable hand to hobnob with the brigade horses at the stables behind the station.

He found Pett in an office that rivaled Cuscaden's for size and splendor. A magnificent teak desk dominated the room, but a fireman's brass helmet and heavy woolen coat and boots told him this was the office of a man who liked to get his hands dirty.

Pett, working at his desk, his shirtsleeves rolled up, jumped up, reaching for his jacket. Seeing Curran, he left it hanging on a hook and came forward, his hand outstretched. "Welcome to my castle, Curran."

"Castle" seemed an appropriate description of the elaborate confection of a building, Curran thought.

"I'd like to show you around if you have time," Pett continued.

"Some other time. I just came to tell you that you were right. It looks like yesterday's fire was deliberately lit as a ploy to destroy the evidence of a murder. The man had been stabbed before being set on fire."

Pett let out a low whistle. "Nasty, but I suppose it is some relief that he was dead before they set the fire. Is there anything I can do for you?"

Curran frowned. "What do you know about people who light fires?"

Pett raised an eyebrow. "One fire does not an arsonist make and I can't say I've had much experience with arsonists," he said. "Although one of my father's firefighters once turned out to be the one lighting the fires. When he was caught, I asked the man why he did it and he said he liked the danger and excitement of fighting fires."

"You're right . . . this is only one fire," Curran conceded.

"What about that chap you caught lighting the fires in Chinatown last year?" Pett said.

"His motivation was money," Curran said. "Do you remember, he damaged buildings he had his eye on to buy and bought them at a reduced price."

"Oh yes," Pett said. "Not the brightest arsonist in the world. When your name is the next one on the title deed, it tends to raise suspicions. It seems to me each case is different." He spread his hands. "Sorry I can't be any more help."

Curran pushed his chair back and stood up. "If you think of anything useful, I'd be happy to hear your thoughts."

Pett also stood and held out his hand. "Come for dinner one night, Curran. Edie would love to meet you."

Curran smiled. "I would like that." Although he knew any dinner invitation would not include Li An.

He took his leave of Pett and retrieved Leopold, who was happily sharing hay with the sturdy brigade horses.

&c; EIGHT

Harriet had been looking forward to the diversion of taking tea with her friend Lavinia Pemberthey-Smythe on Tuesday morning. She had met Lavinia, the no-nonsense widow of a former commander of the First Battalion of the South Sussex Regiment of Foot, during the sad events of August, which had led to the recall of the battalion to England. Lavinia, who had followed the drum even after her husband's death in South Africa, had stayed in Singapore.

A mutual interest in the Women's Social and Political Union had initially drawn the two women together, but a genuine and abiding friendship had grown over the months.

Lavinia had been visiting an acquaintance in Kuala Lumpur and had just returned home after three weeks up north, and Harriet found her friend in passionate debate with her gardener about the pruning of her beloved orchids.

"That man," she said, setting down the trowel she had been waving as the gardener beat a strategic retreat. "I go away for a few short weeks, and he's killed off one of the phalaenopsis orchids. A child can grow those. Honestly, he has no feel for them. I don't know why I persist in trying to teach him."

"Perhaps just leave him to cut the grass," Harriet suggested.

Lavinia put her hands on her hips and surveyed her extensive greenhouse. "You're right, of course, but I really do need help with this lot."

Harriet pointed to the orchid with its simple purple flower Lavinia had been holding. "Does it have a name?"

"It does indeed, it's a Vanda Miss Joaquim. It is the very first hybrid orchid bred here in Singapore by an extraordinary woman, Agnes Joaquim." Lavinia sighed. "I'd love to have met her."

She wiped her hands on the apron she wore over the faded blue *salwar kameez* and threw back her long, graying plait. Lavinia wore European dress only when she was out in public.

"Now, I promised you tea. I've invited Khoo Li An."

"I haven't seen Li An in a couple of weeks," Harriet replied with genuine pleasure.

Harriet had introduced Li An to Lavinia, and the three of them met at least once a fortnight at Lavinia's quaint villa on Scotts Road.

She followed her hostess up to the verandah of the villa, where a setting for three had been laid out, with little plates stacked high with local delicacies such as *kuih ketayap*, a pandan-flavored crepe wrapped around a sweet, dark coconut filling, and *seri muka*, a square of rice topped with a bright-green custard.

"Sit," Lavinia ordered, her years as the wife of a commanding officer not forgotten. Harriet dutifully obeyed.

A ricksha turned into the drive, carrying a slim, elegant woman shaded by a red parasol. The woman alighted, paid the ricksha driver and walked up toward the house. She wore a close-fitting cheongsam of blue with red and yellow flowers and walked with the grace of a dancer, her long, black hair arranged artfully over her left shoulder, a wing of silken tress hiding the terrible scar that transected the left side of her face.

"Li An," Harriet greeted her friend with a kiss.

Despite the friendship that had grown up among the three women over the past few months, there were times Harriet felt no closer to understanding Robert Curran's partner in life. Li An never talked about herself and rarely mentioned Curran. Away from the Straits Settlements Police, the two lived a reclusive life, attracting endless speculation and gossip among the bored European community.

"I am late?" Li An asked, taking the seat Lavinia proffered.

"Not at all. We have just sat down." Lavinia clapped her hands, dispatching her servant to fetch the tea.

She picked up a copy of the morning's *Straits Times* and indicated the small article reporting the unfortunate death of Anthony Dowling in a fire on Emerald Hill. "Harriet, my dear, do tell? Was it really an accident?"

Harriet shrugged. "You know I can't tell you anything," she said. They chatted about the weather and other inconsequential matters until the servant returned with the tray.

Lavinia smiled and picked up the teapot. "Darjeeling," she said, pouring the tea into the chipped and faded once-elegant Wedgwood cups.

"But you must have known the chap?" Lavinia persisted.

"Not very well," Harriet prevaricated.

Lavinia handed Li An a cup. "Li An, did you know that our Harriet has taken to the theater?"

Li An smiled. "Ah yes, the Gilbert and Sullivan. What play is it you are doing?"

"*Pirates of Penzance*. I have a small part."

"Curran does not like the Gilbert and Sullivan. He has purchased a gramophone, but he plays only the Nellie Melba opera recordings." Li An rolled her eyes. "I do not share his enthusiasm. I think I would like the Gilbert and Sullivan better."

Lavinia's eyes twinkled as she raised the cup to her lips. "Harriet, tell me what you think of Madam Sewell?"

"You mean Alicia Sewell? I hardly know her," Harriet said. When Lavinia said nothing, she added, "She is very good. I believe she had been on the London stage before she married."

Lavinia laughed. "So they say, but I have some gossip for you. She was not christened Alicia. Her name was Elsie Williams and far from Covent Garden she was best known for a music hall act."

"Lavinia! How do you know this?"

"When I returned to England after Bertie died, I rather enjoyed visiting the music halls and Elsie was the star attraction until there was a terrible scandal. She had got herself involved with the manager of the music hall at which she performed. He was a married man, and they say that his wife took her own life when she discovered the affair."

"You are a shocking gossip," Harriet said.

Undeterred, Lavinia continued, "Elsie left the country and headed east, where she became Alicia. I believe she met her husband in Ceylon and now here she is in Singapore, lauded as a star of the London theater."

"I agree with Harriet," Li An said. "You are a shocking gossip."

Lavinia shrugged. "But that is the thing about Singapore, Li An, no one is quite who they seem, and many people see it as a chance for a fresh start. You, me . . . Harriet. We have all left our old lives behind."

Li An's cup rattled in its saucer, and she set it down on the table. "Sometimes it is not always possible to escape those old lives, Lavinia."

Harriet set her plate down. "Is something troubling you?"

"You must promise to say nothing to Curran," Li An said, looking up, her gaze traveling from one woman to the other.

Harriet and Lavinia exchanged glances.

"You have my word," Harriet said.

"And mine," Lavinia affirmed.

"You are his friends," Li An said, "and he is going to need his friends."

Harriet leaned forward. "Why? What's happened?"

"Nothing yet, but in a few days I must leave. I am going home to Penang," Li An said.

Harriet frowned. "Penang? But your brother . . . I don't understand."

"For a visit?" Lavinia asked.

Li An sighed. "No, not for a visit. I am leaving Curran. I have a life to return to in Penang and my time has come."

Harriet's breath stopped. She couldn't imagine Curran without Li An. The two were inextricably tied in her mind.

"But he'll be lost without you," Lavinia said.

Li An shook her head. "That is why he will need his friends." She laid a hand on Harriet's. "He will need you, Harriet Gordon. Promise me you will look after him?"

Harriet's mind roiled. Robert Curran was not a man who would be easy to "look after" or who would welcome any attention or sympathy . . . or pity.

"Of course, I will do what I can, but Li An—why?"

Li An touched the scar on her cheek. "It is time to face my brother."

Lavinia straightened, every inch the colonel's wife. "I think it is time for you to tell us the whole story, Li An."

Li An's face revealed nothing, but her long fingers pleated the fabric of her table napkin.

She nodded. "Yes. You have been good friends to Curran and I, and I think I—we—owe you our trust." She looked from one to the other with a piercing intensity. "And I do trust you with our story."

Harriet nodded. The little snatches she knew about Curran and Li An's past never added up to a whole.

"When my father died, my brother Khoo Zi Qiang decided that there was more money to be made in opium and illegal drugs than the honest trade my father had plied. He told me that as his sister I owed him a filial duty to assist him. I was beautiful then and it was not hard to discover what those in authority knew of my brother's activities. Until a new policeman came to Penang and he was not to be bought with flattery and bribes like those before him."

"Curran?" Lavinia interposed, and Li An nodded.

"My brother set me the task of charming him." A tear gathered in the corner of her eye and slid unregarded down her cheek. "It was at a garden party at the governor's house that I first met Curran. My brother was right, he was not like the others. There was a strength in him . . . and a danger. He knew what I was doing, but he didn't care and I . . . I found I was in love with him. I became Curran's spy in my brother's house. Zi Qiang grew suspicious, and he caught me in a lie. He beat me and"—she swallowed—"took me to a *godown* on Penang Harbour. He knew Curran would come, and he and six of his men were waiting. Curran fought them but he did not stand a chance. When he had us both, my brother and his men took us out to a shed on the pier. His men held Curran and"—she faltered—"he knew how to hurt with a knife without killing and Curran was badly injured." She indicated her right side and Harriet recalled the long, ugly scar she had seen on Curran when he had been ill with malaria. "Curran could do nothing to stop what happened next. Zi Qiang made him watch as he cut me . . ." She touched her cheek. "He said no man would ever look on me again with anything but revulsion."

Harriet drew a breath.

"How were you saved?" Lavinia put in, her voice tight with emotion.

"A fisherman heard my cries and rescued us." She drew a shuddering breath. "That is it. That is my story. Dr. Mac saved Curran's life and did his best for me, and Mr. Cuscaden sent Curran to Singapore, where he would be safe." She took a breath.

"Curran is a proud man and that night on Penang Harbour he thinks he failed to protect me and he has not forgiven himself or my brother."

"But you are safe here?" Lavinia said.

Li An nodded. "I am. My brother has business rivals in Singapore who would not tolerate his interference in their doings and Zi Qiang knows Curran cannot return to Penang."

"But you are!" Harriet said. "Li An, this is foolish."

Li An shook her head. "No. I will be safe enough. I have the protection of my mother's family."

"How can they protect you?" Lavinia said. "Your brother sounds like a madman."

"My mother is dying. She and her brother own many businesses and have power to rival my brother's. My cousin has come to Singapore to tell me that it is my mother's intention that I will inherit her share and so I am returning to Penang. Between us, the Teo clan can destroy my brother."

"It's not a trap?"

Harriet thought she could detect the slightest hesitancy in Li An's eyes. "I do not believe so," she said in a flat voice. "And if it is . . . then I am the fool."

Harriet turned her mind back to the time Curran had been sick with malaria and Li An had come to St. Tom's House to nurse him. "But you and Curran have so much more than any other couple I have ever known. How can you just walk away from him?"

The ghost of a smile caught Li An's mouth. "It is not an easy decision. There is blood that binds Curran and me, the blood my brother shed, and those are difficult bonds to sever." She trembled. "I will love Curran to my dying day, but we are from different worlds and it is better for me that I do it this way. He will thank me one day."

You will break his heart, Harriet thought, *and I am not sure he will ever mend it again.* Men like Curran did not love easily, but when they did, it was with body and, more important, soul.

"When . . . ?" Harriet began.

"I don't know. My cousin is making the arrangements."

Lavinia frowned. "That is a terrible secret you have bound us to, Li An. Curran is our friend. He won't thank us for knowing what you were planning."

Li An nodded. "I know and I am sorry but I do not think there will be another time to explain. I must deal with Curran in my own way. It is as you said, Lavinia, we all have our own secrets."

"And this cousin . . . will you strengthen the bond in marriage?" Lavinia asked.

Li An straightened. "My cousin Ah Loong thinks I should marry him but"—she wrinkled her nose—"I think not. I have seen what marriage can do to a woman and I do not want that. He will be a useful ally but my mother's business interests are strong in their own right and I am equal to the task ahead."

"My heart breaks for both of you but it is your decision to make," Lavinia said. "When will you leave?"

"Soon," Li An said. "Within the week, I think."

"Li An . . ." Harriet's heart clenched at the thought of losing her friend and the danger this woman would face back in Penang and it also broke for the man she considered her friend.

Li An looked at her. "Curran will never tell you but you are his friends and you cannot help him if you do not know the truth." She stood up, straightening the creases in her cheongsam. "Now I must go. I do not know if we will meet again."

Harriet jumped to her feet and embraced Li An, the slender woman stiff as a broom within her arms. Lavinia did likewise, and they watched as Li An raised her parasol and walked down the driveway toward Scotts Road.

"You're crying," Lavinia said.

Harriet dashed at the tears. "Silly," she said. "I'm scared for her, Lavinia."

"She is courageous," Lavinia said, "but I have every faith in her."

But Harriet was not thinking of Li An. "She is right. Curran will take it hard. What can we do?"

Lavinia shook her head. "Nothing, Harriet. All we can do is be there when he needs us, even if he doesn't know he needs us."

⊰⊱ NINE

Lovett had sent around the list of addresses of members of the music society to the office that morning. Between the performing members of the company and the backstage crew, there were over thirty names on the list. Curran divided the list between Singh, Greaves and Tan. He took responsibility for Charles Lovett and Alicia Sewell.

He began with Alicia Sewell and it occurred to Curran as he hesitated at the gate to Eltham, the elegant, modern bungalow off Cairnhill Road, that, like Dowling's, the Sewell residence was only a short walk from the old McKinnon property. Unlike that rotting mausoleum, he walked through an immaculate garden, water playing in a fountain in the center of the driveway. It oozed money and good taste, an impression that was not lessened when he knocked on the door to be met by a Sikh *jagar* in a pristine white uniform trimmed with red and gold.

He asked to see Mrs. Sewell and was told to wait in a black-and-white-marble-tiled hallway furnished with a large, round rosewood table on which someone had placed an enormous vase of orchids. The *jagar* returned and bowed him into a large, airy living room. Blinds had been drawn partly down over the windows, leaving the room in semidarkness so it took a moment before Curran could focus on the woman reclining on a daybed.

She raised a languid white hand.

"Inspector Curran, please excuse me for not rising. I have a terrible headache. You've come about Tony, haven't you?"

"Accept my apologies for disturbing you, Mrs. Sewell, but yes, unfortunately I have questions for you."

"Of course."

She did not invite him to sit or offer any refreshment on the hot afternoon. As his vision adjusted to the gloom, he could see her eyes were heavy and red rimmed from crying.

"What have you been told about his death?" Curran began.

Alicia Sewell raised a delicate handkerchief to her mouth and the lace flounces on her peignoir rose and fell as she said, "Elspeth Lovett called yesterday evening. She said Tony had been caught in a fire up at the society's headquarters on Sunday night. I could hardly believe it. I had smelled smoke and heard the fire brigade, but I never dreamed . . ." Her bottom lip trembled, and her large, beautiful eyes filled with tears. "Excuse me, I'm not normally like this. It's just that Tony was a good friend."

He waited for her to compose herself.

"Elspeth said it was murder. Is that correct, Inspector?"

"Yes."

Alicia subsided back on the daybed, one arm thrown dramatically across her eyes. "Poor Tony. Who would do such a thing?"

"I believe you were on friendly terms?"

The blue eyes Alicia turned on him held the glint of steel as she said, "Have you been listening to the gossips, Inspector?"

"Not at all," Curran lied. "However, it is my understanding you and he have shared the leading roles in several productions. From what little I know of such a close professional relationship, I believe it would be hard not to develop some sort of friendship."

She gave a snort of laughter. "Then how little you know, Inspector. Such a close working relationship can certainly develop into a friendship, or it can have the opposite effect." She held up a hand. "But fortunately for us, the former is true. Tony was a dear boy and a lovely tenor, and I enjoyed working with him, but I assure you, Inspector, there was absolutely nothing more to our relationship than just, as you say, a professional friendship."

"What about other female members of the company?"

Alicia stood up and paced the room. She stood for a long moment with her back to him before she turned and said, "Of course he had his admirers. He was young, handsome and charming. Any single lady would have been totally smitten. I am a married woman, Inspector."

The emphasis on "single" lady caused Curran to bite back a smile as he recalled the letters under the mattress. He doubted many of them came from single women. "Of course. May I inquire as to the whereabouts of your husband?"

"He is out on an inspection of a rubber plantation somewhere on the west side of the island. If you want to speak to him, you'll find him at the Balmoral Club this evening."

"What does he do?"

"He is a commodities broker. Rubber, gambier, pepper . . . whatever the commodity of the day is. I don't expect him home till late and I believe he leaves for Johor in the morning."

"Were you both here on Sunday night?"

"Surely you don't think I had . . . we had . . . ? I am shocked!"

Curran said nothing and she continued, "I was here, by myself. The servants can attest to that."

"What about your husband? If you were alone, where was he?"

"At the Balmoral Club, of course. Where else would he be?"

"What time did he get home?"

She shrugged. "Around midnight. I think he was drinking with a friend. One of the planters was up on charges before the magistrate the next day and he and a couple of others were providing moral support."

Curran's jaw tightened. Any friend of Lionel Ellis's was no friend of his.

Alicia sniffed. "What on earth was Tony doing at the society's property on a Sunday night?"

"He apparently went to the bungalow by himself frequently." He paused. "To practice or possibly to meet someone. Did you ever—"

"That's ridiculous," Alicia said. "I am happily married and I have no interest in sordid trysts in dusty rehearsal rooms."

Something in her tone made him wonder if, in fact, she had indeed gained firsthand experience of sordid trysts in dusty rehearsal rooms.

Alicia sank back on the daybed and rubbed her forehead. "Please excuse me, Inspector. My head is swimming. You have my permission to verify my whereabouts with my servants if you wish." She dropped the hand shading her eyes, fixing him with that steel-blue gaze again. "But I assure you Tony's death is nothing to do with me."

Curran thanked her for her time and apologized for his intrusion. He checked her story with the servants and decided the next person he should talk to was Alicia's husband, George Sewell. If the commodities broker was heading off the island the next day, it might be his only chance for a while.

When he had first arrived in Singapore, Cuscaden had nominated Curran for membership in the Balmoral Club on Stevens Road. He paid his dues but rarely visited, preferring the more collegiate atmosphere of the cricket club. Inquiring after Mr. Sewell, the club servant directed him to a back room where two men were smoking cigars, a glass of whisky in their other hands.

It took only a moment for Curran to recognize Lionel Ellis, the man he had prosecuted the previous day. Ellis was in the company of a man with well-oiled brown hair who sat with his back to Curran.

Ellis saw him first and half rose, a scowl beetling his heavy brow.

"What do you want, Curran?"

"My business is with Mr. Sewell, not you, Ellis."

Ellis's companion stood and turned to face Curran. A man in his midforties but still blessed with an athletic build, Sewell had a receding hairline, and he sported a jaunty, well-groomed moustache.

"George Sewell." He held his hand out. "Inspector Curran, is it? I've heard a great deal about you."

"I'm sure you have," Curran responded without looking at Ellis.

"What's your business with me?"

This time Curran shot a glance at the scowling Ellis. "A private matter, Sewell."

"Then step out onto the terrace. Ellis, if you're paying, I'll have another Scotch," Sewell said.

The two men stepped out onto the wide terrace, Sewell still holding his cigar.

"What can I do for you, Inspector? Is it to do with the recent unpleasantness on the Sungei Pandan plantation?"

Sewell referred to Ellis's rubber plantation in the island's west, where the assault for which Curran had charged Ellis had taken place.

"No, nothing to do with Ellis. It's concerning a death at a property on Emerald Hill . . . a young man caught in a fire at the music society's property."

"Oh yes, young Dowling. The news upset Alicia greatly. An accident, I believe?"

Curran ignored the question. "Were you acquainted with Dowling?"

Sewell leaned back against a low wall, his feet crossed at the ankles, and took a drag of his cigar. He watched the smoke curl up to the sky before he answered. "Only casually. Unavoidable when your wife is the leading lady, and he's the leading man."

"At the risk of being indelicate, Sewell, was there anything more to their relationship?"

Sewell straightened, color rising to his face as he drew his brows together. "What the hell sort of question is that, Curran?"

Curran steadied his breath. "I am not implying anything. I am merely trying to get some idea of Dowling's relationships . . . his friendships in particular."

Sewell subsided back on the wall. He looked at the cigar in his hand as if seeking inspiration. "I'll answer your damned impertinent question. He was a friend, nothing more. Alicia is a delight, but she is—was—at least ten years older than Dowling. She can be a bit of a flirt because she's a damned attractive woman, and she likes attention, but she has never given me any reason to doubt her fidelity. I allow her the freedom to indulge herself in theatrical fancies because I trust her implicitly."

Curran noted the word *allow* and tried to imagine the women of his acquaintance being actually forbidden from doing what they wanted. Harriet Gordon would be certain to have a few words to say and as for Li An . . .

"I don't think I have the right to begrudge her doing something that brings her pleasure when I am away from home as much as I am. The society gives her an interest." He paused. "It might have been different if we'd had children, but there it is, Inspector. You take what God gives you." He stubbed out the cigar on the wall and tossed the remnant into a nearby bougainvillea. "I'm not a jealous man, and to tell you the truth when I see her up there on the stage, I'm damned proud of her." He jabbed a finger at Curran. "And I know she'll always be coming home to me."

"Where were you on Sunday night, Mr. Sewell?"

"Sunday? I was at home." He held up a hand. "No. My apologies, I was here dining with Ellis and Lovett and a couple of planters from Perak." Sewell gestured at the building. "Quite a crowd came down to see Ellis's trial on Monday. My work covers a wide territory, and it was a chance to get some important business done."

"Who were these planters?"

Curran made a note of the names Sewell reeled off. His companions were from plantations outside of Singapore, and it would be hard to confirm Sewell's alibi through them. The club staff would be more reliable.

"What time did you get home?"

"Early hours of the morning. Alicia, bless her, was tucked up in bed. She knows better than to wait up for me."

"Can you be more exact?"

Sewell met Curran's eyes without blinking. "No. We consumed a great deal of alcohol. I was lucky to find the key to the front door. Was there anything else, Inspector?"

Curran hesitated, but couldn't resist scratching at one particular wound. "Is Ellis a friend of yours?"

"Not what I would call a friend, but I represent the largest market for rubber and gambier so it is in my interest, or should I say their interest, to keep on friendly terms with the planters."

"You know what he did? Why he went to court?"

Sewell shrugged. "Yes, an unpleasant incident." He paused, looking out over the dark garden. "You have to understand, Curran, these men are isolated on the plantations. It's not surprising they go a bit mad with the heat and the loneliness."

"It doesn't excuse attempted murder."

Sewell shrugged. "I'd like to see how you'd go for months on end with no other white man within miles."

"Is that how he justified beating a man almost to death?"

"It's the way it is, Inspector."

Curran considered the picture Sewell painted. It may have been true for some of the planters on the Malay Peninsula, but the Sungei Pandan property where Ellis worked was only ten miles at the most from the Balmoral Club. Hardly an isolated posting.

"What company do you work for, Sewell?"

"Robert White & Co., London based. I'm their chief commodities broker on the Malay Peninsula."

"Are you indeed. That must keep you away from home a great deal?"

Sewell's eyes narrowed. "It is one of the drawbacks of the posting," he said, "but Alicia understands. Absence makes the heart grow fonder and all that. Was there anything else? I am heading up-country tomorrow. I won't be back until late next week."

"No, not for the moment. Thank you for your time."

They returned to the clubhouse. As they approached Ellis, the man rose to his feet, obstructing Curran's exit. From his heightened color and the general miasma of sweat and alcohol, the man had more than a few drinks under his skin.

"You're not welcome here, Curran."

"I'm here on official business, besides which I am a member."

Ellis scowled. "I should get you blackballed. Can't have nasty little civil servants like you bringing the tone of the place down."

Curran's fingers clenched and unclenched. "You're standing in my way, Ellis."

Ellis's eyes narrowed and Curran tensed in expectation of the man lashing out, but Sewell took the planter's arm. "That's enough, Ellis."

Ellis grunted and stepped aside, but as Curran passed, the man caught his arm and leaned forward. "Watch your back, Curran."

Curran shook off the hand and, without looking at Ellis, walked away.

At the bar, he stopped, glancing into the side room to satisfy himself that Ellis and Sewell had resumed their seats.

He knew the barman, known to everyone as Tom, although his actual name was Yusuf. In fact, all the staff behind the bar were called "Tom," because the members couldn't be bothered learning their real names.

"Can I get you a drink, *tuan*?"

Curran shook his head. "Were you on duty on Sunday night, Yusuf?"

"I was, *tuan*."

"And Mr. Sewell, was he here?"

The barman's face showed no emotion but a slight tightening around his mouth revealed more than his words as he said, "Mr. Sewell was here. He dined with Mr. Ellis and three others."

"Do you know what time he left?"

The man polished a glass as he considered the question. "It was sometime after eleven o'clock. I know because the big clock in the hall struck as he passed it."

Curran held his peace. Sewell's wife had said he'd got home around midnight. Sewell had just told him he had not got home until the early hours of the morning. Sewell was only a fifteen-minute walk from his home on Cairnhill Road. If he'd left here around eleven, where had he passed the intervening time?

Curran thanked the man for his time and ordered a lime juice. He downed the refreshing drink in one draught and walked away from the Balmoral Club, conscious of the hostile glances from other members as he crossed the main room of the club.

He hated clubs.

❧ Ten

Wednesday, 2 November

Harriet had a poor night's sleep as she wrestled with Li An's revelations of the previous day. Now she understood the ties that bound Li An and Curran but what if those bonds were severed, where would that leave them both . . . Cast adrift? She turned her overheated pillow over and lay looking up at the mosquito net above her.

Worst of all, Li An had made her promise to say nothing to Curran. She hated being put in the position of a confidante in this manner, but a promise was a promise. She just hoped that she would not be required to keep her peace for too much longer.

A note that arrived during breakfast did not improve her mood.

Julian looked up as Harriet groaned aloud. "Who is that from?"

"Alicia Sewell. She has asked if I will accompany her to Tony Dowling's funeral this morning. I can hardly say no."

"Why would she ask you? You barely know her."

Harriet shook her head. "I have a friendly face?"

Julian chuckled and returned to the paper as Harriet scribbled a reply for Alicia's messenger.

Alicia's note had said that she would collect Harriet at ten, which seemed rather early, but Harriet dressed in her funeral clothes and was waiting when the blue Rolls-Royce turned in through the gates. Motor vehicles were still a novelty on the island, and this was by far the grandest vehicle Harriet had seen.

Alicia disembarked, dressed like Harriet in black with a heavy veil rolled up over her hat.

"I am terribly early," she said. "Do we have time for a cup of tea?"

Harriet invited her guest to join her on the verandah and sent Huo Jin for tea.

"To the memory of poor, dear Tony," Alicia said, raising her cup. "Such an awful way to die. That nice Inspector Curran says it is murder. It's just too awful to contemplate." She gave a shudder.

"I'm sorry. It's a terrible shock for all of us. You must have got to know Mr. Dowling well over the last few years?"

"He joined the society when he arrived in Singapore about two years ago. It was a pleasure to find a man of his talent. He could have been a professional . . . indeed he told me he had wanted to pursue a career on the stage but"—she shrugged—"the practical need to earn a living prevailed. His sister in New Zealand suffers ill health and he sends money back for her."

"Did I hear someone say he was in insurance?" Harriet asked.

Alicia nodded. "He worked for a New Zealand broker. George had quite a bit to do with him over the insurance of shipments of rubber and gambier. I met him at a dinner party given by my husband's business associates. When I found out he could sing, I introduced him to the society."

"And what does your husband do?" Harriet inquired, adding, "I don't think we have met."

"That's not surprising. He's hardly ever at home. He's a

commodities broker for a London company—rubber, gambier, pepper . . . anything like that, really. The rubber boom has been tremendously good for business so he is always traveling around visiting plantations here and on the peninsula."

Harriet cast a glance at the expensive motor vehicle. The rubber boom had indeed been good for business, Harriet thought.

"And Tony Dowling's business insured your husband's shipments?"

"Mostly. It doesn't always go well. They had a terrible loss earlier in the year. A ship carrying rubber from Port Dickson to Singapore went down in the Malacca Straits and they lost the whole shipment. It was fortunate it was insured. Tony saw to the business side of that." She waved a hand as if magicking away the loss of thousands of pounds' worth of goods.

"And the crew?" Harriet asked.

"I think they lost a couple of sailors but they were only natives."

Harriet swallowed back a response to Alicia's indifference to the loss of human life but she liked the soprano a little less.

Alicia raised a hand to her cheek, her mouth drooped and her eyes brimmed with tears. "I can't quite believe he's dead."

The theatricality of the gesture was not wasted on Harriet.

"Do you know what they are going to do about the show?" Harriet asked.

Alicia swallowed and dabbed the corners of her eyes with a lace-edged handkerchief, managing a wobbly smile. "I believe Charles is going to audition a tenor from the policemen's chorus. He understudied Tony in *Iolanthe*. Not quite the same level as Tony but he will do. As they say in the American circuses, the show must go on. You will stay on, won't you, Mrs. Gordon?"

"Of course. I've been rather enjoying it," Harriet said.

Alicia nodded. "You have a pleasant voice, Mrs. Gordon . . . may I call you Harriet? Have you done much singing?"

"Church choirs and my mother's drawing room." Harriet pulled a face. "Although I doubt my mother would approve of me treading the boards, even in an amateur production." She glanced at her watch. "I think we need to leave if we are going to be in good time, Mrs. Sewell."

"Oh, Alicia, please. I do believe it is going to rain. Do you have a spare umbrella I can borrow?"

Curran hunched beneath the large utilitarian umbrella they kept in the Detective Branch's motor vehicle and reflected that it always seemed to rain on funerals. This internment of Anthony Dowling in the Protestant section of the recently consecrated Bidadari Cemetery off Upper Serangoon Road was no exception.

He stood at a discreet distance, watching the small group of people who had turned out for the occasion. Both Dowling's housemates, Fraser and Butcher, were in attendance, as was his employer, Mr. Henry, and Charles Lovett.

For a man who had been the center of so much feminine attention, only two women were present. Alicia Sewell, wearing black from head to toe, stood beneath a large umbrella, with her arm tucked into Harriet Gordon's, her face shadowed by heavy black net. Harriet, in a funereal black skirt and jacket over a crisp white shirt, met Curran's gaze. He cast her a questioning look; after all, she had said herself that she hardly knew the man. She smiled and cast a meaningful glance at her companion that gave him the answer.

As they waited for the priest to organize himself, Charles Lovett joined Curran.

"Not much of a showing," Curran said. "I had rather gained the impression he was a popular young man."

Lovett looked around the damp cluster of mourners. "The cemetery is a fair distance from town. Perhaps no one wished to come out in this weather." He paused, his mouth curling in a humorless smile. "They do say you know who your friends are by who turns up for your funeral."

"Your wife is not present?"

"Elspeth is rather old-fashioned. She doesn't believe women should attend internments." Lovett's gaze flicked to Alicia and Harriet, and his mouth tightened.

The officiating priest opened his prayer book and cleared his throat, cutting short any further conversation. The rain poured down, and the priest raced through the formalities as quickly as he could manage.

As the mourners dispersed, huddled under umbrellas, Mr. Henry caught up with Curran.

"Inspector, I wonder if you could come to my office tomorrow morning? I have something I wish to show you."

"Of course."

"Good, I shall expect you about ten?"

Curran watched the man hurry away, nimbly avoiding the puddles in the path.

Dowling's housemates were the next to pass him. He greeted them by name, and they stopped.

"Poor old Dowling. We thought there might be a few more people here to see him off," Butcher said.

"Pretty dismal sort of a day for it too." Fraser glanced down the path, where Mr. Henry could now be seen at the gate to the cemetery trying to hail transport on the sparsely populated Upper Serangoon Road. "I suppose Henry had to make the arrangements. He's a dry old stick," Fraser said.

"Do you know him well?" Curran asked.

"The insurance business is a small world, Inspector. We all know each other," Fraser replied.

"How did Dowling get on with him?"

Fraser shrugged. "They were both from the same part of New Zealand, so I think at that level they rubbed along all right."

Butcher shot his friend a sharp glance. "There was that time earlier this year when Henry had to go home, and he left Dowling in charge."

Fraser gave a snort of laughter. "Dowling was in his element. Told us he wanted the manager's role and rather hoped Henry wouldn't come back."

"But he did," Butcher added. He glanced at his watch. "Good of Dowling to give us an afternoon off work. We're off for a beer. Want to join us, Curran?"

Curran declined, and they both bade him good day and hurried away.

Alicia Sewell and Mrs. Gordon were the last to leave, cramped together under the large umbrella that he recognized as belonging to Harriet.

"Allow me, Mrs. Sewell."

Curran held out his arm to Alicia Sewell, and she slipped a gloved hand into the crook of his elbow and drew into the shelter of his umbrella, leaving Harriet to follow.

"Thank you, Inspector. Such a sad day. He was too young," Alicia said.

Curran murmured the appropriate aphorisms.

"He made me laugh, Inspector, and I will miss him." She glanced back at Harriet. "I am so grateful Mrs. Gordon agreed to accompany me. I asked George to stay on, but he insisted he had to go up-country with that awful man, Ellis. Some sort of trouble on one of the Sungei Pandan plantations in Johor."

"Ellis is not a friend?"

"Not of mine. He is a business acquaintance of my husband's, no more. I find the man an insufferable boor. The way he spoke to the servants . . . I was lucky our *jagar* did not resign on the spot after his last visit." She shivered. "I told George that Ellis is not welcome, and if he wished to entertain him, he could do so at the club."

"He is not a man given to respect feelings," Curran agreed.

"I am appalled he got away with what he did to that poor coolie."

"I had hoped for a slightly different outcome," Curran conceded.

A fine motor vehicle stood drawn up at the gates, with a uniformed chauffeur in attendance. The man hurried forward with an umbrella, and Alicia turned to glance back at the cemetery.

"I hope you find his killer soon, Inspector. It is awful to think there is someone out there who could be so cruel. Mrs. Gordon, may I offer you a ride back to your home?"

Harriet looked to be on the verge of accepting, but Curran remembered the letters he had retrieved from Dowling's bedroom.

"Actually, Mrs. Gordon, if you can spare an hour, I've got some work for you at South Bridge Road."

Harriet cast a longing look at the substantial Rolls-Royce and sighed as she glanced at her watch. "Of course, Inspector."

Fortunately, they did not have to wait long in the rain as an empty gharry trundled past. Curran hailed it and they clambered in. The roof leaked and Curran could have sworn the driver deliberately targeted every pothole in the road.

"What is it you want me to do?" she asked.

"I have some letters retrieved from Tony Dowling's room. I thought a woman's eye might read more into them than me."

Harriet laughed. "Billets-doux?"

"I think so."

"And I'm such an expert on love letters? I don't think I've ever received one in my life. Have you?"

"Hardly." Curran smiled in response. "Oh, I think I once received a Valentine from a friend of my cousin Ellie's but it was anonymous, so I never knew who sent it."

"And she's probably nursing a broken heart to this day. Have you had any news from your cousin?"

Curran's favorite cousin, Lady Eloise Warby, known to her family as Ellie, had met Harriet during Harriet's time as a suffragette in London, and in August the news had not been good. Ellie had been involved in a hunger strike in Holloway and had been released close to death.

"Depends on who I believe," Curran said. "According to Ellie, she's back to her old self, campaigning for the WSPU and getting into scrapes but her husband writes her health has been badly affected." He paused and looked at Harriet. "You would know."

Harriet nodded. "It took me months to recover." She touched her throat. "If I get overtired, the cough comes back. The force-feeding causes irreparable damage."

"I can imagine," Curran said. The more he read on the treatment of the suffragettes, the more his sympathy became aligned to their cause.

"Simon tells me that women have the vote in Australia. I don't understand why Britain is so determined—" She broke off. "Sorry, Curran, not a subject to interest you."

"But it does," he said. "I told you when I first met you, I was sympathetic to the philosophy of the cause. What concerns me are the radical actions they are now resorting to."

"'Deeds not words' is Mrs. Pankhurst's new creed." Her mouth tightened and just for a fleeting moment he thought he saw the pain of her own experience in her eyes. She took a breath and turned to him. "Why do you want me to look at these letters?"

"You're better at reading handwriting than me."

"I see." She paused and gave him a cheeky smile. "You just don't want to read all the silly sentimental drivel, do you?"

And that, he had to admit, was true.

He coughed. "I trust you to spot if there is something some- one has written that might point to our murderer."

"You really think it's one of Dowling's lady friends?"

"Or a husband. His preference seemed to be married ladies."

He looked out at the passing streetscape of recent subdivi- sions, where new rows of shophouses were rising from the swamp and the jungle. The boundaries of Singapore itself were stretching out and kampongs were becoming extensions of the town. There was even talk of the tramway being extended north.

"Li An told me she took tea with you and Lavinia yesterday. How did she . . . seem?" He tried to make it sound like a casual inquiry, but his throat constricted.

Harriet said nothing for a long moment, and he turned to look at her.

"She mentioned her mother was unwell. It must be difficult being here in Singapore when your beloved parent is in Penang." Harriet sounded matter-of-fact, but he caught an edge of eva- siveness in her tone and wondered if she knew something he didn't.

"She was very close to her mother," Curran conceded.

Before she met me.

"Does she have much family in Penang?" Harriet asked.

"She comes from an old Straits Chinese family," he said. "They've called Penang home for several generations. So, yes, she has a strong tie to Penang."

And it's calling to her.

As the gharry turned into Victoria Street, Curran fell silent, lost in thoughts that Harriet had no hope of discerning. He obvi- ously had a strong suspicion that all was not right with Li An and it was troubling him.

She blew out her frustration on a breath. Curran and Li An

were entitled to their secrets, and it was no business of hers . . . except she cared for both of them and hated to see them in pain. Curran deserved the truth and Li An had made Harriet an unwitting partner to her deception.

They alighted from the gharry at the South Bridge Road Police Headquarters and Curran placed an arm around her, pulling her closer under the umbrella as they ran for the shelter of the building.

In his office, Curran retrieved a bundle of letters tied up with string and handed them to Harriet.

"I found these in Dowling's room hidden under his mattress. I haven't had time to go through them. I am interested in any that might be relevant to his current . . . current . . ."

"Amours?"

Reading Tony Dowling's love letters promised to be a more interesting assignment than her usual tasks.

The very faint odor of a stale scent, a sickly mixture of rose and eau de cologne, emanated from the bundle, and she grimaced. "I never believed women really perfumed their letters," she said.

"Nauseating, I agree," Curran said.

"It's getting late. Can I take them home with me?"

"If you undertake faithfully not to mislay any of them. They are potentially important evidence."

"Of course," she said, stung by the implication.

As if he read her thoughts, he said, "It's not that I don't trust you, Mrs. Gordon, but you have mislaid evidence before."

She glared at him, and he rewarded her with a smile. Yes, she had mislaid evidence in the past and she didn't need reminding of the fact. She placed the letters in her handbag and headed for the door, bidding Curran good evening as she passed.

Curran glanced at his wristwatch. "I'll escort you downstairs and hail a gharry for you."

"No need—"

Curran smiled. "I insist. You can't go home in a ricksha in this rain."

The deep storm drains that lined South Bridge Road ran like a torrent, lapping over onto the five-foot ways. As always in bad weather, gharries, hansoms and rickshas disappeared, and it took a good fifteen minutes for Curran to hail down a hackney cab.

She arrived at St. Thomas House, damp and out of sorts, to find Julian and Will in the living room playing chess as rain lashed the shuttered windows and dripped from the roof into several strategically placed buckets set around the room.

They both looked up at the bedraggled specter in the doorway.

Julian jumped to his feet. "Harri, come in, sit down. Will, fetch a towel. Drink?"

"What an evening," she grumbled as she accepted the gin and tonic Julian had poured for her.

"I think we will probably get flooding with this rain," Julian agreed as he settled back to the chess game with Will. "I hope it clears up for the weekend."

"Checkmate, Uncle Julian," Will said.

Over the months as they had adjusted to life with their ward, they had settled into "Uncle Julian" and "Aunt Harriet" at home, but definitely "sir" and "Mrs. Gordon" at the school.

"How did you do that?" Julian stared at the board.

Harriet left them to it and retired to her room to change into dry clothes.

After dinner, with the rain still beating on the roof, Julian snoozed in his chair and Will sat at the table working on his homework, and Harriet retired to the sofa with the Dowling letters. She set a kerosene lamp on a table beside her and undid the string binding them.

There were just over a dozen letters written in different hands. The well-schooled young ladies who had authored them may not have signed their names, but they had all dated their letters, which made sorting them so much easier. Unsurprisingly, they began not long after Dowling had arrived in Singapore at the end of 1908. Several were of the "I must leave Singapore but I leave my heart behind" sentiment and these she returned to their envelopes and set aside.

She had loved her husband but they had never been sentimental in expressing their emotions, and she found the lovelorn scratchings and lyrical poetry interesting. Annoyingly, many of Tony Dowling's conquests resorted to silly pet names like . . . "Your dearest kitty cat . . ." or "Your blushing rose . . ." which led Harriet to wonder if the women's names may have been Katherine or Rose.

The clock struck nine, and she sent Will to his bed and returned to the letters. One letter, written on a violet-colored writing paper and exuding lingering traces of eau de cologne, caught her eye.

Darling Tony, the letter writer had scribed. *"When, in joy, I woke to find Mine the heart within thee beating, Mine the love that heart enshrined . . ." When you sing that ballad to HER, my heart weeps, for it describes so perfectly how I feel when I am not near you. When you smiled at me tonight, I thought I would burst with happiness, and I cling to the memory of your caresses that night. When can we meet again?*

Harriet frowned at the quoted words. They sounded familiar. What ballad were they from? She rose and wandered over to the bookcase and picked up the program from the music society's production of *Iolanthe* in July.

She ran her finger down the program and smiled as she saw the title of the Strephon and Phyllis duet . . . "None shall part us from each other." She would have to double-check the lyrics for that song but she would wager the quote came from that duet. The letter writer had either attended the production of *Iolanthe,* or in all likelihood was someone in the society. Her heart raced a little faster at that thought. In the tropical heat, the company's leading man became the focus of attention for the women of the company, but who among them did he single out?

As Tony Dowling's character, Strephon, had sung the ballad with Alicia Sewell, it ruled out Alicia as the letter writer. She was not familiar enough with Alicia Sewell to recognize her writing and she felt it was probably below Alicia's dignity to resort to love letters, particularly written on violet writing paper. Apart from anything else, Alicia, she suspected, would know how to handle an affair without resorting to perfumed pleas.

She turned to the remaining missives but none of them were recent. It seemed after the company's production of *Iolanthe* earlier in the year, Tony's admirers had stopped writing letters or Tony hadn't kept them.

The very last missive, a plain buff envelope inscribed *Tony* with no evidence of it having been through the postal system, contained only a drawing . . . a pencil portrait of Tony Dowling. She held it up to the light and studied it. It had been drawn with confidence and talent, catching the leading man in a pensive pose, his eyes gazing out into the void. It had probably been hand-delivered either in person or slipped under the door to his home. Another of his many admirers at the society, she concluded, sliding the drawing back into the envelope.

She returned to the letter with the quote from *Iolanthe*. It was a common enough writing paper, not one generally used by the few women of her acquaintance but it seemed familiar. Someone had written to her recently . . .

She rose and riffled through her own writing box, finding the letter from the secretary of the Singapore Amateur Dramatic and Music Society thanking her for her interest, advising of her successful audition, offering her the role of Kate and inviting her to the first rehearsal of *Pirates of Penzance*.

She laid it beside the note to Tony Dowling and smiled. Not

only was it the same violet writing paper, but the writing and blue ink were unmistakably that of the billet-doux addressed to *Darling Tony*.

Elspeth Lovett had penned those desperate words. Elspeth Lovett had been one of Tony Dowling's conquests.

❦ Eleven

Thursday, 3 November

From behind the door of the Caldwell & Hubbard Insurance office came the sound of typewriting, the click, clack of the keys moving with a rapidity that would have put Harriet Gordon to shame. When Curran knocked, the typing ceased, and the junior clerk admitted him into the office. The man resumed his seat behind the typewriter as John Henry rose to his feet.

"Good morning, Inspector. This is our clerk, Amir." Henry waved a hand in the clerk's direction.

The young man looked up at Curran with bright, intelligent eyes and smiled.

Henry gestured at a chair. "Take a seat, Inspector. Terrible weather we are having. I wouldn't be surprised if the rivers flood."

Curran took the seat behind what had once been Tony Dowling's desk and made the appropriate response regarding the weather. His boots were already soaked from the ten-minute walk from South Bridge Road.

"What did you want to show me?" he asked as Henry dispatched his clerk to bring tea.

"I realized after you left, I had not disclosed everything."

Henry sighed. "This is very awkward. A week or so ago I received a letter from the head office in Auckland. Several high insurance payouts had been noted, and Auckland requested I conduct an audit of the claims. To my shame I had not begun the inspection until yesterday."

He pulled a letter out of a drawer and handed it to Curran. The request for the audit cited five cases. The top of the list, the most recent was *Claim A3978/10: Loss of Hesperides: Six thousand pounds.*

Henry unlocked one of the wooden cupboards and handed a slender cardboard folder to Curran.

Curran read the title: *Claim A3978/10: Hesperides.*

The folder was empty.

He looked up at Henry. "You brought me here to show me an empty folder?"

Henry shook his head. "But that's the point. It shouldn't be empty. It's a claim Dowling handled while I was away earlier this year. I had urgent family business in New Zealand to deal with and I left him in charge for three months. This claim is heading the list the company has sent me and I know nothing about it. I don't know what I am going to say."

"Is that the *Hesperides* file?" Amir pushed open the door, balancing a tray with teapot and cups.

Curran looked at the young man. "Yes. What do you know about it?"

Amir set the tray down and poured three cups of tea. "The *Hesperides* was a coastal trader. It left Port Dickson on the fourth of February with a cargo of rubber heading for Singapore, where it was to be loaded onto *The Orient* bound for San Francisco. It never made Singapore. It started taking water just out of Port Dickson and sank off Rupat Island. Two hands were lost along with the entire cargo."

"Nothing salvageable?" Curran asked.

Amir shook his head. "No. It sank at quite a depth and was

not considered salvageable or a hazard to shipping so its cargo was written off."

"How much was it worth?"

"As the letter states, the insurance claim was for six thousand pounds," Henry said.

Curran let out a low whistle. "That's a great deal of money. I know the rubber price is high at the moment, but still— Who benefitted?"

Henry shook his head. "I don't know. Every skerrick of paper relating to the claim has been removed from that file." His mouth twisted. "I only found it because I thought it prudent to go through the list I had been sent. I turned the office upside down looking for the paperwork."

"Amir?" Curran directed the question at the clerk.

The young man had returned to his chair and sat with his legs crossed, sipping his tea. "This I cannot tell you either. Mr. Dowling would not let me handle the file. Anything that needed typing he did himself."

"Is that unusual?"

"Very." Amir glanced at his employer. "I hope I am not speaking out of turn if I observe that Mr. Dowling was not one to make extra work for himself if it could be avoided."

John Henry nodded. "I was very fond of young Tony, but his heart belonged to the stage, not the insurance industry."

"How did he come to be here?" Curran asked.

"I know the family," Henry said. "His sister is not in the best of health and his father is . . . not reliable." He made a hand gesture that indicated a fondness for the bottle. "Tony needed a job to support his family, and I offered him a post at Caldwell & Hubbard when he was a lad just out of school. He actually had a good head for the job, and when I was appointed manager here, I asked if he would like to come for the adventure." He shook his head. "It shouldn't have ended so badly for him."

"That was none of your doing."

Henry pointed at the empty file. "I have nothing more than an old insurance agent's instinct, Inspector, but there is something very wrong about this."

"And what is that instinct telling you?"

John Henry's pale-gray eyes met Curran's. "It is telling me that Dowling may have made some bad decisions along the way."

"Did he have regular clients?"

"Of course. Amir, can you put a list of Dowling's regular clients together and pass it on to the inspector?"

The young man nodded.

Curran pulled out a desk drawer. "May I . . . ?"

Henry waved a hand. "Go ahead."

The drawers in Dowling's desk revealed nothing important, except the young man's interest in the theater. He pulled out playbills and newspaper reviews of theatrical and musical productions, a tobacco pouch and cigarette papers and a bag of boiled sweets fused together by the humidity. Conscious of the concealment of important papers behind drawers, he searched every cavity but found nothing hidden in the recesses.

He closed the drawers and opened the empty file cover for the *Hesperides* claim. "Surely you must have a record in your financial accounts of where the payment went?"

"Yes, of course I do. I'll check the ledger. Give me a minute or two." He withdrew a large ledger from the safe behind his desk and resumed his seat, running his finger down the neat rows of writing and figures.

Amir coughed.

Curran looked at him. "Is there something else?"

Amir shot a worried glance at his employer, who waved a hand without lifting his eyes from the ledger. "Go ahead."

"On the day the loss of the *Hesperides* was reported, Mr. Dowling was most upset. I remember he sat at his desk with the newspaper and he was shaking his head."

"It was a large claim," Curran suggested. "I imagine it would be hard on your business."

"Oh no. It was not the money. I heard him say, '*No one was meant to die*.' Then he threw the paper down on his desk and stormed out without another word."

Henry looked up from his perusal of the ledger and frowned. "It's always tragic when there is a loss of life, but it happens, particularly with shipping claims. I imagine the families were compensated."

"Is there anything else you recall about that claim?"

The young man shook his head. "No. There is nothing." Amir looked down at the keyboard of his typewriter and fell silent.

Henry sat back in his chair and looked at Curran. "I am afraid I cannot help you with the ultimate beneficiary of the claim. We paid it out to a firm of solicitors—Lovett, Strong & Dickens. They have offices in Raffles Place."

"I know them." Curran picked up the empty folder. "May I take this?"

"Of course. It's of no use to me."

Curran stood up, circling his helmet in his hands. "You have both been most helpful. If you remember anything else, you know where to find me."

At the door he turned back and held up the empty folder. "Are there any others like this?"

"With missing paperwork? Not that I have discovered, but looking over the ledger here, there seem to be several commodity shipments, handled by Dowling, that have been the subject of claims over the last year. More than I recall in previous years."

"Perhaps if you start by providing me with the details of every claim Dowling worked on since his arrival?"

Henry sucked on his moustache. "That will take a while, Inspector. Are you sure you want *every* claim?"

Curran considered for a moment. "Mr. Henry, I trust your instincts on this. Let's start with every claim that doesn't feel quite right to you. Look for patterns in the claims and the insured."

Henry nodded. "That will still take me a few days, Inspector." He shook his head. "I have to admit, Curran, I find this most unsettling. The reputation of Caldwell & Hubbard Insurance is at stake here."

Mercifully, the rain had abated but the amount of water that still spilled from the overfull storm drains and lapping banks of the filthy river made for a steamy and smelly mess. Curran opened his umbrella and, dodging puddles, set off on the short walk to Raffles Place and the offices of Lovett, Strong & Dickens.

The lawyers occupied an entire floor of one of the commercial buildings on the bustling Raffles Place, which was dominated by the two popular department stores, John Little and Robinsons. Curran entered the office and asked to speak to Charles Lovett. Tony Dowling and Lovett had a direct connection through the society, and it seemed more probable that Dowling's dealings were with Lovett. He had no doubt Lovett would set him straight if he was mistaken.

Charles Lovett rose from behind his desk as Curran walked in. From his impeccably combed steel gray hair to the tips of his polished shoes, Lovett exuded the persona of the successful lawyer. It caused Curran to wonder about the very different Charles Lovett who played the character parts in Gilbert and Sullivan. He regretted missing the production of *Iolanthe*.

"I really am rather busy, Curran. Can this wait?"

"My apologies but the matter is urgent."

Lovett resumed his seat behind his large mahogany desk and waved at the client chairs. "I suppose you had better sit. Is it still raining?"

Another conversation on the subject of the weather followed before Lovett leaned forward.

"Have you caught the blackguard yet?"

"No," Curran said.

"I am not sure I have anything more to add than what I have already told you, Inspector."

Curran let a couple of moments pass before he said, "What do you know about the sinking of the *Hesperides* in February this year?"

Lovett had not been expecting this and he visibly stiffened. "The *Hesperides*?" He frowned. "I recall we acted for the owners of the consignment that was aboard that ship when it went down."

"Were you aware Anthony Dowling was the agent who handled the insurance?"

Lovett shrugged. "I have a busy practice, Inspector. I don't have instant recall of every file in the office."

Curran fixed Lovett with an unblinking gaze. "Caldwell & Hubbard Insurance paid six thousand pounds to this office. Surely you would recall such a sizable amount coming through the books?"

Lovett made a dismissive gesture with his hand, waving aside the sum. "Oh yes, now you mention it, I do vaguely recall the matter. Why is it of interest to you?"

Curran ignored the question. "I would like to know the identity of your client, the beneficiary of the insurance claim."

Lovett leaned forward, resting his hands on his blotter as he said with a smile, "I would like to help you, Curran, but you know as well as I do, I can't provide that information. There is such a thing as solicitor-client privilege and that is a legal principle jealously guarded by the courts."

Curran stared at him. "Dowling is dead, and I am trying to find his killer."

"And you have not told me why you think the matter of the *Hesperides* is connected with his death. One thing I can tell you with absolute certainty, my client was not Mr. Dowling and that, Curran, is all you are going to get from me. Now, unless, there is something else I can assist you with, you can see yourself to the door. I am expecting a client."

As Curran stood up, Lovett said. "You asked about keys to the society's property, Curran. Unfortunately, my wife has not kept the key register up to date. This is the best I have."

Curran looked down at the paper Lovett handed him. It seemed to comprise the names of half the company and included Tony Dowling and Alicia Sewell.

"Your security leaves something to be desired, Lovett."

"Until now it hasn't been needed. Members of the company could come and go freely and I know Tony liked to practice up there because he didn't have a piano in his lodgings. Sadly, we will be discussing taking further security measures at our next committee meeting."

Curran folded the list and stowed it in his pocket. "Will the show still proceed, Lovett?"

Lovett stared at him. "Of course it will. I think we have found a new Frederic."

Curran thanked him and left the lawyer to his important work.

During the wet season, which had begun in late September, it rained in Singapore with a peculiar ferocity, as if someone in the heavens had upended a bucket straight onto your head. It almost made Harriet long for the irritating London drizzle as she stood in the doorway to the Detective Branch, shaking out her umbrella. She seemed to be continually damp.

Curran stood at the evidence table with Singh and Greaves, and she joined them there, her nose twitching at the faint, acrid smell of smoke.

"What's the smell?" she asked.

"All that could be retrieved from Dowling's body," Curran said, and Harriet shuddered.

Singh read out Mac's report. *"I surmise Dowling had been wearing linen trousers, an excellent-quality linen shirt and a blue silk cravat. Unfortunately, very little of these items remained to be of any evidentiary value."*

It would appear that all that did remain—Dowling's boots; an old battered fob watch, the glass cracked and the hands frozen at twelve thirty; the few patches of tartan picnic blanket and the badly singed wallet—now lay on the table.

Harriet picked up the watch. Is that when he died?

Curran shrugged. 'Maybe. The time fits.'

He picked up the wallet and laid out ten dollars in notes, a handful of loose change, a letter and an assortment of scraps of paper and business cards on the table.

"Robbery was not a motive," Greaves observed. "What's this?"

The constable used a pair of long tweezers to pick up a used train ticket from among the ephemera of Dowling's life.

Curran took the tweezers from his constable and squinted at the ticket. "Tank Road Station to Bukit Timah railway station and return."

"Why would he be going to Bukit Timah?" Greaves asked.

"He probably liked the walk up to Bukit Timah Hill," Singh said. "I hear the lemonade at the rest house is good."

Curran shot his sergeant a bemused glance, placed the ticket in an envelope and went through the business cards . . . reading them aloud as he went: a tailor in Little India, a purveyor of cigars and cigarettes in Change Alley and . . . He stopped.

"The Sungei Pandan Rubber Co. Ltd.," he said.

"Ellis?" Singh said.

"It's a general company card, the sort any good insurance agent would have . . . but Lionel Ellis and Tony Dowling? What would those two have in common?"

"Ellis's plantation is only a mile from the Bukit Timah train station," Singh said.

"I wonder . . ." Curran said. He pulled a cardboard folder from his satchel and added it to the evidence table. "This is Dowling's file on an insurance claim for the sinking of the *Hesperides* in February. It was carrying a cargo of rubber from Port Dickson to Singapore—"

Singh frowned. "Port Dickson? That's not the port used for the rubber shipments."

"It was in this case. The cargo was not salvaged and two crew died."

"And the Sungei Pandan was involved?"

Curran shook his head. "I don't know, but this"—he held up the business card—"indicates some sort of connection between Dowling and Ellis's company. Greaves, see what you can find out about the directors of the Sungei Pandan and what the extent of the holdings are in Singapore and Malaya. I think it might require a visit to Port Dickson to find out what I can about the *Hesperides*. Singh, can you do some digging and see if any other shipments of Sungei Pandan rubber have mysteriously vanished in transit? I already have Henry looking at Dowling's other files. There may be something in there."

Singh shook his head. "This will not end well. Ellis will accuse you of harassment, Curran."

"I know, but this is nothing to do with the other matter."

"He will not see it like that."

"But if I can prove the connection . . ."

"Curran, ask yourself if this is not personal."

Curran straightened. "Of course it's not personal, Singh."

Harriet watched his face and saw the flicker of uncertainty behind his eyes. Curran took injustices, such as Ellis's fine for the assault, as a personal rebuke. It was probably his greatest weakness and the reason she admired him as a policeman and a friend.

She rummaged in her capacious handbag and pulled out the bundle of love letters, well wrapped against the rain.

"I went through these letters and there is something that might interest you." Harriet ordered them in piles on the table. "These appear to be from women who have left Singapore," she said, pushing one pile to the back of the table. "These are the most recent and, unfortunately, nearly all anonymous and the sort of sickly-sweet drivel you would expect." She paused for dramatic effect. "Interestingly, there has only been one in the last few months."

She took the letter from the envelope and laid it out. The soft violet of the writing paper provided an odd contrast among the burned remnants of Dowling's life.

Curran picked it up and read it through.

"The quote is from *Iolanthe*." She glanced at Greaves. "Am I right?"

Curran passed the note to Greaves, who nodded. "The Strephon and Phyllis duet."

"Played by Dowling and Alicia Sewell in the July production?"

"That's correct."

"So, the reference to *HER* would imply the writer is not Alicia Sewell?" Curran concluded.

"That would be my guess," Harriet agreed. "Now have a look at this letter."

She handed Curran Elspeth Lovett's letter welcoming her to the society.

"Good Lord," Curran said. "Do you mean that Dowling's anonymous letter writer is Elspeth Lovett?"

He handed both letters to Greaves, who nodded. "Undoubtedly the same hand." He let out an uncharacteristically low whistle. "Mrs. Lovett and Tony Dowling? I would not have picked that."

"You know them both better than anyone here," Curran said.

"Yes, but I would never for a moment have thought . . ." Ernest Greaves removed his glasses and blinked rapidly.

"I don't know why you should be so surprised. Everything we know about him points to a preference for married ladies," Singh said.

"Yes, but Mr. Lovett and his wife appear so devoted," Greaves said. "You'd agree, Mrs. Gordon?"

"They certainly give the impression of being an indispensable team when it comes to the society," Harriet said. "It wouldn't exist without them."

Curran took both the letters and set them down on the table. "But as we all know, appearances are deceiving. And this lot may be amateurs, but they are still actors," he said.

"One last envelope," Harriet said, and held up the buff envelope. She withdrew the drawing. "Undated and not a billet-doux in the conventional sense of the word, but interesting."

"And really rather good," Ernest Greaves said. "Whoever drew this had Tony Dowling to the life."

"But nothing to identify who the artist is or what her relationship with Dowling might have been," Harriet said, adding, "Assuming it's a her."

"It was among the love letters?" Curran said.

Harriet nodded.

Curran set the drawing down on the table. "It will have to remain a mystery for now. I think I need to have a chat with Mrs. Lovett." He glanced at Harriet, a hopeful smile on his lips. "Would you . . . ?"

She knew he wanted her to accompany him, her presence guaranteed to lull poor Elspeth Lovett into imparting information. He'd not been above using her as an unofficial police informer before now, but not this time. She still wanted to be a part of the society, and if the members started seeing her as a police spy, she would have to leave.

"No. I want nothing to do with it. That's your job, not mine,

Curran. I have reports to type. That is, after all, what I am paid to do."

And with that, Harriet retired with as much grace and dignity as she could manage to her corner of the office, flicking the cover off her typewriter with a defiant gesture. Curran just smiled and shook his head.

❧ TWELVE

Curran collected the two Lovett letters and took the motor vehicle to the Lovetts' home, Cairnhill House, built on the highest point of Emerald Hill, rising above the old McKinnon plantation.

It was a house intended to impress; double story with a wide porte cochere under which Tan drew the motor vehicle to a halt. Charles Lovett's business in the law must do them very well, Curran thought as he alighted, straightening his jacket.

An immaculately dressed majordomo met him at the door and he followed the man up a grand, sweeping stairway to the large, airy living space above the porte cochere, where a woman reclined on a rattan daybed, fanning herself with a palm-leaf fan. A girl of about sixteen or seventeen, in a drab, crumpled gray gown, her hair still in two long plaits, sat at the table working on a piece of artwork, a still life of a Chinese basket and palm leaves. She looked up as Curran was shown in, but went back to her drawing without registering any curiosity at his presence.

The woman rose to her feet as he entered. She was one of those women of indeterminate age, her bouffant blond hair swept into a knot on top of her head and arranged in curls around a plump, pretty face. She wore a pink gown, amply trimmed with lace over a heavily corseted figure. The constrictions of women's fashions always struck Curran as bizarre, particularly in this unforgiving climate.

"Mrs. Lovett?"

She stood, swaying slightly as Curran took the outstretched hand. Even at this early hour, he thought he caught a miasma of alcohol about her.

He introduced himself and apologized for the intrusion.

"Inspector Curran. My husband has mentioned your name." Her words slurred. "He's at his office if you wanted to speak with him."

"My questions are for you, Mrs. Lovett."

"Me?" Elspeth's hand went to her throat. "What could you possibly want with me?"

"It concerns the death of Anthony Dowling." Curran glanced at the girl. "I think it best if I speak with you in private, Mrs. Lovett."

Elspeth waved a hand at the girl. "This is my daughter, Eunice. I'm sure there is nothing you have to say . . ."

Hearing her name, Eunice looked up, her gaze traveling from her mother to the policeman. Eunice was as dark as her mother was fair, with a thin, pointed face disfigured with acne. She glowered at Curran from under a heavy fringe of hair.

"I beg to differ," Curran said firmly. "I would prefer to keep our conversation between us alone."

Elspeth sighed. "Very well. You can stay here, darling. We'll use Papa's study."

Curran followed Elspeth back down the stairs to a room that appeared, from its heavy, masculine furniture and wall of books, to be part office, part library.

As the door closed behind them, Elspeth turned and leaned against the desk. She smiled at him and said in a laughing voice, "All so serious, Inspector. Should Charles be here?"

"I don't know . . . should he?" Curran asked.

The coquettishness vanished in the blink of an eye, and she straightened.

"Poor Tony was a lovely young man, but he was just another member of the society, Inspector. I'm sure nothing I can say will add to your picture of him."

"Then perhaps you can explain this."

Curran pulled the letter with its distinctive violet writing paper from his pocket and held it up.

Elspeth's lips parted. "Ahh," she said, subsiding onto the nearest chair and covering her eyes with a well-manicured hand.

He held the letter out for her inspection. She gave it no more than a passing glance, before pushing his hand away.

"Did you write this, Mrs. Lovett?"

"You know I wrote it, or you wouldn't ask me," she said, her tone low and petulant.

Curran waited as Elspeth pulled a handkerchief from her sleeve and dabbed her eyes.

No point in prevaricating. "Were you and Tony Dowling having an affair?"

She squeezed her eyes tight shut as if willing him to vanish, but he was not going anywhere. "Mrs. Lovett?" he prompted.

"You have to understand, Inspector, Charles is so . . . so very English but Tony was different. He was a New Zealander, you know, and he didn't have that sense of upholding propriety. He was irresistible and fun. Yes, that's the word, fun. The colonials are so much less stiff, don't you think?"

Curran thought of Griff Maddocks's friend Simon Hume. Harriet had been stepping out with the Australian journalist for some months, and while Curran had not met Hume often enough to have formed an opinion, he would hardly have described the man as "fun." However, Harriet seemed to like him and he presumed Hume had qualities that distinguished him from the other single men of Harriet's acquaintance.

"He made me feel young and pretty," Elspeth said, her mouth

turning down and making her look anything but young and pretty.

"Was it just flirting, or did it go further?"

Elspeth flinched as if he had raised a hand to her. "Really, Inspector, you've come this far. Why don't you ask me if we were intimate?"

Curran didn't ask but he left the pause long enough for Elspeth to answer it herself.

"Yes, we were lovers. We used to meet up at the society's property where no one would be likely to disturb us." Her lips tightened. "I'm not proud of myself, Inspector. I just wanted a diversion from the tedium of being Charles Lovett's wife. Now you probably think the very worst of me."

"It's not my role to cast judgment on anyone, Mrs. Lovett. I seek only to find who murdered Anthony Dowling."

She blinked. "You know that for certain?"

"Yes. He was dead before the fire was lit."

Her hand went to her high lace collar and tears filled her eyes.

"Can we return to Sunday night?" Curran said.

Elspeth's chin came up. "Very well. If it helps. Charles had gone to the Balmoral Club. He had a client with a big case the next day and he wanted to go over a few points with him." She paused and took a deep breath. "I met Tony at the society property."

"What time did you meet?"

Elspeth sighed. "I slipped out about ten. It's only a five-minute walk from here and who was there to see me? I intended to tell him it had to end. This had to be the very last time, but he had champagne and caviar and I couldn't resist . . ."

She trailed off and more tears trickled down her face. She dabbed ineffectually with her now-sodden handkerchief. Curran produced a clean handkerchief and handed it to Elspeth. She blew her nose loudly and screwed the handkerchief into a ball.

"Why did it have to end?"

"I would have thought that was obvious. I am a married woman, and I had the music society to consider. It wouldn't be long before someone took an interest and then the gossip would start . . . I just couldn't face that."

"Forgive the observation, Mrs. Lovett, but he was considerably younger than you."

She jumped to her feet. "Why should that matter? He said he liked older, more experienced women and he knew how to make a woman feel like she was the only one who mattered, the only woman in the world for him."

Curran thought about the pile of love letters hidden beneath Dowling's mattress. Had all those women felt the same way?

"You said he had food and drink with him. How did he carry it?"

Curran's patience and sympathy had run their course. He just wanted answers and he was now a police officer interrogating a witness.

Elspeth caught the change in tone, and all the bravado leeched from her face.

"He borrowed a picnic basket from one of his housemates. We set it out on the veranda—" The tears were real as she snuffled into Curran's handkerchief. "Just him and me and to hell with the rest of the world."

"What time did you leave him?"

"Just before midnight."

"And he was still alive."

Elspeth gasped. "I assure you, Inspector, he was quite alive. We kissed, and I slipped home. No one saw me. The servants were all in bed."

"Did you see anyone else?"

"No! I told you, no one saw me."

"That wasn't the question I asked, Mrs. Lovett."

Elspeth shrank back against the cushions. "You mean did I see . . . the killer?"

"Well?"

"I . . ." Her eyes darted around the room. "No, Inspector, I saw no one."

He let a long silence pass.

"It was nothing," she said with a dismissive wave of her hand. "I just thought I saw a movement in the trees on the driveway leading up to the old house. I couldn't tell you if it was real or my imagination."

"Man or woman?"

Elspeth shook her head. "Just a flash of something light. I believe in ghosts, Inspector, and it can be very unnerving up there late at night."

"I'm sure it can," Curran said. "What about your daughter?"

Her eyes widened. "Eunice is seventeen. She was at home, asleep in her bed."

"I'd like to ask her a few questions."

"I absolutely forbid it. She is a sensitive girl and Tony's death has already upset her—"

The door opened and Eunice stood in the doorway, her face drained of color.

"Eunice, go back upstairs. This is nothing to do with you."

"But it is, isn't it, Mama?"

"Were you listening at the door?" Elspeth's eyes narrowed. "I've told you before—"

"Of course I was listening. It's the only way I know what is going on in this house. I'm not a child anymore. I knew all about you sneaking off to be with Tony."

"Eunice—"

Eunice cast her mother an unsympathetic glance. "I saw Tony kissing you in the scenery store a few weeks ago. How could you, Mama?" she said in a voice that was low and controlled and filled with so much hurt, so much betrayal . . . her parents' marriage and something else?

Elspeth subsided onto a chair, covering her face with her hands. "I'm so ashamed."

Eunice turned her gaze on Curran. "What do you want to ask me, Inspector?"

Curran looked from mother to daughter and wished Harriet Gordon had agreed to come. He felt completely out of his depth in the face of the outbursts of emotion.

"Where were you on Sunday night, Miss Lovett?"

"Here, at home, in my bed. My maid can attest to that."

"You weren't up at the McKinnon property?"

"No, but I heard Mama go out about half past ten and I heard her come home just after midnight."

"Do you know where she went?"

Eunice's eyes did not move from her mother. "Where she always goes late at night when Papa is not at home. To meet Tony at the society's house."

"And how do you know that is where she always goes?"

Eunice snapped her gaze back to him, a frown creasing her forehead. "I—"

"You know because you have followed her?" Curran suggested.

A muscle twitched in Eunice's cheek. "Yes. I have followed her before . . . but not last Sunday. You have my word, Inspector."

Elspeth held out a hand to her daughter. "Eunice, darling, let me explain—"

Eunice ignored the gesture. "There is nothing to explain, Mama."

She turned and left the room, with every inch of the same rigid control she had shown through the whole interview. The door shut behind her, leaving Curran and Elspeth Lovett alone again.

From beyond the door, the footsteps broke into a run, clattering up the stairs. A door above them slammed, and the muffled sound of weeping drifted through the ceiling.

Elspeth rose to her feet. "I think you have caused enough trouble for one day. I am going to have to ask you to leave."

Curran didn't move.

The woman's bravado faltered. "Will Charles have to know?"

"This is a murder, Mrs. Lovett. What do you think?"

It was not his place to provide the woman with advice on her marital woes.

As he left Cairnhill House, Curran glanced back. Eunice Lovett stood in one of the upstairs windows, watching him.

✺ THIRTEEN

At the end of a long day, Curran went in search of Maddocks and found his friend propping up the Long Bar at Raffles. Seeing Curran, Maddocks raised his hand to beckon him over and pushed a long glass of foaming beer at his friend.

"You look like you need this," Maddocks said.

Curran removed his hat and ran his fingers through his damp hair. "I had a particularly difficult witness to interview. It is one of the less pleasant aspects of this job, unpeeling people's private lives."

Maddocks raised an eyebrow, his journalistic interest piqued.

Curran narrowed his eyes. "Honestly, Maddocks, you are like a dog who smells a bone."

"Anything is better than reports of shareholders' meetings and church bazaars. Have you any leads yet?"

Curran made a show of looking at his watch. "It's Thursday. I'm rather surprised you haven't been dogging my footsteps all week, looking for a story," Curran said.

"I've been a little under the weather. A bad curry in Little India on Monday night." Maddocks grinned. "Come on, Curran. Surely some little morsel for a desperate journalist?"

"As you are on my list of suspects, I am hardly likely to confide in you."

"Me? A suspect?" Maddocks sounded indignant.

"What the hell are you doing treading the boards with the music society, Maddocks?"

Maddocks stiffened, placing a hand on his chest. "How offensive. I'm Welsh. I like to sing."

"Still—"

"I'm particularly fond of *The Pirates of Penzance*, Curran, and I've been enjoying it. At least I was . . . Dowling's death is a trifle unsettling," Maddocks said.

"So, I have one of my constables typecast as a policeman, Harriet Gordon playing a silly sister . . . What part do you play, Maddocks?"

"The Pirate King."

Curran choked on his beer as a laugh caught him. "You? The Pirate King?"

"Now I really am offended. Do you think I lack piratical qualities? I get to swash and buckle and belt out a damn fine tune. It's bloody good fun!"

"I'm sure it is. My aunt dragged us all to the Savoy to see the D'Oyly Carte company at every opportunity. Put me off for life," Curran said. "You couldn't persuade the lovely Doreen to join the merry band of troubadours?"

"The lovely Doreen has been doing weekend duty at the hospital, so I'm at rather a loose end," Maddocks said with a grimace.

Curran smiled. "Remind me how long you have been stepping out with Sister Wilson?"

Maddocks shrugged. "Four months but she doesn't play tennis, loathes cricket and has no interest in Gilbert and Sullivan."

"What do you have in common?"

Maddocks frowned. "She's a killer bridge player, doesn't mind the music halls and is always up for a tea dance."

Curran smiled. Playing bridge, tennis and tea dances were all such normal everyday things a person did with a normal everyday partner. Not things he would contemplate doing with Li An. Their haven was the little bungalow on the Everton estate, and when Curran was at home, they played chess, read or listened to the new gramophone he had recently purchased.

"How did you talk Harriet into joining the society?"

"She took little persuading. She's always up for something new and she sings rather well." Maddocks smiled and drained his glass. "Maybe not as well as she plays tennis though."

Maddocks toyed meaningfully with his now-empty glass, and Curran ordered a fresh round.

"Did you know Anthony Dowling?" Curran asked.

"Are you interviewing me?" Maddocks curled his fingers around his glass and raised it to his lips.

"Yes," Curran said.

Maddocks shrugged. "I knew him well enough to pass the time at rehearsal but not to have a beer with," Maddocks said. He pushed the fresh beer glass to one side and drew a finger in the moisture on the bar. "One thing that puzzles me about his death is what the hell he was doing up at Emerald Hill on a Sunday night?"

Curran hesitated. "Do you have any ideas?"

Maddocks's lips twitched. "I heard gossip."

"And . . . ?"

"Dowling had a key to the property, and he used to go up to the old house for practice and clandestine meetings with members of the fairer sex." Maddocks's eyes gleamed with journalistic fervor. "From what I gather, the man had a positive harem of ladies. It would be the ideal place for a bit of privacy."

"I know all that. His preference definitely seemed to be for married ladies."

"The lonely memsahib with a husband up-country would make the ideal companion," Maddocks agreed.

"Were you aware of any particular relationships within the cast?"

Maddocks rolled his eyes. "The place is seething with under-currents."

The policeman considered that statement. "Was there anything between Dowling and his leading lady, do you think? Did you ever see them together?"

"Not outside rehearsals but they had done a few shows together as the romantic leads so they could certainly give the impression of being romantically involved. You have to understand, Curran, theatrical folk can begin to live their onstage persona offstage."

Curran scoffed. "Spare me."

Maddocks grinned. "Not one for the theater, Curran?"

"No."

"So, do you think Dowling's death may be related to one of his amours?" Maddocks fished.

"It certainly points that way but there may be something else and something you could help me with."

"Go on."

Curran hesitated. He had not been above using Maddocks's access to journalistic sources in the past.

"Apart from his peccadilloes, what else do you know about Anthony Dowling?"

Maddocks frowned. "He was an insurance agent for a New Zealand firm. Been out here a couple of years."

Curran toyed with his glass. "Back in February the firm he worked for, Caldwell & Hubbard Insurance, lost a ship carrying a consignment of rubber in the Straits. Do you remember the incident?"

"I hadn't been in Singapore more than a month." Maddocks frowned. "Yes, I remember it. A couple of the crew went down with the ship. Nothing was recovered."

"Dowling handled the insurance claim but there seems something odd about the whole affair. To begin with, all the paperwork at Caldwell & Hubbard is missing."

Maddocks let out a low whistle. "Yes, I can see how that could look suspicious. You'd like me to do some sniffing around Caldwell & Hubbard?"

Curran shrugged. "Anything you can discover through your sources . . . might be useful."

Maddocks nodded. "Usual terms?"

Curran smiled. "Usual terms" meant Maddocks got to break the story.

"Do you want to go down to the quay and find something to eat?" Maddocks suggested. "Hume is up-country chasing a story in KL and I think my cook has given up on me. I warn you, I'm a bit off curry at the moment."

Curran swilled the last of his beer. "Where do things stand between the charming Australian and Harriet?"

Maddocks shrugged. "Hard to say. When he's in town, they catch up but it's not the sort of things chaps discuss, is it?"

Something wistful in Maddocks's expression caused Curran to wonder, not for the first time, if Maddocks might carry a torch for Harriet. Clearly Harriet saw the journalist as nothing more than a good friend, and now that she had Simon Hume paying court, Maddocks stood no chance.

"Any more trouble from Ellis?" Maddocks asked, clearly changing the subject.

Curran shook his head. "I ran into him at the Balmoral Club. Blew a lot of hot air in my direction but hopefully he's crawled back to his plantation now. He's got no grounds to feel badly done by. None at all."

Maddocks gave a snort of laughter. "I'm not sure he sees it that way. He's a man to hold a grudge."

Curran shrugged. "I did not become a policeman to make friends, Griff. Ellis doesn't scare me."

Griff's eyes widened. "Well, he scares me," he said. "I wouldn't want to work for him."

"Unfortunately, he's not alone. There are too many Ellises

out there," Curran said. "Unless their workers lodge a complaint, there's damn all we can do about it."

Curran glanced at his watch and pushed back from the bar. "Time to go. Thanks for the offer of supper but it's getting late and Li An will be wondering where I am."

Conscious he had consumed several beers and had nothing to eat, Curran stopped in Chinatown, where he bought some satay sticks from a street seller and some *bak kwa,* strips of spiced-and-dried meat much beloved by Li An. The sweet peanut satay sauce on the chicken sticks satisfied the immediate need for sustenance, and knowing Li An would expect him to eat on his return home, he stuffed the packet of *bak kwa* in his pocket and set off to his bungalow on the Everton estate.

Despite the growing late hour, he had no fear of walking alone through Chinatown. Most of the residents knew the tall policeman by sight, and his familiar khaki uniform was protection enough.

The thought of a beer and a chance to sit out on the verandah with the gramophone playing while he and Li An talked put an urgency into his step. He had been working late since Monday, and after the strange encounter with her cousin on Monday night, he felt a growing sense of unease. He didn't consider himself especially sentimental, but he treasured the quiet moments he spent with her and maybe he needed to tell her more often, reassure her she was the first and only love of his life.

Leaving the lights and the five-foot ways and the shophouses, he passed the shanties of the city's poor and turned down the narrow lane that ran from Craig Road to Cantonment Road. Across the railway line, the jungle still dominated, dark and filled with the sounds of a myriad of insects, the chatter of monkeys and the rustle of unseen animals, mostly feral dogs, pigs or goats.

As he drew closer to Cantonment Road, he paused, alerted

to a rustling sound in the undergrowth caused by something larger than a feral pig. There were no more tigers on the island, but that did not mean a predator of a different sort wasn't lurking in the dark. Every nerve prickled, and he took a step back as a dark shape loomed up from the darkness, two legged and definitely human. He appeared to have a dark scarf tied over the lower part of his face and carried something in his right hand . . . something that looked like a club.

He stood between Curran and a still, silent Cantonment Road. The only person likely to be within hearing was his syce, Mahmud, whose hut was only a hundred yards away. Mahmud was over sixty, deaf, and a strong wind would knock him flat, let alone a man of the size confronting Curran now.

Curran barely had time to unbuckle the cover of his Webley as the man made his move, coming at him with a roar.

Only the superb reflexes of an athlete overcame the effect of the beers and he just had time to twist to one side as the cudgel came down, catching him a glancing blow on his upper left arm. It knocked him off-balance, sending him down on one knee, his arm ringing in pain, the fingers of his left hand numbed and useless. The man lifted his cudgel again, but this time Curran was ready, and he rolled out of the way as the man brought the weapon down.

Curran regained his feet and swung around to face his assailant, hauling on the butt of his Webley with his good right hand. He pulled it free and drew back the hammer with an audible click.

"Drop it," Curran said, his breath coming in quick gasps.

The man didn't move.

"No, Inspector, you drop yours." The accent was more East London than East Asia and it accompanied the click of another cocking handle being drawn back.

Something cold and metallic pressed into Curran's neck and he stiffened, releasing the catch of his Webley and letting his fingers fall from the butt. The weapon hung useless from its lanyard, as the second man pressed his own weapon harder against the beating pulse in Curran's neck.

"I'm a policeman," Curran said.

"We know," the first man said. His accent, like his companion's, held a strong cockney twang. "And there's no one here but you and us. Your uniform won't save you from what you 'ave coming, copper."

"*Watch your back on a dark night. Your pretty uniform won't protect you,*" Ellis had said. The wretched man had wasted no time.

"Did Ellis send you?"

"Don't know who you're talking about," the man holding the revolver said. "Get on with it, you big oaf. We don't have all night."

The big man advanced on Curran with an almost deliberate slowness, as if considering what to do next. He opted for a fist in the stomach. Curran went down on his knees, completely winded. As he gasped for breath, a heavy booted foot to the ribs sent him sprawling.

The man raised his cudgel, and Curran curled up, instinctively braced for the next blow. It didn't come.

Out of the dark came an unearthly ululation and a third man joined the fray, leaping onto the back of the man with the revolver. His assailant temporarily distracted, Curran closed his fingers around the butt of his Webley, rolled onto his back, cocked the weapon and fired into the air. A troop of monkeys somewhere in the surrounding trees screeched their protests and flew crashing through the trees. The first thug found himself looking straight into the barrel of the Webley as Curran dragged himself to his feet, his left arm pressed against his ribs.

He pushed the man down to his knees.

"Hands on your head," Curran wheezed.

"Get this bastard off me," the second man complained.

Curran's rescuer had secured the second thug and sat on top of him with the man's arms twisted behind his back. He looked up at Curran, and Curran nodded.

"Let him up."

The young man, an Indian by his dress, released the thug and the man huffed out a breath as he pushed himself up.

"On your knees. Hands where I can see them."

The man complied, casting a sideways glance at his companion.

"Who are you, who sent you?" Curran gasped as he forced the air back into his lungs.

The second man looked up.

"We was sent to give you a warning to leave honest men be," he said.

Curran gave a snort of disgust. "You are both in so much trouble—" Curran began, cutting off as the chug of a motor engine and the blinding light of overbright headlights came around the corner from Cantonment Road.

The sudden illumination momentarily blinded Curran, and he put his hand up to shield his eyes. The two men took advantage of the distraction and turned on their heels, running like the devil was behind them down the lane toward the railway line. Curran turned on his heel, resisting the urge to fire blindly into the dark of the railway cutting, down which his assailants had vanished. He stood in the middle of the road, the Webley hanging from his right hand, and swore volubly.

"I say, is there anything I can do?" The English driver of the motor vehicle drew to a halt, the engine idling. "I just happened to glance down the lane and saw a bit of a tussle going on. Thought you might need an extra pair of hands."

"Nothing to do here," Curran said.

No point in telling the man that in his enthusiasm to help he had allowed the assailants to escape.

"I say, are you a policeman?"

"Yes," Curran managed. Now the adrenaline had begun to fade, the pain in Curran's left arm and his ribs set in with nauseating intensity.

"No point suggesting you report it," the driver said with a forced laugh.

"None at all."

Curran made his weapon safe and returned it to the holster before he went down on his haunches, grasping his arm.

"You're hurt. I could take you to the hospital," the driver of the vehicle said.

Curran shook his head. "Nothing's broken and I live just by here. You've done enough. Be on your way."

"If you're sure. Hope you catch the sods."

No chance of that, Curran thought as he watched the taillights of the motor vehicle round a bend in the road and disappear into the night.

"He is right. They hurt you."

The young man held out his hand to help Curran to his feet.

"Thank you, my friend, you saved me a bad beating." For the first time, Curran looked into the face of the man who had saved him. A tall, young Indian, dressed in tunic and trousers. He held his mud-smeared turban in his hand.

"But not soon enough. Is anything broken?"

Curran moved his arm and flexed the fingers of his left hand. He concluded that he may have a couple of cracked ribs and that by the morning he would have some magnificent bruises, but it could have been so much worse.

"I'll live," he said. "What's your name?"

There was the faintest hesitation before the man replied. "Jayant."

"Thank you, Jayant."

"Let me see you to your house."

"There is no need . . ." Curran began, took two steps and the world began to spin.

Jayant was at his side, his arm around Curran's waist, hooking the policeman's uninjured right arm around his shoulder.

They made slow progress across Cantonment Road and up the narrow lane that led to Curran's bungalow. It was only after the gentle glow of the kerosene lamp that Li An put out for him pierced the dark night that it struck Curran that the young man had not asked where he lived.

Li An stood with one hand on the verandah post as if she had been watching out into the night.

She gave a cry of alarm. "Curran, I heard a shot. What has happened?"

Curran disengaged himself from Jayant's grip and subsided onto a chair.

"A couple of thugs waylaid me, but this young man came to my aid."

Li An turned to the young man. "Thank—" She stopped. "You!"

Li An rarely displayed emotion, but Curran saw fury in the heightened color in her cheekbones and her widened, angry eyes.

"You're acquainted?" Curran asked.

Li An did not take her eyes off the man as she said, "Back in the time of the Hungry Ghost Festival this wretch followed me. He watched the house, and it was he that Harriet and I saw at the temple."

Curran brought his scattered thoughts together, the fingers of his right hand instinctively closing over the butt of the Webley again.

"Who are you? Come into the light."

The man stepped into the light, his head held high. Curran looked him up and down, seeing a man in his midtwenties, his mud-streaked clothing undistinguished, clean-shaven . . . but as his gaze met Curran's without blinking, the policeman felt his world tilt.

Jayant's right eye had the milky film of blindness. He was face-to-face at last with the one-eyed man who, in August, had left notes for Curran written on joss paper, terrified Li An and led her and Harriet Gordon into a dark and dangerous part of Chinatown.

The man who claimed to have information about Curran's father.

"Who are you?" he said between gritted teeth.

"I told you. I am Jayant." The young man raised his hands. "I never intended to cause fright to you, Miss Khoo. My business has always been with you, Curran, and I come as a friend."

Curran rose to his feet, wincing as a cracked rib caught. He drew himself up to his full height and stood eye to eye with this shadow of the past few months.

"What is your business with me?"

Jayant nodded. "It concerns your father . . . our father." He raised his chin and said, "I am the son of Edward Curran."

Curran let his hand fall from the butt of his revolver and for a long moment no one moved.

This man . . . this stranger . . . was his brother?

"How is that possible?" Curran said at last.

"It is a long story, and I have wanted to tell you for so very long."

"It better be good—"

Li An stepped between the two men. "There will be time for talk. Jayant, if that is your name, make yourself useful and fetch the doctor," she said. "You, Curran, sit down before you fall down."

"I don't need the doctor. There is nothing broken, but I do need my sergeant, Gursharan Singh."

"Then I will go and fetch him," Jayant said. "I will be very quick."

Curran gave the young man Singh's address in Little India, and over the man's objections gave him money for transport.

Alone with Li An, Curran laid his head back against the chair. Now that the attack had passed, everything hurt. Li An eased his jacket off and held the lamp up to his injuries. Her face revealed nothing, but he heard the hiss of indrawn breath.

"Is it bad?"

She probed his ribs with ungentle fingers.

"Ouch!"

"You've had worse, Curran, and they didn't hit your face. Be thankful." She took his face in her hands and kissed him. "You will mend." She drew back, still holding his face between her hands. "Do you know who did this?"

He saw the fear in her eyes and knew she suspected her brother.

"It's not Zi Qiang. I know damn well who did it, or at least who organized it. Lionel Ellis."

"Ah. The planter who beat his coolie." Li An shook her head. "What will you do?"

Curran shook his head. "I have plenty of witnesses to his threat, but to prove it, I have to find the thugs he hired first. That's why I've sent for Singh."

Li An straightened. "I will fetch some balm for the bruises."

"I'd rather you fetched a whisky."

"Is that a good idea?"

Curran shifted slightly, his cracked ribs sending a shaft of pain through him. "A very good idea," he said.

He closed his eyes and waited without moving until she returned with a tub of the evil-smelling salve she bought from the Chinese medicine hall in South Bridge Road in one hand and a glass of whisky in the other.

She set to work with the balm, and he took a thankful sip of the Scotch.

"This man," she said as she worked. "This Jayant. Do you believe him?"

Curran tried to shrug, but that hurt too. "I don't know. He

knows something and I need to hear his story before I decide whether he is who he says he is . . . Ouch!"

Li An made a remark in Penang Hokkien that Curran did not understand but he gathered from her tone that it was derogatory. To distract himself, he let his thoughts move to his encounter with Jayant.

It now seemed possible that the rumors were correct. His father had survived the Battle of Maiwand and, if Jayant spoke the truth, had gone on to have a second family.

He closed his eyes and took a deep breath. Was he ready to hear the truth?

❧ FOURTEEN

Sergeant Singh had been and gone, taking with him several burly constables. They were headed for the docks at Tanjong Pagar with the rough descriptions of the two assailants. Singh had retrieved the cudgel and the revolver from the scene of the assault but neither had any useful identifying marks on them, and even with fingerprints, the sergeant was not optimistic about finding the perpetrators among the many ships that crowded the harbor.

Curran waited until the sound of the motor vehicle carrying the two policemen had faded into the distance before turning to Jayant, who lurked in the shadows of the verandah.

"Sit." Curran gestured at one of the battered rattan chairs.

Jayant perched on the edge of the chair as if at any moment he would spring to his feet and flee. Li An took her usual seat, adjusting it so she sat closer to Curran.

"Whisky?" Curran offered.

The man shook his head. "I do not take strong liquor."

Curran poured himself a glass from the bottle Li An had left on the table beside him and downed his drink in one gulp. It did nothing to dull the pain from his injuries, but in this moment, they seemed secondary to the extraordinary conversation that would follow. For that he needed courage.

As if sensing his hesitation, Li An took his hand, her fingers tightening around his.

"Where do we begin, Jayant?" he asked.

Jayant swallowed. "This is hard for me too, and I understand that you may doubt me," he said, "but I have proof that I am the son of Edward Curran."

He fished a cloth bag from his tunic and extracted an envelope. Curran took it from him, still warm from the man's body. He unwound the string that secured it and laid the contents on the table.

The first was a small object in a silken bag. Curran looked up at Jayant and the young man nodded. He undid the strings of the bag and shook out a gold signet ring. Too dainty to have belonged to a man. As he turned it to the light, he let out his breath, recognizing the heraldic symbol of a leopard rampant, the unmistakable arms of his grandfather, the Earl of Alcester. It was one of the family traditions, every woman in the Bullock-Steele family received a ring like this on their eighteenth birthday. His cousin Ellie wore hers on the smallest finger of her right hand. The men of the family, likewise, received heavy signet rings emblazoned with the leopard on their twenty-first birthday.

There had been no signet ring for Curran.

Jayant gestured at the ring. "Our father wore that on a thong around his neck until his deathbed, when he gave it to me. He said a woman had given it to him." He paused. "Your mother. It is yours."

Curran schooled his face to professional impassivity, belied by his own shaking fingers as he set the ring down on the table. He had not missed the word that hit him like a blow to his heart: *deathbed*. So, after all of this, that small light of hope had been extinguished. His father was dead, truly dead.

To distract himself, he unfolded the paper. For a long moment the words danced across the paper, a jumble of letters. He pinched the bridge of his nose and forced himself to concentrate, conscious that Jayant watched him without blinking.

Taking a steadying breath, Curran read:

Robert, my boy.

Only you are not a boy anymore, you are a man grown, probably with a wife and family of your own. If you're reading this, it is too late for us to meet again but there is something I must explain to you. I am sure your mother's family will have told you I died at Maiwand, you may also hear stories that do me no credit. What do they call me? The Coward of Kandahar? Well, this is the truth as I know it and I want you to know I am no coward and I never betrayed my regiment. My patrol was ambushed, and all my men killed. But the bastards spared my life. In the days that followed I had cause to wish myself dead. Ahab Khan had me tortured day and night and it is in those circumstances and those alone that I may have given him information he would use against us. I don't know or I don't remember. Those days are lost to me. What I do know is that on the day of the battle he dressed one of his own men in my uniform and put him in a position at his side, so that the British troops would think me the traitor . . . the Coward of Kandahar. I know this because he forced me to watch the battle unfold . . . the hell he inflicted on my friends and comrades. I prayed for death, but God is not merciful. Ahab Khan held me his captive for months, maybe years. To this day I don't know if he let me escape in the knowledge that I could never return to my fellows without fear of court-martial and disgrace. After all what proof did I have except the scars of torture? I made my way into India with nothing but rags. Your mother's ring I had been able to secrete. It was the only part of my old life I could hold on to. Being dark haired and speaking the language, I could pass as a native, but when I came upon Nira's village, I was on the point of death. Nira took me in and nursed me back to health and I found I didn't want to leave. I helped her as best I could with her business and together we watched our son, Jayant, and our daughter, Samrita, grow as I never watched you, my son, and I found happiness again. It is possible you may hear rumors of those who have seen me. India is a big country but I have had occasion in the city to turn my face from red coats, men I had known. As I write this, I know I have but a short time left on this earth and my greatest hope is that you have lived a good life, free of the taint of my dishonor. I will leave Nira and my children with sufficient means to keep them comfortable and I will entrust Jayant with this letter and your mother's ring as proof of my story on condition he will only seek you out if he has need of your help. Better for you to have thought me dead. God bless you, my boy.

Your father, Edward Curran, LT 1st Battalion South Sussex Regiment of Foot

Curran set the paper on the table beside him, using the empty glass to secure it from blowing away. He stared at it for a long, long moment before picking up the little ring and turning it over in his fingers.

Seeing that arrogant heraldic leopard brought back memories of all the injustices meted out to him by his mother's family. Had his maternal grandfather known Edward Curran had not died at Maiwand? Did his uncle know . . . ? How different would his life have been if Edward Curran had still been a part of it? He gripped the ring tight within his fist, feeling its solidity. When he opened his palm, it had left an imprint of the Alcester coat of arms.

He set it down and picked up the letter again, reading it through several times, committing the words to memory.

Better for you to have thought me dead . . .

How had his life been better for thinking his father dead?

The small child who had cried himself to sleep, until his uncle and his cousin George had convinced him with the strap and fists that "real men" didn't shed tears, stirred in Curran's memory. Only the unconditional love of his paternal grandfather had saved his childhood, but after he had died there had been no escape from his uncle . . . his aunt . . . and his cousin George. No escape.

He reached for Li An's hand again, needing the reassurance of her presence. Something warm and familiar in a world that had just spun off its axis.

Who was he, this young man who had brought him this letter? Who now watched him, his one good eye, brown, not the light gray of his father, unblinking. What help did he seek?

Curran looked up at the young man he should now call his brother. "Do you know what is in this letter?"

Jayant nodded. "Yes. He let me read it before . . . before he left this earth. He was my father too and I mourn him still."

And I have mourned him my whole life.

"Was he a good father?" Curran asked, even though he had not consciously formed the question in his mind.

"He was the best of fathers," Jayant replied.

How did it seem so unjust that Edward Curran had been "the best of fathers" to this man when he had singularly failed to be that for Robert Curran? Did he honestly believe his son would do better in life without his presence—without the truth?

"How did you find me?" Curran, never lost for words, found himself struggling to put thoughts, let alone coherent sentences, together.

"I went first to England," Jayant said. "They would not admit me at Deerbourne Hall. The butler called me a filthy native and accused me of wanting to steal the silver." Jayant's lip curled in disgust. "I have no reason to love the British. I have seen them in India, little nabobs. I long for the day when India will be free of them."

"One day," Curran agreed, "but that is a discussion for another time. Finish your story."

Jayant gave an abrupt nod of his head. "A woman in the kitchen took pity on me. She gave me food and told me you were a policeman in Singapore . . . so here I am."

"Did you tell anyone who you were?"

Jayant gave a snort of derisive laughter. "No. That would have served no purpose, and no one thought to ask. The son of Edward Curran—a dirty native? Would it have been what they expected of our father?"

"Probably, and if it's any consolation, they despise me too. You don't escape the stench of the stables simply by eloping with the earl's daughter," Curran said.

Jayant nodded. "I know the story." He paused. "He loved my mother, but he mourned yours to his dying day."

Curran turned the words over, wondering why they brought him so much comfort.

He brought his attention back to the here and now. "So, Jayant, why have you sought me out? Is my father correct? What help do you want from me? It must be serious if you pursued me to England."

Jayant sighed. "I am not sure if you can help but I had no one else to turn to. It is my . . . our sister, Samrita."

"Samrita." Curran said her name, slowly turning over the syllables in his mind: *Samrita . . . Jayant . . . Robert Curran.* Once more the odd one out.

Curran closed his eyes and leaned his head back against the chair. His arm and ribs throbbed, and he was uncertain how many more revelations he could bear. A hitherto unknown brother and now a sister? This evening had become a delirious dream . . . a sort of wild nightmare in which everything he knew and understood vanished. Surely he would wake in the morning and life would be the same as it always had been?

"Curran, are you all right?"

He caught the anxiety in Li An's voice and brought his attention back to Jayant.

"You asked why I have come to you, Curran," Jayant continued, and Curran straightened, attentive to the man's story. "I am looking for Samrita. Nearly a year ago, not long after father died, a man came to our village, a cousin of the baker. He said he had come from Malaya, where he owned a tin mine. He had much money and a handsome face and he bought Samrita presents. Mumma thought him charming, and he shared our meals and our life. One morning he was gone, Samrita with him."

"Did she go willingly?"

Jayant's lips tightened. "This I do not know. Despite the presents and his charm, she showed little interest." He sighed. "But who knows what a girl is thinking? I tracked them to Calcutta but there I lost them. All we could do was wait, and it was many months before I received a letter. I have it here. Do you read Urdu?"

Curran shook his head.

Jayant pulled a paper from his bag. It was much creased and the paper as fragile as a butterfly wing.

"*Dear brother,*" Jayant read aloud. "*I am in despair. Come to me, take me away from this monster. I do not even know where it is he has taken me, but I know I am in Malaya and I am a prisoner and worse. Your loving sister, Samrita.*"

Curran took the paper from Jayant. The note had been written in pencil, the point of the pencil piercing the paper in several places. On the reverse side was written. *Jayant Kumar, Laxmangarh Sikar, Rajasthan, India.*

So, Jayant did not use the Curran name.

"Kumar?"

Jayant nodded. "That is the name my father took, and that is the name Samrita and I will bear to our graves."

"I see. And this letter . . . it is definitely from Samrita."

"Oh yes. I know her writing well."

"How did it come to you?"

"It came with a letter written by a letter writer. The man who sent it said she gave it to a workman who came to the house. He took it to the letter writer to explain how it came into his possession and in his turn placed it in an envelope and mailed it to me." He paused and took a visible breath. "I have come to you because I need your help to find her."

"Malaya is a big place, Jayant."

Jayant raised a finger. "Ah. I am a detective too. The letter was posted from Kuala Lumpur. I know the name of the man who was her abductor. The name of the bounder is Gopal Acharya. I went to Kuala Lumpur to seek her out and I found the house where she was being held. Here."

He thrust a piece of paper at Curran. Curran did not know Kuala Lumpur well, but he recognized the address as being in one of the better parts of the city.

"I was too late," Jayant continued. "The house was shut up. I asked, but no one knew where they had gone. No one knew a girl called Samrita. I am desperate and so I come to you."

Curran's professional mind started to piece together the puzzle, and he knew the answer before he asked the question: "What did you find out about the activities at this house?"

Jayant shivered, despite the warmth of the evening. "It was a house of ill repute. Many visitors, European and Asian men, the servant at the next-door house told me. He never saw the girls, but he heard them singing."

"Singing?"

"Oh yes, and a gramophone playing. Maybe they entertain their clients? My parents did not bring me up to know about these places, but I think of Samrita, and I despair. You are a policeman. You can find her . . . rescue her?"

The hope in the man's face cut Curran to the quick. "It's not that simple, Jayant. I have no jurisdiction in KL. It is one of the Federated Malay States and it's not as if prostitution, if that is the trade she is involved with, is illegal." The hope faded from the young man's face and Curran added, "But you were right to come to me. I will see what I can do."

He closed his eyes, trying to pull the scattered threads of his thoughts together. He could do nothing for his father, now twelve months in the grave, but this girl, whether or not she was his sister, needed help.

"I have one more thing for you."

Jayant fumbled in his bag and produced a creased and worn studio photograph of a family group and handed it to Curran. For the first time in his life Curran realized he was looking at an image of his father, a thin gray-haired man with a heavy moustache, dressed in turban, tunic and loose trousers, looking every inch a native of Rajasthan. He sat beside a woman dressed in a formal sari. Behind them to the right a slender young man in an embroidered tunic and turban.

"You?"

Jayant nodded. "Mumma and Dada and my sister. She was fourteen when that likeness was taken. She is now nearly twenty."

Curran studied the girl on the edge of womanhood. She had a perfect oval face, large eyes and curved lips. If she was now nineteen, she would be a beauty.

"Her eyes—" Curran said.

"She has her father's eyes . . . your eyes. Light eyes are not so unusual in the north of India but once seen they are not forgotten. Maybe that is why he took her?"

Curran nodded. That feature alone would surely make her distinctive and, hopefully, easier to find.

"May I keep this?"

Jayant nodded. "I have been carrying it for you."

They sat in silence for a long minute, a silence broken when Li An asked where Jayant was living. Curran squeezed her hand, grateful for her practical question. His own head spun with the events of the evening—and too much whisky.

"I have employment in Chinatown," Jayant replied, and his eyes slid sideways.

Li An snorted. "In the opium den of Madam Lim?"

Jayant shot her a quick glance. "I needed work and Madam Lim gives me a place for a bed. What happens in her house is no concern of mine." He rose to his feet. "I have taken enough of your time tonight. You are injured and need your rest."

Curran nodded. "I have a lot to think about, Jayant."

Jayant turned to Li An. "I am truly sorry that I caused you and your friend trouble in Chinatown that night. I was afraid that Curran was not interested in what I had to tell him and maybe I was not ready—"

Curran held up a hand. "Wait. That was months ago, Jayant. Why have you not been in contact before now? I waited for you that night at Change Alley."

"I had an urgent telegram to say my mother was very ill. I am sorry I did not send you word, but all thoughts except for Mumma were driven away. I had to return to India and my ship sailed that night. She is now dead without seeing her beloved daughter again."

"I'm sorry," Curran said, and meant it.

"When I returned from India, I went to Kuala Lumpur and that is when I found I was too late. Believe me, I would not have come to you if I had anywhere else to turn."

Curran rose to his feet and held out his right hand. "You are my brother," he said, his tongue tripping on the unfamiliar word. "Please call me by my given name, Robert."

Jayant took the proffered hand in both of his, his grip warm and firm. "Robert Curran. My brother."

He threw his arms around Curran, leaping away just as quickly in response to Curran's yelp of pain.

"Oh, sorry . . . so sorry," Jayant said.

Curran managed a smile. "It's fine. I'll live and thank you for your help tonight. I'm not sure I'd be standing here if you hadn't been there."

Jayant nodded. "I have come many nights, but my courage would fail me and I would go away again. I saw you tonight buying satay and followed you, and the gods sent those men."

"It was no god that sent those thugs," Curran said. "I know exactly who it was, and I will deal with him."

Jayant nodded. "I will go now. You will find me at Madam Lim's." He stepped back, bringing his hands together at his chest. "*Shubh ratri*. Good night, my brother."

Curran stood with his good arm around Li An's shoulders, watching as the dark swallowed up the tall, one-eyed man . . . the man who shared his blood.

❧ FIFTEEN

Friday, 4 November

Gursharan Singh loomed over Harriet's desk, and she looked up from typing Curran's notes on his interview with Elspeth Lovett. They made fascinating reading. She had had no inkling that Elspeth had been having an affair with Tony Dowling but then she remembered the argument at the last rehearsal. Her instinct had been correct, it had not been about costumes.

The Detective Branch had been in an uproar all morning as news of the attack on Curran became general knowledge. Curran had sent a message to say he was not badly injured but was recuperating at home. If anyone needed him, they knew where to find him.

Singh and a bevy of constables had scoured the docks the previous night but could not locate the offenders. They had gone out again in the morning and had just returned.

"What news?" Harriet asked.

"It would appear the miscreants were crew aboard the *Sally Anne*, which sailed at midnight bound for Hong Kong. We were too late." Singh's scowl deepened. "I have reported to Curran and sent word to Hong Kong but they are gone."

"How is Curran?" Harriet asked.

Singh shrugged. "Bruises and cracked ribs. I am sure he has had worse. I have told him there is nothing urgent for him but then I arrive here and find this has come from the bank." He held up an envelope and pulled out a sheaf of papers. "Mr. Dowling's banking details. I have to pursue inquiries in another matter, but I am certain the inspector would want to see these. Mrs. Gordon, out of the goodness of your heart, would you consider taking this to him at his bungalow?"

Harriet pulled the finished statement from her typewriter and placed it in a cardboard folder. "I have finished the reports from yesterday." She held out her hand and took the envelope from Singh. "I will drop everything with him on my way home."

"Thank you. That would spare one of my men," Singh said.

Harriet left the ricksha in Cantonment Road and walked up the lane leading to the bungalow Curran rented from the owner of the Everton estate. Curran sat on the front verandah, his feet up on a stool, reading a book. He looked up as Harriet approached, and he set the book down on the table beside him.

"Mrs. Gordon . . . Harriet . . . forgive me not standing. I am a little stiff today and I can't say I got much sleep last night."

He looked terrible. There were deep lines of pain around his mouth and eyes and she realized how narrowly he had avoided what could have been a fatal beating.

"Sergeant Singh told me you have cracked ribs. That can be very painful," Harriet said.

Something flickered in his eyes. "Not just the ribs."

"It's all anyone can talk about," Harriet said. "Gursharan told me the ruffians got away. Do you think it was Ellis?"

"I'm certain Ellis paid the thugs," Curran said, and sighed, "but I can't prove it and Singh tells me their ship has sailed. What have you got there?"

Harriet handed over the folder. "Yesterday's reports and an envelope with Dowling's bank statements."

Curran broke the seal on the envelope and scanned through the papers.

He let out a low whistle. "See this, Harriet? Dowling received a deposit of six hundred pounds in June. That's a lot of money for a lowly insurance clerk."

"And exactly ten percent of the value of the *Hesperides* claim," Harriet noted.

He looked up. "Well spotted. It is."

He returned the papers to the envelope. "Sorry, I can't even offer you a cup of tea. Li An went out this morning and isn't back yet."

"I am quite capable of putting a kettle on to boil if you would like a cup as well?"

"Thank you. If you can see to the tea and you're not in a hurry, I would welcome your advice on another matter. Not related to the Dowling case."

It could only be Li An, the last subject on earth she wanted to discuss with him.

She forced a smile. "Now you have me intrigued."

As Harriet busied herself with the tea-making ritual, she wondered how best to react if he was to tell her that Li An had left or had told him she was leaving.

I must appear surprised. She paused in her work and leaned on the table to gather her thoughts. *What can I say? The truth? That I have known for days?*

She carried the tea tray out to the verandah and poured them both a cup. Curran stared into the depths of the chipped china.

"Did you want something stronger?" Harriet asked.

He looked up. "No. I was just wondering where to begin with a story that seems as strange to me as it will to you."

"As the king in *Alice's Adventures in Wonderland* said . . . 'begin at the beginning and go on until you come to the end,'" Harriet said, and her betraying heart hammered against her chest as she steeled herself for a difficult conversation.

Curran set the cup down and ran a hand through his hair.

"Do you remember that business in August with the one-eyed man?"

Harriet stared at him. Of all the conversations she had been preparing for, it had not been about the one-eyed man. How was this related to Li An?

She gathered herself and managed a smile. "Yes. I can hardly forget. You were so angry with us."

Harriet and Li An's well-meaning pursuit of the one-eyed man through the streets of Chinatown in the mistaken belief he was connected with a case, only to find they had interfered in some private matter of Curran's, had accomplished nothing except raise his ire.

Curran cleared his throat. "He crossed my path again. In fact, he probably saved my life last night . . ."

"And is the mystery solved?"

"Yes . . . no . . . maybe. Between us, Harriet, I am struggling to understand the whole story."

Harriet frowned. "Understand, what exactly?"

"He claims to be . . . no, he is . . ." Curran narrowed his eyes and the words "my brother" came out in a rush.

"What?" she squeaked.

Out of all the possible scenarios Harriet had imagined about the one-eyed man, this had not even been in consideration.

"I know . . . it sounds absurd."

Harriet leaned forward. "Go on . . ."

Curran took a visible breath and winced as his cracked rib caught. "It's a long story, but he brought me sufficient proof for me to accept the truth. He is my father's son. His mother is Indian. So technically he is my half brother."

Harriet studied him, but his face revealed nothing. "And your father?" she ventured.

He met her eyes. "Dead but only in the past year." He shook his head. "All this time and I never knew."

"I'm sorry," Harriet said.

"That is the hardest part. The part I am really struggling with," Curran said. "He could have contacted me at any time in the last thirty years. Instead . . ."

He looked away.

"You are absolutely sure?" Harriet ventured.

He looked back at her. "He wrote me a letter."

"That doesn't necessarily prove—"

"It is definitely my father's hand. After Jayant left last night, I remembered I have a letter he wrote to my grandfather when he left for India. There's no mistake. The letters were written by the same hand. See for yourself."

He opened the book he was reading and took out two sheets of paper—one much folded and yellowed with age, the other more recent, the folds crisper—and handed them to Harriet.

As she took them, Curran held up the book. "This is all I have that was his."

Now Harriet could see the title on the spine—*Gulliver's Travels*.

A dozen questions roiled in Harriet's mind. She knew the story of Curran's father, the so-called Coward of Kandahar, whose betrayal had led to the disastrous defeat of the British troops at the Battle of Maiwand. How had he survived to father another son in India?

She turned her attention to the letters. One thing her work as a typist and stenographer had given her was an appreciation of handwriting, and it seemed to her cursory inspection that the handwriting was indeed from the same hand.

"You can read them," Curran said as she made to give them back to him.

The older letter, dated 3 August 1876, began: *Dear Da. Well, this is it. Ship sails on the tide. God alone knows when we will return. This is the best for Robbie and me. Hold him tight and don't miss the chance to tell him that what I am doing is be-*

cause I love him. He will be better off with Georgina's family. He'll have everything I can't give him. Education and opportunities will open up for him. I will write when I reach Bombay. Tell Robbie that I love him. Ned

She refolded the letter and handed it back to him and turned to the second, more recent letter written on Edward Curran's deathbed. She read it through twice before she looked up at him, blinking back tears for a man she had never known and for this man who had been denied the chance to know his own father.

"Harriet?"

She fumbled in her sleeve for her handkerchief. "Silly me," she said. "Something in my eye." She handed back the letter, her fingers brushing his. "Curran, I can only imagine what went through your mind when you read this."

He managed a smile. "Hence the sleepless night."

"I suppose it answers all your questions, but tell me more about this long-lost brother you knew nothing about?"

Curran shrugged and winced as he shifted position. "His name's Jayant Kumar and he's been tracking me for almost twelve months. He even went looking for me in England."

"Why?"

"He is looking for his . . . our . . . sister, Samrita. He believes she was, for want of a better word, kidnapped and is somewhere in one of the Malayan states."

"Kidnapped? Forced into marriage?"

Curran shook his head. "No. It sounds more like prostitution. Her trail has gone cold, and he thinks I have a better chance of finding her than him."

Harriet stared at him. "That's awful. Where do you even begin to look?"

He shrugged. "At the last place she was known to be . . . Kuala Lumpur."

"Does he look like you? I only had the quickest glimpse at the temple that night. All I remember was his blind eye."

He handed her a studio photograph of a family; father, mother and two youngsters in their best clothes posed stiffly for the camera. The stiff poses gave nothing away about the dynamics of the family but they looked easy with each other. Jayant's hand rested on his mother's shoulder and Edward Curran . . . his light-gray eyes, so like his son, discernible even in the grainy image.

"That is the only likeness of my father I have ever seen," Curran said. "I have no memory of him."

She looked up and saw the pain in his eyes. Without conscious thought she took his hand, twining her fingers in his. This private, reserved man was reaching out to her, and she wanted nothing more than to take him in her arms, share the burden of the pain.

But it was not her place or her right and she released her grip and withdrew her hand.

"That's it. I just wanted you to know that one little mystery is now solved."

Harriet studied Curran's face, seeing the troubled lines around his eyes. There was more, much more to the story.

"Your father left you a difficult legacy," Harriet said.

He smiled, a gesture not echoed with his eyes. "He has turned my world upside down."

"And this Jayant . . . your brother . . ."

"We are very different men from very different backgrounds. Sharing the same blood does not instantly bring us kinship. It is going to take time."

"And you do believe him?"

"Yes," Curran said. "If it had been about money, that would have been an end to it, but this is personal. He probably would not have come to me at all if he had not reached the end of his own initiative and resources."

"And if he is telling the truth, there is a young woman somewhere out there who needs you both."

He nodded. "Exactly. Thank you for understanding, Harriet."

"Harriet!"

Curran stiffened and Harriet turned to see Li An, carrying a basket, coming up the hill. Harriet waved in response. So Li An had not left yet and, she guessed, neither had she told Curran of her plans.

Li An reached the verandah and set the basket down on the table with a thump.

"What brings you here, Harriet?" Li An asked.

"I had some papers to deliver."

Li An's gaze flicked to the letters Curran had left on the table. "He has told you about our one-eyed man?"

Harriet nodded. "Quite a relief to know the truth."

"Maybe." Li An laid a hand on Curran's shoulder. "How is my wounded soldier this afternoon?"

He reached up and patted her hand. "Stiff and sore."

"I have been to the medicine hall, and I have a tea for you. Let me make you a cup."

Harriet rose to her feet and picked up the basket. "Let me carry this in for you, Li An," she said.

"I . . ." Li An began but Harriet had already headed toward the kitchen.

Alone with Li An, Harriet looked at her friend. "Li An—"

Li An held up a hand. "You are going to ask me, how I can leave when he needs me?"

"Well?"

"It changes nothing." Li An's eyes filled with tears. "I have to go, Harriet. Curran is strong and he will find that strength that sustained him before he met me. He has good friends and now he has a brother and a sister who need him."

"Is there nothing I can say to change your mind?" Harriet ventured.

Li An shook her head and Harriet sighed.

The trauma that had bound Curran and Li An had been

powerful but whatever drew her back to Penang exerted a greater power.

There was nothing more to say. Li An's feet now trod a path that diverged from what she had shared with Curran.

Harriet left Li An brewing her healing tea and returned to the verandah.

Curran looked up from *Gulliver's Travels* as she picked up her hat and bag.

"I must get home," she said.

"Any plans for tonight?"

Harriet shook her head. "No, Simon's pursuing a story in Kuala Lumpur. I don't expect him back until next week."

"So how will you pass your time?"

"I have a rehearsal tomorrow and church on Sunday."

Curran smiled. "Ah, the rehearsal . . . that will be interesting. Do they have a new Frederic?"

Harriet shrugged. "I don't even know if the show will continue. What about you?"

"I'll go to Port Dickson on Monday to follow up on the *Hesperides*."

"Are you up to it?"

"I'll be fine." He rose to his feet, but she didn't miss the grimace as he walked with her to the lane. When she was fifty yards down the lane, she turned and he raised his hand. She returned the gesture and with a determined step walked away.

❦ Sixteen

Despite Li An's objections, Curran took himself off to watch the Saturday cricket match on the Padang. He had been looking forward to playing but had to be content with a seat in the back of the stands where he could watch the match and, most important, think. He did his best thinking in the back row of the pavilion.

The Singapore Cricket Club batted first, and although they lacked Curran's talent, the two opening batsmen were doing well and looked set to make a good score. As Julian Edwards's talents lay in bowling, not batting, it would be some time before he was required to bat, and seeing Curran in the stand, he climbed the stairs to sit beside him, his pads and bat in hand, just in case he would be required to go in.

"Not disturbing you, am I?" Julian asked.

Curran shook his head and moved over to accommodate his friend. Julian gave him a good, long, hard look. "I heard about Thursday night. Who have you annoyed this time?"

"I have my suspicions, but I can't prove it," Curran replied. "Did you bring Will today?"

Julian pointed to a gaggle of young boys leaning against the fence. "I'll make a cricketer of him yet, although he has become rather sidetracked with an enthusiasm for the Boy Scouts."

Julian's mouth tightened, and Curran cast the man a sympathetic glance. Even though Julian was the principal of a well-respected school, money was always tight. Will's father had died penniless, and Harriet got no remuneration for her work at the school. It was fortunate that a grace and favor house was part of the arrangement.

"Harriet insisted on going to the rehearsal for *Pirates* today despite the awful tragedy." Julian tapped his cricket bat on the floor, betraying his unhappiness at his sister's decision.

"She seems to be enjoying it," Curran said.

"Hmm," Julian responded. He set the bat down. "Are you any closer to finding the perpetrator?"

That very question had been occupying Curran's thoughts when the reverend had joined him.

"No. There are a couple of possibilities."

Julian brightened, and Curran smiled. In the months he had come to know the Reverend Edwards, he had discovered the highly respectable reverend gentleman had a great interest in crime. Like his sister, he had an insatiable curiosity, although unlike his sister, his curiosity tended to be satisfied intellectually.

"Go on," Julian said.

"Between us, the most likely is a connection with the sinking of a ship back in February."

Julian raised an eyebrow and said, "Insurance?"

"Yes."

"And the other possibility?" Julian urged.

"Jealous husband."

"Oh yes, Harri told me that the young man had an eye for the married ladies." Julian left a pause, and when Curran did not respond, he added, "You're not going to tell me any more, are you?"

"No."

Curran cast Julian a sideways glance. The thing about this man of God, he made a good confidant, and in between his musings on the Dowling case, the other matter—the appearance of Jayant and the disappearance of the girl who was possibly his sister—kept pulling at the corners of his mind.

"Did Harriet tell you about the one-eyed man?" he ventured.

Julian shook his head. "That miscreant from August? Has he been bothering Li An again?"

So, Harriet had not rushed home to her brother with this juicy piece of gossip. There was so much he respected and liked about Harriet Gordon.

He took a breath and related the story of his meeting with Jayant.

Julian listened, hardly blinking. "That's an extraordinary tale," he said.

Curran fumbled in his pocket and pulled out his wallet. "He gave me this."

He handed over the studio photograph of Edward Curran and his second family.

Julian studied the photograph and nodded. "Your father? The likeness to you is unmistakable."

Curran took the image back and studied it, frowning. "Do you think so?"

Julian smiled. "Yes, Curran. It's in the eyes. What are you going to do?"

Curran squinted at the image, trying and failing to see what Julian saw. "Do? I've always been alone. Now I apparently have a hitherto unknown half brother and a missing sister. What am I supposed to do?"

Julian leaned forward, his hands clasped, his elbows on his knees. This time his silence invited Curran to continue.

"I know nothing of their lives," Curran went on, talking more to himself than to the man beside him. "Or they of mine. I must be at least ten years older than Jayant. All we have in common is this man." He touched the sepia face in the photo-graph. "Edward Curran may have been my father, but I didn't know him." And in the sympathetic company of this man of God, the words he had been holding on to so tightly came out. "Jayant and his sister had something I never had—a father they knew and loved."

"Does that make you angry?" Julian said.

Curran paused. Who should he be angry with? His father? Jayant?

His father was dead but Jayant had tilted his comfortable world off its axis and he felt himself falling out of control.

He shook his head. "No. I'm not angry . . . just saddened, I suppose, for all those wasted years. A family I never knew." He huffed a humorless laugh. "I'll reserve my anger for the family I did know."

"I think you just have to give yourself time, Curran. Get to know this man . . . your brother." Julian ran a hand through his hair. "And if you ever need someone to talk to, I'll be here." Julian jumped to his feet. "Oh, good shot!"

The two men politely clapped the six that had just gone sail-ing into the spectators and sat in silence watching a few more balls before Julian said, "Is there something else troubling you?"

Curran shot his friend a murderous glance. "I swear you re-ally can see into my soul."

Julian shrugged. "It goes with the job."

"I think Li An is going to leave me," Curran blurted out.

"What on earth makes you think that?" Julian asked.

"Her cousin is in town. He's been to visit her a couple of times and she's become distant, preoccupied. I know it's some-thing to do with her mother, but she won't talk to me. I think she is planning to go back to Penang, and I know there is noth-ing I can do or say to stop her from walking into a dangerous situation." He ran a hand over his eyes. "It's all going wrong and there's not a damn thing I can do to stop it."

Julian frowned. "What is the situation she will face in Penang that worries you?"

Curran paused. While he was in the confessional, he may as well continue. "Her brother is Khoo Zi Qiang, head of the Khoo clan. After his father died, Zi Qiang took over his import-export business. He turned to importing opium and other drugs into the Malay Peninsula. When I first arrived in Penang, Cuscaden assigned me the case of bringing the man to justice, but we needed evidence. Zi Qiang set his sister, Li An, on to me to win me over, feed me false information and prize details of the operation out of me."

Julian drew in his breath. "Curran!"

Curran shot his friend a self-deprecatory smile. "I'm not a complete fool, Edwards. I knew what she was doing and played it to my advantage. The unfortunate complication came about because neither of us had counted on falling in love." He gave a hollow laugh. "Stupid, unprofessional . . ." He shrugged.

"We can't help where love finds us." Julian's gaze stayed fixed on the cricket pitch, but his jaw tightened, leaving Curran to wonder if Julian had his own story of love lost. "Go on."

Curran hesitated and slowly, painfully, he told Julian the story of the night on Penang Harbour, the night he thought would be his last on this earth.

When he had finished, Julian said nothing, didn't move for a long, long moment. He turned at last to look at Curran. "Thank you, Curran. We knew . . . we suspected there was something fundamentally powerful holding you two together. When was this?"

"Toward the end of '08. Fortunately Mac was posted to Penang at the time and I would have died if it hadn't been for him." He leaned forward, forgetting his cracked ribs, and winced as he straightened. "Mac is the only other person apart from Cuscaden who knows the whole story. When I was fit for duty again, Cuscaden transferred me to Singapore and I brought Li An with me and we've been happy . . . at least I thought we were." He shook his head. "I don't know why I'm telling you this. It's no one's business but ours."

"You and Li An have built a fortress around yourselves and now that is threatened. You need to talk to someone, Curran, and if nothing else, as you have observed, I'm a good listener." He paused. "When Harriet arrived in Singapore, I tried to get her to talk about her time in Holloway but she pushed me away. I watched it eat away at her and I couldn't help her. I have much to thank Lavinia Pemberthey-Smythe for. She got Harriet to open up and it's been like a weight off her shoulders. Sharing a trouble is not a sign of weakness, Curran."

Curran had no answer for that. Never showing weakness had been beaten into him since childhood. He was a Bullock-Steele. His ancestors had arrived with William the Conqueror and plundered and pillaged their way to an earldom. Personal problems never entered into the family story, let alone talking about them.

Julian was not done. "As for Li An . . . If she is intent on returning to Penang, you can't stop her. She has to face her own demons."

A bubble of grief and loneliness welled inside Curran's chest.

"I can't imagine my life without her, Edwards." He grimaced at the humiliating crack in his voice as he said the words that had been crashing around his mind since the night he had encountered Li An's cousin. "Li An has always said we are bound by blood . . . but now . . ."

"Now she has healed. If she wants to go, Curran, you can't hold her."

Curran swallowed back the fear of being left alone, of a life without Li An . . . of admitting to himself that his need for her was greater than hers for him.

He sighed and lowered his head. "I know that."

"All relationships change," Julian continued. "You couldn't

keep clinging to each other and keeping the world at bay. Something would force a change and it's not just Li An. In the months I have known you, I sense something different in you too, a renewed confidence."

A roar from the crowd followed by a smattering of polite applause as the Singapore Cricket Club batsman started the long walk back to the pavilion caused both men to look up. "I'm in next," Julian said, rising to his feet. "You know where to find me."

Julian strapped on his pads and left Curran, jogging out onto the cricket pitch. No one expected him to make much of a score.

Curran pulled his pipe from his pocket and tapped it in his hands as Julian took strike. He had found the conversation with Julian had eased the pain and put his thoughts into some sort of context. Julian Edwards was that rare thing, a man of the cloth blessed with abundant common sense.

He allowed himself a smile as Julian swung wildly at his first ball. He may have been a man of many talents but Julian Edwards could not hit a cricket ball if it was tossed to him by young Will.

A lingering odor of smoke from the recent fire still hung over the old McKinnon property as Harriet joined the SADAMS company, gathered, as they had been instructed by a note on the door of the house, around the pile of blackened beams and twisted metal that had been the scenery store.

She found Griff Maddocks among the assembled company and slipped her hand into the crook of his arm.

"This is so bizarre," she said. "Why are we gathering here?"

Griff shrugged. "Lovett does like a grand theatrical gesture."

"Have you any thoughts on Tony's death?" Harriet asked.

Griff shook his head and glanced around at the other somber

faces. "There must be plenty of aggrieved husbands on the suspect list, but Curran has me chasing up an insurance matter involving Dowling."

"The *Hesperides*?" Harriet asked.

Griff nodded. "We can't seem to find out who benefitted from the loss of the cargo."

Harriet started, a half-forgotten conversation with Alicia Sewell coming back to her.

"But I know," she said.

Griff stared at her. "Who? . . . How?"

"Alicia Sewell told me it was her husband."

Griff frowned. "George Sewell? But if that's so, he would be acting on behalf of the rubber companies he represented, surely?"

"I only know what Alicia told me."

Griff's eyes took on a familiar gleam, and she smiled. She knew him well enough to recognize when her friend sensed a story.

"Sorry we're late." A perspiring Charles Lovett came hurrying up, with Elspeth and Eunice following. Elspeth looked terrible, deathly pale with dark circles under her eyes and her normally immaculate coiffeur replaced with a rather crooked bun on top of her head. Having read Curran's notes on his interview with Elspeth Lovett, Harriet suspected that an uncomfortable conversation with her husband probably accounted for the down-in-the-mouth appearance.

Harriet's nose twitched at the unmistakable miasma of alcohol that surrounded Elspeth as she stopped beside her.

"How are you, Mrs. Lovett?"

Elspeth cast her a glance, her eyes bloodshot and red rimmed, but she managed a watery smile. "Fine," she said. "Just saddened by Tony's death, as we all are."

Charles Lovett stepped between the assembled company and

the burned-out ruin of the scenery store, his face set in an expression of deep mourning. He glanced around at the ruins and removed his hat, holding it to his heart.

Once a ham actor, always a ham actor, Harriet thought.

He began in a sonorous tone. "To lose one of our own in such awful circumstances is unthinkable, but I have every confidence that the police will see justice is done for poor Tony. And of course, our scenery stock is gone too." His expression brightened. "I want you all to know that we will not let this tragedy prevent the show from proceeding. Tickets are already selling fast and the committee has decided that a percentage of the proceeds will be sent to poor Tony's family in New Zealand."

"The committee . . ." mumbled Elspeth. "He means he decided."

The announcement provoked a smattering of applause and nods of approval from the company.

"Of course, you are probably wondering how we will proceed without a lead tenor and I am delighted to announce that we have found a new Frederic." He gestured to one of the chorus members, who stepped forward, his cheeks pink with embarrassment. "Mr. Dixon has been hiding his light under the bushel of the male chorus and he is a worthy successor to Tony Dowling. Mr. Dixon, dear chap, perhaps I could prevail on you and Mrs. Sewell to cheer us?"

Mr. Dixon was no Anthony Dowling, being several years younger, and his receding hairline and chin detracted from the physical presence of the former leading man, but without the benefit of accompaniment, he and Alicia Sewell sang the rather lovely duet "Ah, leave me not to pine" to rapturous applause from the company.

"He'll do," muttered Griff to Harriet.

Back in the rehearsal room, Lovett, his face now sheened with perspiration, his jacket off and his shirtsleeves rolled up, raised his voice to be heard over the rabble of small conversations.

"Ladies and gentlemen, we're going to try for a full run-through to accustom our new Frederic to the flow of the show. I see some of you are still holding scripts. Next week . . . NO SCRIPTS. Pirates, places, please."

As it lacked a little while until the women were required, Harriet removed from her bag the crumpled nightgown Elspeth had given her at the last rehearsal. She had done nothing to it during the week and she realized she had forgotten to collect the quantity of green ribbon required for the trimming.

The door to the costume room stood ajar and Harriet pushed it open, her gaze falling on the worktable and the spools of different-colored ribbon. She pulled out the green ribbon and picked up a pair of long sharp-pointed scissors from among the selection and cut off a couple of yards.

A cough made her start, and she turned on her heel to see who had entered the room. At this point, she was not above believing in ghosts. But the other occupant of the room was real enough. Elspeth Lovett had pulled a chair into a shadowy corner and sat with her hands in her lap, her hair coming down in rat's tails around her face and the unmistakable odor of brandy exuding from her. In her right hand she held a silver flask.

"Mrs. Lovett, I—" Harriet began.

Elspeth Lovett held up the flask. "Just had to have a little drink," she said, her words slurring. "The self-righteous prig pontificating about wonderful bloody Tony—"

Harriet shook her head and hunkered down in front of the woman. "I think you may have had enough for the moment, Elspeth."

"'S'all gone." Elspeth held the flask upside down and shook it. Only a few drops splashed onto the dusty floor. "I 'spose you're going to tell everyone that Elspeth Lovett is a lush." She gave a humorless snort of laughter. "I 'spose you know it all. You work for that bloody policeman. They'll all know sooner or later. Elspeth Lovett is a foolish old woman who fell for the charms of a lothario and made a complete and utter fool of herself."

"What I hear in the course of my work is confidential, Elspeth. I don't gossip and as for this"—Harriet took the flask from her and stoppered it—"it's nobody's business but yours . . . and your family's. But why today? Why here?"

"So you do know? 'Bout Tony and me?"

"Yes."

Elspeth moaned and ran a hand through her already-disordered hair. "After that bloody policeman came and raked it all up . . . I had to tell Charles. Tell him everything. I wanted him to yell and scream, show some emotion, but he just folded his paper and stood up. He said it changed nothing and if I wanted a divorce, he quite understood, but I was his wife for better or for worse and we would get through it. *It* . . . what's *it* that we have to get through? I confess, throw myself on his mercy, and he acts as if nothing happened. Saint bloody Charles Lovett. We will just carry on as always. He'll go to work and play God with the society while I run around after him." She poked a finger at Harriet. "You know something, Harriet . . . I can call you Harriet? I hate Singapore. Maybe I should just go back to England at Christmas and stay there. To hell with Charles." She lowered her head. "I really loved Tony. He made me feel special and now he's dead. What choice do I have, Harriet?"

Harriet had no words of advice to offer. If she had been in Elspeth Lovett's position, a strategic withdrawal to England would probably be her decision too.

"You wait there, Elspeth. I'm going to get you a cup of tea and then see about getting you home. You're not fit to walk. Did you bring the motor vehicle today?"

Elspeth nodded and sank back in the uncomfortable chair, like a broken puppet.

In the kitchen, she found Eunice Lovett setting out the cups and saucers for the rehearsal break.

"Your mother is feeling unwell," Harriet said. "I'm just going to take her a cup of tea."

Eunice's lips tightened. "Mother needs more than a cup of tea," she said. "She's been drinking since breakfast today. In fact, she's been drinking steadily since that policeman came."

Harriet didn't quite know how to respond to the hard, cold statement of fact. It occurred to her that everyone thought of Eunice as a child but she was on the verge of womanhood and more than aware of the undercurrents that seethed around her. No one ever seemed to notice Eunice. She was always there but somehow absent.

"I am not naive," Eunice continued. "Tony's death upset her and this is how she copes. It's how she always copes."

"What about you, Eunice?"

"Me?" Eunice looked up from dispensing tea into the pot.

"Yes. It can't be easy for you with a busy father and . . . your mother."

Eunice shrugged. "It's been no different, but ever since I was little, I would come up here when I needed to get away," she said. "I like it here. It's my secret place." She handed Harriet a cup and saucer. "There you are, for all the good it will do," Eunice said. "I'll have the motor vehicle brought up and take her home before she embarrasses us all."

When Harriet returned to the costume room, Elspeth was sprawled in the chair, her head back, snoring, a line of spittle running down her chin onto her blouse.

Harriet set the cup down and shook the woman awake. "Drink this, and then we'll get you a little tidy."

Elspeth took the cup in shaking hands and downed the tea almost without taking a breath.

"Be a dear and pass my cigarettes," Elspeth said. "In my bag."

Harriet had never seen Elspeth smoking but now she could

detect the lingering odor of tobacco combined with the alcohol, overlaid with a sickly rose perfume. She picked up the woman's capacious handbag and set it on the table. It contained a jumble of accumulated rubbish, sweet wrappers, old ticket stubs and crumpled handkerchiefs. She found the discreet silver cigarette case and a box of Takasima brand safety matches. She stood looking at the matchbox in her hand and tried to recall where she had seen a box of Takasimas recently.

Her breath caught as she recalled the objects on the evidence table in the Police Headquarters. She made a quick decision and slipped the matches into the pocket of her skirt and turned back to Elspeth.

"Sorry, my dear. I can't seem to find any matches."

Elspeth pulled a face and set the cup down on the floor. "I'm gasping for a cigarette," she said. "They're the only things that keep me sane. Charles does not approve of women smoking . . . says it's unladylike."

With quick fingers, Harriet tucked the loose strands of hair behind Elspeth's ears and, using one of the crumpled handkerchiefs, wiped her face.

Eunice appeared in the doorway.

"Poor Mama," she said, with a face that betrayed not a skerrick of sympathy. "Mrs. Gordon said you had one of your headaches. Ahmed has brought the motor vehicle up. Let me take you home. Papa can walk."

Elspeth swayed on her feet. "Yes. One of my headaches," she said. "You're very kind, dear. Take me home."

Harriet helped Eunice escort her mother to the motor vehicle and saw her safely gone, before she pulled the matches from her pocket and turned the box over. An unremarkable piece of everyday ephemera that anyone would carry. She tried to imagine Elspeth Lovett stabbing Tony Dowling, setting fire to his body and calmly destroying the evidence. Whatever Elspeth had felt for the young man, surely she was no murderer. Then again, a woman scorned . . .

She thrust the matches back in her pocket and turned back to the rehearsal room, where the last strains of "Oh false one, you have deceived me!" was her cue for the entrance of the Major-General's daughters.

⚭ SEVENTEEN

Sunday, 6 November

S imon!"
  Harriet gathered up her skirts and ran down the steps of St. Tom's House as the green Maxwell tourer came to a halt, spraying muddy water from a puddle. Harriet jumped back just in time to avoid a dousing.

Simon pushed back his goggles and vaulted from the driver's seat.

"How wonderful to see you," Harriet said, and meant it.

He circled the car and lightly grasped her by the forearms. "And it's great to see you too, Harriet."

He bent his head, and their lips met. He smelled of spice and man, and they kissed with a confidence that she had missed on their first exploration. She returned the kiss, enjoying the sensation of being in his arms.

A cough from the verandah made them both jump apart. Julian stood at the top of the steps, pipe in hand.

"*Pas devant les domestiques*, Harri," he said.

The servants to whom he referred were nowhere to be seen.

Simon threw his arm around Harriet's shoulders, and they joined Julian on the verandah.

"Tea or something stronger?" Julian offered.

"Is it too early for a gin and tonic?" Harriet inquired.

"Never," Simon agreed.

Julian rolled his eyes and turned to the front door to fix the drinks. He glanced back. "I'm not Harriet's bodyguard," he said. "If you two would prefer to be alone . . ."

Harriet laughed. "Don't be silly, Ju. Bring us all a drink and Simon can tell us what he's been up to."

Seated comfortably, drinks in hand, Simon raised his glass. "Good health. I must say it's a relief to be back. It was rather an unpleasant story that took me to KL."

"We've had our own share of unpleasantness this week," Julian said.

Simon nodded. "Maddocks told me about the murder up at the society's property. Any suspects yet?"

Harriet shook her head. "Curran has a couple of lines of inquiry. Tell us about your story."

"Not much I can tell you and I don't think it's going to go anywhere."

Harriet put her hand over Simon's. "I've never seen you discomposed by a story, Simon."

"It's a sordid smuggling ring . . . smuggling girls from India into Malaya to service"—he coughed—"gentlemen's establishments."

Harriet stiffened. She had heard this story in the last two days, from Robert Curran.

"Go on," Harriet said.

"The girls targeted are middle class, educated and naive. They are wooed by the procurer who lures them into his trap and literally smuggles them out of India. The establishments they go to are not common garden brothels, but high-class, catering to men of wealth, and they move them around so by the time they come to the authorities' notice, they have gone. I spoke to one girl who had escaped. She told me the girls are regularly drugged and threatened. They are told their families will be punished if they try to escape. After a while they just give up."

"But this one girl didn't? What was her name?" Harriet said, hoping against hope that maybe Simon's source was Curran's sister, Samrita.

"Jameela. She got away because one of her clients made it his business to get her out. She married him and is happily settled with two children. Another girl was not so lucky. She turned up dead in the Klang."

Harriet stared. "Murdered? Did she have a name?"

"The newspaper report mentioned a star-shaped birthmark on the woman's upper arm and Jameela thought it was a woman called Lakshmi. Officially though she remains unidentified . . . and no one can say whether she jumped or was . . ."

"Murdered?" Julian shook his head. "How awful."

"Jameela's contact inside the house said one girl had gone missing. Wouldn't say which one. With the description of the birthmark, she drew her own conclusions."

"And how did you find Jameela?" Julian asked.

Simon smiled and tapped his nose. "I'm a journalist . . . Actually, through her husband. He's a successful Anglo-Indian department store owner, and I got talking to a friend of his in the bar of the Spotted Dog and he introduced me. He told me about the racket."

Harriet snorted. "But the man patronized the place. What a hypocrite."

Simon shrugged but his scowl echoed Harriet's sentiment.

"What are you going to do with the story?" Julian asked.

Simon shook his head. "I don't have enough for a proper story, and even if I did, I doubt my paper would print it. Not what the good people of Melbourne want to read over their breakfast." He shivered, despite the warmth of the evening. "That sort of story just makes me despair for mankind, and I do mean *man*kind."

Harriet jumped to her feet. "Simon, you have to share this story with Robert Curran."

Simon frowned. "Why?"

Harriet had to think fast. "He has a similar case of a missing girl and you may shed some light on it for him."

"A similar case? Maybe a bit of an exchange of information..." Simon mused aloud. "I'll try to catch up with him next week—"

"No. Now . . . you need to see Curran right now."

"Come on, Harriet. I thought we could go to the tea dance at the Hotel Europe—"

"Another time. This is important, Simon. Really important."

Simon cast a despairing glance at Julian, who shrugged. "I think Harriet's right."

Harriet cast her brother a questioning glance. How did he know it was important to Curran?

Simon's sharp journalistic gaze moved from brother to sister. "What's going on?"

Harriet returned his gaze. "Nothing. Stay there. I'll be right back and we can drive over to Curran's bungalow."

Harriet dashed to her bedroom to fetch her hat and a scarf and reached the motor vehicle before Simon bade Julian good-bye.

She directed him to Cantonment Road. He stopped the car and looked at the narrow lane that led up the hill to Curran's bungalow.

"I'll have to park here. It's too narrow to drive," he said.

They left the car with Mahmud and climbed the steep lane to the bungalow. Simon was puffing by the time they turned the corner and the bungalow came into view.

"Why on earth would anyone choose to live in such an isolated spot?" Simon wheezed.

Curran sat at the table on the verandah, unlit pipe clenched between his teeth, apparently poring over old newspapers with Griff Maddocks. Both men started, rising to their feet when Harriet cleared her throat.

"What brings you both here on a Sunday afternoon?" Curran inquired.

"I thought you were taking Harriet to a tea dance," Griff addressed his housemate.

"So did I," Simon grumbled.

"Simon has an important story to share with you, Curran." Harriet swung her gaze to Griff Maddocks. "What are you doing here?"

Griff indicated the newspapers. "Curran had me looking at reports of unsolved insurance losses," he said. "We can account for at least six in the last two years."

Curran tapped his empty pipe on the edge of the table. "Take a seat." He indicated two battered chairs and Harriet and Simon drew them up to the table.

"I told Simon you have been working on a case involving a missing girl," she said.

Curran glared at her, and she silently willed him to believe that she had made no disclosure of his true interest in the case.

"And how does this concern Hume?" Curran said, his low tone full of warning.

"I've been investigating a story about forced prostitution in KL. Girls, drugged and brought over from India," Simon said.

Curran's hand tightened on the pipe, his knuckles white. "Go on," he said.

As Simon related his story, Harriet watched Curran's face, but he betrayed nothing in his expression except that of the professional policeman.

"I don't understand why the administration doesn't step in?" Maddocks said.

"Prostitution is not illegal," Simon said.

"Slavery is," Harriet said.

"That is the kernel of the problem that I hit. Whoever is behind this ring has friends in high places. From what Jameela told me, they would get a report that someone was showing an unfriendly interest in the operation and they'd simply up and move to another premises. They are always one step ahead."

"This girl you spoke to, do you think she would talk to me?" Curran asked.

Simon shook his head. "No. You're a policeman. I suspect the establishment numbers the police among its clientele. She doesn't trust anyone in a uniform."

Curran leaned forward. "Nevertheless, can you give me her address?"

"No." Simon held up his hand. "I would have to ask her permission to speak to you."

Harriet, knowing Curran so well, detected the flicker of impatience behind his eyes. "Could you do that, Hume?" He paused. "Perhaps you could assure her my interest is personal, not professional."

"What do you mean, personal?" Hume glanced at Harriet. "You said it was a case he was working on."

Curran held up a hand. "I have no jurisdiction in KL but I agreed to help a friend find his sister."

Hume leaned forward, his journalistic interest piqued. "That's interesting. If he could share his side of the story, I can make something of this."

"I can't tell you anything more," Curran said.

Hume sat back and shrugged. "I'll ask." He glanced at his watch. "Harriet, there is still time to catch the tea dance."

Harriet shook her head. "Thank you, Simon, but I have a busy week ahead of me. I would rather go home."

She stood, prompting the three men to push their chairs back and rise.

"Is Li An here?"

Curran shook his head, his lips compressing in a thin line. "She went out this morning. I hope she's back soon. I've got a ticket on the night train to KL."

Griff looked at him. "The case of the missing girl?"

Curran shook his head and tapped the pile of newspapers. "No. I've got some questions for the port authorities in Port Dickson so I'll be disembarking before KL."

"If there's nothing more you need me for, Curran, I'll head back to my digs with Hume," Maddocks said.

"Thank you for this information, Maddocks. It will be a great help," Curran said.

"I'll let you know about the girl, Curran. Might take a few days to get a letter to her and for her to reply," Simon said.

Curran thanked the journalist, and Harriet and the two men left Curran standing on his verandah, his hands thrust into his pockets.

As the motor vehicle turned off Cantonment Road, Hume glanced at Harriet. "Can you tell me what his real interest in the prostitution story is?"

Harriet looked at him. "You know I can't, Simon."

"But you know."

Harriet fixed her gaze on the road ahead. "Yes, I know," she said.

"It's no good, Hume, she won't say anything," Maddocks said from the backseat. "Absolute secrecy and confidentiality . . . that's Harriet's motto in life."

Li An returned to the bungalow as Curran was in the throes of packing his traveling bag. He kissed her, returning to his packing as she leaned against the doorjamb, watching him.

"I was afraid I might miss you," he said. "Where have you been?"

"I had some business with Ah Loong."

His heart sank. Business with Ah Loong did not sound good.

"What time is your train?" she asked.

He glanced at his watch. "Just over an hour." He turned to

face her. "What was your business with Ah Loong?" His words faltered as he studied her face. "Or don't I want to know?"

Her lips parted, and she swallowed. "Curran, I will not be here when you return. I have passage booked on the steamer leaving for Penang in the morning."

He took a breath. "Is this it, Li An?"

"It?"

"Are you leaving me or just going to visit your mother?"

Her eyelids fluttered, and he wondered if he caught the glint of tears on her lashes, but he couldn't bring himself to move. "My mother is dying, and that will change everything. She is naming me her heir in her family business, and I will be an equal partner with my uncle. I must go and claim my place." Her face softened, her eyes almost pleading as she said, "You knew I would leave you one day, Curran."

He shook his head. "No. No, I didn't. I want to marry you, Li An. God knows I've asked you enough."

Her eyes flashed. "And I have always said no. We do not belong in each other's worlds, and we are fooling ourselves to think otherwise. I know the other *ang mo* talk about us. They call me your 'woman.' They say you have gone native. I do not want that anymore. Not for you and not for me."

"But if we married—"

She laughed. "Can you see me at the cricket club, being polite to the governor's lady?"

"You did it in Penang. Your father—"

Anger flashed in her eyes. "My father . . . my brother . . . and you. Yes, you, Curran. I have always been the property of a man to use as they think fit. I do not forget that you used me to get to my brother as much as my brother used me to get to you. No more. My mother is offering me freedom and I would be a fool to walk away."

Appalled, Curran stared at her. "Li An. I have never thought of you that way."

She took a step toward him, reaching out to touch his face. He put his hand over hers and pressed her fingers to his lips as she said, "Maybe not now, but in the beginning you did. Men will not use me anymore."

"Li An, I love you—"

"No!" she flashed, pulling her hand away. "Do not speak of love, Curran. It is not enough. Not anymore."

Stung, he dropped his hand. "What do you want? What can I do to make you stay?"

She shook her head. "Nothing. My mind is made up."

He studied her with the terrible realization that the woman he thought he knew so well stood before him a complete stranger. "What is this really about, Li An?"

A faint, hard smile caught her lips. "You would not understand."

"Try me."

She brought her gaze up to meet his and her dark eyes glittered in the light from the lamp as she touched the scar on her face.

"Revenge," she said. "Ah Loong and I together, we can bring down Zi Qiang."

She was wrong—he did understand. Understood too well . . . he had failed to defeat Zi Qiang so she had taken control of revenge for both of them.

The complex balance of clans in Penang went deep. Li An's mother came from the powerful Teo clan, and if Li An was to hitch her fortunes to her mother's clan, together they could well be a serious rival to the illegal machinations of Khoo Zi Qiang. If that was the road Li An chose, then he could not follow, however much he loved her. This was a drama that had to be played out behind the mysterious gates of the clan houses in Penang. One that he, an *ang mo*, could have no part in.

He picked up his bag, and as he took a step toward her, she said, "You don't need me anymore, Curran."

He dropped his bag and stood within an arm's length of her. "Who are you to say that I don't need you, Li An? You are everything to me."

She shook her head. "We have clung to each other like a sailor clings to wreckage, but once you reach shore and safety, the thing that brought you there is no longer needed." She took a step across the void that lay between them and laid her hand on his cheek again. "If it is not clear to you now, you will understand what I mean in time."

Her cool fingers burned into him like a brand, but she let her hand drop before he could catch it up again.

"Li An . . ." Her name came out in a strangled gasp.

She picked up his traveling bag and handed it to him. "Goodbye, Curran. If you do not go now, you will miss your train. When we meet again, I hope it will be as friends."

He took the bag and dropped it again, taking her in his arms and pressing his lips to hers, seeking the unspoken answer to an unspoken question. When they drew apart, he held her gaze, willing her to understand his next words.

"If I have to let you go, Li An, don't think it means I will ever stop loving you."

Her lips parted, and a single tear ran down her unscarred cheek.

As he turned to the door, she whispered, "Or I you, Curran."

He stepped out into the soft, warm night, where the faintest scent of frangipani lingered in the heavy air. But even as he strode away from the home he had shared with Li An, the knot of grief and loss tightened in his heart.

⚘ EIGHTEEN

Monday, 7 November

The overnight train from Singapore to Kuala Lumpur arrived at Seremban station at five A.M. Despite the comfort of a sleeper, Curran had passed a restless night, his sore ribs protesting at every lurch of the train and his mind churning with thoughts of a life without Li An. He fell asleep just before Seremban and the conductor had to wake him.

He stood on the platform, looking with bleary eyes after the departing train. Less than two hours farther on lay Kuala Lumpur. If he had time in the afternoon, he would continue his journey to KL and seek the address Jayant had given him, but right now he had business in Port Dickson and he needed to give it his full attention. He checked the timetable, and as it lacked a couple of hours until the connecting train to Port Dickson, he ate breakfast in the station's adequate cafeteria, shaved and changed into a clean uniform.

He got into Port Dickson at nine. It was his first visit to the port, which lay on the coast between Malacca and the major port and harbor for the west coast of Malaya, Port Swettenham. Like many of the smaller west coast ports, it existed to service the booming tin industry, and the area around the station had an industrial feel to it with railway trucks filled with the raw material mined from the hills and mountains of Malaya and bound for the industrial north of England.

He found the customs office and introduced himself to the young man in charge, a lad of probably no more than twenty-five with a shock of fair hair, who greeted Curran like an old friend as he wrung his hand.

"Alfred Simmons," he said. "Good to see you, Inspector. What can I do for you?"

Curran asked to see the records of the February sailing of the *Hesperides*.

"That old rust bucket?" Simmons commented as he pulled out his ledgers. "Funny thing is, you're the first person to ask about it. Here you go . . . She sailed on February fourth with a local captain and six crew. She carried a cargo of thirty thousand pounds of crepe rubber shipped by Robert White & Co." He looked up at Curran. "Brokers, aren't they?"

Robert White & Co.—Sewell's company?

Curran nodded and almost held his breath as the man's finger moved to the last column. "Insured value, six thousand pounds. That can't be right. Rubber was fetching about two shillings a pound. The stated insured value is double its actual value."

Curran restrained himself from punching the air. There it was . . . the fraud.

He steadied his breath and noted the details in his notebook before asking, "Do you get much rubber going out of here?"

"That's the other thing. Hardly any. Most of it goes by rail down to Singapore or out of Port Swettenham. They mostly use this port for tin." Simmons shut his ledger and looked at Curran. "Why the interest?"

Curran saw no reason to prevaricate. "I'm investigating a possible insurance fraud."

The young man clapped his hands. "At last something interesting. I tell you, Curran, day in, day out, this job is killing me. Since you're investigating, there was indeed something decidedly fishy about that cargo. Let me show you."

Curran followed Simmons to a secure *godown* on the quayside. At the water's edge, he paused to look out to the Straits of Malacca. The steamer carrying Li An back to Penang would pass this port in the next few hours. The breath constricted in his throat at that thought and he swallowed hard.

"Inspector?" Simmons's voice brought him back to the problem at hand. "In here." The man unlocked the heavy door and threw it open. "We keep the contraband and seized goods in here. When some of the local villagers brought this in, I stowed it here against the day when someone came asking questions. Of course, no one came."

It took Curran a moment or two to adjust to the gloom of the warehouse, and he picked his way through wooden crates and strange packages. The place smelled of mold, mildew and dust.

"Ah, here it is."

Simmons stopped in front of a large, irregularly shaped object covered with a stained canvas tarpaulin. He whipped off the cover, revealing a collapsed, moldy rubber bale covered in a rotting hessian cloth through which the sheets of crepe rubber could be seen.

"I believe this came off the *Hesperides*." Simmons put his hands on his hips. "It washed up on a beach just south of here after a severe storm a month after she went down and the locals brought it in. Thought there might be some money in handing it in."

Curran stared at the unprepossessing article. "How do you know it came off the *Hesperides*?"

Simmons grinned and held up a finger. "I'll get to that. This is what I wanted to show you."

He produced a knife and cut into the bale. Forcing the cut apart, he pulled out a handful of moldy straw. Curran sucked his breath in and went for a closer inspection. Beyond the outer layer of rubber, someone had filled the core of the bale with disintegrating straw. It smelled vile.

Clearly enjoying the excitement of uncovering a genuine crime, Simmons continued, "If we're talking fraud, it looks like there was something in the center. I'd guess a bag of something heavy, like rocks, inserted to bring the weight up to the usual weight of two hundred and twenty-four pounds. As the straw and hessian rotted, the weight fell out, making it light enough to drift ashore."

Curran took a step back and considered the unlovely object.

"Would I be right in thinking that the entire shipment may have been similar?" he asked.

Simmons shrugged. "No way of knowing, of course, but I've seen enough shifty deals to recognize one when I see it. It was quite simple, really. Pack a rust bucket of a boat with a heavily insured cargo, and when the ship sinks, so does the evidence. Only this one washed up on the shore." He ran a hand over the top of the bale. "Here's the proof it was on the *Hesperides*. You can just make it out. This snake is the mark of the Sungei Pandan Rubber Company and the number of the bale tallies with my records of the cargo loaded on the *Hesperides*." He turned to Curran and grinned. "Enough evidence for you, Inspector?"

Curran almost let out an uncharacteristic, and unprofessional, whoop. He had the connection with Lionel Ellis. Ellis was the managing director of the Sungei Pandan Rubber Company. While Ellis lived on the main rubber plantation in the east of Singapore island, the company had other plantations scattered through southern Malaya. It was one of the biggest rubber-growing enterprises in the area. The shipment could have come off any of the Sungei Pandan plantations. Would it be enough?

The grin faded from the young man's face. "Sad thing was, two of the crew had to die. My betting is the captain scuttled the boat but two of his chaps didn't get off it in time."

"The newspaper reports said it was caught in a storm."

Simmons snorted. "Calm sailing all that week."

Curran made arrangements with the young man to have the remnant of the bale, together with copies of the bills of lading, escorted to Singapore as soon as possible.

"I'll bring it myself. God knows I'm owed some leave," Simmons said.

"Just make sure you deliver it intact to South Bridge Road," Curran said.

Simmons grinned. "It's not like I want to keep company with a stinking bale of rotting straw, Inspector. Do you have time for tiffin?"

Curran declined, and the young man blew out his breath, his face crestfallen. "Not even time for a beer, Inspector?"

Curran felt a flash of guilt. The young man was obviously lonely and desperate for company, but he couldn't linger.

"I have business in KL and need to make the one o'clock train to Seremban," Curran said apologetically. "I will buy you a beer when you get to Singapore."

As he sat waiting at the station at Seremban for the KL train, he turned over the information he had discovered at Port Dickson. All the evidence pointed squarely to a conspiracy between Dowling as insurance agent, Sewell as broker, and Lionel Ellis or at least the Sungei Pandan Rubber Company as the producer of the rubber shipment. He would lay good money of his own that Dowling's six-hundred-pound windfall was his payoff for his part in the scheme. Now he knew of other, similar "accidents," the trail would be easier to follow.

Nothing would give him greater pleasure than to bring Ellis to court again, but this time it would have to be a watertight case so that a sympathetic judge could not give the man a slap on the wrist. To do that he needed more direct evidence. Dowling was dead, Ellis was off-limits, which meant that the one link in the chain that he could pull in would be George Sewell. Sewell's name was on the shipment. He had to be complicit in the plot.

He turned his thoughts back to Dowling's death. It seemed to point less to an aggrieved lover or husband of a lover, and more to a connection with the insurance fraud. Dowling was an essential cog in the conspiracy, so why did he have to die? Did it come back to the passing remark he had made to his clerk? Did Dowling have a conscience about the death of the innocent sailors? Or was it the threat of an audit?

The round note of a train's horn announced the arrival of the KL express and he put away his notebook and turned his thoughts instead to the matter awaiting him in Kuala Lumpur.

Curran arrived in Kuala Lumpur well after four P.M. The night train to Singapore departed at eight thirty in the evening, which gave him ample time to do what was needed.

Kuala Lumpur was not one of the Straits Settlements, but one of the Federated Malay States, which meant that while it was nominally under the control of the sultan of Selangor, it operated to all intents and purposes just like every other colonial state in the British Empire with a "Resident-General," instead of a governor, suitably installed in an impressive "residence" on a hill overlooking the town.

In the circumstances, Curran had no jurisdiction in KL, as it was generally known by the expatriate community, and courtesy demanded that he should have paid a call on his equivalent, but he decided that required too much explaining. It didn't concern him. The police commissioner for the Federated Malay States, Henry Talbot, was a friend. Talbot, like Curran, had played first-class cricket in England and their paths had crossed on several occasions. Nevertheless, Curran took the precaution of changing into civilian clothes, leaving his bag at the left luggage office at the station.

He strode out of the station and looked around for the ricksha stand.

"Curran!"

At his name, he turned on his heel, his heart sinking as he recognized the familiar khaki uniform and solid build of Inspector John Keogh of the Federated Malay States Police. He knew Keogh from his time in Penang. A policeman of no imagination and a stickler for rules and regulations to the point of pedantism.

The two men shook hands, and Keogh clapped him on the shoulder. "Good to see you, old man. What brings you to KL?"

"Private matter, Keogh."

"You got time for a beer at the Spotted Dog? It's just been reopened. Looks absolutely spiffing."

The Spotted Dog was the local name for the Royal Selangor Club, the popular and exclusive haunt on the edge of KL's own *padang*. Curran had heard the nickname could be traced back to the wife of one of the club's founders, who would leave her two dalmatian dogs at the entrance whenever she attended.

Curran shook his head. "Sorry, not this time. I've got to be on the train back to Singapore tonight."

"Pity. Got a lot of catching up to do. Aren't you in the middle of a murder investigation? Some chap got himself caught in a fire I read in the *Straits Times*."

"That's correct. That's why this is a flying visit. Maybe next time? What are you doing haunting the train station?"

"Nothing more exciting than meeting some bigwig on the next train from Port Swettenham," Keogh said.

They shook hands, and Curran hailed a ricksha. As the ricksha trundled through the unfamiliar streets, Curran wondered if he could trust Keogh to help with the search for Samrita. Keogh's obsession with the rule of law would make that difficult so probably better not to involve him.

"This is the address, *tuan*." The ricksha wallah set the ricksha down in a tree-lined street of elegant villas. If the house had been a brothel, it was far removed from the stews of Petaling Street.

He told the ricksha wallah to wait for him at the end of the street and turned to the house at the address. His policeman's instincts prickled as he scanned the high stone wall, bristling with shards of broken glass to discourage anyone from climbing over it, surrounding the property on all sides. A heavy, solid metal gate decorated with curlicues of wrought iron barred entry. No amount of fancy work disguised the purpose of the gate, which was both to keep casual visitors out and the residents in. The gate itself had a metal grille through which visitors could be screened, but it was shut tight and the whole gate secured with a heavy chain and padlock.

He found a bell pull beside the gate and tugged on it. No one came.

He pulled the rope again and could hear the distant, muffled clang of a bell, but nothing stirred beyond the gates. As he bent to look through the gap where the chain ran through the gate, a woman passed him, took a couple of steps and turned back.

"What is your business with this house?" she demanded.

He straightened. "That is my business."

She snorted. "If you are looking for the ladies of that house, then you are too late. They are gone."

The ladies of that house?

An icy chill ran down his spine.

"Do you live in this street?" he asked the woman.

She raised her chin. She wore expensive western clothes with her graying hair coiled in a tidy bun at the nape of her neck, and in keeping with the neighborhood, he guessed her to be a member of a wealthy Chinese household.

"I have the misfortune to live next door. When my neighbor died a few years ago, *he* bought the house, built the walls, brought in the girls and then the visitors came."

"Who do you mean?"

"We called him Gopal the Procurer. I do not know his other name."

"How many girls were in this house?"

"What a question. I never went in there and we never saw the girls on the street . . ."

Curran gave her what he hoped was a winning smile and she sniffed.

"Maybe five or six."

"Indian girls?"

"Some but all races, even *ang mo*," the woman said.

Curran swallowed. "Did you hear any of the girls called Samrita?"

The woman assumed a horrified expression. "I have told you, I never set foot in the place but," she relented, "I heard a girl in the garden calling that name, or something like that."

Curran took out the photograph Jayant had given him. "This girl?"

She shrugged. "Maybe, but I cannot say for sure. I never . . ."

"I know, you never set foot in the place." Curran would have laid a bet that this lady had her ways of spying on the goings-on next door. "Can you describe the man, Gopal?"

She narrowed her eyes. "You talk like a policeman."

Curran ignored the remark. "I am looking for the daughter of a friend."

"Then tell your friend that she is lost. If she was once of a respectable family, it is better she stay lost."

Curran's breath constricted. His sister . . . .and she was lost . . . but he would find her.

"Gopal?" he prompted.

"Indian," the woman said. "About a head shorter than you, solid build. He had a disgusting moustache."

It was not much, but it was something.

"Do you know where they have gone?"

The woman shrugged. "I do not know. One night a few months ago, they left." She looked at the gate and her face twisted. A stream of invective in Straits Chinese followed, causing Curran to smile. "Good riddance." The woman reverted to English. "This is a respectable neighborhood. We do not need such scum plying their wares here."

Curran thanked the woman. He waited until she had entered her own property, casting him a last suspicious glance, and the street was empty once more. He bent and peered through the gate again. The last light had faded during his conversation with the neighbor, and in the dark, he could barely make out what appeared to be a low, pleasant villa surrounded by a wide verandah. The windows were shuttered, and the grass looked as if it hadn't been cut for many months. No doubt about it, the place had been abandoned, and if he believed in ghosts, an unpleasant air hung over the property.

He glanced at his watch and grimaced. As much as he would have liked to find a way into the property, time had run out. He ran back to his dozing ricksha wallah and told him to hurry.

He just made the Singapore train, dined well and retired to his cabin, exhausted. His shoulder and ribs hurt like the very devil, and he lay awake listening to the creaks and squeals of the train as it traveled through the night, thinking, not about the sinking of the *Hesperides* but about the girl who had been held prisoner in the compound in Kuala Lumpur.

"Gopal the Procurer" had taken his girls and disappeared. Why move an obviously prosperous business unless you did not want to be discovered? Hume had suggested that the establishment enjoyed protection from high up so maybe someone had warned them it was time to change premises. He took out the photograph and studied the beautiful, innocent face of his sister.

Samrita, he thought as sleep finally claimed him, *I will find you.*

The train got into Singapore the following morning at quarter past eight, leaving Curran with the decision of going straight to South Bridge Road or returning home to an empty house for a wash and a change. His heart rebelled against the latter, but he needed a clean uniform and the reality of Li An's departure had to be faced eventually.

As he walked up the lane from Cantonment Road, his footsteps became slower as the silence engulfed him. No monkeys chattered in the trees, and even the insects, normally a lively chorus in the surrounding jungle, had fallen silent. He stood looking at the unassuming little bungalow that had been both haven and retreat from the worries of the world. The scent of the frangipani tree hung in the heavy air, almost nauseating with its sickly sweetness.

When he tried the door handle, he found the front door locked. He stared at his hand on the latch in bemusement. It had never occurred to him to take the key. Li An had always been here, either sitting on the verandah reading or busying herself inside.

He had to stop and think about where she would have put the key. He ran a hand across the top of the lintel and checked under the doormat, to no avail.

"*Tuan.*"

He started and turned to look at Mahmud, who had crept up behind him on silent feet.

"You will get yourself shot, sneaking up on me like that, Mahmud," he said without anger.

Mahmud held up the key to the front door. "Miss Li An gave me this to give to you, but I did not hear you go past my hut."

The old man had probably been dozing.

Curran took the key with grunted thanks and inserted it into the lock.

Mahmud hadn't moved. He stood looking at Curran, the corners of his mouth downturned and his shoulders stooped. "Is it true? Miss Li An is gone?"

Curran forced a smile. "I hope not, old friend."

Mahmud shook his head. "I do not think she is coming back."

With another shake of his head, the old man turned and trudged away.

Curran opened the door and stepped into the house.

It had been only twenty-four hours, but the house had the fug of desertion; dust and mold and stale cooking smells hung in the air. He dropped his bag and looked around. Everything was just as he had left it. His books in the bookcase, a mildewed print of early Singapore on the wall, but the essential element that had made it a home was gone, and for the first time since he was a boy, he felt a prickle at the back of his throat.

He swallowed back the grief and opened the cupboard where he kept the whisky bottle.

❦ NINETEEN

Tuesday, 8 November

Julian let out a heavy sigh and set the letter he had been reading down on the table. Pushing his glasses up, he rubbed his eyes.

Harriet paused in buttering her toast. "Something the matter?"

He pushed the letter across to her and she picked it up. It was from Julian's old school, Ashburn, where he had been both student and teacher.

The headmaster began with all the usual pleasantries and self-congratulations at winning rugby against Harrow. It was only by the third paragraph that she reached the heart of the matter.

> *. . . We have considered your application along with the excellent references for the boy William Lawson, but on consideration I regret to inform you that we do not consider the lad a suitable candidate for a scholarship. His academic record, while good, is not of a sufficiently high standard. You are of course welcome to enroll him as a paying student. A leaflet with our current fees is enclosed . . .*

She glanced at Will, who paused with a spoon of boiled egg halfway to his mouth.

"Why are you both looking at me?"

"You have egg on your nose," Harriet lied, and made a pretense of wiping it off.

She and Julian exchanged glances. Ashburn had been something of a forlorn hope but Julian had prayed, both literally and figuratively, that his long association with the school might hold some influence. He had been mistaken and now they were faced with the very real dilemma of what to do with Will when he finished at St. Tom's at the end of school year in July.

"I better get going." Julian pushed his chair back and Harriet watched her brother stomp across the garden, his academic robe billowing behind him as he headed to the gate in the hedge, the shortcut to the school.

"What's wrong with Uncle Julian?" Will asked.

"Just some bad news this morning," Harriet replied. "Finish that egg and off you go."

Will hurried inside to fetch his school things, and as he emerged onto the verandah, Harriet stooped and kissed him on top of the head.

"What was that for?" Will looked shocked.

She smiled. "Work hard at school today and you can be a doctor or a lawyer or an engineer, like your father."

Will screwed his face up. "I don't want to be any of those things," he said. "I'm going to be a police inspector like Mr. Curran."

He was gone before Harriet could respond, scampering off on the same route Julian had taken just as the school bell began to toll.

Alone with her cold toast, Harriet picked up a piece and carried it over to the verandah rail to try and scrape the worst of the blackened crumbs from it. She considered the unedifying morsel and the flock of hopeful mynah birds who gathered below her.

As she crumbled the toast to breadcrumbs for the birds, a gharry turned into the driveway. Brushing her fingers on her skirt, she moved to the top of the steps as Eunice Lovett alighted from the carriage. The girl told the driver to wait and ran to the steps.

"Eunice, what on earth is the matter?"

The girl looked terrible. Her hair had been wrenched back in one untidy plait that was already coming loose and the pimples on her pale face stood out like dark blotches. She stopped at the bottom of the steps and looked up at Harriet.

"I didn't know who else to go to," she said. "It's Mama . . ."

"What about your mother?" Harriet's blood ran cold with dread.

"Mama's maid went to wake her this morning. Her bed's not been slept in. We've searched the house and grounds but there's no sign of her."

"When did you last see her?"

"At bedtime last night. She kissed me good night and went to her room . . . This morning . . . she's gone."

"Have you asked your father?"

Eunice shook her head. "No. He's not here. He went to Johor yesterday to see a client and I don't expect him back until this evening. Please, Mrs. Gordon. I think I know where she is, but I don't want to go by myself."

The feeling of dread intensified as Harriet hurried inside to fetch her hat and tell Huo Jin she had to go out.

Once they were both in the gharry, she asked Eunice where they were going.

Eunice swallowed. "The society's property."

"Why do you think she'd be there?"

Eunice shook her head. "Just a feeling."

Harriet reached over and patted the girl's hand, trying to

summon an encouraging smile, but she shared Eunice's feeling that all was not right.

The gharry dropped them at the gate to the old McKinnon property. Harriet told the man to wait, and he rolled his eyes. Only when she offered him extra money did he find he had no other pressing business.

On all the previous occasions she had been to the SADAMS property, it had been a place alive with music and people, but today it felt lonely and isolated, far removed from the bustling city just a few hundred yards away. Harriet and Eunice walked up the carriageway, the old pepper and gambier trees forming a dark canopy alive with the buzzing of unseen insects. The humidity seemed to close in around them.

As they rounded a corner, the old house loomed above them, dark and foreboding, and Harriet wondered about Tony Dowling and his romantic trysts in this place. Was it the very isolation and forbidding nature of the house that was the attraction? Then her gaze fell on the ground at the base of the disused staircase leading up to the verandah.

At first she thought, with a flutter of hope, that she was looking at a bundle of old rags, but as her vision cleared, the bundle of blue cloth took shape and substance and her heart swooped. She put out a hand to prevent Eunice from going any farther.

Eunice had seen what she had seen and moved forward with a heartfelt cry of "Mama."

Harriet grasped the girl by both arms, forcing her to look into her eyes. "Stay here, Eunice. That is an order."

Eunice nodded, and Harriet walked toward the crumpled body that lay at the bottom of the rickety front steps.

Elspeth Lovett lay on her back, one arm flung out and her right foot resting on the bottom tread. Harriet looked up toward the house. The gate at the top of the steps stood open. It appeared that Elspeth had fallen down the rickety steps.

Harriet knelt beside the woman and looked into Elspeth's

wide, staring eyes. An ant casually strolled across the woman's eyeball and Harriet recoiled. She had no official medical training but ten years of marriage to a doctor and helping him with the sick and injured of the Bombay slums had given her a rudimentary knowledge. She didn't need to be a doctor to see from the angle of Elspeth's head that she had broken her neck and had probably been dead for several hours.

"Mrs. Gordon?" Eunice's voice came from close behind her.

"I told you to wait," Harriet snapped, coming to her feet. She took Eunice by her arms, turned the girl and marched her into the shelter of the trees, away from the sight of the dead woman.

Eunice looked up at her. "Is she . . . is she dead?"

Harriet nodded. "I'm so sorry, Eunice."

"No!" The word came out as a strangled cry and Harriet folded the girl in her arms again, but Eunice pushed away from her.

"I have to see her," she said, and as Harriet made a grab for the girl's arm, Eunice shook her hand off and ran back to her mother.

Harriet caught up with her, but was too late to prevent Eunice from reaching the body.

The girl stood still, looking down at her mother.

"Don't touch her," Harriet said. "We need to fetch the police."

Eunice didn't seem to hear. She continued to stare dry-eyed and drained of color.

Harriet grasped Eunice by the forearms again and turned the girl to face her. "Eunice!"

Eunice blinked, her glazed eyes coming back into focus. Her lips trembled, and she pressed her hands to her eyes.

Harriet relaxed her grip and drew the girl in to her. "Eunice. I need you to be calm. Please take the gharry and go to the police post in Orchard Road and report that there has been an accident at this property. Ask them to send for medical assistance and Inspector Curran from South Bridge Road. The matter is urgent."

Eunice swallowed and nodded.

"What about Mama?"

"I will stay with her until help arrives. Go . . . now!"

Her ragged plait swinging behind her, Eunice turned and ran down the drive, disappearing around the bend and leaving Harriet alone with the dead woman.

Harriet knelt down beside Elspeth again and looked up at the open gate fifteen feet above her. If Elspeth had fallen from the verandah, was it an accident? She could just as easily have jumped or . . . been pushed.

She stood, brushing dirt from her skirt. There was nothing she could do for Elspeth Lovett, and she probably had quite a long wait until help arrived. She felt a little light-headed, most likely from the heat, the shock and the lack of breakfast.

She walked around to the service area of the property to fetch some water from the tank by the kitchen and to look for something to cover the woman. Her footsteps slowed as she saw the back door standing wide open. The temptation to investigate further was almost irresistible, but she had been with the Detective Branch long enough now to know that she should disturb nothing.

That would be a job for Curran, when he got here.

Blood . . . blood everywhere. Li An was moaning, her hands covering her face, blood oozing through her fingers. Lying curled up on the filthy boards of the noisome shed, Curran watched with a strange sense of detachment, his own blood dripping through the ill-fitting boards into the azure waters below the pier. He had an obscure thought about sharks, but the world had begun to roar in his ears and his only thoughts became thoughts of death. They were going to die here, Li An and he . . . their bodies probably not discovered for days. He tried to think of Li An, but saw only his own failure . . .

"Curran! Wake up." Someone was shaking his shoulder. "Wake up!"

Curran groaned. "Go away." His words sounded slurred even to his own ears.

"Are you inebriated?" The voice, which now seemed vaguely like that of Gursharan Singh, came from a long way above him.

There were footsteps and the sudden, terrible shock of cold water on his head. He sat up spluttering, wiping water from his eyes and swearing volubly.

"What the hell are you doing?" he demanded of his sergeant, who stood with his hands on his hips, regarding him with no sympathy.

"What the hell are *you* doing?" Singh countered. "We have a dead body and you are needed."

Curran swallowed. His mouth felt like one of the ten courts of hell.

Singh picked up the empty whisky bottle between the fingers of his right hand and made a disapproving click of his tongue.

"It is the middle of the day and you have plainly been drinking for some hours. Chai!" Singh ordered someone else, who hovered just outside the door to the bedroom. "Where is Li An?" he asked.

It took Curran a moment to remember. "She's gone . . . to visit relatives in Penang."

"I see, and that is a reason for you to drink Singapore dry?"

"I won't be lectured by you," Curran said, rising to his feet, conscious that he still wore the clothes he had traveled in. "And I'm not drunk. I didn't sleep well on the train last night."

"Wash and change . . . sir," Singh said, his lips compressed tightly. "There will be chai when you are respectable again."

Humiliation mingled with anger and a drinker's regret as

Curran plunged his head into a basin of cold water. When had one small whisky become half a bottle?

He rested his hands on the basin and stared at his reflection in the mirror. His eyes were red rimmed and bleary, and he needed a shave. The body, whoever it was, could wait a few more minutes.

❧ TWENTY

"Harriet?"

Harriet looked up as the shadow of Robert Curran fell across her. She had pulled a chair into the shade of a rain tree where she could watch for the arrival of help and make sure Elspeth's body was not disturbed. Out of deference to her own sensibilities, she had found a painter's drop sheet in one of the outside storerooms and covered Elspeth. Although the sheet, covered in splodges of garish paint, seemed an irreverent covering, she found it easier to look at an anonymous lump of canvas than the body of someone she had spoken with just days before.

Beneath his tan, Curran looked gray, his eyes bloodshot and red rimmed. As she stood to face him, she caught the unmistakable whiff of whisky.

"Curran, are you all right? Is it Li An—" she began, and stopped as his eyes narrowed in warning.

"You knew?" he said.

She couldn't lie, and her silence gave him the answer he sought.

He looked away, the muscle in his cheek twitching. When he turned back to her, his eyes blazed with anger. "Why didn't you tell me?"

"Because I made her a promise."

His nostrils flared. "Absolute secrecy and bloody confidentiality," he said.

She laid a hand on his arm, feeling the muscles tense beneath his sleeve. He was strung so tight that the slightest wrong word would cause him to snap, to shatter into pieces before her.

"Curran, this is a discussion for another time. See to Elspeth Lovett."

She let out a breath as she watched him stride away. He was angry with the world . . . not with her, not with Li An . . . just the world.

She resumed her seat and watched him hunker down beside the body and lift the canvas sheet. He removed his hat and ran a hand through his hair before replacing the sheet covering Elspeth's face with deliberate care. He paused for a moment before standing up. He looked up at the house, at the open gate at the top of the stairs, and she wondered if his thoughts were the same as hers. Accident . . . suicide . . . or something else?

Curran returned to her, his hat in his hand and a frown creasing his brow.

"What on earth possessed you to come looking for her up here?"

Harriet raised her chin. "Eunice Lovett came to my door about nine this morning in a terrible state. She said her mother had gone out during the night and not returned. She asked me to come with her because she thought her mother might be up here."

"Why would she think Elspeth had come here?"

"She wouldn't tell me."

"Where is the girl?"

"I sent her to the Orchard Road police post."

"And Lovett?"

"According to Eunice, he's with a client in Johor Bahru. Expected back this evening." She frowned as Curran blew out a breath and rubbed his forehead. "Are you all right?"

"I didn't sleep well on the train," he said. "I've got a crashing headache."

He was lying. The cause of the headache came from a bottle.

"It's not malaria?" she asked with wide, innocent eyes. Curran was prone to recurrent malaria.

"No, not malaria," he growled.

Their eyes locked, and he gave her a rueful smile. "I may have drowned my sorrows."

"I'm sorry about Li An but you have work to do, and I need to show you something," she said, and led him to the service area and the open back door.

"This is how I found it."

Curran pushed the door open and stepped inside. He made no objection to Harriet's following him, and the close, fusty atmosphere of the old house closed in around them.

The heels of their boots echoed on the old wooden floor as they passed into the main part of the house. They looked into the costume room first. Even in the gloom, nothing seemed amiss.

Curran threw open the door to the main rehearsal room.

"Is there anything out of place here?" he asked.

At first, she saw nothing wrong, the usual clutter of chairs in a semicircle around the piano, the chalked marks on the floor where scenery had to be imagined. She lifted her gaze, scanning the room.

"That door should be shut." She pointed to the main door that led out onto the verandah. "And"—she frowned—"there is no reason for a kerosene lamp to be there."

Someone had placed an old lamp with a cracked glass on the floor beside the daybed.

Curran nodded. "I'll get Greaves to dust it for fingerprints," he said. "Anything else?"

Harriet turned to the open door, but a glint of something

bright and metallic from beneath the daybed caught her eye. She knelt down and fished in the dust, her fingers closing on Elspeth's silver flask. The stopper was missing, and it was empty. She handed it to Curran.

"Elspeth Lovett carried this flask in her handbag."

"Then where is her handbag?" Curran asked.

They searched every corner and recess of the house but failed to find the capacious leather handbag.

Harriet frowned. "I've never seen her without it, but then again, she may have come down here to drown her sorrows away from the eyes of the servants and her daughter, and a handbag would probably not be necessary."

"So assuming she sat on that daybed and drank the flask dry before falling down the stairs, where is the stopper?" Curran asked.

"In her pocket?"

"If it is, Mac will find it," Curran said.

She followed him onto the verandah. The bolt that held the gate at the top of the stairs shut had been pulled back. She stood at the top of the steps, looking down the steep fall of stairs.

"Whoever designed these stairs should be shot," Curran said. "Even when new, they must have been treacherous without a handrail." He frowned. "You knew her, Harriet. Is it possible she might have jumped?"

Harriet looked up at him. "She was deeply unhappy."

Curran shook his head. "There's nothing to suggest she was here to meet anyone else," he said. "I have to finish up here. If Lovett's in Johor, the daughter is by herself. Could I prevail on you to take Musa and go down to the Lovett house and keep her company until other arrangements can be made?"

"I have a pile of correspondence at the school needing my attention, Curran."

"I know, but at the moment there is a seventeen-year-old girl who has just lost her mother alone in a house by herself."

She gave a curt nod and turned back to the house to make her way to the back door.

"Harriet."

Curran's voice stopped her at the door to the house. She turned to face him.

"She isn't coming back, is she?"

It took a moment to comprehend he was talking about Li An.

"I honestly don't know, Curran," she said.

He took a breath and looked up at a point well above her head. "She said I didn't need her anymore." His shoulders rose and fell. "But she was wrong."

"Curran . . ." Harriet took a step toward him. She wanted to hold him in her arms and tell him that if Li An didn't need him anymore, someone else did. The realization of the depth of her feelings for this man hit her like a dousing of cold water.

Only a few yards of rotting floorboard stood between them, but it could have been a mile. If she took that step, if she so much as touched him, their relationship changed forever and neither of them was ready for that.

He needed time to grieve, and she needed . . . what?

She turned and left him leaning on the rail surrounding the verandah, a solitary figure in a khaki uniform.

Harriet had yet to be invited to the Lovetts' home, and it surprised her how close Cairnhill House was to the old McKinnon plantation. A ten-minute walk at the most. She walked up the steep carriageway, past an immaculate garden, to the porte cochere. An ominous silence hung over the grand house and the servant who answered her ring of the doorbell looked as if he had been crying.

"We are not receiving visitors," he said. "There has been a death."

As he made to close the door, Harriet stepped forward. "Constable Musa bin Osman has been sent by Inspector Curran and I am a friend of Miss Eunice."

"She already has a memsahib with her," the man said.

Before Harriet could ask who, the front door was thrown wide and Eunice flung herself into Harriet's arms.

"I thought you'd never come," she said. "Mrs. Sewell is here."

Harriet left Musa in the front hall and allowed Eunice to take her by the hand and lead her into a formal living room, filled with stiff, over-upholstered, heavy European furniture. Alicia Sewell rose from a chair and set the cup of tea she was holding down on the table.

"Harriet, I am so pleased to see you," Alicia said.

"How did you come to be here?" Harriet asked.

"Eunice telephoned me from the police post so I fetched her home. Such a terrible thing."

Eunice sat on the edge of one of the overstuffed chairs, twisting a handkerchief in her hands. "Has Papa been told?"

Harriet shook her head. "Not yet. Do you know whom he is visiting in Johor?"

Eunice shook her head. "Someone at his office will know."

"Eunice, would it be all right if I take Constable Musa and have a quick look at your mama's bedroom? He needs to make sure nothing is touched before Inspector Curran arrives."

Eunice's eyes widened. "Why do they need to look in Mama's bedroom? It's private . . . it's—"

Alicia laid a hand over the girl's. "Eunice. The police have a job to do."

"Why?" Eunice burst out.

"The police have to look at your mother's room. She died in a very strange way and they have to find out why," Harriet said.

Eunice's shoulders slumped, and she nodded. "Very well. Please make sure *he* doesn't touch any of Mama's things." Eunice glared at Musa, waiting patiently beyond the wide-open double doors to the withdrawing room. He met the girl's hostile gaze with a friendly smile.

Alicia looked up at Harriet. "Do what you have to," she said.

Harriet exchanged a knowing glance with Alicia Sewell, glad for the other woman's sensible presence.

Eunice summoned the majordomo and he showed Harriet to a pleasant room on the first floor of the villa.

"I took the liberty of locking the door," he said, producing a key. "Miss Lovett wanted to . . ." He shrugged. "I do not know what she wanted to do, but I told her that the police would have to look first. She was not happy but I insisted."

"That was good thinking," Musa said.

"My brother is a policeman," the majordomo said, and the two men exchanged sympathetic glances.

"May we have the key?" Harriet held out her hand.

A good servant, he hesitated for a long moment before removing it from the ring he carried and handing the key to Musa.

"I'm sorry Miss Lovett was so rude, Musa," Harriet said after the servant had left them.

Musa shook his head. "The child has just found her beloved mother dead. It is an excuse and I will honor her wishes. I will stand here at the door, if you would care to do a search? We are, I think, looking for a note."

A note? It took Harriet a moment to realize he meant a suicide note.

At first glance she could see nothing obvious, like an envelope that might contain such a missive. Nothing seemed out of place. The bed had been turned back, the mosquito net lowered, and a nightdress laid out on a chair, but it had not been slept in. The items on the dressing table were those she would expect. It was the pretty, feminine room of a woman who left no indication of any turmoil in her mind that may have led to her taking her own life.

She left the matter of a more extensive search for Curran, shut the door, and Musa locked it. Downstairs she sent the majordomo for sandwiches and rejoined Alicia and Eunice in the living room. Musa took up a position by the front door to wait for Curran.

"We've locked your mother's room. No one will go in there except the police," she said. "Now, let's have something to eat."

"I've told Eunice she can come home with me after the police have been," Alicia said.

Harriet nodded, not without a little relief. That seemed a sensible suggestion and she was not sure she would cope well with Eunice's histrionics.

Curran arrived in the early afternoon. He still looked gray with fatigue combined with the surfeit of alcohol for breakfast, but the years of hard training were holding him together.

Eunice looked up at him with wary eyes as he sat down facing her. Her hand, holding Alicia's, tightened.

"I have sent a message to your father," Curran said.

Eunice's lip trembled. "Poor Papa."

He pulled a key from his pocket. "Constable Musa has given me the key to your mother's bedroom and I am just going to have a look, Eunice, and then I have some questions for you."

Eunice glanced at Alicia. "I really want to go to Alicia's house now."

"I promise I won't be long," Curran said. "Is it all right if Mrs. Gordon comes with me?"

"But she's already been in there."

Curran glanced at Harriet.

"Just a very quick look," Harriet said. "Musa can verify I didn't touch anything."

"What are you looking for?" Alicia asked.

Curran glanced at Eunice and said, "I'll know if I find it."

Comprehension dawned in Alicia's eyes. "You think—" She bit back the next words at a warning glance from Harriet.

Alone in the bedroom, Curran turned to Harriet. "Are you sure you didn't touch anything?"

Harriet stiffened. "Of course not. I know how you work."

Curran began his search with the woman's writing desk. It revealed very little beyond a copious stock of violet-colored writing paper. He moved on to the wardrobe and dressing table and bedside cabinet. An adjoining room contained a single bed and Charles Lovett's clothes and possessions and Harriet wondered if Elspeth's recent confession of adultery had led to Charles removing himself to the dressing room.

"Nothing," Curran said, straightening from the sewing cabinet. "No note, no journal. Not even a day diary."

"Neither have we found her handbag," Harriet pointed out.

Curran nodded. "We've searched the grounds of the McKinnon plantation and it hasn't turned up there yet. On that subject, Mac says he didn't find the stopper for her flask in the pockets of her dress either."

"So what do you think? Accident? Suicide? Or something else?" Harriet said.

Curran shrugged. "I think until something more concrete turns up, we will consider this an accident."

"But you don't think that it is?"

He shook his head. "Just my instinct. Suicide is a definite possibility. Murder? Who and why? I'll keep an open mind for now, Harriet, and if anyone asks you, it was an accident."

She nodded. "Which begs the next question, What was she doing up there?"

Curran rolled his eyes. "That question again? What is it about that godforsaken property? It's an unpleasant thought, but if she had been drinking heavily, it is not beyond the realm of possibility that she wandered down to the old house to"—he shrugged—"I don't know . . . revisit happier moments?" He tossed the key in his hand. "I suppose I should ask the girl a few questions."

They found Eunice pacing the drawing room. "I want to go," she said. "I can't bear being in this house . . . not without Mama."

"You can leave shortly," Curran said. "But I've got a couple of questions for you, Miss Lovett. Why did you think your mother would be at the McKinnon house?"

Eunice stopped pacing and returned to her seat beside Alicia. She bit her lip and shook her head.

"Just a feeling."

"When did you see her last?"

"When I went to bed at about ten o'clock."

"Where was she?"

Eunice looked up. "Upstairs in the parlor."

"What was she doing?"

Eunice's mouth tightened. "I can't say."

"Was she drinking?" Curran suggested.

Eunice shot him a look of pure distaste. "Yes. She had been drinking all day. I try to hide the bottles but she had found a bottle of brandy somewhere. Probably Papa's study."

"Did you hear her go out?"

Eunice shook her head. "My room is at the other end of the house. I don't know what time she went out. Her maid woke me when she found Mama's bed had not been slept in. That's when I thought she might have gone to the society's house."

"Why would you think that?"

"She was talking about it last night. How she'd been happy there. How happy Tony Dowling had made her." Eunice pulled a face. "Frankly, it was nauseating. I told her she was lucky to have Papa and she should be grateful he was so forgiving."

"Did you go to the house this morning after you found your mother missing?"

Eunice shook her head. "I didn't want to go by myself." She glanced at Harriet. "Mrs. Gordon understood about Mama so I thought she would be a good person to come with me."

Alicia Sewell rose to her feet. "If there are no other questions, Inspector, I think I should take poor Eunice home with me."

Eunice looked from Alicia to Curran. "What about Papa?"

"I'll break the news to him," Curran said. "Leave that to me, Miss Lovett."

Harriet returned home just as it was going dark, too tired to feel anything other than mild annoyance at the sight of Simon's familiar green motor vehicle pulled up in front of the house. All she wanted was a quiet supper, a bath and bed.

Julian and Simon were seated on the verandah, glasses in hand. They both came to their feet as she walked up the steps.

"Harriet, thank heavens," Julian said. "When I got your message to say you wouldn't be at the school today because of an accident, I didn't know what to think."

"Elspeth Lovett is dead," Harriet said.

As Julian handed her a glass of Scotch and soda, she recounted the events of the day, omitting any reference to Curran and Li An.

"That property is cursed," Julian said.

"You don't believe in curses," Harriet said. "You're a man of God, remember?"

Julian shrugged. "I maintain an open mind."

"I don't believe in curses," Simon said, "but it seems an odd coincidence to have two deaths at the same property within a week."

"It appears to have been an accident," Harriet said. "She fell down the front steps and broke her neck. The stairs were treacherous. It could have happened to anyone."

"You sound doubtful," her perceptive brother said. "Is it possible she might have taken her own life?"

"She was unhappy but was she at the point of taking her own life . . . ? I don't know. She didn't leave a note."

Harriet looked at the glass in her hand and set it down. When had one evening drink become two or even three? In her years in India she had met women like Elspeth Lovett, lonely, neglected wives for whom alcohol became their daily crutch. It got them out of bed and it sent them to sleep.

Elspeth had been in love with Tony Dowling. Had the revelation of their affair been too much to bear? Or at their last meeting had Tony rejected her and she could no longer live with the guilt of his death?

They would never know now. Elspeth was dead, and if she had taken her own life, she'd left no clue.

"What does Curran think?" Simon asked.

Harriet started at the mention of Curran's name.

"He's not saying," she said.

"Another funeral," Julian said. "I swear you live at that cemetery, Harri."

Simon clapped his hands together. "Change of subject," he said. "I bring good news. A friend has loaned me the use of his beach villa at Katong this weekend and I wondered if you would"—he glanced at Julian—"all of you, Will included, like a weekend away from the cares and troubles of Singapore." He held up a hand. "And don't tell me you have rehearsals. I don't think your little play will be going on this year, not after another death. I'll invite Griff and Doreen too. We could have quite a house party."

"That sounds wonderful," Harriet said, and meant it. A weekend at the beach with friends away from the dramas of the dramatic society and Curran would do her good.

She glanced at her brother. "Julian has cricket and school commitments."

"Nothing I can't get out of," Julian replied. "We could all do with a couple of days off."

Harriet rose to her feet. "We shall look forward to it. Now I really am rather tired. I'd like a wash and my supper."

She left Julian to see their guest off and lay, still fully clothed, on her bed, listening for the sound of the motor vehicle dying away, followed by footsteps on the floorboards outside her room.

A quick rap at the door and Julian stood in the doorway looking down at her.

"What's troubling you, Harriet Jane?"

"Nothing," Harriet snapped. "I'm hot, tired and hungry and it's been a trying day."

"You were a bit peevish with Simon."

"I was a bit," she admitted. "I wasn't in the mood for his particular brand of good humor." She blew out a breath. "Li An has left Curran."

"Ah. He thought she might."

Harriet raised her head to look at her brother. "You know?"

"Yes. Curran and I had a bit of a chat at the cricket on Saturday and he confided that he thought she was about to leave him." He narrowed his eyes. "But you already knew, didn't you, Harri?"

"Yes, she told Lavinia and me last Tuesday when we were at tea. It's been hell not being able to say something."

"How's Curran?"

Harriet clenched her jaw. "I think he started the day with whisky for breakfast," she said.

"That's not a good sign."

"No. He's taken it hard."

She wanted to say that his heart was breaking, but that wasn't the right thing to say about a man like Curran. That wasn't what was expected. Keep a stiff upper lip, never show your emotions . . . carry on until the weight of the burden you were carrying became unbearable.

"Harri . . ." Julian began.

She knew that tone of voice, that of a priest ready to hear

confession. Well, she wasn't ready to confess . . . and she had nothing to confess except her own confusion.

"I'm tired, Ju. I think I'll have a bath and go straight to bed. Ask Huo Jin if she can bring me a little soup. That's all I want."

She rolled onto her side with her back to the door. She heard it click shut and closed her eyes, fighting the betraying tears.

Curran paced the platform of the Tank Road Railway Station as he waited for the evening train from Johor Bahru. As he paced, he tried to compose the words he needed to address Charles Lovett. Telling an unsuspecting man that his wife was dead had to be the one part of the job he hated the most.

Lovett swung the carriage door open and dismounted from the train. He wore a crumpled beige linen suit and a fedora and carried a battered leather briefcase. Curran stepped forward to intercept him.

"Inspector? To what do I owe the honor of a welcoming party?"

The man looked unutterably weary, his face sunk in deep lines and his chin in dire need of a good shave.

"I think it best you come with me," Curran said. "This is not a conversation for a busy railway platform."

"Good Lord, am I under arrest?" Lovett may have sounded jocular, but there was no humor in his eyes.

"No, nothing like that. There's been an accident."

Comprehension flashed into the man's face, and his mouth drooped. "Tell me . . ."

"In here." Curran guided the man into the stationmaster's office, which he had commandeered by arrangement.

Lovett sat heavily in a wooden chair and Curran poured him a glass of water from the jug on the desk. He perched on the edge of the desk and waited until Lovett had removed his hat and drunk the water. As he set the glass down, Lovett looked up at him.

"Well?"

"It's your wife," Curran said.

"What's that stupid cow done now?"

This was not the reaction Curran had been expecting, so he ditched the gentle breaking of the news he had been rehearsing and settled with, "She's dead."

Lovett stared at him. "Oh God, I thought . . . maybe . . ."

"What did you think?"

He shook his head. "I don't know. She's always tripping over things, but I suppose you wouldn't have been waiting here if she'd just sprained her ankle. Tell me, Inspector, what happened?"

Curran frowned. *Always tripping over things?* What exactly did that mean? He studied Lovett with renewed interest.

"How . . . how did it happen?" Lovett asked.

"She died of a broken neck. Fell down the stairs at the society's property during the night."

Lovett screwed up his face. "What? Where? Why was she there, for heaven's sake?"

Curran shook his head. "We don't know. I hoped maybe you'd know?"

"Me? No idea. I wasn't in Singapore last night. Who found her?"

"Your daughter and Mrs. Gordon."

Lovett reached for the glass again. "Oh no, not Eunice. Where is she now?"

"Eunice is with Mrs. Sewell at her house."

Lovett nodded. "Good, best place for her—and Elspeth?"

"At the hospital mortuary. I will need you to formally identify your wife."

Lovett blew out a breath. "Very well. Let's get it over with."

"My motor is outside," Curran said, throwing open the door.

Lovett said nothing on the drive to the hospital. Mac met them and conducted the man to the morgue. The formalities were brief and Lovett didn't flinch as Mac flicked the sheet away from the dead woman's face.

He gave a cursory nod of his head and said, "Yes, that's my wife. Now take me home, Curran."

"I just need to have a quick word with the doctor," Curran said. "Can you wait for me in the courtyard?"

Alone with Mac, he looked down at the body of Elspeth Lovett. She had been a comely woman in life, now whatever remnant of beauty she may have had was slipping away from her as the hours since her death passed.

"Definitely broken neck," Mac said. "Broke her left leg too."

"The injuries are consistent with a fall down the stairs?"

Mac nodded.

"What if she jumped?"

Mac thought about that for a long moment. "I honestly can't say, Curran. Sorry."

"What are you going to say in your report to the coroner?"

"Just what I just told you. It's for the coroner to draw his own conclusions."

Curran slumped against the wall and ran a hand over his eyes. "It's been a hell of a day, Mac."

"What else has happened?"

"You'll know soon enough, if half the island doesn't know already. Li An's gone back to Penang."

Mac said nothing for a long moment.

"You don't look surprised," Curran said to break the silence.

"I'm not. She is a Khoo. Did you really think she would be content being your housekeeper and bed warmer for the rest of her life?"

"That's not fair. I asked her to marry me but she refused . . . several times."

"Are you going to go after her?"

Curran ran a hand through his hair. "I don't know, Mac. What should I do?"

Mac laid a hand on his shoulder. "I'm not the one to advise you. Affairs of the heart are only of interest to me when they stop beating." He dropped his hand and glanced at the door. "Now you better get going. You can't keep Lovett waiting any longer. Get him home to his daughter."

❦ TWENTY-TWO

Wednesday, 9 November

Where's Mrs. Gordon?" Curran asked as he entered the Detective Branch on Wednesday morning.

Nabeel looked up from his filing. "She sent a message that she is unwell and will not be coming in today."

"That's inconvenient," Curran said, more to himself than to his assembled colleagues.

Singh pointed to a large, odiferous, hessian-wrapped object in the middle of the floor. "This was just delivered," he said.

"Excellent. Unwrap it, Greaves."

Greaves wrinkled his nose, and with some reluctance cut the rope binding. The smell grew worse as the wrappings fell away. Everyone took a step back. Even Curran had to resist the urge to cover his face.

"What is it?" Greaves asked.

Curran explained the importance of the falsified bale of rubber and pointed out the stamp of the Sungei Pandan Rubber Company.

The normally phlegmatic Singh smiled. "Is there enough now to charge Ellis?"

Curran nodded. "I think so, but we'll have a look at it in a moment. Greaves, can you photograph this object and have it taken away and stored somewhere safe?"

Even after the bale had been removed, the smell lingered. Musa opened all the windows and shutters and Nabeel sat with a handkerchief pressed to his nose as the Detective Branch gathered around the blackboard and the evidence table.

"We've really got two cases," Curran said. "They may be related, or it may just be coincidence. On the one hand, we have an insurance fraud that implicates the deceased, Tony Dowling, the broker George Sewell and Lionel Ellis of the Sungei Pandan Rubber Company in at least one, but possibly more, insurance frauds, the last one being the sinking of the *Hesperides* in February this year. Dowling's death could well be related to this little triumvirate."

"In what way?" Greaves asked.

"From what the clerk at Caldwell & Hubbard said, Dowling could have developed a conscience following the death of the two sailors when the *Hesperides* went down," Curran said.

Singh nodded. "Maybe he was turning his hand to a little blackmail or maybe he just wanted to walk away." He flicked through the statements. "His employer was getting suspicious and had asked his manager to instigate an audit. That could have caused a degree of nervousness on the part of Dowling and his fellows."

"Agreed, and if that is correct, it points to either Sewell or Ellis being the murderer. They were both at the Balmoral Club at the time he was murdered, but as I can attest," Curran said with a grimace, "Ellis is not above hiring others to do his dirty work."

"But if Dowling's death is not related to the insurance fraud, then we are looking at a crime of passion," Greaves said. "An aggrieved husband or a cast-off lover?"

Curran nodded. "It doesn't look like he had any other current lovers except Elspeth Lovett."

"Not Alicia Sewell?" Singh asked.

"The lady says not. A professional friendship, nothing more, and I'm inclined to believe her."

"And Mrs. Lovett's death?" Greaves asked.

Curran huffed out a breath. "There is nothing about her death that suggests murder. She had keys to the property. She was deeply unhappy and had been drinking heavily. The house was secluded and private."

"Are you saying she took her own life?" Musa said. "But there was no note."

"Not all suicides leave notes," Curran said. "And in the circumstances, an accident while intoxicated is just as plausible a reason for her to stumble and fall down the stairs."

Greaves shook his head. "I know these people," he said. "Mrs. Lovett was not a happy woman but I'd never have said she was suicidal."

"Would you have guessed she was having an affair with Tony Dowling?" Curran countered.

Greaves shook his head. "No. That surprised me. She must have been ten years older than him, if not more. Do you think he rejected her, and she killed him and then took her own life in remorse?"

Curran considered the young constable for a long moment. "That's a possibility," he said. He frowned. "We've missed one thing. Where was Tony Dowling killed? In the house or where we found him? If he was killed in the house, how would a woman like Elspeth Lovett have carried his body out to the scenery store?"

Greaves frowned. "There would have been blood but I didn't see anything in the house. Perhaps I should have another look?"

Curran nodded. "When you have some time, Greaves."

Singh stroked his beard. "There is one person common to both scenarios," he said. "The lawyer, Charles Lovett."

Curran took his pipe from his pocket and clenched it, unlit, between his teeth as he considered the blackboard. He picked up a chalk and drew lines from Elspeth Lovett and Tony Dowling to Charles Lovett. Until this point he hadn't seriously considered Lovett a suspect but now . . . ?

"Lovett was in Johor on the night his wife died and he has something of an alibi for the night of Dowling's death." He looked at Singh. "What about Ellis?"

"Lionel Ellis is an unpleasant individual," Singh said. "But you cannot let your own prejudice against the man cloud your judgment."

Curran removed his pipe and used the stem to point to Ellis's name. "There is no denying his involvement in the fraud. The rubber shipment purports to come from his company."

"That is not evidence that he himself knew or condoned the fraud," Singh said.

Curran glared at his sergeant. He hated to admit Singh was right, and it was his own blind spot where Lionel Ellis was concerned that obscured his clear sight of the case.

"Singh, follow up with the manager of Caldwell & Hubbard Insurance about the other cases Dowling may have been involved with, starting with the cases that had been identified as requiring an audit."

"What about you, Curran?"

He replaced the pipe in his pocket and turned on his heel. "I think we might find some answers with the man whose name is on the shipping documentation. It is time to have another talk with Mr. Sewell."

Curran began his search for Sewell at his home off Cairnhill Road. He didn't need to ask if the lady of the house was at home. Music and a lovely soprano voice lifted in an operatic aria drifted out of an open window as he walked his gelding, Leopold, up the driveway.

The majordomo showed him into a cool room, with large French windows opening onto the verandah. Thin muslin curtains fluttered in the breeze, and seated at a grand piano, Alicia Sewell looked up at him and smiled, but didn't stop until the beautiful aria was finished. In the subdued lighting, with her hair loose around her shoulders, she looked dazzlingly beautiful. He thought he now understood what *stage presence* meant and felt a momentary pang of regret that he hadn't seen her perform.

"Inspector, what can I help you with?" she said, dropping her hands from the keys of the piano to her lap.

"What were you singing?"

"Handel's 'Lascia ch'io pianga,'" she replied.

"That's a long way from Gilbert and Sullivan," he commented.

"There are actually some lovely ballads in G and S," she said, "but my first love is opera."

"They tell me you were on the stage in London," Curran said.

Alicia laughed. "Do *they*? Have you noticed, Inspector, that no one in Singapore is quite who *they* say they are? Yes, I was on the stage." A mischievous smile caught the corners of her mouth. "But between us, Inspector, it wasn't Covent Garden. I was a music hall singer."

Curran smiled. "And were you a star?"

"Oh yes," she said. "But alas my career ended in scandal. When you fall in love with a married man, it will never end well."

"I am learning that in the world of the theater the lines between marriage vows are somewhat blurred," Curran said.

A frown creased her brow. "The line between the fantasy of the stage and reality is where the blurring occurs, Inspector."

"What about you, Mrs. Sewell? I believe Tony Dowling had a penchant for married women," Curran said.

She studied him for a long time. "And you are curious as to whether I had a taste for my younger costar? I think I have told you before that in the case of Tony Dowling, as attractive as he may have been, we were never anything more than professional colleagues."

He studied her for a long moment. "Your husband is absent for long periods. Do you ever seek the company of other men?"

Her lips twitched. "Really, what a question? I like you, Inspector, but I do not feel inclined to confess my deepest desires and sins to you. You are not a priest."

"And yet in my experience I have found confession good for the soul," Curran said.

Alicia rose to her feet and crossed to the window. She parted the curtains and looked out into the well-kept garden, her arms around herself.

After a long moment, she turned to face him. "Why are you here, Inspector? Is it just some prurient interest in my love life?"

"You haven't answered my question."

"And I have no intention of doing so. I am faithful to my husband. That is all you need to know."

Curran considered the woman and realized she hadn't exactly denied some sort of entanglement beyond her marriage. It may not have been fully realized, but the possibility existed.

"Is Miss Lovett still staying with you?"

"No. She returned to that mausoleum of a house and her father last night."

"And is your husband in Singapore at the moment?"

"He is and you will find him where he usually is when in town . . . the bar of the Balmoral Club."

Curran consulted his watch. "At ten in the morning?"

"Yes," she said. "He spent the night at the club. Why do you need to speak to him?"

"That's between him and me."

"Are you planning to arrest him?"

He frowned. "Why do you think I would want to arrest him?"

She sighed. "I am tired of this game, Inspector. Whatever your intentions, remember I am his wife, and I will say nothing against him."

Curran rarely found himself backed into a corner, but for once he had nothing to say, despite the myriad of questions churning in his mind.

"If that is all, Inspector, I would like to return to my music."

She returned to the piano stool, and her fingers strayed over the keys. Curran knew he had been dismissed.

Curran returned to South Bridge Road organized a couple of his men and suitable transport to accompany him before confronting George Sewell. For a man with a wife as attractive as Alicia, George Sewell didn't seem too eager to spend time with her and Curran found the man, as his wife had suggested, by himself at a table in the bar of the Balmoral Club, a half-empty glass of beer in front of him and a pile of papers on the table.

Sewell glanced at his watch as Curran approached.

"Sun's over the yardarm somewhere in the world," he said. "Sit down. Care to join me for a beer?"

Curran declined both the beer and the offer of a seat, preferring to stand.

Sewell narrowed his eyes. "You look serious, Curran."

Curran lowered his voice. "I would like you to accompany me to South Bridge Police Headquarters, Sewell."

Sewell shook his head. "No, thank you. I'm meeting some chaps for lunch." He tapped the paperwork. "Business."

"It's not a social invitation, Sewell. I suggest you come with no fuss or I am going to have to arrest you here and now and I'm sure you would like that even less than missing lunch with the chaps."

Sewell stared at him. "Arrest me? What the hell for?"

"I would prefer to discuss that at South Bridge Road. Let's just say I have some questions in relation to the sinking of the *Hesperides*."

A muscle twitched in Sewell's cheek, and he set his glass down on the table. "I see. Tom," he hailed the barman. "When Coghill and Jennings turn up, give them my apologies. I've been called away on urgent business."

Curran had arranged for the false rubber bale to be placed in the room where he intended to interview Sewell. The smell of the rotting straw combined with the airless room caused the man to recoil as Curran opened the door.

"What is that disgusting smell?" he demanded.

Curran removed the canvas cover from the bale. "I thought you might recognize this."

Sewell pressed a neatly laundered handkerchief to his nose. "What is it?"

"It's part of the cargo off the *Hesperides*." Curran made a show of consulting the bill of lading. "It comprised fifty bales of high-grade rubber consigned by your company and, unless I am mistaken, signed by you. That is your signature?"

He passed the paper to Sewell, who nodded. "I don't see the problem. The ship was lost in a storm in the Straits of Malacca."

"It's interesting that it was insured for six thousand pounds. For fifty bales, that would make its insurance value twice its actual value, I believe."

He had Sewell's interest now. Sweat broke out on the man's forehead and he dabbed at his face with his handkerchief.

"So what? The insurer paid up. No questions were asked at the time."

Curran stood up and walked over to the stinking bale of straw. "Come over here, Sewell."

The man crossed the room on leaden feet, his handkerchief pressed to his mouth and nose.

Using a ruler, Curran parted the ragged cut made by the customs official at Port Dickson. "As you can see, it is a bale of straw covered in a layer of rubber to make it appear like a regular bale of rubber. We believe it was weighted with rocks, or similar, to give it the correct weight for shipment. Whatever was used fell out as the straw rotted."

"How the hell do you know it's connected with the *Hesperides*?" Sewell lowered his handkerchief, his eyes blazing defiance.

"These stamps." Curran indicated the faded stamp of the Sungei Pandan Rubber Company. "This washed up on a beach south of Port Dickson a month after the *Hesperides* sank. The number tallies with the bill of lading and the name of the shipping agent as we have already established was you, Sewell. As Robert White & Co.'s sole representative on the Malay Peninsula, you can probably understand why I believe you are responsible for this shipment."

"Can we talk elsewhere? I feel quite nauseated," Sewell said. The color had drained from his face and a sheen of sweat shone on his forehead.

Curran ushered him into a nearby room, giving orders for the bale to be returned to storage.

Sewell sat down, and the constable produced a cup of strong black tea.

Curran waited until the man had composed himself.

"If I am to understand you correctly, Inspector, you are accusing me of involvement in a fraud?"

"That is correct."

Sewell's eyes widened, and the color returned to his face as he rose to his feet, thumping the table. "That is an outrageous accusation, Inspector. I am a well-respected businessman. I—"

"Then tell me why the insurance value was inflated?"

"It was a valuable cargo . . . we had an important client waiting on it in San Francisco."

"But it wasn't the only overinsured shipment Tony Dowling handled for you, was it?"

Curran produced the records found by John Henry and passed on to Singh, together with the newspaper reports from Griff Maddocks.

Sewell shrugged. "It's just business. Nothing more."

"Did you get greedy? Six thousand pounds is a sizable sum of money. How were the proceeds disbursed, Sewell? Tony Dowling got ten percent and I just need to inspect your financial records to see how much you got. No doubt some went to the captain of the vessel. A few officials to bribe along the way. And then of course there were the two men who died—"

"They were only natives. Their families were compensated."

"But it bothered Tony Dowling, didn't it?"

"It's the insurance business, people die. I don't see why it should have bothered him more than any other lost cargo."

Curran laid his hands flat on the desk and leaned forward. "Because it was a deliberate scuttling, Sewell. Those men were murdered for the sake of your six thousand pounds."

Sewell swallowed. "Look here, Curran, I strenuously deny this accusation. I have only ever acted in good faith. I knew nothing about the cargo being falsified."

"Someone else masterminded the plot, Sewell? If it wasn't you, who was it? Your very good friend Lionel Ellis, perhaps? It's his company stamp on the bale."

Sewell crossed his arms. "I'm not saying another word."

Curran shrugged. "That's your prerogative, but I am curious as to why Tony Dowling had to die. Was he worried about an audit? Did he threaten to report the conspiracy to the authorities? Or was it simple blackmail?"

Sewell jumped to his feet. "I had nothing to do with Tony Dowling's death."

Curran straightened. "That remains to be seen. In the meantime, I have more than enough evidence to charge you with fraud, theft, falsifying documents and, oh . . . manslaughter."

Sewell's eyes widened. "Manslaughter?"

"Those two sailors who died. They were put aboard a ship that was intended to be scuttled. If it wasn't murder, it was certainly manslaughter."

"I've had enough of this nonsense. I'm going home."

He turned for the door, but Gursharan Singh stepped in front of him.

Curran continued, "I've got more questions for you, Sewell, and while you can probably apply for bail, for the time being, I am detaining you here while we do the paperwork."

Sewell turned back to Curran. "You're arresting me?"

Curran pretended to consider the question for a long moment. "Yes," he said, "I am."

He recited the formal arrest charges, leaving it to the constable to lead Sewell away to the cells.

"You enjoyed that," Gursharan Singh said.

"You have no idea how much," Curran replied. "But not nearly as much as I am going to enjoy seeing Ellis behind bars."

❧ TWENTY-THREE

After the events of the previous day, Harriet had slept badly and woken with an atrocious headache. Finding her bedroom too stuffy, she lay on the daybed on the verandah, a damp cloth over her eyes and Shashti on her lap. By midafternoon, her headache had eased enough to allow her the indulgence of flicking through the months-old copies of *The Lady*, loaned to her by Louisa. It made lighter reading than the back issues of *Suffragette*, which reproached her from the table in front of her.

A carriage turned in through the gate, and Harriet's heart sank. She really was in no mood for visitors. Her despondency increased as Alicia Sewell stepped from the carriage and sashayed up the steps with a smile and an apology for calling unannounced.

Good manners overcame Harriet's initial resentment and she invited Alicia to join her for a cup of tea.

As they waited for Huo Jin, Alicia picked up a copy of *Suffragette*. "I had heard a rumor that you were involved with the WSPU in London," she said. She raised an eyebrow. "And you served time in Holloway?"

Harriet bit her lip. While it was a fairly open secret among a few on the island, she didn't like her history being bandied about in casual gossip. She had too much at stake.

"You can't believe every bit of tittle-tattle in Singapore," she said, and added with unusual cattiness, "For instance I've heard that your fame in London was on the music hall stage."

Alicia threw back her head and laughed. "Touché. It is quite true. Elsie Williams, as I once was, was the darling of the Mulherrin company of music halls." The humor died in her eyes. "You have lived in our colonies for a long time, Harriet. It is my observation that out here the most ordinary person can imagine themselves extraordinary."

"But you do have a wonderful voice," Harriet said.

"Thank you. I once harbored ambitions of Covent Garden," Alicia said, "but nothing could get me past my origin, the stews of Whitechapel."

"But your husband—"

Alicia shook her head. "George may sound like he was born with a plum in his mouth but I can assure you he comes from the docks of Liverpool." She paused, turning the cup on its saucer. "Your Inspector Curran, he's the genuine article, isn't he?"

"He's not *my* Inspector Curran," Harriet protested.

"Is it true that he is the grandson of an earl?" Alicia said.

"I believe so," Harriet conceded, but despite Alicia's hopeful look, did not elaborate.

"He came to visit me this morning." Alicia bit her lip. "And he's arrested George. Do you know why?"

Harriet could answer with complete honesty. "I've no idea."

Alicia's mouth tightened. "I went to the Police Headquarters, but they wouldn't let me see him. I'll speak to Charles Lovett. He'll know what to do."

As Alicia showed no sign of taking her leave, Harriet reverted to the previous subject. "How did you escape the music hall?"

"My position became untenable. Mulherrin's son took a fancy to me. It was fun at first, but there was one problem. He was married and it all ended messily when his wife stuck her head in a gas oven and left a vile note telling the world it was my affair with her husband that had led to her act of desperation. I packed my bags and decided to try my luck in the colonies. I never got further than Singapore. I met George Sewell and he was the answer to my prayers—or at least that's what I thought."

"What do you mean?"

Alicia managed a small, tight smile. "He drinks too much, and he has something of a temper." She rubbed her arm and Harriet understood.

"He hits you?"

She touched her face. "It's never anywhere the bruises can be seen and he's always sorry. There will be flowers or a piece of jewelry tomorrow, I'm sure."

She rolled up the loose sleeve of her muslin gown. Dark, ugly bruises on her forearm told their own story. Harriet had never met George Sewell, but if he had appeared on her doorstep at that moment, she would have . . . would have . . . what? What could a woman in these circumstances do?

One thing she could do was tell Curran even if Alicia bound her to secrecy. She had more than her share of other people's secrets.

"I'm sorry, Alicia," Harriet said.

"We make our own decisions in life, don't we?" Alicia let the sleeve fall back. "When he's sober, he's sweetness itself, but he got back from his trip yesterday and it was plain he'd been drinking. I made the mistake of challenging him about it."

Alicia looked away, resting her chin on her hand, the very picture of a thoughtful ingenue. "Fortunately George is often away, and when he is home, he finds far more congenial company at the Balmoral Club." Her shoulders tensed. "And in the brothels of Kuala Lumpur."

Harriet straightened. "I beg your pardon?"

Alicia turned to look at her. "He is far too concerned about his reputation to sully his nest here in Singapore. There are girls in KL he visits when he is there."

"Any particular brothel?" Harriet asked.

Alicia stared at her. "What a strange question. I didn't know you had an interest in brothels, Harriet?"

"It's a case Curran is working on."

"Very well. I believe it is an expensive brothel catering to the tastes of the higher end of our society." She frowned. "The Topaz Club or some such name." Alicia's mouth curved in a moue of disgust. "I don't know anything more about it. I don't want to know."

"I'm sorry, Alicia."

She shrugged. "I am just grateful I don't have children. It would be no life for them." She looked around, her gaze fixing on Will's cricket bat propped up against a wall. "Do you have a child, Harriet?"

"My son died in India a few years ago. Julian and I have a ward."

And she could no more imagine life without Will than she could have imagined a life without her own son.

The headache was creeping back, and she rubbed her eyes. "Forgive me, Alicia. I'm a little under the weather today. Was there something in particular you wanted to ask me?"

Alicia nodded. "I feel I should attend Elspeth's funeral tomorrow—for Charles's and Eunice's sakes," she said. "She is being buried tomorrow at eleven in the morning."

"And you want me to keep you company again?"

Alicia smiled. "You are a steady companion, Harriet, and I am humble enough to accept that sometimes I need a person like you at my side. Charles has taken her death hard, although frankly the woman could be a terrible trial. I can say it now, although we all knew. She was an alcoholic and thoroughly miserable. She wanted to be back in England, dispensing tea and cake in her living room." Alicia's lip curled. "As you know, this climate, this atmosphere, is not for the fainthearted. As for her daughter . . . neglected and ignored. Basically allowed to run wild. Charles is sending her back to England as soon as it can be arranged. She needs the discipline of a proper English school, not the halfhearted attention of a score of governesses."

"Poor Eunice," Harriet said.

Alicia's lips twisted. "Yes indeed, poor Eunice. She deserved a better upbringing."

She picked up her elegant, beaded handbag from the table. "I should be going. I have some errands to run in Raffles Place and I need to talk to Charles about getting George released." A small, tight smile marred the beautiful face. "Although I rather like the idea of him rotting in a stinking jail cell for the time being."

Harriet, thinking of the nasty bruises on the woman's arm, had to agree with that sentiment.

Alicia stood up. "The motor vehicle has developed a problem, which didn't help George's mood yesterday. Do you mind awfully ordering a hackney and coming to my home tomorrow morning about ten and we can go on from there?"

Harriet hadn't actually agreed to go to the funeral, but it seemed the decision had been made. "I suppose so, yes."

Alicia cast her one of her radiant smiles. "Good. I shall see you at ten."

✥ TWENTY-FOUR

Curran left George Sewell stewing in a hot, unpleasant cell at the back of Police Headquarters and rode Leopold out to the Lovett home, Cairnhill House. Since he had first visited it the previous day, the pleasant villa had become a house in mourning. The shutters were bolted and black crepe hung from the front door. The majordomo showed him into the front hall, leaving Curran to cool his heels for at least ten minutes before admitting him into Lovett's study.

The pleasant room, where he had interviewed Elspeth Lovett, had an unmistakably masculine air about it, from the tiger skin on the floor to the heads of various local fauna who glared at him from the wall with dead glass eyes.

"You hunt?" Curran asked.

"Not for some years." Lovett did not rise from his seat behind a large teak desk. He gestured to a leather upholstered chair of the sort found in gentlemen's clubs in London. "What do you want to ask me? If it's about my wife, I have nothing new to tell you." He waved a hand at the papers on his desk. "I am afraid I will have to cancel the current production. Hardly seemly to proceed in the circumstances."

Curran frowned. "You were considering continuing?"

Lovett sat down at his desk and rested his head in his hands.

"It may seem strange to you, Inspector, but there is precious little in my life that gives me as much joy as bringing pleasure to other people with the stage shows."

"That's an admirable sentiment, but your wife is dead, Mr. Lovett, and you have a daughter who needs you."

Lovett looked up. "Of course, but grief works in strange ways, Inspector, and while it might seem odd that my preoccupation is with the society, it prevents me from thinking of my loss and what must be done for Eunice. Now, what is it you wish to discuss with me?"

"The sinking of the *Hesperides*," Curran said.

Lovett blinked. "What has that to do with my wife's death?"

"I don't know," Curran said. "Maybe something, maybe nothing."

Lovett looked away with a sour laugh. "Don't waste my time, Inspector."

"As we have discussed before, the proceeds from that insurance claim, which had been handled by Tony Dowling, flowed through your trust account. You wouldn't divulge the beneficiary but I believe I have a name now."

Lovett said nothing, but he brought his gaze back to Curran.

"Your client was George Sewell?"

Curran took Lovett's silence as tacit agreement and continued, "Sewell saw to the insurance of the *Hesperides* cargo using Tony Dowling as the insurance agent so I assume the money from the claim, which was paid over to you, went to Sewell? Am I correct?"

Lovett waited a long, long moment before he let out a sigh. "That is correct, Inspector. There is nothing suspicious about that. Just a normal commercial transaction. Sewell was acting in his capacity as a broker and agent for the consignment owner."

"As you say. Did you know who Sewell's client was?"

Lovett gave a small, noncommittal shrug.

Curran plowed on, "The shipment came from the Sungei Pandan Rubber Company . . . another of your clients, Lionel Ellis."

"What of it?"

"Let me tell you what I think happened. Sewell and Ellis conspired with Dowling to insure the shipment for double its value. Someone either swapped or made up a shipment of rubber with the stamp of the Sungei Pandan, only it wasn't rubber. It comprised weighted bales of straw with a veneer of sheet rubber, enough to satisfy the cursory inspection. They chose an obscure port for the shipment and a notoriously unreliable ship. The shipment passed the examination for weights and measures. There may even have been a couple of genuine bales produced for inspection. The shipment was loaded, and once out of the shipping channel in the Straits, the captain scuttled the ship, escaping with his crew either back to Malaya or across to Sumatra. Either way, we have no chance of tracing them. I presume the captain sent a telegram from wherever he ended up, reporting the loss of the ship and the crew."

Lovett nodded. "We tried to trace the man, but he had vanished, but what's this nonsense about the cargo being fraudulent? I'm sorry, Inspector, I can't accept that George Sewell would be implicated in such a plan."

"What about Lionel Ellis?"

"I know your thoughts on Ellis, Curran, and they are not without justification, but none of this has anything to do with what happened to Dowling."

"Doesn't it? He was complicit in the fraud," Curran said.

Lovett stared at him. "Fraud? That's a bit much."

"You're a lawyer, you know as well as I do that it was fraud and there are a raft of other charges I can add but that will do for now."

Lovett rose to his feet, resting his knuckles on the desk. His eyes blazed from a reddened face as he all but shouted, "I can assure you, Inspector, I had nothing to do with such a venture. Nothing. I was a completely innocent party."

Curran met his gaze without blinking. "But you were the lawyer who received and disbursed the funds. You had to be complicit."

Lovett sank back on his chair and, his hand on his mouth, turned to look at the moldering head of an antelope. "Sewell and Dowling had a number of similar arrangements." He turned to face Curran again, his hands now clasped together on his blotter as he leaned forward. "Dowling would arrange the insurance at Sewell's behest and I would handle the payout, but I swear on my life, Inspector, I took them entirely on trust." He paused. "Although now I think on it, it seems strange that quite so many shipments resulted in claims."

"Were they as big as this one?"

Lovett shook his head. "No, and not always rubber. Gambier, even pepper."

"Nothing that would attract attention?"

The man sat back in his chair, his face gray and drawn, his eyes bloodshot. He looked like a man whose world was crashing in around him.

"Did they get greedy?" Curran said.

Lovett looked up. "George Sewell is a friend. If I am guilty of anything, it's of taking the man's word on matters I should have investigated further. But I still fail to see what this has to do with Dowling's death?"

"You tell me."

"For the last time, I know nothing about it!" The color rose in the man's face again.

Curran persisted. "Dowling wanted more? Or did the deaths on the *Hesperides* scare him? Did he have to be silenced?"

"If you're implying either Sewell or Ellis had anything to do with his death, I absolutely refute the suggestion. We were all at the Balmoral Club when he died." Lovett's eyes flickered from one corner of the room to the other, like a trapped animal looking for an escape.

"But your wife wasn't. She was with Dowling."

"Curran, you have gone too far."

"Have I?"

"If you are implying Elspeth killed him because of an insurance fraud she knew nothing about, that is ridiculous."

"I'm not suggesting she did, but it would not have been hard to find someone willing to kill him. God knows, Ellis tried it on me last week."

Lovett slumped back in his chair, silent.

"Do you think Elspeth's death may be connected to Dowling's?" he said at last.

Curran shook his head. "To be honest, I don't know. It just strikes me as coincidental that there are two deaths at the same property within days of each other."

Lovett shook his head. "Elspeth's death was an accident. You said so yourself." Lovett's mouth worked. "I have to believe that is what happened, Curran. I am struggling to come to terms with the sad truth that she was conducting an affair with Dowling. We exchanged words . . . cruel words before I left for Johor. It was almost as if she was trying to deliberately provoke me, and as I was sitting here this evening, I did wonder if maybe . . . maybe . . . she jumped. I suppose I will never know if she intended to end her life or just to hurt herself for the attention."

"That's harsh."

"Elspeth was not an easy woman. She was . . . inclined to be emotional, particularly after too much to drink. She liked people to make a fuss if she was ill or indisposed. Maybe she thought if she broke her leg, all would be forgiven. Now, do you have any more questions, Inspector? I have a funeral to arrange."

"Is your daughter here?"

"Eunice? What do you want with her?"

"Just tidying up loose ends, Lovett."

Lovett stood up and crossed the room and opened the door. He called his daughter's name and Eunice appeared with a promptness that indicated she had not been far away.

"You called, Papa?"

"The inspector has some questions for you," Lovett said, and stood aside to admit his daughter into his study. Eunice perched on the edge of the desk and looked at Curran with an intensity that he found unnerving.

"You had a terrible shock yesterday, Miss Lovett. Do you mind answering some more questions?"

Eunice shrugged.

Her father moved beside her and laid a hand on her shoulder. "I'll be right here, Eunice. If there's anything that upsets you or you don't feel like answering, just say and I'll ask the inspector to leave."

Curran turned a level gaze on the man. He understood a father's protectiveness but he still needed answers to his questions.

"I will be asking Eunice questions about things she might have seen at the old house."

"What do you want to ask me, Inspector?" Eunice interposed.

"Eunice, you told me you had, on occasion, followed your mother to her evening meetings with Mr. Dowling."

Lovett bristled. "Inspector—"

"It's all right, Papa. The inspector is right, I saw Mama and Tony together at the old house on several occasions."

"Were you there the night he died?"

Eunice returned his gaze without blinking. "No, Inspector. It felt like rain, and I preferred to stay at home in bed."

"Are you often in the habit of going to the society's property when no one is there?"

"I've already told you I do." She glanced at her father. "I've been going up there since I was young."

"And do you have a key to the building?" Curran asked.

For the first time, the self-confidence slipped a little, and she looked down at the floor. "Yes."

"Eunice!" Her father interposed.

Eunice raised her chin. "I don't see why I shouldn't have a key. After all, it is always me who has to do the odd jobs around the place. Neither you nor Mama really cared where I was or what I was doing so I'd slip away. It is my private place."

Curran felt a jerk of pity for the lonely child, neglected by her self-absorbed parents.

"I am conscious that your mother allowed a certain degree of freedom quite inappropriate to a girl of your age. That's all going to change. I will be writing to your aunt in Cheltenham and you will be going to stay with her while she arranges for you to go to a proper school for young ladies," Lovett said.

Eunice jumped off the desk and faced her father across its expanse. "No, Papa. Please don't send me away. I don't want to go to England."

"We should have sent you years ago."

"Is this so you and Alicia—" Eunice gasped, her hand going to her mouth.

"Go to your room," Lovett said in a low voice that brooked no opposition.

The door slammed behind the girl, and Lovett turned to Curran. "You don't have children, do you, Curran?"

"No."

"I was only blessed with Eunice and there are days I wonder how much of a blessing she is."

"What did she mean about you and Alicia . . . I assume she meant Alicia Sewell?"

Lovett made a dismissive gesture with his hand. "There is nothing between Alicia Sewell and myself. The trouble with theatrical productions is that sometimes the line between make-believe and reality can get a little blurred. I blame her mother filling the girl's head with stories of fairies and whatnot."

It occurred to Curran that if Eunice grew up in a house obsessed with Gilbert and Sullivan, then it was not just her mother to blame for notions of fairies and "whatnot." Hadn't the society's last production been *Iolanthe*?

Lovett subsided into the chair behind his desk and rested his head in his hands. "Please leave, Inspector. I have nothing further to say to you and I have my wife's funeral to arrange."

Curran took his leave, retrieved Leopold from the syce, and rode back to Cairnhill Road, deep in thought. It had been a passing remark, but a telling one . . . Was there something more than just a professional relationship between Alicia Sewell and Charles Lovett?

He glanced at his watch. Time for one last visit and then he'd call it a day.

"Harriet?"

Harriet raised a corner of the cloth covering her eyes and, seeing her visitor, replaced it. "Go away, Curran. I've had enough visitors for one day."

"Sorry to disturb you."

"No, you're not."

"No . . . I'm not," he agreed. "If it's any consolation, you look terrible."

She squinted up at him. "Did you think I was faking a headache to avoid you? I get them now and then, a legacy of my time in Holloway. Why are you here?"

"I feel I owe you an apology for being out of sorts yesterday."

"Half a bottle of whisky for breakfast will do that," she said.

"It won't happen again. I have a case to distract me but it will be later . . . that's when I will miss her."

Harriet sat up, dislodging the drowsing cat. "She may come back."

He sat down and circled his hat in his hands. "Harriet, I am nearly thirty-eight years old, not a lovelorn boy of eighteen, and I know Li An. She has set a new path and it doesn't include me."

She looked up at him and for a long moment time stood still before she summoned the courage to say, "Then you will just have to cut your own path, Curran."

He shifted his gaze to the interior of the house, from which the distant sound of Lokman and Huo Jin arguing drifted through from the kitchen.

"Lavinia Pemberthey-Smythe has taken me in hand," he said. "She turned up last night with a meal and has organized someone to keep the place tidy and ensure I don't starve."

"I thought she might. She takes a motherly interest in you."

He rolled his eyes. "You must all think me such a fool. Seemed I was the last one to know."

"We see what we want to see, Curran, and you had your suspicions. Don't deny you discussed it with Julian last Saturday."

Curran's eyes widened. "So much for confidentiality of the confessional."

"He's Church of England and vicars love a good gossip." Harriet reclined again, replacing the cloth over her eyes. "If that's all, Curran, please leave. I've already had Alicia Sewell on my doorstep this afternoon."

"What did she want?"

"She wants me to go to Elspeth Lovett's funeral with her tomorrow."

"It must be flattering to be her choice of funeral companion." Curran's tone was dry and Harriet was glad she had her eyes covered and didn't have to look at his amused expression. "On the subject of Alicia Sewell, I have something to ask you."

Harriet pulled the cloth away and squinted at him. "What?"

"Do you think there is the remotest possibility that Charles Lovett may be having an affair with Alicia Sewell?"

She stared at him, trying to bring her fuzzy thoughts into

some semblance of order. "She's close to him and her marriage is not a happy one. Why do you ask?"

"Something Eunice Lovett said."

"Eunice . . ." Harriet paused, thinking back over the times she had seen Alicia and Lovett together. "I don't think I have seen anything in their behavior toward each other that would indicate anything particular about their relationship. Eunice is overlooked and neglected and in that situation it is easy for her to observe what is going on with the adults in her life. But she surely lacks the judgment to really understand what it is she is seeing."

"She seemed to be under no illusions about her mother and Dowling, why not her father and Alicia Sewell?" Curran said.

Harriet frowned. "Does that change anything?"

Curran sat down in Julian's chair, his hands clasped in front of him, his brow furrowed. "I don't know. It certainly muddies the water even more." He shook his head. "Either this case is about an insurance fraud or love. I still think my prime suspects are George Sewell and Lionel Ellis. They had plenty of reasons to want Dowling dead."

"Do you consider Charles Lovett a suspect?"

"Yes, but he was with the others at the Balmoral Club on the night Dowling died and in Johor when his wife died. Of the three of them he seems the least likely, but as I have said before, that doesn't prevent any of them from hiring someone to do the deed for a few dollars."

Harriet shook her head. A mistake. She winced. "I don't know. The murder of Dowling didn't seem to be premeditated. Remember the missing kerosene tin on the shelf? Someone just grabbed that because it was there." A wave of nausea threatened, and she closed her eyes shut. "Can we continue this conversation another time, Curran?"

Curran stood up. As he turned for the steps, he said. "I've arrested George Sewell."

"I know. Keep him there. He hits his wife."

Before Curran could respond, she waved a hand at him. "Go!"

She fell back on the cushions and squeezed her eyes shut, the pain a welcome distraction from the conversation about Li An. Shashti returned to Harriet's lap, indignant at being ousted, and Harriet let her fingers play with the cat's soft brindled fur.

Yes, Li An's departure changed everything. Curran had a new path ahead of him, but she was entertaining a vain hope if she thought even for a moment that it would cross hers.

"That is a path that can only lead to pain," she told the cat.

✦ TWENTY-FIVE

Curran restocked his whisky supply, and after consuming the meal of chicken curry Lavinia had arranged to be left for him, he retired to the verandah and sat in the still night, with just the hiss and glow of the kerosene lamp and the chatter of the neighborhood macaque monkey troop for company.

He had spent most of his life alone but now, as he poured his second glass, he understood what loneliness meant. Li An's absence tore at his heart with an almost physical pain.

To lift his mood he contemplated putting on the gramophone, and as he stood to fetch the machine out onto the verandah, a figure loomed out of the dark. Curran tensed, relaxing as Jayant stepped onto the verandah.

Curran hesitated, uncertain how to greet his visitor. Jayant solved the problem with a polite salaam. Curran returned the gesture and motioned to a chair . . . Li An's chair.

"Where is Miss Khoo?" Jayant asked.

"She's . . . she's away, visiting relatives. Have you eaten?"

Jayant nodded.

"A drink?" Curran proffered the whisky bottle.

"I told you, I do not take strong liquor."

Curran subsided with his glass. It would be his last for the night. After his unfortunate encounter with the whisky bottle on his return from KL, he had to be careful.

"Do you have any news?" Jayant broke the awkward silence.

"I went to Kuala Lumpur," Curran said.

Jayant leaned forward. "And . . . ?"

"The house is as you found it . . . deserted but I spoke with a neighbor and I am certain Samrita was there."

Jayant's good eye gleamed in the lamplight. "Do you know where they have gone?"

Curran shook his head. "The neighbor neither knew nor cared."

Jayant threw his head back, running his hands up his face and through his hair.

"Where has he taken her?" he shouted to the universe.

Curran waited until the young man had composed himself. "Did you know a girl called Lakshmi?"

Jayant visibly started. "Lakshmi?"

"She had a distinctive star-shaped birthmark on her upper left arm."

"Had?"

"She's dead. Found in the Klang."

Jayant's mouth fell open, his hand flying to his chest. "Lakshmi? Dead?"

"I take it you did know her? What aren't you telling me about this matter, Jayant? I can't help you unless I know the whole story."

Jayant gave a shuddering sigh and looked up. "Lakshmi was my sister's best friend, and as the gods would have it"—he swallowed—"we were betrothed. When Gopal came to our town, I thought him a good fellow. We spent much time together and it was I who introduced Gopal first to Lakshmi and it was Lakshmi who fell for his charms. She told me she wanted to end our betrothal. We argued. I told her she would bring shame on our families. I said other words. The last words." He dropped his gaze. "They will haunt me forever. The next morning Gopal had gone, taking with him Lakshmi and Samrita."

"So if Lakshmi went willingly, how did she persuade Samrita to go with her?"

Jayant shook his head. "I do not believe Samrita went willingly. There was a witness at the train station who saw a girl fighting with a man to prevent boarding the first-class carriage. The witness thought it a lover's tiff. I think that girl was Samrita."

Curran turned this information over in his mind and he studied Jayant for a long, long moment.

"What were the other words that were spoken?"

"To my eternal shame I took my hand to her. No one had ever done that before. She told me I would regret my action. I had no thought of how very much I would regret it. I think she punished me by taking Samrita."

Curran swirled the last of the whisky in the glass as he ran through the story Jayant had just told him.

"Why didn't you tell me the whole story when we first met, Jayant?"

"I was ashamed and I thought maybe you would not help me."

"Are you looking for Samrita or Lakshmi?"

Jayant hunched his shoulders and looked down at his hands. "I was searching for both of them, Curran. You have to believe me. Now you tell me Lakshmi is dead. Did this man Gopal kill her? What will he do to Samrita?"

Curran had been a policeman too long not to imagine exactly what men like that were capable of doing to Samrita. The thought made his flesh crawl.

"Tell me more about Samrita, Jayant."

My sister.

"What is there to tell you?" Jayant said. "She was . . . is beautiful and always a good and dutiful daughter. My parents insisted on a proper education so she could read and write. She wanted to be a teacher."

"Was she liked?"

Jayant laughed, the first time Curran had heard the young man laugh. "So many girls always at our house, laughing and teasing—not just Lakshmi. There was a young man in our town who was courting Samrita but after she disappeared he married another."

Curran snorted. "So much for love," he said.

Jayant shook his head. "You know how it is, Curran. His parents would never have permitted a marriage to a girl not of the proper caste."

Curran nodded. He knew how it was.

"So the people of your town knew her father was a foreigner."

Jayant nodded. "It was no secret. It is one thing to fool people in passing but not year after year in close proximity, but he earned their respect, and they kept his secret."

Curran took the photographic image of the family from his wallet and set it on the table.

"Am I . . ." he ventured, as he touched the two-dimensional face of his father. "Can you see anything of him in me?"

Jayant nodded. "Yes. It is in your eyes. He had gray eyes like you."

"That must have made him stand out?"

Jayant tilted his head. "And you have his smile. You say you never really knew him but it is strange how I see his shadow in the way you move."

Curran fought back a sudden, desperate longing to ask the most inane questions about his father. He still wrestled with a sense of injustice that he had been deprived of the man that Jayant and his sister knew so well.

"Why did he never try to contact me?" He heard the naked pain in his voice and Jayant responded by briefly laying a hand over his.

"I think he was ashamed. He heard what the British called

him, the Coward of Kandahar, and he didn't want to bring more shame on you."

"I never heard him called that until this year."

Curran had no doubt that if his uncle and aunt and his odious cousin George had known of that particular sobriquet, it would have been used to taunt him unmercifully. Thankfully, it did not seem to have gone beyond the close-knit ranks of the South Sussex Regiment.

"You see his hands?" Jayant pointed to the image and the hands of the man resting lightly on his knees. "They broke his fingers . . . one by one. He had other, terrible scars, but he never spoke of his time as a prisoner."

Curran flinched, unconsciously straightening his own fingers in silent sympathy.

"He helped our mother in the shop where she sold saris and beautiful fabrics and he taught himself to carve, despite the pain in his hands."

"You loved him?"

"He was my father." Tears glistened in the corners of Jayant's eyes. "They were happy . . . he and my mother. Samrita and I never felt anything less than loved."

Jayant could have had no idea how those words cut deeper than any knife. Curran thought back to his own miserable childhood. He had been clothed, fed and educated but loved?

No, never loved, except perhaps by his grandfathers, the earl and his stable hand, very different men who had both died when he was too young to really understand the depth of their affection for him.

He looked up at the younger man. "And you, Jayant? What road were you following in Laxmangarh?"

"My parents were insistent that I get the very best education, and when I finished school, I sat for the civil service exams. I had a good job in the courts, but when Samrita disappeared, I resigned and vowed to not rest until I found her."

They sat in silence for a long time. Jayant showed no sign of leaving and Curran eyed the empty glass and the whisky bottle but resisted the urge to pour himself another drink.

"Here's another question," Curran began. "How did you lose the sight in your eye?"

Jayant touched the milky eye. "A childhood game that went wrong," he said. "My turn, I think, to ask you a question."

Curran tensed. "What do you want to know?"

Jayant studied him. "I want to know why Miss Khoo has left you?"

Curran's instinct was to deny the assertion. "We have come to a natural parting of the ways," he said, adding, "Not that that is any of your damn business."

Jayant muttered an apology and they sat in silence.

Jayant fidgeted, his long fingers drumming a tattoo on the arm of the chair before he blurted out, "Curran, what are we to do about Samrita?"

"We'll find her, Jayant."

"How? What can I do?"

Curran hesitated. "Nothing for the moment. I'm in the middle of a difficult case. Give me a few days and we'll work out what to do next." Lightning cracked in the south, followed by a roll of thunder. "I think there is a storm brewing. If you want to get back to your bed before the rain, I suggest you leave now."

Jayant rose to his feet. "Good night, Curran. I will not trouble you again until you are ready to speak with me. You know where to find me."

Long after Jayant had left, Curran remained on the verandah, watching the lightning split the sky as the gods sent down the rain in torrents, and despite his best intentions, the bottle beside him slowly emptied.

❧ TWENTY-SIX

Thursday, 10 November

Curran woke to a heavy pounding on the door of the bungalow. He lifted the mosquito net and peered at the clock by his bed. The fluorescent dial swam before his eyes but he could swear it said something past three o'clock.

He wrapped a sarong around his waist and staggered to the front door, opening it on Sergeant Singh, immaculate in his uniform. Singh looked down at him, his gaze going to the nearly empty bottle that still sat on the verandah table where Curran had left it.

"This better be important," Curran said, rubbing a hand over his eyes.

"There is a suspicious fire we must attend."

"We're not the fire brigade," Curran responded.

"Superintendent Pett sent for us," Singh said. "I will boil some water while you get dressed."

It seemed to take forever to dress, and Curran's hand shook so much, he cut himself shaving.

Even after Singh's mug of strong chai, Curran's head felt as if it were stuffed with kapok. The rain had passed and the night was clear. Curran sat back in the motor vehicle, looking up at the starry night as they sped through the quiet streets. Gursharan Singh sat beside him, formidable and disapproving. His sergeant did not drink alcohol, but then again, his sergeant enjoyed a happy marriage with three children, on whom he doted. He did not expect Singh to understand.

Curran came to life as the vehicle turned onto Cairnhill Road.

"Where's the fire?" he asked his sergeant.

"I wondered when you would ask," Singh said. "The Sewells' bungalow."

Curran glared at Singh. "Why didn't you say?"

Singh shrugged. "I'm not sure you would have absorbed the information," he said. "We are here, I think."

The motor vehicle came to a shuddering halt in the well-kept carriageway behind the Merriweather fire truck. Smoke and the smell of burning hung heavily in the air. Fire had reduced the pretty bungalow that he had visited the previous day to a smoldering ruin.

Monty Pett stood with his arms crossed, watching his men dealing with the last of the flames.

Curran straightened his jacket and Sam Browne, cleared his throat and strode over to him.

"You took your time," Pett said.

"It's the middle of the night," Curran mumbled.

Pett consulted his watch. "Four thirty to be precise," he said. "The building was well alight when we got here an hour ago."

"Is everyone safe?"

Pett glanced across at the gaggle of servants gathered beneath a tree, arms around one another, watching the firemen work.

"Servants are all accounted for, but according to the majordomo, the lady of the house was alone. Unfortunately, she didn't make it," Pett said. "We found her body a few minutes ago."

Curran shook his head, the stab of pain and grief real. If he closed his eyes, he could almost hear Alicia Sewell's beautiful voice singing the Handel aria.

"Alicia Sewell is dead?"

"Yes. Do you know where her husband is?"

Curran swallowed. "In a cell in South Bridge Road."

"Well, he can count himself fortunate."

Curran ran a hand over his stinging eyes. Not so fortunate was the police officer who had to impart the bad news to George Sewell.

"By the time her majordomo smelled the smoke, her bedroom was well alight. He tried to get to her, but . . ."

"Where is he?"

Pett indicated the man, unrecognizable out of his pristine white uniform. He sat on the low parapet of a fountain while one of the female servants bandaged his hands.

Curran turned his attention back to Pett. "Where did you find her?"

Pett heaved a sigh. "In her bed—what was left of it." He nodded toward the house, where two firefighters were negotiating the fallen walls with a stretcher covered in a sheet of canvas. "Looks like they're bringing her out."

Steeling his nerves and his uncertain stomach, Curran stepped forward and stopped the men. He lifted the canvas and his stomach heaved as he fought back the nausea. He couldn't have the men present think the sight of a corpse overcame him when the reality was a surfeit of alcohol. Even in the light of the lanterns, the blackened, contorted object on the stretcher was still vaguely recognizable as human but any trace of the beautiful woman who had serenaded him with Handel the previous day had been obliterated.

He replaced the canvas.

"We've sent for the mortuary cart," Pett said.

Curran nodded. "That will be a pleasant job for Dr. Mackenzie in the morning. Do you think it's an accident?"

"From what we can see, the origin of the fire was her bed. She may have knocked her lamp, and the kerosene caught the mosquito net. It would have gone up like a roman candle. She never stood a chance, but I'll know more in the morning," Pett said.

Curran left Pett to get on with his job and walked over to the Indian majordomo. His right hand had been crudely wrapped in a rough bandage and the girl who had been seeing to her injured colleague stood back as Curran hunkered down in front of him.

Curran looked down at the man's unbandaged hand. Even in the light of a lantern, the blisters and blackened skin on his left hand told its own story.

"You must go to the hospital and see to the burns," he said.

The man looked down at his hands as if seeing them for the first time. "I tried to get to her, sir, but the flames were too fierce."

"You were very brave to have even tried."

A tear trickled down the man's cheek. "She was so sad. She played sad, beautiful music."

"What was she sad about?"

The man's eyes slid sideways. "If the sahib had been here."

"We'd probably have two deaths instead of one. Why was the mem sad?"

"She and the sahib . . . there had been a terrible argument when he came home on Tuesday night. He went out and did not come home that night or last night. I think he may be at the club."

Curran knew exactly where Sewell had been, and it wasn't the club.

"What was the argument about?"

The man shook his head. "I cannot say."

Cannot . . . would not . . . a loyal servant, despite his own pain. He nodded to the girl holding the bandages and turned back to rejoin Pett, but she came after him, tugging at his sleeve.

"I cannot say in front of . . ." She glanced back at the major-domo. "The argument he talks of, it was very bad. Tuan Sewell, he hit the mem." The woman touched her arm. "Knocked her to the ground."

"Did you hear what it was about?"

The woman hesitated. "Mem was angry about something the *tuan* had done in Kuala Lumpur. My English is not so good." She shook her head and spread her hands apologetically.

Curran thanked her and with his hands in his pockets he returned to the fire chief. Harriet had been right, Sewell did hit his wife. If he had not taken to the man before, he disliked him even more now.

"Nothing more you can do here," Pett said. "We'll secure the scene, keep a presence to make sure it doesn't flair again. Come back in daylight and we'll have a better look."

Curran nodded and turned to Singh. "We've got to tell Sewell."

Singh looked up at the sky. "Maybe it can wait until daylight," he said. "I think it would be wise for you to have a couple of hours' sleep."

Curran was about to protest but his spinning head suggested Singh was right. A couple of hours' sleep would be best.

Curran made his way to South Bridge Road at eight in the morning. He wasn't entirely certain that the two hours of sleep he had managed really made much difference to his hangover, but a steamed bun and a strong chai from his favorite street vendor had eased his growling stomach. This was going to be a hell of an interview, and although he would have given his soul for a whisky right then and there, he was conscious that half a bottle of the best Scotch still swilled around his bloodstream.

He commandeered one of the better offices in the main building and sent for Sewell.

Sewell looked like a man who had spent the night in a police cell; gray faced, unshaven, rumpled and stinking. Far from the respectable commodities broker he purported to be.

Curran gestured at the upholstered leather chair and Sewell collapsed into it, almost snatching at the cup of tepid tea Curran handed him.

He set the cup down and looked around the well-appointed office. "Why am I here?"

Curran took a steadying breath. "I needed somewhere more congenial than the interview room to talk to you, Sewell."

Sewell narrowed his eyes. "About what? I told you yesterday, I've got nothing to say to you about that bloody boat."

"It's not about the *Hesperides*. It's about your wife . . ."

"Christ!" Sewell half rose. "What tales has the little bitch been telling you? That I slapped her around a bit? She asked for it . . . needed reminding who was in charge."

Curran let the man rant, struggling to disguise his disgust at the words coming from Sewell behind professional indifference. He waited until Sewell had finished.

"I'm sorry to tell you, but she's dead," he said.

Like Lovett before him, Sewell stared at him. He blinked rapidly, as if he could not comprehend the words.

"She was fine yesterday," he said. "I didn't hit her that hard . . ."

With a hard eye Curran fixed the man. "Tempted as I am to pursue this admission of abuse, Sewell, your wife's death had nothing to do with you."

Sewell stared at him.

"Then, how . . . ?" the man asked in a low voice.

"There was a fire in the early hours of the morning. Your wife was asleep in her bed, and by the time the alarm was raised, it was too late."

The color drained from Sewell's face.

"Bathroom . . . now." Curran hauled the man up by the arm, and between himself and Singh they got him as far as the nearest conveniences before Sewell was violently ill into one of the toilet bowls.

The two policemen waited outside for Sewell to pull himself together.

"You don't look much better," Singh remarked.

"Don't be insubordinate," Curran said, but without conviction. He knew Singh was right. "It was the curry from last night."

Singh snorted.

Sewell emerged, ashen and sweating, mopping his face with a handkerchief.

Curran had taken the precaution of ordering more tea, and an orderly brought the tray into the office as Sewell collapsed back into the chair and sat with his elbows on his knees and his head in his hands as Curran recounted as much as he knew of the circumstances of Sewell's wife's death.

Sewell raised his head, his mouth a thin, grim line. "This is your fault, Curran. If I hadn't been locked up in your bloody cell last night, I would have been at home. I could have saved her."

"Save me your righteous indignation, Sewell. You had no intention of being at home last night. What was your argument about?"

"What argument?" Sewell licked his dry, cracked lips, his eyes darting to the corner of the room.

"The argument you and your wife had before you stormed out the night before last."

Sewell hunched his shoulders. "Just a stupid domestic matter. She had expensive tastes, and she'd overspent again."

"You hit her for that?"

Sewell's gaze swiveled back to Curran, and his mouth fell open.

Curran closed in on the man's discomfort. "Did you hit her often?"

"No . . . she just . . . she just drove me to distraction. I'd just walked in from a visit to some backwater in Johor to be met with her bleating about how I didn't give her enough allowance."

The beads of sweat dotted Sewell's brow and his eyes darted to every corner of the room. The man was lying, and he was a terrible liar.

Curran pushed a bit further. "The argument was not about another man?"

Sewell's eyes widened. "No! I told you the first time we met, my wife was faithful."

"And what about you?"

"No!" The momentary hesitation made a lie of his denial.

As if sensing Curran didn't believe him, Sewell ran a hand through his hair and tried, unconvincingly, to smile. "We're both men of the world, Curran. I'm away from home a great deal, and well, it can get lonely. You know how it is."

"I'm not sure that I do," Curran said. "Was the argument about your womanizing?"

Sewell swallowed. "You don't have a cigarette on you, do you?"

Curran patted his pocket, but he had left his cigarette papers and tobacco in his office. "No, I don't. What was the argument about, Sewell?"

"I told you it was about money. I was going to buy her some pretty little trinket to give to her when I saw her again and all would have been forgiven and forgotten." Sewell's shoulders slumped. "Where have they taken her?"

"The hospital mortuary."

"Can I see her?"

"I don't advise it. She was burned beyond recognition. Remember her how she was, Sewell."

"No!" Sewell moaned. "Not my beautiful Alicia." He gave a choked sob and buried his face in his hands and Curran thought that this time the grief was genuine. "I can't bear to think our last words were angry and that I . . . I behaved like a cad."

Curran had no sympathy left for the maundering recrimina-
tions of a self-confessed wife beater. He stood up and looked
down at the man.

"I'm letting you go for now, but we'll talk again, Sewell. The
matter of the *Hesperides* still needs to be cleared up."

But he didn't think the man heard him. Sewell leaned forward, his head still buried in his hands, the tea on the table
untouched.

Curran touched the man on the shoulder. "Sewell? Can I
organize a hackney to take you back to the club?"

Sewell raised his head and swallowed. "Can you take me to
the house? I have to see for myself."

❦ TWENTY-SEVEN

The last thing Harriet wanted to do was attend a funeral. The headache of the previous day had left her feeling drained, and on days like this, the inescapable humidity just sapped the life from her. She toyed with sending her excuses to Alicia Sewell but duty and curiosity got the better of her and she dressed appropriately, cursing the heavy, dark clothing.

As the hackney cab she had hired rounded a curve in Cairnhill Road, she noticed a sizable crowd gathered at the closed gate to Eltham, the Sewell home. Unable to proceed any farther, she dismounted and told the driver to wait as she hailed the young constable at the gate.

"Musa!"

Musa raised his hand in greeting. Holding her hat to stop it being knocked, she pushed through the crowd to reach the constable, who stood in front of the solid gates. As she approached, the unmistakable acrid scent of burning grew stronger.

"Mrs. Gordon, what are you doing here?"

"Mrs. Sewell and I are going to Mrs. Lovett's funeral. What's happened? Why are you here?"

"Fire in the night," Musa said.

Harriet gasped. "Anyone hurt?"

Musa looked at a point somewhere above Harriet's shoulder.

"I cannot say, but perhaps you come in? Mr. Pett can tell you more, I think."

He opened the gate wide enough to allow her to slip in. She stood in the driveway, staring at the ruins of what was reputed to have been one of the prettiest villas in Singapore. The house itself remained largely intact, but the roof at the front of the house was gone and the whitewashed walls were blackened. The stench of burning hung over the property.

The fire brigade's smart new truck stood in front of the house and brass-helmeted firemen were picking their way through the ruins. The fire chief, Monty Pett, stood with one hand resting on the bonnet of the truck as he directed his men. Harriet knew both Monty and his wife, Edie, who were regulars at St. Andrew's.

"Superintendent Pett," she greeted him.

Monty Pett started. "Mrs. Gordon. What brings you here?"

"I am supposed to be going to a funeral with Mrs. Sewell. Is she here? Is she all right?"

Pett shook his head. "I'm sorry, Mrs. Gordon. She was caught in the fire."

Harriet stared at him. "She's dead."

He nodded. "She was a friend of yours?"

"More a close acquaintance."

But we could have been friends, Harriet thought with genuine sorrow.

A klaxon sounded from beyond the gate and Harriet and Pett turned to see the Detective Branch's motor vehicle make its way into the driveway, the curious crowd beyond pressing in for a better look at the ruined house. Tan was driving, and Curran sat in the passenger seat. She didn't recognize the man in the rear seat, but she could guess his identity.

If this man was Alicia's husband, he looked terrible, unshaven and unhealthy color, his linen suit crumpled and stained. As the motor vehicle slowed, he sat quite still, staring at the house, his mouth open. The vehicle had hardly stopped before he threw the door open and ran toward the house.

Moving with surprising speed, Monty Pett intercepted him, holding him by the arms.

"That's far enough, sir," Pett said. "Too dangerous to go any further."

"But it's my house!"

"It may be, but at the moment, it's *my* house," Pett replied. He glanced at Curran. "I take it this is Sewell?"

Curran nodded. "You can let him go, Pett."

As soon as the fireman released his grip, Sewell's knees gave way and he went down on his haunches, his hands over his face.

Pett placed a hand on the man's shoulder. "Please accept my condolences, sir."

After a few moments, Sewell dragged himself to his feet. He thrust his hands into his pockets, producing a crumpled handkerchief. He blew his nose, stuffed the handkerchief back and looked at Pett. "Did she suffer?"

Pett hesitated. "Hard to say, sir. The fire was fast."

Sewell shook his head. "How did it happen?"

Harriet caught the quick glance that went between Pett and Curran.

"We believe she must have knocked over a lamp, and it caught the mosquito net," Pett said. "Mosquito nets act like a wick." He shook his head. "I've seen too many fires started by kerosene. I'll be glad when electricity becomes more widespread."

Sewell nodded. "How bad is the damage?"

"You can see the bedroom is destroyed and the rooms on either side are badly damaged. The roof is in a dangerous condition. In short, the building is uninhabitable. Do you have somewhere to stay?"

Sewell nodded. "The club. I have some things there, but everything else . . ." He stared at the house. "Gone."

"Some things will be salvageable, sir. The fire hardly touched the rooms on the left side of the building. I will do the appropriate report for your insurer."

"Caldwell & Hubbard Insurance. They're in Finlayson Green," Sewell replied.

Curran signaled his driver. "Constable, would you be so good as to take Mr. Sewell down to the Balmoral Club?"

Sewell cast around the grounds. "But Alicia. I should be with her."

"Nothing you can do for her," Curran said. "I will let Dr. Mackenzie know he can contact you at the club."

He summoned his driver, and as Tan led Sewell away, Pett shook his head. "Poor man," he said.

"Don't feel too sorry for him. Last time he saw his wife, he left her with a backhander."

Harriet nodded sadly. "Mrs. Sewell came to see me yesterday afternoon. She showed me the bruises. The man is a brute."

Noticing her for the first time, Curran turned to her. "Mrs. Gordon, what are you doing here?"

She explained about the funeral for the third time, and Curran ran a hand over his eyes. "Elspeth Sewell's funeral. I should go to that." He turned back to Pett. "Before I leave, I've heard the official version but what do you really think caused the fire, Pett?"

Pett looked around and lowered his voice. "As I told her husband, it started in her bedroom in the vicinity of her bed. We found a broken lamp, but we also found that . . ." He pointed to the twisted, blackened remains of a familiar can that one of his men had placed on a sheet of canvas, the writing mostly burned but some letters still identifiable: a *K*, an *E*, *S* and *N*.

Harriet looked up at Pett and asked, "Why would she have a can of kerosene in her bedroom?"

"I don't think she would," Curran said.

Pett nodded. "What I didn't say to her husband is it's my

opinion the bed was deliberately doused in kerosene and set alight."

Curran let out a low whistle. Harriet looked up at the house and shivered, despite the heat.

"Any chance the husband lit the fire?" Pett asked.

Curran shook his head. "No, I had him locked up. His alibi is beyond reproach, and unless he had prearranged the immolation of his wife, I've no reason to think his reaction is anything but genuine. We will have to wait for Mac before we know if she was alive or dead when the bed went up."

Pett nodded. "We can only hope it was postmortem. Hell of a way to die. Poor woman."

Curran glanced at Harriet. "Are you all right? You look pale."

Harriet nodded, ignoring the rising bile. "I . . . I should still go to the funeral. I have a cab outside if you want to accompany me, Curran."

"Do you need me here?" Curran asked Pett.

The fireman shook his head. "No. I'll make sure anything of evidentiary interest goes with your constable."

"Did you get any sleep last night?" Harriet asked as the hackney turned into Upper Serangoon Road.

Curran looked like he had hardly slept, his eyes sunk in exhaustion and the shaving papers adhering to his chin testimony to haste, a shaking hand or a hangover.

"Not a lot. I got called out to the fire at three."

"Do you think—"

"Harriet, I don't know what to think at the moment." He looked up at the bright blue sky. "I do know one thing, it isn't raining for once."

Unlike Dowling's funeral, a huge crowd had gathered for Elspeth's internment, most connected in some way with the society. On the far side of the grave, Lovett stood with his daughter. Eunice wore an ill-fitting black linen dress with a wide cream-colored collar. If she had been called upon to play the part of a puritan maid, she would have been appropriately dressed.

As Harriet and Curran walked toward the graveside, Louisa Mackenzie looked up at them and prodded Griff Maddocks, gesturing for Harriet to join them.

"Good morning to you, Curran," Maddocks said.

"Nothing good about it," Curran said. "Excuse me. There is someone I must talk to."

"He's in a dour mood," Louisa remarked. "I thought you said in your note that you were coming with Alicia Sewell. Where is she?"

"Alicia Sewell is dead," Harriet replied. The words sounded hard and unforgiving but there really was no easy way to impart the morning's events.

Louisa stared at her. "Alicia? How?"

"A fire at her home in the night."

"I heard there'd been another fire on Emerald Hill," Maddocks said. "How did it start?"

"It looks like she knocked a lamp onto her bed," Harriet said. The truth would come out sooner or later, but for now the official story would do.

"How awful!" Louisa exclaimed. "What about her husband?"

"He was away," Harriet said, not wishing to muddy the waters with the exact whereabouts of George Sewell.

"Oh no, this is really too bad." Louisa reached for a handkerchief and dabbed her eyes. "Tony, Elspeth and now Alicia? I'm beginning to think the music society is cursed."

"So am I," Harriet said.

A sharp cry rent the air and everyone fell silent, heads turning to Charles Lovett. From the posture of Lovett and Curran,

Harriet guessed Curran must have broken the news about Alicia Sewell. The scream had come from Eunice, who fell into her father's arms, sobbing in a way she had never wept for her mother.

"Really! I do think Curran could have waited," Louisa said. "What are you doing, Griff?"

Both women looked at the journalist. Griff had his notebook and pencil in his hand.

"This is Elspeth's funeral and you're here as a mourner, not a journalist," Harriet said.

"You know very well that I'm never off duty," Maddocks responded.

"Put it away, Griff," Louisa added to the approbation.

Charles Lovett put an arm around his sobbing daughter and turned to face the gathered crowd. "Ladies and gentlemen. One woe doth tread upon another's heel. I've just been informed that our much-loved leading lady, Alicia Sewell, died in a tragic accident last night so we will bury my beloved Elspeth today only to return and bury Alicia in a few days."

Lovett looked up at the sky, his mouth set in a hard line, the very picture of a man barely in control of his emotions. Harriet wondered if his grief was for his wife or for Alicia Sewell, who may have been his lover. Then again, for an amateur, the man was a consummate actor.

"Anyone would think we were putting on a production of *Macbeth*," Maddocks said in a loud whisper.

The canon of St. Andrew's, standing robed and ready beside the grave, coughed and Lovett nodded.

"Man that is born of a woman hath but a short time to live, and is full of misery. He cometh up, and is cut down, like a flower; he fleeth as it were a shadow, and never continueth in one stay. In the midst of life we are in death . . ." the priest began, and heads were bowed reverentially.

Curran slipped into place behind his friends.

Louisa turned and glared at him. "You could have waited until after he had buried Elspeth," she said in an angry undertone.

"I was interested in his reaction," Curran replied in a whisper.

"And?" Harriet asked.

Curran quirked an eyebrow. "I got the answer I was after."

❧ TWENTY-EIGHT

Curran left the cemetery before the end of the service and went straight to the Singapore General Hospital.

He found Mac in his office, leaning back in his chair, a cup of tea in his hand as he gazed out of the window.

"I had a look at the body you sent me." Mac set his cup down. "There are days, Curran, when I think you should find yourself a new police surgeon."

"And I should take a job as a greengrocer," Curran agreed. "What can you tell me?"

Mac sucked in his breath. "Unlike her young friend, the body was incinerated. Nothing much to see from the exterior."

Curran sat forward. "But?"

Mac's eyes gleamed. "It is highly likely she was dead before the fire."

"How can you tell?"

Mac placed a finger on his neck. "Like Dowling she died from a puncture wound to the carotid artery. She'd have bled to death in seconds. The fire was used to cover up the evidence and there would have been a lot of blood."

Curran stood up and paced the floor. "Same weapon?"

Mac shrugged. "I'm not that good. It was just lucky I found

a nick on one of the bones in her neck. This time I knew what I was looking for. All I can tell you, the weapon would have to have been long and pointed and your murderer pushed the blade in hard." He frowned. "There was some evidence of other stab wounds, which may have been inflicted postmortem. Impossible to say how many, given the state of the body, but it was almost like a frenzied attack."

"We found a kerosene tin in her bedroom. Too similar to Dowling to be a coincidence," Curran said.

Mac let out an uncharacteristic whistle. "I think we are looking at the same hand being responsible for both murders. What are your thoughts?"

Curran shook his head. "I've been working on the Dowling case being connected to an insurance fraud . . . but Alicia Sewell? Now I'm not so sure. Can I have a word with her majordomo?"

"Yes. He'll be fine. His hands are burned and there is some smoke inhalation, but you'll find him on the general ward. Did you want to see Mrs. Sewell before you—"

Curran shook his head. "I don't think there's anything to be gained from doing so."

"You just dislike burn victims," Mac said.

Curran managed a smile. "I am sure your report will be thorough. Thank you, Mac."

Curran found the Sewells' servant in a bed in the long ward. "I need to ask you some questions," Curran said.

"The mem is dead," the man replied.

"She is and you tried to save her. When did you last see her?"

"When I shut up the house. It would have been about ten of the clock."

"And she was alone?"

The man nodded. "She was playing the piano and singing." A tear dribbled down his face. "She sang often . . . such a pretty sound. It made us happy."

"You locked all the doors and secured the windows?"

He nodded. "I did, but the mem sometimes opened her doors onto the verandah. I warned her it was dangerous . . . There are bad men . . ." His lip trembled.

"I have been told that the mem and her husband argued?"

The man visibly stiffened. "Terrible argument. A vase was broken, and he left before his supper."

"Did Mrs. Sewell have any visitors yesterday?"

The man stared at him. "You came, sahib."

"Apart from me?"

The man shook his head. "No. She went out to visit a friend in the afternoon. Her maid said she went to bed at about eleven of the clock and I heard nothing, nothing at all until I smelled the smoke and the house, it was well alight." Another tear dribbled down his cheek and he held up his bandaged hands. "I tried to get to her, but her bedroom, it was on fire."

"The fire was just in the bedroom?"

He nodded. "And then it started to spread. The house, it is gone? Where will we go? What will we do?"

Curran had no answer to those questions. "The house is badly damaged but it could be repaired. It is up to the sahib. Was the mem a good person to work for?"

The majordomo looked up. "She was a kind person. We were very fortunate."

"And Sahib Sewell?"

The man's face closed over. "He could be hard."

"Did he beat the servants?"

The man's eyes flicked sideways, and it was a long moment before he answered, "Sometimes, but it was always deserved. He did not take insolence or carelessness."

"And he hit his wife too?"

The man lowered his gaze to the bandages. "It is not my place to say."

Curran didn't need an answer. George Sewell was a hard master with a quick temper and he had a significant argument with his wife before she died. Frustratingly he would have made a prime suspect if he had not been locked in a cell at South Bridge Road Police Headquarters at the time his wife was murdered.

"The sahib went away often," the man continued, "and the mem was happy."

"When he was away, did the mem have many visitors?"

"Mr. Dowling, he came often and they would sing together." A sad smile curled the corners of the man's mouth. "We would listen."

"And Mr. Lovett?"

The man's eyes darted to the right. "Sometimes he come."

"Alone?"

"Sometimes with his wife or his daughter, other times alone. They also would sing and he would take a meal."

Curran wrestled with the next question. "And were there times, when her gentlemen callers stayed late?"

The old man met his gaze and the creases deepened. "No. I will not speak ill of the mem." He spread his hands.

Curran took a steadying breath. That was not the answer he wanted, but Alicia Sewell had told him that she had been faithful to her husband. Could it have been true?

"Were there other visitors? Any other arguments with someone?"

The man shook his head. "No. There were lady visitors and Mr. Lovett's daughter but the mem she was loved by all."

Not everyone loved her. Someone hated her enough to stab her multiple times and leave her to burn and it looked like that might be the same person who also murdered Tony Dowling.

Curran left the man to rest and leaned against the wall of the hospital, smoking a cigarette as he turned the facts of the case, as he knew them, over in his mind.

What did Alicia Sewell's murder have to do with the insurance fraud?

Nothing, he concluded. Tony Dowling's and Alicia Sewell's murders were nothing to do with the insurance fraud. If that was the case, what did that leave?

Love . . . This was a story of love, but quite who loved whom and in what order, he had yet to work out.

Curran walked slowly back to South Bridge Road. The injuries he had sustained in the ambush the previous week were aching and the aftereffects of a second night with the whisky bottle coupled with disturbed sleep were telling. He stopped at an Indian street vendor outside the Sri Mariamman Temple and bought a cup of chai and a couple of pakoras, the spiced vegetable fritter of which he was rather fond. The food and drink put new life in him and by the time he reached his own office he felt ready to take on the world again.

As he walked into the Detective Branch office, a young man rose from a bench outside and he stopped in his tracks. Tony Dowling's housemate John Butcher stood circling his hat between his hands.

"Can I help you?" Curran inquired.

The young man swallowed. "I rather think it is I who can help you, Inspector. I have been wrestling with my conscience and I am afraid I haven't been entirely straight with you about Dowling."

Curran ushered the young man into his office and offered him a cigarette. Butcher tried to disguise a shaking hand as he took it.

Curran waited until the young man had taken a few deep draughts of the cigarette before he leaned forward and asked, "What do you have to tell me?"

"Dowling . . . Dowling was involved in a few suspect transactions." The words came out in a rush as if the young man had been rehearsing them.

"You mean he was involved in wholesale insurance fraud," Curran responded.

Butcher's eyes widened. "You know?"

"Some of it. The question is, What do you know?"

Butcher stubbed out his half-smoked cigarette in the ashtray. "You know about the sinking of the *Hesperides* back in February?" When Curran nodded, he continued, "I told Dowling he should never have got involved. That it would only lead to trouble."

"Go on."

"Dowling's manager went back to New Zealand just after Christmas, leaving Tony in charge. Dowling approached me with a proposal that would, he said, make us some money. It was quite simple. Stand the insurance on a shipment of rubber that would never reach its destination and I would be guaranteed a percentage of the insurance claim. No questions asked. I declined and he got quite annoyed with me. I told him what he was proposing was fraud . . . theft, in fact, and I wanted no part of it."

"Why did he want your company to take on the insurance?"

"I gained the impression he may already have been involved in a couple of similar schemes on a smaller scale and this one was big and could attract attention. He wanted to put it at arm's length but I don't know why he thought I would take it on."

"Did he mention who was involved?"

Butcher shook his head. "No, but I can guess. He did a lot of work for George Sewell and his company, Robert White & Co. I thought he had decided not to go ahead, and he never mentioned it again. Then the *Hesperides* sank, and two lives were lost and that really shook him. He wasn't a venal man, Inspector, and as long as it was just money, he probably justified it in his own mind. His sister in New Zealand is an invalid and I think he was supporting the family. I honestly didn't want to know but I could see he was upset."

"In what way?"

"Took to the bottle hard and would talk about 'making it right.'"

"What did he mean by that?"

Butcher shrugged. "It is not to my credit that I asked no questions, but I've been thinking about it and it's my theory that the last thing his fellow fraudsters needed was one of their number losing his nerve and maybe threatening to tell all."

"So, he had to be silenced?"

Butcher said nothing for a long moment. He took a shuddering breath. "That's what I think happened."

Curran sat back in his chair. "Did he ever mention Alicia Sewell?"

"The soprano? They were friends through the society and of course she introduced him to George Sewell."

"Did she have any involvement with the insurance frauds?"

Butcher's eyes flickered. "I doubt it. The few times I met her she seemed entirely focused on the current musical production."

"What about Charles Lovett?"

Butcher gave a snort. "Slippery fish like all lawyers, Inspector. Lived for the society but was he involved in Dowling's business? I honestly don't know."

"Did he ever mention Lionel Ellis?"

Butcher shook his head. "The name's familiar. He's a planter, isn't he? Wasn't he in court last week, something about killing a coolie?"

"Assault," Curran said.

"To answer your question, no. I think all Dowling's dealings, in so far as they were suspicious, were with Sewell."

Curran stood up. "I wish you had come to me sooner with this information, Mr. Butcher."

Butcher had the grace to color. "I wish I had too. It has been on my conscience. A promise made to a dead man."

"I hope you can sleep better at night," Curran remarked drily as he showed the young man the door.

Butcher failed to catch the sarcasm; he smiled and nodded. "Oh, I am sure I will. Thank you for your time, Inspector."

Curran shook his head as the door closed behind the insurance agent.

"Anything useful?" Singh asked. "He wouldn't talk to me. He'd been waiting for you for over an hour."

Curran recounted the conversation and the events of the day, concluding, "If he had come to me yesterday, I would have closed the case on George Sewell but now the death of Sewell's wife has muddied the waters, Singh. I am going to need a much longer and franker conversation with Mr. Sewell."

"What about Lovett?" Singh asked.

"Definitely a conversation is needed there too, but the man only buried his wife today so it can wait until tomorrow."

❧ TWENTY-NINE

Curran had a hunch that Lovett would be back at his desk on Friday morning and paid his first visit of the day to the offices of Lovett, Strong & Dickens.

Both he and Sergeant Singh were shown without preamble into the man's large, well-appointed office. Lovett made no effort to rise. He leaned back in his chair, replacing the lid on his fountain pen. Curran sat unbidden on one of the padded leather chairs. Singh stood behind him, his hands behind his back.

Annoyance flickered in Lovett's eyes. "Inspector, really. I have nothing more to tell you. What is it this time?"

Curran brushed a piece of imaginary lint from his tunic and looked the man in the eye. "Were you and Alicia Sewell lovers?"

Lovett's eyes widened and he took a visible breath. Whatever he had been expecting, it was clearly not that question.

"I . . . I . . . no . . . of course not!"

"I'm tired, Lovett, and I've no patience with lies. We can talk here, or I can walk you out through your office and take you to South Bridge Road."

"My wife is dead, Alicia is dead. Whatever my relationship may or may not have been with Mrs. Sewell is irrelevant."

Curran studied the man. "Very well. Where were you on Wednesday night?"

"At home with my daughter. I went to bed—alone. I have slept badly since poor Elspeth died so I took a sleeping draught. My manservant can vouch for me."

"And Monday night? The night your wife died?"

"You know very well I was in Johor. You met me off the train on Tuesday."

"And the night Tony Dowling died?"

"You cannot seriously be accusing me of . . . of these terrible deaths."

"I am not accusing you of anything. I just need to know where you were."

Lovett adopted the patronizing tone he would use on a recalcitrant child. "I have told you before, I spent Sunday evening at the Balmoral Club with friends. I probably got home about midnight. The house was in darkness. My family all in bed."

"Did you notice the fire at the society property?"

Lovett blinked.

"You can see the property from your home. Did you notice flames. Smell smoke?"

"Now you mention it, I did smell smoke, but I didn't think much of it. I had dined rather well at the club and I was anxious for my bed."

"Was your wife already in bed?"

"I didn't want to disturb her, so I slept in my dressing room."

"So you can't be certain that she was in bed?"

A flicker of hesitation crossed Lovett's face. "I suppose not." He rose to his feet, slamming his palms on his desk. "Now if I have answered your questions, you may leave."

Curran stood. "You still haven't told me if you and Alicia Sewell were lovers."

"And I have no intention of doing so. George Sewell is a friend. I would not betray his trust. If it satisfies your prurient interest, Alicia and I were close friends with a love of musical theater in common. Nothing more." His eyes widened and he pointed the fountain pen at Curran. "This is because of what Eunice said, isn't it? Eunice is a difficult child with an overactive imagination. She has just lost her mother and is jumping at shadows. Take no notice of anything she says." The lawyer continued before Curran could respond, "And what's this I hear about you arresting George Sewell?"

"He would still be behind bars if it had not been for the death of his wife."

"Are you still going on about that business over the *Hesperides*?"

Curran had to bite back a sharp retort. "Two men died, Mr. Lovett, and I have sufficient evidence of the fraud, sitting in a locked room at South Bridge, to lay charges. Regardless of any involvement in Tony Dowling's death, your friend Sewell will be charged over the insurance fraud."

Lovett's lips tightened and he subsided back in his chair, fiddling with the fountain pen. "I am an officer of the court, Inspector. I have always acted entirely in good faith in all my dealings with Sewell. I have stated and will swear on a Bible to a court that I was not a party to any conspiracy to defraud the insurer. Is that all?"

Curran rose with deliberate slowness, circling his helmet in his hands. "For the moment, Lovett."

Lovett stood up and pointed at the door. "Please leave."

Outside the office, Curran looked at Singh. "What do you think?"

"He is a very bad liar," Singh said. "There was more than just an interest in musical theater between himself and Mrs. Sewell."

"I agree," Curran said, "but I am inclined to believe him on the insurance fraud. He didn't need to be a party to it, just the conduit through which the money flowed."

"Where to now?" Singh asked as they stepped out onto Raffles Place.

Curran looked at his sergeant. "Time to have another chat with George Sewell."

The rules of the Balmoral Club left Sergeant Singh fuming on the doorstep and Curran went in alone. He found George Sewell in a corner of the main bar deep into what looked like a heavy drinking session that would have started early.

The man looked up at Curran with pure hate in his eyes.

"Go away. I've nothin' to say to you." Sewell's accent had reverted to its roots in Merseyside.

Curran removed the half-empty glass from the man's reach and sat down.

"I'm sorry about your wife, Sewell, and I'm not here to talk about the insurance matter." He took a breath—the next part of the conversation would not be easy. "Your wife's death was not an accident. She had been stabbed multiple times before her bed was set alight."

Sewell's mouth fell open. He blinked rapidly. "She was . . . she was, murdered?"

Curran nodded.

The man jumped to his feet, jabbing a finger at Curran's chest. "This is your fault, Curran. If I'd been there . . ."

Curran brushed the man's hand aside. "I have no time for false sentiment, Sewell. You had no intention of being there." Conscious of a few curious glances, he took the man by the arm and propelled him outside onto the terrace.

"Pull yourself together, Sewell. I need your help. We need to find who murdered her."

"You 'aven't found who did for Tony Dowling. You are incompetent, Curran . . . bloody incompetent."

"It takes time," Curran said.

Sewell raised his gaze to Curran's. "So, am I a suspect?"

"No, but I do have questions for you."

Sewell looked around the terrace. "Can we talk 'ere? I don't ever want to go back to your stinkin' police station."

Curran summoned the waiter to bring tea and sandwiches and gestured Sewell toward a table in a shady corner, far from curious ears.

"You're a member 'ere?" Sewell asked.

"Yes."

"Never see you."

"I prefer the cricket club," Curran said, clearing room for the tea and sandwiches. "Now I suggest you eat something."

Sewell obediently picked up a cucumber sandwich and munched it while Curran poured them both tea.

"Where are you from?" Curran asked.

"What do you mean?"

"Liverpool, by your accent?"

Sewell nodded. "My da worked on the docks."

"How did the son of a dockie get to be managing a broker-age business in the Far East?"

"Hard work," Sewell said. "Started as the office boy, went to school at night. Taught myself to talk proper."

"And where did you meet your wife?"

"In Ceylon. She was in a traveling show. Alicia Merveille, the Songbird of the East. Weren't her real name though."

"Go on."

"She was born Elsie Williams," Sewell said. "Toast of the music halls was Elsie. 'Alicia' is the name she assumed when she left England."

"Why did she leave England?"

"Got caught in some scandal about the manager of the music hall. His wife stuck her head in a gas oven and blamed Els. She reinvented herself in Ceylon as Alicia Merveille—sang in the opera house in Colombo and all. I first saw her there, and when she came to Singapore . . . well, the rest is history."

"When was that?"

"Five years ago." Sewell looked into the teacup. "I wasn't the best 'usband. I traveled too much to give 'er the attention she wanted. Then there were the temptations." He snorted. "Picked up an unmentionable from some girl in Johor. Couldn't tell Alicia and she thought I was just rejecting her because I didn't love her anymore. I never told her the real reason." He looked up. "Stupid thing was I worshipped her, but she drove me crazy with her demands and her nagging. I'm not proud of how I treated her but the drink . . ."

"Is that why she began her affair with Lovett?" Curran cast caution to the wind. He'd had Lovett's denial. Sewell could now either confirm or deny it.

He fell into the trap. "Yes. What she saw in 'im, I don't know. I guess it was the music." His shoulders slumped. "He made her 'appy in a way I didn't seem to be able to."

"How did you know they were having an affair?"

"A husband always knows, don't he? Mind you, I'm not sure if they ever actually . . . you know, but she told me to my face that she'd leave me for 'im in a heartbeat if he was free but he'd never leave his wife. Couldn't risk the scandal."

"Did his wife know?"

Sewell shook his head and held up a finger. "Couldn't see her nose in front of 'er face or I guess she chose not to see. Besides she had pastures of her own to explore, if you know what I mean."

"Dowling?"

Sewell's face clouded over. "That self-righteous little . . ."

"Business associate?" Curran finished the sentence.

Sewell lowered his head. "He developed a bloody conscience, didn't he? Happy to take the money as long as no one got hurt."

They had arrived back at the insurance fraud and Sewell had

no more defiance left in him. "Do you want to start at the beginning, Sewell?"

The man heaved a heavy sigh. "It was Ellis's idea to lose a
few insured shipments. A bit of extra cash for us, nobody hurt . . .
too easy really, except we needed someone in the insurance
business. Dowling came to dinner with Alicia one day and he
was talking about his invalid sister and how every spare cent
goes home to New Zealand. It wasn't too hard to persuade him
to help us out. The first couple were small shipments, no one the
wiser, but Ellis got greedy, thought we could manage a major
loss." He looked up at Curran, his bloodshot eyes begging Curran to believe that he was nothing more than an innocent dupe.
"It was all his doing. He organized the consignment of fake
rubber bales. I admit I organized the ship and Dowling arranged
the insurance. Dowling's manager was away so he could do it
easily. No one to ask questions and it all went to plan."

"Except two men died."

Sewell shrugged. "They were only natives. I arranged for the
families to be paid but Dowling's conscience got the better of
him. Didn't realize he'd been brooding on it, until he caught up
with me a few weeks ago and said his employers were getting
suspicious and wanted to do an audit. He threatened to go to the
police if we didn't pay him extra so he could slip away if things
got too hot."

"What did you and Ellis do?"

"We didn't kill him," Sewell said, emphasizing his innocence
by slamming his hand on the table. "We paid up, three hundred
pounds in cash. But Ellis made it clear if he ever opened his
mouth, he would end up in a boating accident on Keppel Harbour. I think, by then, he knew Ellis well enough to know that
when he said something, he meant it."

The additional money had not shown up in Dowling's bank
account so Curran made a mental note to check for any trans-
fers of large amounts of money to the family in New Zealand.

Sewell picked up the last sandwich and looked up at Curran. "That's it, Curran. That's my full confession. What happens now?"

"What do you think?"

Sewell shook his head. "You can charge me with the insurance fraud, Curran, but I had nothing to do with Dowling's death . . . or Alicia's. Just find the bastard who did it." He looked up. "Did she suffer?"

Curran shook his head. "If it's any consolation, she was dead before the fire." He didn't need to elaborate on the frenzied stabbing attack. Sewell would find out in due course.

"Just like Dowling?"

"It would seem so."

Sewell closed his eyes and sighed. "I can't bear that our last words were angry . . . and that I hit her. I'll never forgive myself."

The man was clearly in the mood to unburden his own conscience, so Curran asked, "What did you really argue about that day?"

Sewell's eyes slid sideways. "She found a little present I'd bought for a girl in KL. Nothing more than a silly trinket really, but I had promised Alicia to stop visiting the Topaz Club. Couldn't help it . . . a business associate took me, and the girls are beauties. There's one girl there, had a bit of Anglo in her, I think. She would melt the hardest heart."

Curran stared at the man. He had to swallow hard before he asked the next question. "What is this place?"

"The Topaz Club is top end. Very exclusive. You need a personal introduction to get in . . . and this."

He took out his wallet and pulled out a gilt-edged card. It had nothing written on it, just a yellow circle printed in the center.

"And this girl you mention, did you know her name?"

Sewell shrugged. "Not her real name. They use flowers . . . she was Lily, but I heard one of the other girls call her Samera? Samrita? Something like that."

A red mist rose before Curran's eyes, and it took all his strength to stop himself from wringing the story out of Sewell. He steadied his breath and asked, "And how do you get a personal introduction?"

Sewell shook his head. "It was a chap I met in the Spotted Dog. Can't recall his name."

Curran steadied himself. This conversation had turned onto dangerous ground. His first duty was to find the murderer of this man's wife.

"We will talk about this later," Curran said, pocketing the card with the yellow circle.

Sewell looked up at him. "Why? It's nothing to do with Alicia or Dowling. Do you fancy a bit of high-class—?"

"It's another case I'm working on," Curran snapped, and stood with such abruptness, his chair toppled over. "Time to go. Stand up, Sewell."

Sewell rose more slowly. "You're arresting me?"

"What do you think?" Curran said.

With Sewell back in custody at South Bridge Road, Curran, Singh and Tan drove out along Holland Road to Clementi and the Sungei Pandan plantation, several hundred acres of rubber trees on the banks of the Pandan River, the Sungei Pandan, where Lionel Ellis lived. The company owned several other rubber plantations in Johor and Selangor, and Ellis had overall management of the company plantations. To all intents and purposes Ellis was the Sungei Pandan Company.

The police motor vehicle turned in through the gates, the carriageway lined with the scraggly rubber trees scarred by the V-shaped tapping cuts. The largely Tamil workforce, engaged in the cutting or collecting of the liquid rubber, looked up as the vehicle passed. They stared at the motor vehicle with dull eyes, their thin, scarred bodies saying everything that needed to be said about their employer. Ellis paid poorly and was a hard task-master, as his recent court case had demonstrated, and Curran wondered what kept most of the workers in Ellis's employ.

But if you are poor, then it is a matter of taking work where it could be found.

The plantation house, built on a slight rise, came into view. Like many similar buildings, it sprawled on its stilts, a wide verandah and heavy thatched roof giving the impression of a straggly fringe over the eyes of the house. Ellis sprawled in a planters' chair, a reclined chair with wide arms, one booted foot propped on the verandah rail and a bottle of beer in his hand.

He showed no curiosity about his visitors and did not rise as the motor vehicle came to a halt. Curran and Singh dismounted and stood at the foot of the steps, looking up at the planter.

"Excuse me for not inviting you in," Ellis said, "but you're not welcome. Now get back in that fancy machine and go back to South Bridge Road."

The afternoon sun beat down on Curran's helmet and runnels of sweat gathered in the starched collar of his uniform. He would have sold his soul for a beer, but he couldn't show any weakness in front of this man.

"I would like you to accompany me," Curran said.

Ellis's lip curled. "I don't think so. I have nothing to say to you, Curran."

Curran put his hands in his pockets and squinted up at the blazing tropical sun. "That's unfortunate because I will have to arrest you."

"What for this time?"

"Let's start with the assault on me last week and then we might move on to fraud and theft."

Ellis dropped his booted foot to the verandah with a thump. He jumped to his feet and came forward, leaning his hands on the railing.

"What are you talking about?"

Curran cocked his head. "Do you remember the *Hesperides*, Ellis? Two men drowned. I am considering adding manslaughter to the charges."

"You're being ridiculous, Curran." But the certainty had gone from his voice.

"Then come with me and explain to me why I am being ridiculous?"

Ellis's refusal was blunt and colorful.

Curran shrugged and turned away with a quick nod to Singh and Tan. When Ellis continued to protest, Curran ordered handcuffs to be used and had great pleasure in watching Ellis being led to the car, red-faced and swearing, his hands cuffed behind his back.

As they drove away, the man's hard-put-upon workers crept out of the trees to watch the *tuan* being taken away like a common criminal.

Back at South Bridge Road, Curran sat in his office and smoked his pipe as he considered how best to tackle the interview with Ellis. He had Sewell's confession and a similar admission from Lionel Ellis would close the case of the sinking of the *Hesperides*.

But if he entertained any thoughts Ellis would roll over quietly, he was mistaken. The man sat in the interview room, his legs spread, and his beefy arms crossed over his chest.

"You don't bloody give up, do you, Curran?"

"Not when men like you are getting away with murder . . . and I do mean murder."

Ellis snorted.

The sight of Ellis's smug, self-satisfied face played on the tightly wound cord of Curran's temper.

"Two men died on that boat," he said between gritted teeth.

Ellis shrugged. "They were only natives." He sat back in his chair, his hands behind his head. "You've gone soft, Curran. Comes of living with that Chink girl. Gone native yourself." He leaned forward. "I hear she's left you and gone back to her own kind. Left you with a taste for the exotic, has it? I can recommend a nice piece in Serangoon Road."

The fragile cord of Curran's self-control snapped, and the red mist flared in his eyes. All the frustration of the last case against this man, the physical assault by Ellis's thugs, the whispered gossip of his years with Li An and now the loss of Li An, boiled together and he launched himself across the table, grabbing Ellis by the shirt front, toppling them both onto the floor. Ellis's head hit the concrete with a thump, and he flailed wildly in his attempt to dislodge Curran.

Curran raised his fist and smashed it into Ellis's face. The man's nose exploded in a mist of blood, and he roared with pain.

Ellis had strength and size on Curran, and he threw the policeman off, dripping blood onto Curran's uniform. His ham-sized fist came down and Curran just managed to twist away before it connected with his own face, but the fist slammed into his already-bruised shoulder. The pain was so intense he thought he would be sick, but Ellis was not done; he planted a knee in Curran's chest and it was only Singh's intervention, pulling the red-faced planter off Curran, that saved him from a worse beating.

"Curran!" Gursharan Singh shouted in his ear.

He took his sergeant's outstretched hand and let him pull him to his feet, wiping the blood and sweat from his face with the back of his hand.

A pair of uniformed constables had Ellis by the arms. The man's face was a mask of blood and the small, piggy eyes glittered.

"I want that bastard charged." Ellis spat blood. "You saw it, Sergeant. An unprovoked attack on an innocent man."

Singh's grip on Curran's arm tightened, warning him to say nothing more.

"Take Mr. Ellis to the cells and clean him up," Singh ordered.

The anger had begun to die away and something Curran vaguely recognized as shock washed over him. He let Singh push him out of the interview room and into the corridor. Singh threw open the door to the bathroom and thrust him inside. Still gripping Curran by one arm, Singh turned on a tap, and before Curran could protest, his sergeant thrust his head beneath the tepid water.

He dragged him back and turned the tap off, leaving Curran gasping for breath, his sodden hair falling in his eyes.

"What the hell are you doing?" Curran spluttered.

Singh pushed Curran back against the wall and held him by the arms, scanning his face.

"I shouldn't have to keep doing this. How much have you had to drink?" Singh demanded.

"Nothing," Curran responded, trying to salvage some semblance of dignity. "I swear I haven't touched a drop today! Now let me go."

Singh obeyed and Curran straightened, running his fingers through his sodden hair. His right hand hurt like hell, the knuckles reddening from the impact with hard cartilage and bone.

"Inspector Curran." Singh shook his head. "What have you done?"

Curran let out a breath and shook his bruised hand. "Probably screwed my career, but by God it felt good."

Singh put his hands on his hips and regarded Curran. "I'm not denying Ellis didn't deserve what you gave him, but he's screaming blue murder and he has some powerful friends."

Chastened, Curran tugged at his blood-spattered uniform jacket. "I let him get to me," he said.

Singh shook his head. "Yes, you did. We both know it was nothing to do with the case, he knew the way to break you was through Miss Khoo and it worked."

"Leave my private life out of this," Curran sparked again.

"I can't. Your private life is affecting us all. You are drinking too much, and it is affecting your judgment, Curran. Once Cuscaden hears about today . . ."

Curran slid down the wall, crouching on his heels, his head in his hands.

"Ellis . . ." He mumbled through his fingers. "Charge him with the *Hesperides* and keep him under lock and key. I don't need him to confess to anything. I've got George Sewell's signed confession . . . That case is closed."

"What about the murders?"

Curran raised his head. "I can see them being responsible for Tony Dowling's death but not Alicia Sewell's." He rose slowly to his feet. "I don't think either of those deaths or Elspeth Lovett's accident has anything to do with the insurance fraud." He ran a hand through his wet hair. "I can't even think straight."

Singh laid a hand on his shoulder. "Go home, Inspector, and don't come back until you have pulled yourself together. I will tell Cuscaden that you are suffering from a bad curry."

❧ THIRTY

Harriet had spent a tedious day at the school, in her unpaid role as the school's administration assistant, typing up requests for the payment of overdue school fees. While the work left much to be desired, she loved being around the boys and hearing their happy chatter and noise. Julian's school had become quite sought after by the mamas of Singapore and was now, happily, at full capacity with a mixture of boarding and day attendees.

She waited at the door of the classroom for Will to come bursting out. Will missed the boardinghouse, but even if Julian and Harriet could have afforded the cost of boarding, Will now lived next door in the headmaster's house, so it would have been a pointless expense. Since Will had come into her life back in March, he had given her a sense of purpose. Will had to be clothed, fed, educated and, above all, loved and she could no longer imagine a time when the boy had not been part of her life.

The vexed question of where to send the boy after St. Thomas preyed on her mind as they walked together across the playing field to St. Tom's House. She listened attentively to his chatter about his day; the A+ for mathematics, his dismal failure at Latin and his plans for his new adventures with the Boy Scouts. As they rounded the corner of the house, Harriet stopped. Curran sat on the top step leading up to the verandah, hatless, his elbows resting on his knees, his shoulders slumped. She looked around for Leopold but he had apparently arrived by other means.

"Curran?"

He looked up and she read a naked pain and despair in his face she had never seen before. As he rose to his feet to greet them, she told Will to go around to the kitchen and see what Huo Jin could arrange for their afternoon tea.

Skirts in hand she sat on the step. He sank down beside her, ran a hand across his forehead, pushing his hair back. "Sorry to bother you, Harriet. I didn't want to go back to the bungalow, and I didn't know where else to go. I needed a friendly face."

And you came to me? Harriet thought, letting a warm glow light her heart.

"You know you're always welcome here." She looked up at him, noting the dark circles under his eyes and an unhealthy pallor beneath his tan. It seemed to her that he was being held together with string and packing tape that had begun to unravel.

"Something's happened," she said.

He sighed. "I punched a suspect. I think I broke his nose."

He rubbed the skinned knuckles on his right hand and she pointed to the spattering of dark spots on Curran's normally immaculate tunic.

"Blood?"

"His, not mine," Curran said.

"Ah," she said. "Who did you punch?"

"Lionel Ellis."

"I presume he deserved it?"

He glanced at her from under the unruly fall of hair and his lips quirked. "He . . . said things about Li An."

"Of course he did. He was trying to get a rise from you, Curran."

"He succeeded." Curran looked down at his hands, his shoulders sagging. "There will be hell to pay with Cuscaden."

Whether it was the instinct of one human being to comfort another in pain, Harriet couldn't have said. She reached out and took his hand, curling her fingers around his. He made no move to pull back and they sat together for a long moment in silence.

"Tea, mem."

At Huo Jin's voice, Harriet pulled her hand away. "Come and have something to eat, Curran, and stay for supper. You don't need to go home to an empty house. You don't need to go home at all. We can make up the spare bed for you."

He nodded. "Thank you. I can't face an empty house tonight."

"Julian will be home soon," she said. "If you need to talk . . ."

He shook his head. "I've said enough."

"Give me that jacket. I'll find one of Julian's shirts for you. I'm not sitting through a meal staring at Ellis's bloodstains."

As Huo Jin set the table with their afternoon tea, Harriet stood in the doorway to Julian's bedroom watching as Curran undid his Sam Browne. He moved stiffly, shrugging off the khaki jacket. She took it from him and stood holding it while he buttoned on Julian's shirt. He wore a simple cotton undershirt, but it was enough for Harriet to see the yellowing bruises from the previous week's beating.

He glanced around and caught the expression on her face.

"Ellis deserves more than a bloodied nose," she said. "He's a thug and a bully. Is he also a murderer?"

"Not the murders at the music society. However, there is more than enough evidence to convict him on the insurance fraud and possibly the manslaughter of the two crew from the *Hesperides*. There will be no friendly magistrate to give him a rap over the knuckles this time."

Over tea and sandwiches and cake, Will told Curran about the Boy Scouts and the promised camping trips.

"I met Baden-Powell," Curran said. "He—" But stopped

short of continuing as Will stared at him with undisguised admiration. "I think it all sounds jolly good fun," Curran finished.

"Gosh, wait till I tell the others that you know Baden-Powell. I've got his book."

Without asking for permission to leave the table, Will scampered off.

"What were you going to say about Baden-Powell?" Harriet asked.

"That I thought he was a terrible soldier," Curran said. "Hundreds of men died at Mafeking because he chose to be besieged instead of breaking out. He had superior forces. He could have done it easily." He shook his head. "But who am I to question a man's judgment?"

Will returned with *Scouting for Boys*.

"Were you at Mafeking?" he asked Curran.

Curran shook his head. "No."

He took the book from Will and opened it to the page about the boys of Mafeking. Man and boy sat together on the verandah discussing the Siege of Mafeking, or at least Baden-Powell's sanitized version of it, until Julian came home.

Julian, used to the comings and goings in his home, greeted Curran without surprise and Harriet followed him inside.

"What's going on, Harri?" Julian asked in a whisper. "Why is Curran wearing one of my shirts?"

Harriet recounted the afternoon's events and Julian let out a low whistle. "He looks like he hasn't slept in days. Hardly surprising Ellis pushed him over the edge."

"I've offered him a bed here tonight, Julian. Maybe a decent meal and a good night's sleep will help."

"Maybe," Julian said without conviction.

After Will had been sent to bed, Harriet, Julian and Curran sat on the verandah, watching the distant display of lightning and listening to the resulting rumble of thunder amidst the crackle and chirrup of insects and the crash of monkeys through the trees.

Curran declined Julian's offer of a drink with what might have been a shudder. "I'm sorry to land myself on you tonight," he said.

"Nonsense. That's what friends are for. Where are you at with the case or is it cases?" Julian asked.

"The latter. Ironically, we have solved the insurance fraud case," Curran said. "Although I probably had a few more questions for Ellis before I broke his nose."

"Is it connected with the murder of Dowling?" Julian asked.

"I thought it was and then Alicia Sewell died—"

"She was murdered?" Julian almost started from his chair. "The newspaper report said it was an accident."

Curran shook his head. "She was stabbed multiple times before her bed was set alight."

Julian shook his head. "Poor woman." He sat back, steepling his fingers. "So, she and Dowling both died in a similar fashion? Stabbed and burned?"

"Yes."

Julian, who loved solving puzzles, frowned. "Who are your suspects and why?"

Curran took a deep breath, as if collecting his thoughts. "Very well. Start with George Sewell. He may have wanted to silence Dowling about the insurance fraud after Dowling started to blackmail the conspirators."

"Was Dowling having an affair with his wife? It would give him a motive to kill them both."

Curran looked at Julian. "You know, for a priest you have an interesting mind!"

Julian had the grace to color slightly. "I am also more aware than many of the weaknesses and failings of men and women, Curran."

"To answer your question," Curran said, "I don't think Alicia Sewell and Tony Dowling's relationship went beyond friendship and Sewell had no motive to murder his wife for that reason. Besides, I had him locked in a cell when Alicia died."

"What about when Dowling died?"

"At the club until about eleven. No witnesses to say what time he returned home."

"So, he could have had time to kill Dowling."

"Possibly but I don't think so. He's a wife beater and a bully but I don't think he's a murderer."

"What about Ellis?"

"Ellis spent the night of Dowling's murder at the club. No evidence he ever left, and he was at the plantation the night Alicia died."

"But that doesn't rule him out entirely. He's not above hiring others to do his dirty work, as you can attest, Curran."

Curran rubbed his shoulder. "Whatever his motives could have been in relation to Dowling, he had no reason to kill Alicia and I do think the same hand is responsible for both of those murders."

"Who does that leave?" Julian asked.

"Lovett," Harriet said.

Both men looked at her.

"He denies any guilty involvement with the insurance fraud, and I tend to believe him," Curran said.

"But what if it's nothing to do with the fraud?" Harriet said. "And you're leaving out Elspeth Lovett's death. Three people closely associated with Lovett are dead."

"He was in Johor the night his wife died," Curran said. "Her death is unfortunate, but I lean toward the theory she jumped or fell to her death without the aid of a third party."

"But you don't know."

"No, I don't."

"Elspeth Lovett was having a physical affair with Dowling . . ." Harriet began.

Julian looked at her. "What a den of iniquity your music society is."

Harriet ignored him. "Was Lovett having an affair with Alicia?"

Curran took a long moment to answer. "There was certainly something between them, but I'm not entirely sure I'd go as far as to say it was an affair. Besides, if his motive was to be with Alicia, why would he kill her?"

"Good point. You can see him bumping off Dowling and helping his wife to end it all, but for what purpose if it was not to be with the beautiful Mrs. Sewell," Julian said.

"Unless she turned him down," Harriet said.

Curran rose to his feet. "If you two have finished solving my case for me, I'm going to bed."

Harriet and Julian both rose.

"It's getting late, and you look dead on your feet, Curran," Julian said. "I think I'll shuffle off too. Good night, Harri."

Harriet waited until she heard the respective bedroom doors shut and sank back on her chair, pulling Shashti with her. There was something about Dowling's death that no one seemed to have raised. For someone to have stabbed him in the neck, they would have had to get close. While it was perfectly possible to hire a killer, would Tony Dowling have allowed a total stranger so close that he could be so easily stabbed? Surely it had to be someone he knew and trusted?

Absently she ruffled the little cat's brindled fur. Enough of death. It was Friday and tomorrow she was supposed to be going away for a weekend at the seaside with Simon and her friends. Something fun to look forward to.

✇ THIRTY-ONE

Saturday, 12 November

Curran returned to his bungalow on Saturday morning. He had slept like the dead in Harriet and Julian's narrow, lumpy spare bed and the brief reprieve had been a godsend but now the world had to be faced.

After an early breakfast he returned to his own bungalow to be met by Mahmud with an envelope with his name scrawled in a familiar handwriting. The inspector general of the Straits Settlements Police requested Inspector Curran's presence in his office at ten o'clock.

Curran glanced at his watch. It was just past nine. He felt human for the first time in over a week, but the wrath of his senior officer had to be faced and memories of being hauled into the master's office at his college in Oxford for fighting with his cousin George surfaced. That hadn't ended well, and he had no doubt that the coming interview with Cuscaden would have a similar outcome.

He dressed in his crispest uniform. The dhobi organized by Lavinia did not spare the starch and the tunic all but stood up on its own. He shaved, combed his hair and polished his boots and Sam Browne. If nothing else, he would go to his fate looking immaculate.

Sensitive to the inspector general's moods, the icy atmosphere descended the moment he stepped into the South Bridge Road office. If they hadn't been in Singapore, frost would have clung to the light fittings. For an agonizingly long minute, Cuscaden said nothing. His eyes raked Curran from head to toe, while all the time he toyed with his fountain pen.

He set the pen back in its holder and leaned forward, resting his elbows on his desk.

"You know why you're here?"

The calm, low tone Cuscaden used did not fool Curran.

He cleared his throat. "Yes."

"You assaulted Lionel Ellis. Broke his nose, in fact."

Good, Curran thought.

"He provoked me."

"Provoked you? Curran, the first rule of good policing is not to give in to provocation. You know that better than anyone else." He held up a hand as Curran opened his mouth to protest. "I have no interest in my officers' personal lives until it starts affecting their work and you've been off your game since that girl of yours left you."

Curran swallowed. "I assure you that—"

"I'm sorry for it but this simply won't do. Pull yourself together, man."

"Yes, sir. Can I go now, sir?"

Cuscaden leaned back in his chair, folding his fingers across his stomach. "Look, Curran, you have to admit you are a mess. I've had reports of you being inebriated on duty. It's not like you, man. You need some time to sort yourself out, get over the girl, remember you are a senior officer in the Straits Settlements Police, not a lovesick youth."

Curran felt the heat rising to his face at the same moment his heart sank. "What do you mean, sir?"

"I am suspending you from duty."

"No . . . I need to be working. I have . . ." Curran stumbled around, suddenly desperate and afraid of being set adrift.

Cuscaden held up his hand. "I'm not firing you, but you need a break from all of this. Go to Ceylon, shoot a tiger or something."

"But the department needs me."

"No, it doesn't. Kuala Lumpur is sending Keogh down to take over while you're on leave."

"Bloody hell. Keogh's an idiot. He'll screw everything up."

If Curran had not been so low, he would never have stepped over this line. Now his boss narrowed his eyes.

"That's enough, Curran. I don't want to see or hear from you until I'm ready for you to come back. You need time to pull yourself together. Do I make myself clear?"

"Suspending me is not going to help me pull myself together, with respect, sir."

"It's my opinion you never really got over that incident in Penang. You were back at work far too soon."

"Because I need to work—" Curran began but fell silent.

Nothing he could say would change the outcome of this conversation. He had been suspended and that was Cuscaden's prerogative.

"When's Keogh arriving?" he asked.

"Monday."

Curran swallowed. "Then give me the next two days, sir. Apart from anything else, I need to finalize the report and charges relating to the insurance fraud, and if I can find Dowling's and Sewell's murderer—"

For a long moment, Curran didn't move. He stood in front of the massive desk, suddenly light-headed with fatigue and grief. If he moved, he might pass out and that would be the final humiliation.

"Do you know who it is?"

"I'm so close, sir. I just need to pull the threads together."

"And you can do that in two days?"

"I'm damned if I am leaving it to that idiot Keogh."

Cuscaden coughed and Curran wondered if the hand the man put to his mouth might have concealed a smile.

"Two days, Curran."

Curran took several deep breaths, drew himself to attention and saluted.

"And stay away from Ellis." Cuscaden delivered the parting shot at Curran's back as he left the room.

Curran had no intention of going anywhere near Ellis. He had his quarry in mind. He just needed to corner him long enough to get a confession.

Curran found Singh at his desk in the Detective Branch going over the formal charges that had been laid against Sewell and Ellis. He looked up as Curran crossed the floor to him.

"Well?" Singh asked.

Curran looked around the room. They were quite alone. "Suspended indefinitely," he said.

Singh said nothing for a long moment. "I say this with the greatest respect, sir, but you have only yourself to blame."

"Yes, thank you, I don't need you moralizing at me. I've had enough from Cuscaden this morning. He's bringing in Keogh from Kuala Lumpur."

Singh was not a man to swear but he said something in Punjabi that Curran gathered may have been a less-than-flattering expression of his thoughts on Inspector Keogh.

"It's not all bad news," Curran said. "I have two days to finalize the Dowling and Sewell murders."

Singh quirked an eyebrow. "Two days?"

Curran put his pith helmet on and tightened the strap. "Are

you coming, Singh? We are going to have a chat with Mr. Lovett but first we need to find Tan and Musa."

An additional atmosphere of misery seemed to hang over the Lovett house with its shuttered windows and black crepe still hanging limply from the door as Curran knocked. They left Tan and Musa with the motor vehicle and Curran and Singh were admitted into the hallway and told to wait. Lovett himself appeared at the door to his study.

"Really, Inspector. I have nothing more to say to you."

Curran gestured at the man's study. "Shall we talk privately, Mr. Lovett?"

Lovett hesitated. He gave an impatient shrug and stood aside to admit Curran and Singh, who closed the door behind him. Lovett took his seat behind his desk and picked up a paper knife. Curran eyed the object and wondered how sharp it was and if the man had the speed to leap across his desk and use it as a weapon. He decided to remain standing. Singh took up a position beside the door, the patient observer of what was about to unfold.

"Well?" Lovett tapped the hilt of the paper knife on his blotter.

"I have arrested Sewell and Ellis."

"Have you. Do they have legal advice?"

"Your partner Clive Strong will represent them," Curran said.

"But I'm—"

"You're lucky not to be keeping them company," Curran said. "It would just take one of them to implicate you."

Lovett's mouth opened and shut as the import of Curran's words hit home.

"I told you, Inspector. I was as much a dupe in this as the insurance company."

"That remains to be seen, but that's not why I'm here."

Lovett stiffened. "Well?"

"Let's start with the death of Tony Dowling, your leading man, Lovett. You knew about his dalliance with your wife."

"I've already told you this. Elspeth was hardly subtle, particularly when she was drunk. She boasted about it, in fact."

"Did she know about your relationship with Alicia Sewell?"

Lovett's nostrils flared. "I did not have an affair with Alicia Sewell."

"Maybe not physically but you're not going to deny the mutual attraction?"

"We were both married. Nothing happened."

"And then quite suddenly, you weren't married, Mr. Lovett."

"My wife only died a few days ago. I was hardly going to jump into bed with Alicia Sewell. Good God, man, this may be Singapore and things are different here but I still have a reputation to maintain and—"

"Yet you turned a blind eye to your wife's dalliance? Did you put it down to the tropical heat and the pent-up passion of Gilbert and Sullivan?"

"Very well, to be honest, I didn't particularly care about Elspeth and Dowling as long as she was discreet. If she was happy, I was happy, but people had started to notice. She had become an embarrassment, hanging around him with great cow eyes like a foolish debutante. I told her to end it and she agreed."

"So, she arranged one last meeting with him?"

"Apparently."

"Where were you?"

"At the club with Sewell and Ellis."

"Until what time?"

Lovett shrugged. "I've told you all this before several times. Midnight . . . thereabouts."

"And you came straight home?"

"Yes, and went to bed in the dressing room. Really, Inspector, I am repeating myself."

"But you are wrong about one detail, Lovett. You left the club at eleven."

"That's not right."

"It is because that is the time the barman closed up for the night. The three of you were the last men left in the bar. Ellis went to bed, and you and Sewell departed."

Lovett swallowed. "I am not proud of myself but we'd both had rather too much to drink and we ended up in Geylang. Sewell knew a place with clean girls." He closed his eyes and shuddered. "Unlike Sewell, it is not my habit or custom to . . . to visit such places and I was sufficiently disgusted to leave before anything happened. I left Sewell there and got home, as I have stated, just after midnight."

"But you can't be sure Sewell didn't leave shortly after you. However, while he may have had a motive to murder Dowling to keep him silent about the insurance fraud, he did not murder his own wife, and they were both murdered in too similar a fashion as to be a coincidence."

The color drained from Lovett's face. "Alicia was murdered?"

The shock seemed genuine and for a long moment Curran's confidence wavered until he recalled the man was an actor and quite a good one, by all accounts.

"How . . ." Lovett swallowed. "How exactly did she die?"

"The same way as Dowling. Stabbed and set alight."

Lovett dropped the paper knife and covered his eyes with his hand, his elbow on the desk. His shoulders heaved.

"But you already know that," Curran said.

Lovett looked up. "How would I know?"

"Because you were the one who killed her."

"Why would I kill her? I loved her."

"There could be any number of reasons. She wouldn't leave her husband? She knew you killed Dowling and you had to keep her quiet? Shall I go on?"

"You've said enough." Lovett had gone quite still, his gaze fixed on the door behind Curran.

"Lovett?"

He shook himself and brought his attention back to Curran. "You are absolutely correct, Inspector. I killed Tony Dowling and Alicia Sewell."

"What?" Curran stared at him, the about-face taking him completely by surprise. "You're confessing to the murders."

"Yes. I'm tired of lying, Inspector. I killed Tony Dowling because of the affair with my wife. It was unplanned and unintended, but yes, Alicia . . . she challenged me about it and I knew she had to die too. Take me in, Inspector, charge me. I will give you a full written confession."

Curran tried to bring his scattered thoughts together. "How did you kill them?"

"You already know that. I stabbed them and then set fire to the bodies to try, unsuccessfully apparently, to hide the evidence of my crime."

"What weapon did you use?"

Lovett looked down at the paper knife on the blotter. "A knife."

"That one?"

Lovett shook his head. "No, a knife I found in the kitchen."

"Where is it now?"

"I threw it away."

"Where?"

Lovett shrugged. "In the river. Just arrest me, Curran, and be done with it." He stood up and walked out from behind the desk.

"You claim Dowling's death was an accident, but you took a knife from the kitchen and confronted him at the McKinnon plantation?"

Lovett raised his chin. "I'm not saying another word. I killed him. That is all I am going to say." He held out his wrists. "Are you going to handcuff me?"

Curran stared at him. "I don't think there is any need for that. Singh, can you escort Mr. Lovett to the motor vehicle?"

As they walked out into the hall, Eunice appeared at the top of the stairs. "Papa? What's happening?"

"I am so sorry, my dear," Lovett said. "I have to go with the police. It is a terrible thing and I don't want you to hate me. I have told the Inspector that I am responsible for the deaths of Tony and Alicia. It's all over now."

"No!" Eunice screamed, and ran down the stairs, throwing herself at her father.

He stroked her head and disengaged her, holding her at arm's length. "I am so, so very sorry, my darling."

She turned on Curran, beating her fists against his chest, striking the bruises with an unerring accuracy that made him wince. He took hold of her wrists and held her off.

"My daughter," Lovett said. "Is there somewhere she can go? Maybe Mrs. Gordon? She seems a sensible woman."

Curran nodded. "Miss Lovett, I will leave Constable Musa here with you for a little while. Pack a bag and I'll send the motor vehicle back to take you to Mrs. Gordon."

Eunice's mouth drooped and her eyes filled with tears. She looked up at her father. "Daddy?"

Lovett kissed her forehead. "It will all be for the best, my dear."

❦ THIRTY-TWO

Harriet sat on the verandah of the pleasant seaside villa, fanning herself gently with a pretty painted fan she had picked up for a few cents in Chinatown. Beyond the wide expanse of beach the languid waters of the Singapore Straits, dotted with distant green islands, stretched to the Dutch East Indies island of Batam. The seaside villa came equipped with a full staff, ample bedrooms and direct access to the beach, where Julian and Will were building a sandcastle. It was perfect.

"You're very quiet," Simon said, handing Harriet a cup of tea.

Simon sat down on the chair next to her, stretching out his long legs as Harriet took a sip of the tea.

"What are you thinking about?" he inquired.

"I was wondering about how to take a trip to Batam or Bintan. I really haven't traveled at all since I've been in Singapore," Harriet said. "I haven't even been across to the mainland."

"You could come to Australia."

Harriet's cup tipped, spilling tea into the saucer. She set it down, her heart hammering. "Australia?"

"Why not? It's not as far as London. The residents are friendly . . . and they speak the King's English."

"It's a big country, Simon. Where would I go?"

"Well, personally, I reckon Sydney's overrated. Come to Melbourne with me, Harriet. You'd love it. An elegant city, fabulous theaters and shops and out of town there are mountains and wide-open spaces. A little bit of everything. I could take you out to visit the family property in the Western District."

"Are you serious?" Harriet looked at him.

"Completely serious." He held up a hand. "Don't look like that, Harriet. I'm not asking you to marry me, just give me a chance to show what life in the Great Southern Land can offer a lady like you."

"Oh, Simon, as tempting as you make it sound, I can't possibly leave Julian or Will."

"Not forever. Just a holiday. Face it, for someone who came out to Singapore to recover from what you've been through, you've had a hell of a year, Harriet."

She looked at him. "Are you planning to go back to Melbourne imminently?"

Simon shrugged. "I don't know. Depends—"

"Halloo!" came a cry from the front of the house.

"Sounds like Maddocks," Simon said.

A clattering of booted feet from inside the house and Maddocks burst onto the verandah, hand in hand with Sister Doreen Wilson from the Singapore General Hospital. Harriet had never been so glad to see Griff and Doreen in her life.

"I say, this is a bit upmarket for us. Thanks for the invite," Maddocks said.

The two women embraced and Doreen collapsed onto the chair vacated by Simon, fanning herself with Harriet's fan.

Maddocks waved at Julian. "I'm going for a swim. How about you, Hume?"

Simon glanced at Harriet. "Harriet?"

She shook her head. "Tomorrow, maybe. I'm quite happy just sitting here doing nothing."

"Doreen?"

"I've got the latest book by E. M. Forster," Doreen said, pulling the volume from her capacious handbag.

"*Howards End*," Harriet read the title. "May I borrow it after you? I read *A Room with a View*."

"Of course. Now off you go, boys," Doreen said, her Lancastrian accent growing stronger. "Time for Harriet and me to have a bit of a natter."

As they watched the men, clad in their woolen bathing costumes, run barefooted toward the water, Doreen let out a long sigh. "Oh, that Simon Hume. You're a lucky lass, Harriet Gordon. I can't see why you aren't jumping into bed with that one."

Harriet stared at her. "Because we're not married . . . we don't . . ." She didn't like to say they had barely kissed, let alone anything else. She looked at Doreen with new eyes. "Do you and Griff . . . ?"

Doreen met her gaze. "Of course we do. It's a bit of fun, that's all. You've been married, Harriet, have you forgotten what it's like?"

Had she forgotten what it was like to lie in a man's arms, to share the intimacy of a man's body? Harriet took a shuddering breath. It was not James she recalled but another man, asleep with another woman curled in his arms. A moment between two people that she had no business sharing.

"Of course not, I just don't think of Simon that way," she said.

"Oh my gawd," Doreen said. "How can you not? Look at him, Harriet. He's got a body like a Greek statue, and trust me, I'm something of an expert when it comes to the male anatomy."

Woolen bathing suits were not the most flattering of costumes and, when wet, drooped and sagged in the most unflattering way but even the ugly garment could not disguise the man's broad shoulders, narrow hips and strong, muscular legs from a youth spent in the outdoors, probably on horses. He was beautiful, if men could be described as beautiful, but he was not the man that set Harriet's heart racing when he walked into a room or when he smiled at her.

She took a deep breath and stood up to pour herself a glass of lime juice from the jug that stood on the table, while waiting for the beach party to return.

"Penny for your thoughts." Doreen's voice brought her back to the moment and Simon's suggestion she should go to Australia.

Absurd, she thought. Leaving aside the complexities of Simon and his motives in wanting her to go to Australia, such a trip was out of the question. While she was certain Australia in general, and Melbourne in particular, would be every bit as wonderful as Simon rhapsodized, she couldn't just abandon Julian and William. She had responsibilities in Singapore. It could wait for a more suitable time, preferably when her relationship with Simon had moved to a firmer footing, rather than the shifting sands on which it stood at the moment.

"Mem Gordon?" A houseboy appeared at the door. "There is a policeman at the door. He has a message for you."

Harriet turned on her heel and followed the man to the doorway, where a young local constable stood, balancing a bicycle with one hand and breathing heavily as if he had just pedaled like the wind.

He whipped off his hat. "I am Constable Ahmed from the Katong Police Post. I have a message for Mrs. Gordon."

"I'm Mrs. Gordon."

With obvious relief the constable handed over the note.

"Does it require an answer?" she asked as he turned his bicycle back toward town.

"No, mem," he replied.

She unfolded the note. *Mrs. Gordon. L has confessed to deaths of Dowling and Sewell and is now in custody. Urgent assistance required with daughter. Can you please come to Lovell residence as matter of urgency. C*

She understood exactly what had happened. Curran had arrested Lovett, leaving Eunice by herself. Curran needed her help.

Curran needed her help. Her heart sang.

She walked slowly back through the house to the verandah, where the men were emerging from the water with smiles and laughter. Simon ran a hand through his hair and guilt racked her as he saw her and waved. He stooped to pick up the abandoned beach robe and belted it on before striding up the steps of the verandah.

"That was brilliant," he said. "Come for a swim, Harriet."

She tapped the note on her hand. "I'm sorry to do this, Simon, but I have to go back to Singapore."

"Whatever for?"

"I'm needed by the police."

"Urgent typing?"

She winced inwardly at the hurt in his voice.

"Something like that. There's been an arrest in the Dowling and Sewell murders."

"Curran snaps his fingers and you come running?" Simon's eyes flashed.

Harriet straightened. "Please remember that I have to earn my living, Simon. I'm not a kept woman with a man's income to support me. So, yes, if urgent typing is required, then I have to make myself available."

"What's this?" Julian wandered up to the pair. Griff had been waylaid by Will, who appeared to be constructing Windsor Castle.

"Your sister is abandoning us," Simon said.

Harriet handed Julian the note.

"He's arrested Lovett?" Julian said.

"And he's asking me to deal with Eunice."

"If that's the issue, why don't you bring her here?" Simon said.

"You haven't met Eunice," Harriet said. "She's hardly the

life of the party at the best of times, and in the last week, her mother has died and her father's been arrested for murder."

"Then a nice distraction is probably what the girl needs," Doreen said. "I agree, Harriet, bring the girl here for the night. There's a spare bed for her."

"Give me ten minutes to get changed and I'll drive you," Simon said.

Harriet started to protest but she had no other means of getting back to Singapore and she would have been a fool to refuse it.

Simon let out a whistle as they drew up under the porte cochere of the Lovett house. His glance took in the shuttered windows and the black crepe on the door.

"Quite a place," he said. "Lovett must be worth a bit."

Harriet shivered. The gloomy atmosphere of the house seemed to seep into her bones.

"The quicker I can get Eunice out of here, the better," she said.

Constable Musa bin Osman answered the door.

"Where's the majordomo?" Harriet asked as she and Simon walked into the echoing silence of the front hall.

"Miss Lovett has sent all the servants away," Musa said.

"Why would she do that?" Simon asked.

Musa shook his head. "I do not know. She wished me to go too, but I am here because the inspector ordered it and here I will stay."

"Where is Miss Lovett?"

Musa glanced up the stairs. "She said I was to remain here."

"I'll go and talk to her," Harriet said. "Wait here, Simon. I'll try not to be too long."

Her heels echoed in the silent house as she climbed the stairs.

She glanced back at Simon and Musa, who stood at the bottom of the stairs, watching her with anxious looks on their faces.

She found Eunice Lovett in what had been her parents' bedroom. She sat in an armchair beside the shuttered window, a framed picture hugged to her thin body. She wore the same drab, ill-fitting black dress she had worn at Elspeth's funeral, the wide linen collar now crumpled and stained. Her hair had come loose and hung in disordered rats' tails around her face.

She barely looked up as Harriet crossed the room toward her.

"Eunice?"

"What do you want?"

"Inspector Curran has asked me to take you home with me until something can be arranged. In fact, we are having a lovely weekend at the beach and there is plenty of room in the villa for you, so let's pack your things and we'll be on our way."

Eunice glared at her from under her heavy fringe. "I'm not going anywhere. I'm not leaving this house. I don't care what Inspector Curran says. He took Papa away and I'm staying here until Papa comes home."

Harriet took the framed image from Eunice's unresisting hands. She glanced at it and frowned. It was a wedding photograph of Charles Lovett and a woman who was not Elspeth Lovett.

She looked at Eunice. "Your father has been married before?"

The girl nodded. "That's my mother, my real mother. She died when I was five. Father married Elspeth within a few months, and we moved to Singapore."

"So, Elspeth was your stepmother?"

Eunice nodded and Harriet set the wedding photograph down on the nearest table as she digested this information.

"Do you remember your mother?"

Eunice's face screwed up. "Sometimes I think I do, but then it goes away." She looked up at Harriet. "Please don't take me away. I want to stay here."

"Eunice, you sent away the servants. You can't stay here."

Eunice gave a gulping sob. "Just tonight. Please!"

"I will have to stay with you."

Eunice shrugged. "Please yourself but I am not leaving."

Harriet stood looking down at the girl, torn with indecision. She could hardly drag her bodily from the house.

"If you promise you will come with me in the morning," she said at last, "I will spend the night here with you."

"Would you?"

"Of course. You can't be by yourself."

Harriet returned to the front hall, where Simon and Musa waited.

"She's very distressed and won't leave so I'll stay here with her tonight and hopefully in the morning she will be more amenable."

"I can't leave you here, Harriet," Simon said.

"Nonsense. Musa is here and you have guests at the beach house. Go back to them and I'll rejoin you tomorrow morning, with Eunice."

Simon glanced at Musa. "If you are sure . . ."

She smiled and laid a hand on his chest. "Musa will be here. Go, Simon. I'll see you in the morning."

She stood at the front door, waving as Simon drove away.

"Send the policeman away too."

Harriet turned. Eunice stood at the top of the stairs, looking down on the hall. Harriet wondered how long she had been there.

"I can't. Musa is under orders from Inspector Curran."

Eunice sniffed and turned back to the bedrooms. Harriet gave Musa a shrug and went in search of Eunice. The girl led her down a dark corridor and threw a door open. "You can sleep here. I think the bed is made up. I will find one of Elspeth's nightdresses for you."

"Thank you. Which bedroom is yours?"

Eunice hesitated. "You want to see my bedroom?"

"I thought I could help you find something clean and fresh to wear."

Eunice blinked. "Oh." She looked down at her dress. "I suppose so."

Harriet wasn't sure what she had been expecting. Her knowledge of young girls was limited to her niece, Fleur, who was much the same age as Eunice. While Fleur lived in a confusion of lace and frills, flowers and furbelows, Eunice's bedroom could not have been more different. Nothing was out of place . . . the bed had been made with military precision, shoes were neatly lined up beside the wardrobe and every item on the girl's dressing table looked like it had been arranged with a ruler.

"I don't like untidy places," Eunice said. "Elspeth was always leaving things around the place. I would have to pick up after her."

Interesting that she now referred to her stepmother by her given name.

"May I . . . ?" Harriet indicated the wardrobe. Like the room, it had been ordered by type of garment and color. There were some blouses and dresses in bright colors trimmed with lace and ribbons, which had probably been selected by Elspeth. She had never seen Eunice wear them. She selected a light-gray frock and held it out.

"Will this do?"

Eunice nodded. "I don't care much for clothes and such things," the girl said, stepping out of her sad mourning dress. "Elspeth wanted me to be more like normal girls but I hated the clothes she chose for me. I had to wear them when I was little, but when I turned fifteen, I refused to let her buy me anything more."

"It is important to be true to yourself," Harriet said, helping to button the dress at the back. "Sit down and I will do something with your hair."

Eunice sat down on the stool at her dressing table and stared at her wan expression in the mirror. "Elspeth was so pretty. All the men liked her," she said. "No one ever noticed me."

"You're only young. Some people take a little while to grow into themselves." Harriet picked up a silver-backed hairbrush embellished with the letter *S* entwined with ivy leaves. "Was this your mother's?"

Eunice nodded. "Her name was Sarah."

Harriet pulled the pins from the inadequate roll of hair and began brushing it out. From the knots and snags, it hadn't been given a good brush in days.

Tears started in Eunice's eyes and Harriet stopped. "Am I hurting you?"

"No. You just made me remember that Mama used to brush my hair every night . . . before she died."

"How did she die?"

Eunice wiped her eyes with the back of her hand. "Papa said she slipped and fell in the river near where we lived."

"I'm sorry," Harriet said.

"She was very unhappy. I remember her hugging me and saying how much she loved me."

"That's a lovely memory to have."

"Except she was crying."

"Elspeth was kind to you though?"

Eunice shrugged. "She wasn't unkind but she had been on and on at Papa about sending me to school in England. I wouldn't leave. I've lived here nearly all my life. I don't know anyone in England." Her voice rose.

"You'd soon make friends at school."

Beneath Harriet's hands, Eunice shook her head with a vehemence that caused Harriet to drop the hairbrush.

"Alicia said the same thing. Alicia wanted Papa all to herself. That's why she . . ."

Harriet's blood ran cold. "Why she . . . ?"

"Nothing."

Eunice lapsed into silence and Harriet wound the girl's hair into a loose, flattering knot in the nape of her head. "There," she said. "Do you like that?"

"Thank you," Eunice said. "Can you put this into the knot?"

She opened a drawer on her dressing table and took out a tortoiseshell hair comb inlaid with silver.

Harriet took it, turning it over in her hands. The very touch of the object sent a cold shiver down her spine. She forced a smile as she said, "This is lovely. Didn't Alicia Sewell have one very similar to this?"

Eunice nodded. "Alicia gave it to me. She said as Papa had given it to her, it was only right I should have it."

Harriet positioned the beautiful comb in the knot she had just made, and for the first time in all her acquaintance, Eunice Lovett smiled, twisting her head so she could see better.

Harriet studied the girl's reflection in the mirror. Eunice Lovett . . . plain, unloved, neglected . . . a killer? Maybe Alicia really had given her the comb, maybe . . . but Harriet's instinct was screaming at her.

Had Eunice been harboring a fancy for Tony Dowling? Harriet recalled the incident with the cup of tea she had saved for him, the callous way he had taken it without acknowledgment. Had she followed Elspeth on her rendezvous with Tony out of spite for her stepmother or her own infatuation with the young man? Jealousy could be a powerful motive to hurt someone.

Oblivious to Harriet's dark thoughts, Eunice swiveled on her stool. "I like you, Mrs. Gordon. Would you like me to show you my secret place?"

"Is that at the old house?"

Eunice nodded. "No one knows about it except me."

"I would very much like to see your secret place," Harriet said. "But first I better check in the kitchen and see if there is anything to eat for our supper."

She left Eunice still sitting by the mirror admiring her reflection and hurried down the stairs.

She signaled to Musa, and he followed her into the kitchen area.

After checking to see Eunice hadn't followed her, Harriet took a breath.

"I need you to take a message to the inspector," she said in a low voice.

"I cannot leave my post."

"You can for this. Tell him to come to the old McKinnon plantation house as fast as he possibly can."

"Are you in danger, mem?"

Harriet shook her head. "No. I don't think so, but I think the inspector may have arrested the wrong person. Go, Musa."

Before she left the kitchen, she took the precaution of finding a small sharp knife, which she tucked into her pocket.

She found Eunice waiting in the front hall. "Where is the policeman going?"

"I've sent him to the nearest market to find us some supper. There is nothing in the kitchen."

Eunice shrugged. "I'm not hungry."

"But I am, and I am sure Constable Musa is too. Shall we go?"

Eunice led her down the long drive. The quiet tree-lined street was silent, the neighboring properties set well back behind gates and a fence, and across the road, the drowsing silence of the old McKinnon plantation, surrounded by a decaying wall. Harriet turned right, heading for Cairnhill Road and the main entrance to the property, but Eunice grasped her sleeve.

"There is a shortcut," she said, leading Harriet away from the main road.

Harriet pulled back. She had told Musa she had no fear for her own life and she still believed that, but the girl was unpredictable and could turn on her.

"It's going to be dark soon," she said. "Let's go back to the house and wait for the constable."

"We'll be really quick. I just want to show you my secret place," Eunice said, and before Harriet could stop her the girl jumped a ditch and disappeared behind a large bush, leaving Harriet with no choice but to follow.

Behind the bush, the wall had fallen into disrepair and Eunice scrambled over it, looking back to ensure Harriet was behind her but always staying just beyond Harriet's reach.

The short twilight had already faded, plunging the property with its ancient, overgrown trees into darkness. If there had been a path, Harriet couldn't see it and she had to rely on keeping Eunice in sight as she tripped and stumbled over the undergrowth.

They reached the edge of the tree line and the old house loomed above them. Eunice stood looking up at it.

"Isn't it beautiful?" she said as Harriet, puffing from the unaccustomed exertion and damp with perspiration, joined her.

Beautiful was not a word Harriet would have used. Every hair on the back of her neck prickled and her breath came in short gasps.

✵ THIRTY-THREE

South Bridge Road on a late Saturday afternoon drowsed in the tropical torpor. The little interview room with its one window, high up in the wall, was unbearably stuffy and the sweat trickled down the back of Curran's neck as he sat across the battered table from Charles Lovett.

"You have my confession," Lovett said. "I'm not saying anything else."

Curran looked at the notes in his notebook. In effect all he had was *I did it*.

"Tell me more about the weapon you used?" he pursued.

Lovett shrugged. "A knife."

"Describe it."

"It was just a knife." Lovett's voice held a nasty edge to it. "Really, Inspector, I've had enough of these questions. Just let me sign the confession and be done with it."

Curran sat back in his chair and surveyed the man. He knew without a shadow of a doubt that Lovett was lying.

"And your wife . . . ?"

Lovett's head snapped up. "I had nothing to do with her death. It was an accident."

"Or suicide?"

The man's mouth tightened.

"Or . . . murder?" Curran suggested.

"Murder? Not murder," Lovett whispered, and lowered his head into his hands. "I've said enough. Just be done with it, Curran."

A knock on the door came as a welcome relief. Singh opened it and Constable Musa stood outside.

"May I speak with you, Inspector?" he said.

Curran left the interview room and gestured to the courtyard. He pulled out his battered cigarette case, annoyed to find it empty. Shoving it back in his pocket, he took a deep breath of what passed for fresh air.

"You should be at the Lovett house," he said.

Musa shifted from one foot to the other. "I have a message from Mrs. Gordon. She says you are to come at once to the McKinnon house."

"Why?"

Musa paused. "She says you may have arrested the wrong person."

Curran frowned. "What did she mean by that?"

Musa shrugged. "I do not know. There is only her and Miss Lovett at the house."

Curran stared at the young constable as the import of Harriet's words fell into place.

"The wrong person," he repeated.

The murders had nothing to do with insurance frauds or jilted lovers and everything to do with an overlooked, underestimated young girl. Lovett's confession had never rung true because he was protecting the one person in his life he had a duty to protect—his daughter. Had Eunice been jealous of her mother's relationship with Tony Dowling and, more chillingly, her father's relationship with Alicia Sewell?

Eunice Lovett was the one common thread binding all three deaths and he had left Harriet alone with her.

He ordered Musa to find Tan and bring out the motor vehicle and returned to the interview room.

Lovett sagged in the uncomfortable chair, his tie undone and his hair sticking damply to his face. He hardly bothered to straighten himself at Curran's entrance.

"For God's sake, get this over with, Curran," he said, his tone low and flat . . . and resigned.

Curran leaned his hands on the table and looked down at Lovett. "I know why you're lying to me. It's because you know who the real murderer is."

The color drained from Lovett's face. "I don't know what you mean."

"You think the murderer is your own daughter."

Lovett sprang to his feet. "You don't understand . . . she's fragile . . . she's only a child."

"She's seventeen. Not really a child, Lovett, and she has murdered two, if not three, people," Curran said grimly.

Lovett flinched. "You don't know that." But his words lacked conviction.

"It certainly wasn't you," Curran said.

"Where is she?"

"She is alone at the McKinnon house with Mrs. Gordon. Is Mrs. Gordon in danger?"

"No, she has no reason to hurt Mrs. Gordon." An unspoken "but" hung in the air.

Curran turned to his sergeant. "Get the motor vehicle, we need to get up to the McKinnon property."

"I'm coming with you," Lovett said. When Curran hesitated, he added, "Please. She'll listen to me."

Curran gave a curt nod. He just hoped Lovett was correct and Eunice would not hurt Harriet. If anything happened to her . . . He shook off the paralyzing sense of foreboding and made for the door.

❧ THIRTY-FOUR

Eunice stood looking up at the old house. "Papa says it will be torn down. His client has lots of wealthy people, Peranakan mostly, who want to buy properties in this area. He says it will be a very good investment . . ."

"You think a great deal of your father," Harriet said.

Eunice nodded without taking her gaze off the house. "He's clever and he's so funny when he is on the stage. Don't you think so, Mrs. Gordon?"

"He is," Harriet agreed with complete honesty. She gathered her jangling nerves together and said, in what she hoped sounded like a normal voice, "So, where is this secret place?"

Eunice turned and looked at Harriet. "Are you coming?"

Harriet resisted the urge to turn and run, but she closed her hand on the knife in her pocket as she followed Eunice across the grass to the old house.

As the house had been built up and into the hill behind it, there was by necessity a void beneath, which had been covered from view by a wooden lattice, covered in rampant bougainvillea and other creepers growing up and around it. Harriet followed Eunice to the farthest end of the building, where the verandah wrapped around the house. Eunice stopped and lifted aside the creeper, revealing a gap in the rotting latticework.

"In here," she said.

"Are there spiders?" Harriet asked. "Snakes?"

Eunice looked pained. "No, I keep it very tidy."

"What about ghosts?" Harriet said with a forced smile.

Eunice turned to look at her, her eyes unfathomable in the dark.

"Oh, there are ghosts," she said, "but they won't hurt us. They're afraid of me."

Harriet took a breath and followed where the girl led, convinced she felt a spider crawling down the back of her neck. A match struck and a kerosene lamp hissed. Eunice held it up, revealing a small whitewashed room, immaculately kept like her bedroom.

A shelf held books and a notebook and a neatly arranged array of sharpened pencils. An old armchair that must have been difficult to wrangle into the space had been covered with a bright sari and on the wooden walls, affixed with thumbtacks, were pencil drawings, expertly done, and all of Tony Dowling in different poses and moods. It left no doubt as to the identity of the creator of the anonymous drawing that had been sent to Dowling.

Harriet crossed to the wall of drawings. "These are terribly good. I would love you to do a drawing of my son."

The word *son* had come out without conscious thought. She had, of course, meant Will but saying *ward* felt so clinical.

Eunice reached out and touched one of the drawings, tracing the lines of her pencil with her finger. "He was so beautiful," she said. "I loved drawing him."

"Did he sit for you?"

The girl's eyes widened. "Oh no. I used to sketch him in rehearsals when he couldn't see me."

Harriet turned around to scan the room, her eye on the door through which they had come. "You've made this very comfortable. It looks like you come here often."

"Nearly every day. It was difficult when I had a governess so I made sure they never lasted long."

Harriet's gaze came to rest on the one incongruous object in the room . . . a woman's large leather handbag had been placed on the shelf beside the books. She recognized it at once. Elspeth Lovett's missing handbag. Beside it the silver stopper for a brandy flask sat like a trophy.

Her blood ran cold.

Eunice's eyes crinkled with pleasure as she lifted the lamp, looking around her den. "But there's more. You see that door?"

The light shone on a low doorway at the far end of the room. Eunice lifted the latch and beyond it Harriet could see a narrow flight of stairs winding up, presumably to the verandah.

"The stupid policemen never found it." Eunice walked toward the door.

Harriet would be having strong words with the "stupid policemen" when she next saw them.

"Coming?" Eunice turned to look at her.

Harriet had to duck her head to avoid hitting it on the lintel. The circular stairs ended in a trapdoor. Eunice lifted it easily and it opened silently on oiled hinges. As Harriet climbed out through it, she could see the stairs came out onto the very end of the verandah, concealed behind a lattice screen. Nobody would have thought to look beyond the lattice, thinking it just covered the dirt bank into which the house had been dug. In the days of the working plantation, the room below could well have been servants' quarters or a storeroom or even a wine cellar.

"You need to crawl here," Eunice said, going down on her hands and knees. She swung a part of the lattice away, revealing an opening large enough to crawl through. Harriet followed. They came out under a rickety old table that had been pushed hard against the lattice.

Harriet straightened and looked back at the way they had come. All the people who attended rehearsals here over so many previous years would not have thought twice about the table and the secret it concealed.

"No one would know you were there," Harriet said aloud. "What a wonderful hiding place."

"Isn't it?" Eunice giggled, "But it's our secret now. Don't tell anyone else."

Harriet crossed her fingers behind her back. "Of course not."

She followed Eunice around to the front of the house, where the gate to the entrance stairs still stood open. Eunice set the kerosene lamp on the floor beside the door to the house and produced a key from a chain around her neck.

She unlocked the door and opened it. Standing to one side, she turned back to Harriet and threw her arms wide. "This is all mine when no one is here. I can pretend I am a princess in a castle."

Eunice picked up the kerosene lamp and carried it into the house. She executed a pirouette in the middle of the floor of the rehearsal room.

"I am the star of every show," she said, and not for the first time, Harriet felt a pang of sympathy for the overlooked and neglected child. Sympathy that evaporated with the thought that Eunice was also a killer.

In the costume room, Eunice set the lamp on the table.

"I get to wear all the costumes," Eunice said. "Phyllis in *Iolanthe* is my favorite." She selected the Arcadian shepherdess's costume and held it to her. "Of course, Alicia was too old to play Phyllis. It would look much better on me and then I could have kissed Tony. I told Papa I wanted to be in the next show but he just laughed and said I had no talent."

Eunice replaced the costume and wandered idly around the room, skimming the racks of clothes with her fingers before returning to the table. She picked up the long-bladed, pointed scissors Harriet had used to cut the ribbon for her costume, only a week earlier.

"These are so sharp," Eunice said, running a thumb over the edge. "Elspeth hated blunt scissors." She opened and shut them several times. "They were so hard to clean."

"Clean?" Harriet asked, and when Eunice gave her a quizzical glance, she realized she was looking at the murder weapon . . . in the hands of the murderer.

"Put them down, Eunice, and let's go home. I'm sure the constable will be back with our supper." As she spoke, she took several steps back, ensuring she had a clear escape route if Eunice decided to turn the scissors on her.

"Tony kissed me, you know?" Eunice said.

"Did he?" Harriet's fingers tightened on the knife in her pocket. She drew it out, hiding it in the folds of her skirt.

"He kissed me, and I let him touch me." Two spots of color appeared on the girl's cheeks, and she looked up at Harriet. "It was terribly wrong, but I thought if I let him touch me like he touched Elspeth, he would love me."

"When was this?"

"Just after *Pirates* started. He came out to the kitchen, where I was making tea. That's when I gave him a drawing I had done. He said it was so good, he would send it to his sister and that's when he kissed me. Not a proper kiss at first, but I put my arms around his neck and made him kiss me properly and . . . the other thing."

"Was that the only time?"

Eunice's mouth drooped. "He said it was our secret and I was not to tell anyone but he never seemed to find the chance to be alone with me."

I'm not surprised, thought Harriet. Even Tony Dowling had some scruples.

"Did you used to come to your secret place on the nights Tony brought his friends up here?"

She scowled. "Tony would bring women here all the time. Sometimes in the rehearsal room but mostly on the verandah.

He didn't know about my secret place and I would watch them. I wanted it to be me so badly. Then he started bringing Elspeth and I knew that was wrong. It would make Papa unhappy if he knew Elspeth was seeing Tony . . ." She paused. "It made me unhappy. I thought he liked me better than Elspeth."

"What happened that last night, Eunice?" Harriet tried to keep her voice calm and reassuring.

"Which night?"

"The night Tony died."

Eunice used the scissors to point in the direction of the verandah. "They were out here . . . doing *it*. I was so angry. He loved *me*, not Elspeth. I had to make Elspeth see that it was me he wanted, not her."

"What did you do?" Harriet's mouth had gone dry, and the words came out in a high, tight voice.

"I didn't mean to hurt him." Eunice turned her gaze on Harriet, her eyes wide and pleading.

"I'm sure you didn't."

Eunice held the scissors up and examined them. "I had heard Papa telling Elspeth it had to end but she didn't listen. I had to help Papa so I slipped in through the back door and picked these up and went out onto the verandah. When I shouted at them to stop, he jumped up and ran at me . . . he just sort of ran into the scissors," she said. "Elspeth was screaming and he fell down on the blanket and just lay there with blood coming out of his mouth and he was gurgling." She blinked a few times. "And then Elspeth said he was dead."

"What did Elspeth do?"

"She took the scissors and hugged me and told me it was an accident." She looked up at Harriet, her eyes wide. "It was an accident, Mrs. Gordon. You have to believe me."

"I believe you," Harriet said, her mouth dry.

"It was Elspeth's idea to make it look like he had been caught in a fire. We used the blanket to drag him to the scenery store.

It took so long. He was so heavy. We put his clothes back on. That was embarrassing . . . men are very funny-looking, aren't they, Mrs. Gordon?"

Harriet said nothing, letting Eunice paint a vivid picture of the events of Sunday, 30th October.

"There was a lot of blood so we cleaned it all up. Mama found the can of kerosene and we splashed it everywhere and tossed in the rags we'd used to clean the floor. She had some matches and we stood at the door and threw matches in." Eunice's eyes widened. "It was magical. I couldn't stop watching but Mama shut the door and bolted it and said we had to go home."

"What did she do with the scissors?" Harriet asked.

"She washed them and put them back in the costume room."

Harriet's flesh crawled at the thought of picking up those scissors and cutting the ribbon.

"I think, Eunice, you need to tell Inspector Curran everything you just told me. If you explain it was an accident—"

"Why? Why should I tell Inspector Curran?"

Harriet stared at the girl. "Your father knows what you did, Eunice."

"I didn't tell him."

Harriet thought about Curran's short note to her. "I think your papa guessed and he has told Inspector Curran he was responsible. He is trying to protect you."

Eunice blinked. "That's what he said to me, he told me it would be all right. He always makes things right." Her eyes widened. "What will happen to him? What will happen to me?"

Harriet ignored the question. Charles Lovett would hang and his daughter would be sent to relatives in England, who would be ignorant of the fact they were harboring a murderer.

"What about your mother? Was that an accident too?" Harriet prompted. The knife in her hand was slick with sweat and she shifted her grip slightly.

Eunice bit her lip. "It was her own silly fault. She came looking for me up here. She didn't know about the secret place. She climbed the front steps, even though we're not supposed to use them, and left the gate open. When she couldn't find me, she sat down on the daybed in the rehearsal room and drank her flask empty." Her nose wrinkled. "She had been drinking all day so I waited until she had finished and then I came to the front door and told her to come out onto the verandah and I hid. I threw a rock into the garden and she came to the stairs calling my name and she . . . she lost her balance and fell."

"Did you push her?"

Eunice said nothing, leaving Harriet in no doubt that Eunice had assisted her stepmother's tumble to her death. It wouldn't have taken much if Elspeth was already unsteady on her feet.

"And Alicia?"

Eunice stiffened, brandishing the scissors. "Alicia." She spat the name out with such venom that Harriet took a step backward. "I thought Alicia was my friend, but she wasn't. It was Papa she wanted. She came to see Papa." The bitterness in the girl's voice sent a cold shiver down Harriet's spine. "The study door was partly open, and I saw them kissing and I heard Alicia tell Papa that I should go to school in England while she got a divorce from her horrid husband."

"So, you took your scissors and went to her home in the dead of night?" Harriet said between stiff lips.

Eunice nodded. "It was so easy. She was asleep so I made sure she didn't wake up again."

"Oh, Eunice," Harriet said.

Eunice opened and shut the scissors with an ominous click. "I shouldn't have told you any of that," she said. "You'll probably tell that beastly policeman."

"Why don't you give me the scissors?" Harriet tried to keep her voice calm.

Eunice turned the weapon over in her hand, as if studying it, while she calculated her next move. Harriet tightened her grip on the knife and started to edge toward the door.

Eunice looked up. "What was that?"

Harriet heard it now, the unmistakable growl of a motor vehicle coming up the driveway.

Eunice turned to her. "You told him! You betrayed me . . ."

Harriet didn't wait to hear any more, she turned and ran, through the open door, across the verandah and down the rickety flight of steps, stumbling to her knees at the bottom. A strong hand seized her arm and pulled her up.

Curran.

He didn't relinquish his grip on her, pushing her behind him as he drew the Webley from its holster. Eunice stopped at the top of the stairs, the scissors brandished in her right hand. She stood, swaying slightly, her gaze fixed on a point over Curran's shoulder. Harriet followed her gaze.

Charles Lovett stood beside the motor vehicle with Sergeant Singh.

"Eunice!" her father shouted. "Put those scissors down, and come down here like the good girl I know you are."

Eunice shook her head. "But I'm not good, Papa."

"I know what you've done, sweetheart. It will all be fine."

Eunice's gaze swung to Curran and she pointed at Harriet.

"I'm not silly," she said. "I've told her everything and there's nothing you can do to make it right, Papa."

She turned and walked back into the house, reappearing with the kerosene lamp. She raised it over her head and dropped it to the ground a few feet behind her. The glass shattered and the light went out. She turned and kicked it back toward the house.

Below her, no one moved for a very long moment.

One tiny pinprick of light briefly illuminated Eunice Lovett's face as she struck a match. It fell from her fingers to the floor and the kerosene from the broken lamp ignited in an instant.

"Eunice, no!" Lovett screamed.

Curran pulled Harriet to him, pressing her face into his chest. Harriet twisted in time to see Eunice Lovett poised at the top of the steps, a dark silhouette against the flames that greedily lapped at the tinder-dry wood of the old house. As flames caught at the hem of her dress, she spread her arms wide and fell forward, tumbling down the stairs before coming to rest on the ground, one leg resting on the lower risers, the other bent beneath her.

Above her the fire had taken hold of the ancient building, flames licking around the doorway, spreading into the rehearsal room and the costume store.

Singh ran to the girl, his own weapon in his hand. The fall had doused the flames that had caught her dress and Eunice lay quite still in much the same position as her stepmother had been found only a few days earlier.

Singh looked up at Curran and shook his head, holstering his Webley. "Neck's broken. Probably a mercy."

Lovett sank to his knees, his face buried in his hands, sobs racking his body.

Harriet turned back to Curran and buried her face in his tunic again. The arm around her shoulder tightened.

"You shouldn't have had to see that," he said, and he wrapped both his arms around her.

She closed her eyes and embraced the moment, safe in this man's arms—where she belonged.

Distantly she heard the clang of the fire brigade truck coming up the hill toward them. Curran disengaged her, straightening his tunic as he turned to meet Monty Pett.

As the old house burned, Singh had moved the body of Eunice Lovett away from the flames and laid her on the grass.

Lovett knelt beside his daughter, holding her hand, a broken man. His jacket covered her head and torso. Swallowing her revulsion, Harriet walked over to Lovett and laid a hand on his shoulder. He rose to his feet.

"You were with her?"

Harriet nodded.

"What did she say?"

"Everything," Harriet said.

Lovett sighed and ran a hand across his eyes. "I knew she was a troubled child, but I had no idea that she was capable of murder. Her mother was not well. She took her own life, that's why I kept Eunice with me. I thought I could protect her." He spread his hands. "But I got distracted with work . . . the society. Elspeth had known my first wife and I married her with the understanding that Eunice was special and needed to be watched. Maybe I just didn't pay enough attention."

No, Harriet thought. *You were too busy to notice your wife was an alcoholic and your daughter was running wild without any firm hand to guide and control her.*

"I honestly don't think she intended to kill Tony Dowling," Harriet said, "but your wife and Alicia Sewell—"

"Elspeth? She was responsible for Elspeth's death?" Lovett's voice cracked.

"From what she said, I am fairly certain Eunice pushed her down the stairs."

Lovett groaned and he glanced down at his daughter's body. "Perhaps it is as well that she ended it. Her life would have been unendurable."

Harriet thought about Eunice's fate. She probably wouldn't have hanged for her crimes but she would have spent the rest of her life in an asylum. Death would have been preferable.

"Lovett?" Curran strode across to them both.

The man straightened. "I think I would like to go home, Inspector." Even as he spoke, he started to walk away.

Curran nodded to Musa. "Go with him and stay. Make sure he is safe."

Musa nodded and turned to follow the Englishman, who wove an uneven path back down the driveaway toward the main road.

Curran watched until Lovett was out of sight. Taking Harriet's arm, he guided her to the bench under the rain tree and they sat for a moment in silence watching the old McKinnon plantation house burn to the ground.

At Curran's prompt, Harriet went through the events of the night and the conversation with Eunice. He said nothing, just let her talk.

"What an utter mess," he said when she was done. "All those lives shattered because of a child's obsession."

"She may not have intended to kill Tony Dowling but the others?" Harriet shivered. "She took souvenirs—the stopper from Elspeth's flask and the hair comb from Alicia . . . and fire. She liked fire . . . The way she described watching the fire in the scenery store . . ." She shivered.

"I should never have put you in such danger, Harriet. I knew Lovett was lying. I should have guessed the reason."

"Why? You had no real reason to suspect Eunice. That was how it was with Eunice. No one ever really saw her for who she was. We all overlooked her."

Curran shook his head. "If I hadn't been so caught up with— Enough. You've had a hell of an evening. I am guessing there's no one at home?"

"Just Aziz. Huo Jin and Lokman are visiting family while we're away."

"Then I will take you to Lavinia's," he said.

He stood up and held out a hand, pulling her to her feet. He put an arm around her shoulder, and as they walked down the driveway to the motor vehicle, she leaned into him, grateful that he had taken charge and none of it was her responsibility anymore.

✂ THIRTY-FIVE

Sunday, 13 November

Whatever Lavinia Pemberthey-Smythe had put in Harriet's drink, it had the desired effect. She slept long and deeply and, more important, without dreams.

On a bright, sunny morning that seemed a long way removed from the dark events of the previous night, she sat with her hostess on the verandah enjoying the last of a leisurely breakfast. She'd also enjoyed a long bath and, with her own clothes reeking of smoke, Lavinia had loaned her a dark-blue *salwar kameez*.

"I expected Robert before now," Lavinia remarked, rising to greet Curran as he swung off the horse and tethered Leo in the shade before striding up the steps to the two women. Lavinia gestured at an empty chair, poured a cup of tea and gave him a long, hard, appraising look.

"Did you get any sleep last night, Curran?"

He shrugged. "An hour or two, maybe." He looked Harriet up and down and smiled. "Good morning, Mrs. Gordon. That is a fetching ensemble."

An unexpected heat rose in Harriet's cheeks. "It is certainly comfortable," she said.

"I've just come from seeing Charles Lovett," Curran said.

"How is he?" Harriet asked.

"Shattered," Curran said.

"From what Harriet tells me, the sad fact is the child was deeply troubled," Lavinia said. "An unstable mother, a father too busy to notice her and a stepmother who had little or no interest in her. Little wonder she lost herself in a world of her own. In some ways, we should be thankful she is at peace," Lavinia said. "I suppose you're here to speak to Harriet?"

"I wrote down everything I told you last night while it was still fresh." Harriet handed him a sheaf of notepaper.

Curran sat back and read through her notes. When he was done, he set them on the table. "I'm glad to shut the book on this case before tomorrow."

"Tomorrow?" Lavinia said.

"I've been suspended."

"Good heavens. How long?" Lavinia said.

"Indefinitely."

Harriet stared at him. "Was this because of Ellis?"

"Yes."

"What did you do?" Lavinia asked.

Curran smiled. "I broke his nose and I would do so again."

"Oh, Robert. You really should have known better," Lavinia said.

"Of course. Sometimes we can't always be sensible," Curran said. "I'm damned if I'm going to apologize. So Cuscaden has told me to cool my heels."

"But who is going to replace you?" Harriet hoped she didn't sound as despondent as she felt.

He glanced at her. "A man called Keogh from Kuala Lumpur."

He didn't elaborate and neither woman pressed him.

"What will you do?" Lavinia asked.

"I have a personal matter to pursue," Curran said.

"You're going to look for your sister?" Harriet put in.

"Maybe." He rose to his feet. "I better be going. I need to get the paperwork in order before I hand everything over to Keogh. Harriet, what do you want to do now? I can take you back to the beach house, or home—"

"On the back of a horse?" Lavinia snorted.

Curran shot her a sharp glance. "I can send a motor vehicle."

"I can get myself home," Harriet said. "And then I'll come into South Bridge Road this afternoon and type up your final reports."

Curran's gaze met hers and she found herself unable to look away.

"That would be a kindness. I would prefer to leave with a clear desk," he said. "Harriet, I nearly forgot. I collected your handbag from the Lovetts'. I thought you might be missing it."

Harriet hadn't given her bag a second thought but now she realized she had left it behind when she had gone out for the last fateful walk with Eunice Lovett.

She followed him down to Leopold, who lifted his head and nickered a greeting. She stroked the horse's long nose while Curran retrieved her handbag.

She took the proffered object, which looked a bit the worse for wear for being stuffed in a saddlebag. She thanked him and stood back as he swung into the saddle. She raised a hand in farewell as he turned Leopold back out onto Scotts Road.

Lavinia poured them both another cup of tea and the two women sat in silence for a long moment before Lavinia set her cup down. "You know, my dear, it is a very bad idea to fall in love with men like Robert Curran."

Harriet started, the cup rattling in her saucer. "What on earth do you mean?"

"I'm not blind, Harriet Gordon." Lavinia leaned over and

patted her hand. "I see the way you look at him. But Curran has his own dragons to slay before there will be room for another woman."

"That is an unfortunate analogy," Harriet said.

"I don't mean literally. The bond with Li An is one not so easily severed as either would believe and now there is his father's legacy to resolve."

Harriet looked down at her hands in her lap. She felt like she had been caught playing truant by one of her school mistresses.

"And then there is the matter of your Australian?"

Harriet sighed. "He's not *my* Australian, Lavinia."

"I'm not sure he sees it that way."

"He wants me to go with him to Australia—just a visit. No expectations."

Lavinia raised her eyebrows. "And what did you say?"

"Nothing. I haven't given him an answer."

"But the answer was written on your face when you looked at Curran, Harriet. I am just asking you to be careful."

Harriet stood up and paced the verandah. "But that's the problem, Lavinia. I'm always careful."

"Are you? May I remind you that you are the one person of my acquaintance with a criminal record. There is a degree of impetuosity about you, Harriet, that you hide behind a very thin veneer of sensibility. I am just suggesting that whatever you and Curran enjoy in the way of friendship is also something precious and something you should not want to damage."

"Oh, I know," Harriet said, and her voice cracked. "I know . . . and you're right." She glanced at her watch. "I really must leave you and go home. I need a change of clothes if I am going into South Bridge Road. Thank you for your hospitality."

Lavinia stood up and folded the other woman in her arms.

"Just think about what I said, Harriet. Don't do or say anything you will regret."

Harriet pushed away and shook her head. "I have too much at stake to risk my heart so easily, Lavinia."

Lavinia patted her cheek. "My brave suffragette. Remember, deeds not words!"

❧ THIRTY-SIX

Monday, 14 November

The strong scent of a familiar tobacco smoke caused Harriet to pause at the gate to St. Thomas House. She knew at once who waited for her. She picked up her skirt and hurried around to the front of the house.

Curran sat on the top step leading up to the verandah, casually dressed in gray flannel trousers and a linen shirt, no tie and with the sleeves rolled up. He looked the picture of insouciance, his forearms resting loosely on his knees and a pith helmet on the ground beside him.

Seeing Harriet, he knocked out his pipe and stood up.

"Curran." His name came out in a breathy rush. "I'm getting used to finding you on my front doorstep."

"Sorry to bother you again," he said, "but I have a small favor to ask."

Anything.

"That entirely depends on what it is," Harriet said.

He stood aside and indicated two wooden tea chests. "I'm rather hoping you can look after these for me."

The breath caught in her throat. "You're leaving Singapore?"

He shrugged. "Yes."

"But you'll be back?"

"Maybe. I've given up the bungalow. When . . . if . . . I come back, I'll go into the police lines so it seemed pointless keeping the house."

"But you're only suspended . . ." The note in her voice rose. He couldn't be leaving . . . not forever.

He took the few steps toward her, catching her hands in his. He looked down at her ink-stained fingers as if seeing them for the first time. When he looked up at her, she saw a softness in his face she had never seen before and his smile lit his gray eyes.

"You have taught me the value of friendship . . . You and Julian and the rest, but I think you understand why I have to go. I have to find my sister—Samrita." The name sounded stilted as if he were still getting used to saying it.

Her fingers tightened on his. "I understand," she whispered, although her heart broke. "Just promise me you will come back."

"Curran!"

At the sound of Will's voice, Curran drew back from her, stuffing his hands into the pockets of his trousers.

"Master Lawson, I am pleased to see you," he said.

Will looked from Curran to Harriet and his eyes narrowed. "What's happened?"

"I came to tell Mrs. Gordon that I have to go away for a little while."

Will's face dropped. "But the cricket club will miss you."

Harriet bit her lip to stop the laugh escaping.

"The cricket club will be fine without me," Curran said.

"You were going to show me how to do a leg sweep," Will persisted.

Curran pointed at the boxes on the verandah. "When I get back. In the meantime can you look after my cricket bat while I'm away. It will need oiling at least once a week. There is a jar of linseed oil in the box."

"I promise," Will said.

"And I am lending you all my gramophone," Curran said. "I even found a recording of *Pirates of Penzance* in Robinsons this afternoon."

Harriet shivered. "I think I have lost my taste for Gilbert and Sullivan. If you've given up the bungalow, what will happen to Mahmud?"

"He comes with the bungalow. I've paid him enough to keep him in comfort for a while."

"And Leo?" Will asked.

"I have left Leo with one of the racehorse trainers. He'll be quite happy and well looked after."

Will scooped up Shashti, who wound around his ankles, no doubt anxious for her evening meal. "Shashti will miss you."

Curran scratched the little cat's ears. "I will miss all of you. Tell the reverend I was sorry not to see him."

He turned and started to walk away, but when he had gone a few steps, he turned back and his eyes met Harriet's. "To answer your question, I will be back, Harriet. I promise."

She summoned a smile. "God keep you safe, Robert Curran."

Will leaned against her and she put an arm around his shoulders and swallowed back the tears that pricked the back of her eyes. She couldn't cry in front of the boy. That would be too shaming.

"Let's get Aziz and find a space in the box room," she said.

Will looked up at her and said with absolute certainty, "He always keeps his promises, Aunt Harriet."

THIRTY-SEVEN

Curran thrust his hands into his pockets and pulled his felt hat down low as he pushed past temple worshippers and the hawkers selling food from the pans they carried across their shoulders, and dodged around the large family groups sitting on stools along the five-foot ways. Pagoda Street at this time of night came alive but no one seemed to pay him much notice and he wondered if anyone recognized him out of his uniform.

He had hated lying to Harriet Gordon but he could give her no promises about his return from suspension because he had not been suspended.

Cuscaden had come to Curran's bungalow late on Sunday night, when Curran, exhausted from the events of the last few days and several whiskys, was drowsing in the chair on the verandah while he considered his plans.

He didn't think the inspector general knew where he lived, let alone would deign to come to his home at such an unusual time. Unbidden, Cuscaden sat down and poured himself a whisky.

"You know this was never about Ellis," Cuscaden said, without any preamble.

"I thought that was exactly who it was about," Curran replied.

"As far as I am concerned, you could have beaten the man

black-and-blue and I would have stood by and applauded, but you gave me the excuse I needed."

"To do what?"

Cuscaden drank down his whisky in one gulp. "I have a job for you, Curran."

"Too bad. You put me on suspension, and I have my own plans, Cuscaden."

Cuscaden shrugged. "Ah yes, your missing sister?"

"Damn it, how do you know that?"

Cuscaden smiled. "You keep forgetting I'm first and foremost a policeman, Curran. I make it my business to know things. You're quite free to continue your mission to find her." He paused, swilling the liquid in his glass. "I believe you will find that the two things may be related. Hear me out . . ."

And Curran had listened, and when the inspector general had finished, he had agreed to Cuscaden's proposal and to absolute secrecy.

Now he had one destination in mind, a noisome alley and the dark house with the heavy wooden door, Madam Lim's opium den. He hammered on the door with his fist and the grille slid open. A baleful eye regarded him without speaking before the bolt was slid back and Curran was admitted. The sickly smell of the opium almost threatened to overwhelm him, but he needed his wits about him.

Madam Lim . . . four and a half feet of vengeful spirit, looked up at him. "What you want, Curran?"

"You have a man working here. Jayant Kumar. I have to speak with him."

"What is your business with him?"

Curran regarded the woman for a long moment. "I suspect you already know."

She shrugged. "You want him, you fetch him. He's in there." She pointed to the main room, where the benches were filled with the bodies of the victims of opium and the heavy, sickening scent of the poppy hung in the humid air.

His face must have registered his disgust and dismay because she cackled, "You didn't know? I like to call it payment in kind. He keeps my books and I reward him."

Curran entered the den, his eyes adjusting to the dim light. The recumbent forms were drawn from all nationalities and all walks of life, including European. The fug of opium exacerbated by the airless humidity made his eyes water and he had to press his handkerchief to his nose and mouth to try and dissipate the effect of the atmosphere on his own senses.

He found Jayant at the farthest end of the room, the tray with opium pipe and equipment beside him. He drowsed, his eyes no more than narrow slits. Curran swore and grabbed the man by the front of his tunic, hauling him into a sitting position. Jayant was as boneless as a puppet in his grasp.

A slow smile spread across Jayant's face.

"Curran."

"You're coming with me."

"I don't think so." Jayant batted at Curran's hand.

Curran dragged the man to his feet and put one arm around his waist. Jayant's protests were lost as they made slow, clumsy progress through the room before encountering Madam Lim at the front door. She nodded to her doorman, and he opened the door. Curran turned to the woman. "Have his possessions sent up to my house."

She smiled beatifically. "Of course, Inspector Curran. My pleasure, Inspector Curran."

Curran spent an uncomfortable night in an armchair, while Jayant slept off his opium session in Curran's bed. He emerged close to lunchtime, unshaven, gray faced and wreaking of sweat.

Curran set down *The Decline and Fall of the Roman Empire* and looked his brother up and down without speaking.

"I am ashamed that you found me like that, Curran," Jayant said.

"Sit."

Curran gestured at the spare chair and poured the man a cup of tepid tea from the pot he had recently made for himself. Jayant downed the unedifying brew in one gulp.

"Tell me why?" Curran said.

"When I came to Singapore to look for you the first time, I fell into bad company. They took all my money, and I woke up in the gutter outside Madam Lim's. I don't know why she took me in, but she did. She needed a good bookkeeper and I needed a bed."

"Bookkeeper? I thought you worked in the kitchen."

"I did for a little while until she found my skills lay in other areas. I did not . . . indulge until my mother died and I returned to Singapore and found my way back to her door. I wanted to forget about Samrita, our mother . . . our father . . . and you."

"Are you addicted?"

Jayant looked straight at him. His pupils were still too large and in his silence he gave Curran the answer he sought.

Curran sighed. "I need you sober, Jayant."

"Why?"

"We are going to look for Samrita."

"You and I?"

"Yes . . . but before we start looking we are going to spend a few weeks in a place I know on the coast of Johor. I have another task to prepare for and I need to be absolutely sure you are not going to be looking for your next hit of opium."

Jayant blinked. "What is your other task?"

"I can't tell you just yet, but we are going to become people we are not. I am going to be an English m'lord and you are going to be my private secretary."

Jayant's eyes flashed. "Your servant? I am no one's servant."

"No. My private secretary. My manservant resigned and returned to England and I haven't replaced him."

Jayant shook his head. "I don't understand. Why must we go in disguise?"

"Because it will also help us find Samrita. You can stay here if you wish, but I would rather have you with me."

Jayant nodded. "No. That is all good, Curran. I am your brother. I will stand by your side."

Curran stood up. "Excellent. Now you can clean yourself up and we'll find something to eat in Chinatown. Then we will go shopping for some proper clothes for you." He considered his brother for a long moment. "Can you handle a weapon?"

"No. I am a man of peace."

Curran grinned. "If you want to come with me, you are going to learn how to handle a weapon . . . in a peaceful manner."

❧ THIRTY-EIGHT

Tuesday, 15 November

A dark cloud hung over the Detective Branch as Harriet entered it on Tuesday morning. Nabeel huddled at his desk, his head down. Gursharan Singh was notable by his absence and a European sergeant sat at his desk and several unfamiliar constables occupied the other desks. Only Constable Greaves looked up and gave her a wan smile.

A portly man of middle height sporting a large moustache and wearing an inspector's rank stepped out of Curran's office.

"Mrs. Gordon, I presume?"

She forced a smile and held out her hand. "Inspector Keogh? I'm here to help with the typing. I also do shorthand . . ."

She trailed off as he did not take her hand. Embarrassed, she withdrew it, clutching the handle of her bag tightly.

"In here." Keogh stood aside to admit her into Curran's office.

Not Curran's office, she had to admit. All evidence of Curran had been removed and replaced with a large photographic image of a plain woman and three children. Mrs. Keogh, Harriet presumed. She glanced at a chair, but he did not invite her to sit.

Keogh shut the door. He took up a position behind his desk

and picked up a paper that he appeared to study for a long, long moment before he looked up at her.

"It has come to my attention, Mrs. Gordon, that you are a criminal."

Harriet stared at the man. "I most certainly am not."

Keogh brandished the paper. "You have a criminal record and spent several months in Holloway. They don't put innocent people in Holloway. I don't know what lies you told to gain employment with the Straits Settlements Police—"

"I told no lies. Inspector Curran was aware of my history as, I believe, is the inspector general. My record pertains to an arrest and conviction for my involvement in the suffrage movement—"

"Something of which I strongly disapprove," Keogh said. He glanced at the photograph. "As does Mrs. Keogh. She calls you so-called suffragettes an insult to womanhood. Regardless of how you may view your past history, Mrs. Gordon, your continued employment in a position of trust cannot be tolerated. I am terminating whatever agreement you had with Inspector Curran, effective immediately."

Harriet's chin came up. She had no grounds to protest, and he knew it. She wasn't going to beg.

"Who will type your reports?" she inquired.

Keogh smiled. "The inspector general has no cause to complain about my handwriting," he said. "You may leave now. You may submit a final account and I will ensure that whatever money owing to you is paid in full."

Harriet paused only long enough to collect her few possessions from her desk. She bade Nabeel and Greaves farewell and with heavy steps made her way out into the courtyard, where she bumped into Gursharan Singh. She had a feeling he had been waiting for her.

She recounted her interview with Keogh and he shook his head.

"I am so sorry, Mrs. Gordon," he said.

"So am I," she said.

"If it is any consolation, he has relieved himself of my presence as well. I have been reassigned to traffic. Constable Musa has been returned to Changi and I think he has only kept Tan because he is useful with the motor vehicle and Greaves because he is—"

English, Harriet thought. "Useful with everything?" she said aloud. "But surely Curran is returning?"

Singh shrugged. "Who can say."

A weight settled on Harriet's shoulders. "Do you know where he is going?"

Singh shook his head. "No. It is none of my business . . . or yours, I fear, Mrs. Gordon. He will be back, or he may not. Let me walk you to the street."

With his hands behind his back, he matched his stride to hers.

"So many changes, Mrs. Gordon. Just last night my son, Hardit, tells me he does not wish to follow me into the police force. He wishes to go back to India and join the fight to rid our motherland of the colonial oppressors . . . his words, not mine," Singh said. "He was born here in Singapore, as was I, and yet he talks of India as his motherland. I do not think of it as such."

"I think," Harriet said slowly, "we are seeing many changes, Gursharan. My fight for the right of women to vote, for example, has just seen me lose a job I loved."

"What will you do now, Mrs. Gordon?"

Harriet shrugged. "I still have my work at the school." But even as she said it, a wave of fear washed over her. If word was getting around about her "criminal past," at some point the school's governors would have to confront it. "And I can always take private clients," she added.

Singh smiled. "Like Sir Oswald Newbold."

"Yes, but preferably not dead."

* * *

Julian took the news of her dismissal with surprising calm.

"We'll work things out, Harri." He glanced at the ceiling. "The good Lord has a plan."

Harriet was not quite sure she had such confidence in Julian's assertion, and when Simon arrived unexpectedly and asked her to join him for dinner, she viewed the distraction as more than welcome.

Over an excellent roast lamb with mint sauce at Raffles, she told him about losing her position with the Detective Branch. In turn he cross-examined her about the Lovett case and its sad outcome.

As she concluded her account of the events of Saturday night, Simon shook his head. "I knew I shouldn't have left you there alone. It didn't feel right."

Harriet shook her head. "You weren't to know . . . and I had no idea what I was walking into, but I'm safe, and it is all ended, albeit tragically."

He reached out and took her hand.

"Harriet . . . I've got something to tell you, and before you say anything, the telegram only came yesterday so I had no idea when I was speaking with you on Saturday."

Harriet's heart stopped for a fleeting moment.

He's not going to ask me to marry him! Please, not that . . .

"I've been summoned back to Melbourne," Simon said, and a wave of relief washed over Harriet.

"Oh," she said. "Is that unexpected?"

Simon shrugged. "Yes and no. When the boss whistles, we scribblers have to go."

"Do you know why?"

He smiled. "A promotion? Seriously, I have no idea. Perhaps there's a story they want me to chase." He paused. "You're free of obligations now, why don't you come with me?"

"I . . . I . . ." she stuttered. "I told you on Saturday, I can't just up and leave."

"But you've lost your job with the police."

"But I still have other responsibilities . . . Will, Julian . . . the school."

He looked away. "I know, but they can manage without you. I just hoped the offer of adventure . . ."

"You are the second person who has accused me, wrongly I might add, of being impulsive. Besides, from what you told me of Melbourne, it is a civilized city, hardly an adventure."

He smiled. "You're right, but I thought you might enjoy a bit of refinement you don't get here."

"I'm sorry, Simon," she said in what she hoped was a firm tone. "I have responsibilities here. I just cannot leave."

The disappointment in his face caused her to reach out and lay her hand over his. "I'm sorry. Not this time. Do you know when you will be back in Singapore?"

"Depends on the reason they want me in Melbourne." Simon shrugged.

Harriet summoned a smile. "I'll still be here."

"You're a good egg," he said. "I can hear the band striking up. How about we have a dance or two and forget about the world for the evening?"

As he drew her into his arms, Harriet found her mind wandering to her life here in this little corner of the world and she decided she really didn't want to leave. Despite the loss of a job she loved, she was fortunate to have Julian and Will and her friends: Griff Maddocks, Louisa and Euan Mackenzie, Lavinia Pemberthey-Smythe, Gursharan Singh and his wife, Sumeet Kaur and even the irascible Huo Jin.

Only two ghosts drifted on the outer fringes of her happiness . . . Khoo Li An and her new life in Penang and Robert Curran, cast adrift and lost somewhere, searching for his lost sister and his lost self.

HISTORICAL NOTES

One of the joys of research is populating the story with real people. You have already met the inspector general of the Straits Settlements Police, "Tim" Cuscaden, and "Mad" Ridley, the director of the Botanical Gardens. In this story you get to meet Montague Pett, who was responsible for the foundation of the professional fire brigade in Singapore. In my past life, I have worked with firefighters and I was delighted to find Monty. He came from a family of firefighters, served in the army in South Africa and came to Singapore in 1905 to set up the fire brigade. His legacy, the rather quaint red-and-cream fire station, is still to be seen on Hill Street. From Singapore he moved to Shanghai, where he served until 1926, bringing all manner of innovations to improve the fire service. He and his wife, Edie, lived in a delightful bungalow on the hill above the fire station in Singapore (which is now a restaurant, I think). It's definitely on my "must visit" list for my next trip to Singapore.

Another real person who is mentioned in the story is Frank Cooper Sands, the founder of the Singapore Scout movement. He formed the First Sands Troop with thirty boys (all English) with, I believe, the active support of Cuscaden. I hope we see a little more of Will and his scouting adventures in another story.

Again this is a bit of a personal side trip as I have also worked for the Scout Association in my past life.

Harriet and her friends and family and St. Thomas School are fictional as is the Detective Branch as I have imagined it (although there was a real detective branch in the Straits Settlements Police Force). Likewise the Balmoral Club, Caldwell & Hubbard Insurance and Robert White & Co. are also fictional.

As for the (also fictional) Singapore Amateur Dramatic and Music Society . . . I am sure such a society existed at the time (a similar society was still in existence when I lived in Singapore and did, in fact, use an old bungalow as its headquarters but any resemblance between that society and the one I depict is purely coincidental). I do, however, confess to drawing on my own experience in amateur dramatics and I once had a role in *The Pirates of Penzance* (as Isabel . . . a whole two lines!) so it has happy memories for me, but mercifully nobody died during our run!

The inspiration for using a theater device came once again from the *Straits Times* 12 February 1909 . . . "For more than two solid hours, last night, *The Pirates of Penzance* pirated and pirouetted before a crowded audience, in the (newly opened) Victoria Theatre . . ." Sadly at the end of the day I wasn't able to take the SADAMS production to the theater but I am thrilled that my clever cover artists incorporated the still extant Victoria Theatre on the cover of *Evil in Emerald*.

A quick word of clarification. As this book originates in the US, we have used US spelling (although my own natural spelling is UK/Australian). On one word I am a stickler and that is "whisky." My characters drink copious amounts of Scotch whisky (no *e*), not Irish or American whiskey.

What's next for Harriet and Curran? For the next book, we will break the bounds of Singapore Island and spend some time on the Malay Peninsula. Unfortunately my plans for a research trip to Malaysia are well and truly on hold for the time being but I have my memories and my imagination to keep me going. If you want to know more, please sign up for Harriet's newsletter!

You will find a character list and glossary (and other information!) on my website www.amstuartbooks.com.

Acknowledgments

I would like to acknowledge and thank my readers who have taken Harriet and Curran into their hearts. In the darkest days of the seemingly endless lockdowns here in Melbourne, the personal notes and lovely reviews kept me going. As did my wonderful cheer squad, the Saturday Ladies Bridge Club (which is about writing, not card games!), and my ever-patient (and beta-reading) husband, David, who routinely fell asleep during my performances of Gilbert & Sullivan. And of course, a huge thanks to my "team" at Berkley—the cover artists, the audio production team and everyone who puts so much work into making sure the book is the best it possibly could be.

Finally, I would like to thank my agent, Kevan Lyon, and my editor, Michelle Vega, particularly for their understanding when it all got a bit much. Thank you all!

Helen Beardsley Photographer

Australian author A. M. Stuart, creator of the popular Harriet Gordon Mysteries, lives in Melbourne, Australia, but over her life she has traveled extensively and lived in Africa and Singapore, experiences which she brings to her writing. Before becoming a full-time writer, she worked as a lawyer across a variety of disciplines, including the military and emergency services.

As well as the Harriet Gordon series, she is also multi-published in historical romance and short stories with settings in England and Australia and spanning different periods of history.

CONNECT ONLINE

AMStuartBooks.com
AMStuartBooks
AMStuartBooks